The Fantastical Exploits of
GWENDOLYN GRAY

The Fantastical Exploits
of
GWENDOLYN GRAY

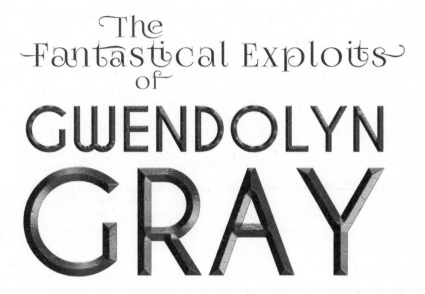

B. A. WILLIAMSON

JOLLY FiSH PRESS

Mendota Heights, Minnesota

First Edition
First Printing, 2020

Book design by Jake Slavik
Cover design by Jake Nordby
Cover illustration by Sanjay Charlton

Jolly Fish Press, an imprint of North Star Editions, Inc.

Library of Congress Cataloging-in-Publication Data (pending)
978-1-63163-435-2

Jolly Fish Press
North Star Editions, Inc.
2297 Waters Drive
Mendota Heights, MN 55120
www.jollyfishpress.com

Printed in the United States of America

For my mother, who would have loved this,
even if someone else had written it.

And for my students, whose delicious tears
only make me more powerful.

A TABLE OF CONTENTS

PART ONE: GREEN

PART TWO: BLACK

PART THREE: BLUE

PART ONE: GREEN

CHAPTER ONE

No Story . . .

Once upon a time, in the City of No Stories, Gwendolyn Gray was surrounded by zombies.

Though you may have encountered stories of zombies before, Gwendolyn had not, but if she had, she would certainly agree it was a fit word to describe the mindless creatures shuffling toward her.

But we are getting ahead of ourselves.

Yesterday, Gwendolyn had not been in this predicament. Yesterday, light had streamed in through the window of her dull grey bedroom. But Gwendolyn was already awake. The nightmares saw to that. Always the same—black clouds, grasping tentacles, and rumbling thunder.

Three weeks since she'd returned from Tohk. Three weeks since she'd had a decent night's rest. She rose from her bed and brushed a frizzy waterfall of red curls out of her face. She rubbed tired and itchy eyes, and looked around.

Pictures stared back at her. Hundreds of them, wallpapering

the room. Sparrow. Starling. Tohk. Copernium. She'd been drawing nonstop, though she could no longer make the colors appear like she used to. She thought she caught the two children in the pictures waving at her now and again, but it was, of course, just her imagination.

She touched a picture of Sparrow, feelings swirling inside her. I would like to describe those feelings to you, but though I have some skill with words, they fail me here. When attempting to describe the sensation of falling in love with an imaginary friend that you have accidentally brought to life and then lost forever, I find myself at a loss. It is a very specific sort of feeling.

Gwendolyn sighed and opened the closet to see some of the only color she had left: the red dress of her own creation and the green, puffed-sleeve dress from the Mainspring Marketplace. The faithful green dress was a bit ragged, not to mention weighed down with too many memories to fit comfortably. So she threw on the red one and went downstairs to her family's stylish living room, full of glass and chrome and black leather cushions.

Father was reading his paper, and Mother was busy in the kitchen. Gwendolyn crept toward the door, hoping to escape without any hassle.

"And just where do you think you're off to this fine morning?" Father asked. Behind the newsprint, Danforth Gray was a handsome man with an outrageous mustache and a twinkle in his eye.

Gwendolyn froze. "The School," she lied.

Father lowered his paper. "Did you hear that, Marie? She's off to the School. Do you know, I daresay she's forgotten?"

Mother came out of the kitchen, wiping her hands on a rag. Her platinum hair was up in its usual bun, her sharp features unusually soft this morning.

"Forgotten? Of course not. Even our distracted daughter wouldn't forget her own birthday." Her tone was teasing, but a flicker of worry passed between her and Father.

"Oh, yes. Birthday . . ." Gwendolyn said. May fifteenth. She *had* forgotten. "Happy birthday. I mean . . . no, that's what *you* say, isn't it?" She forced a small laugh. Another set of motions to go through. But she would try, for her parents' sake.

Father shared another glance with Mother, then coughed. "Yes, happy birthday! It's not every day one turns *thirteen*, after all."

"Yes!" Mother said, with extra cheer ladled on top. "Now, into the kitchen with you. I've whipped you up a special breakfast."

Gwendolyn cringed. She'd had enough experience with her mother's cooking to beware the word *special*.

There were no balloons or cake or candles, not in the City. But Gwendolyn's parents always made some effort. Mother proudly presented a plate of poached eggs, fried meat-from-a-tin, and a square of colorless gelatin that Gwendolyn supposed was meant to be festive.

At least it wasn't boiled cabbage again. She took a bite and forced a look of appreciation.

"So," Father said, preparing to ask the same question he asked *every* year. "Do you feel older?"

"Umm . . . I suppose so?" She never knew how to answer. Who woke up feeling a whole year older all at once?

Mother wrung her hands. "Well, eat up. A birthday is no reason to be late to the School. Although, must you wear *that* dress again? You've worn it so much recently, it'll be threadbare soon, and I've had to do the wash that much more often—"

"Now dear, don't nag the poor girl. It's her birthday, let her wear what she wants." Father winked at Gwendolyn.

Mother put up her hands in apology. "I'm sorry. It *is* your day."

Gwendolyn pushed her chair back and stood. She'd had her fill of awful birthday food and awkward birthday talk. "Thank you, both. Mother's right, I really should be going. I, um, promised I'd be there early today . . ."

"Ah!" Father said, latching onto the thought. "Meeting some friends before class, eh? Wonderful! Why don't you invite your School chums over for games tonight? I'm sure we can find some somewhere . . ."

Gwendolyn presumed he meant games, not friends, though she didn't know where to find either. Neither had ever been seen in the apartment. "Yes, that's it," she lied. "I'll be sure to ask them. Though I won't get my hopes up, it's very short notice . . ."

She grabbed her bag and checked that her treasures were safely snuggled inside. The powerless Figment gem, which had once held enough magic to take Gwendolyn between worlds. The red book, *Kolonius Thrash and the Perilous Pirates*, into which she had traveled on her last adventure. Starling's goggles, which the older girl had left behind. And her pencils, about the only thing from the City itself that she cherished.

Her parents followed her to the door, and Mother wrapped

her in a sudden and unexpected embrace. Gwendolyn cringed. She hated being touched, especially lately, but she endured. Mother noticed the cringe, which made her hug Gwendolyn all the tighter.

They parted, and Mother held Gwendolyn at arm's length for a moment. The changes in their daughter were not lost on Father and Mother, but they had no idea how to break through her depression to find the girl they loved within. Mother gave Gwendolyn a slow, meaningful look. "We love you, Bless. Happy birthday."

Father held out a package wrapped in white tissue. "Here you are."

Gwendolyn took it, and opened it. "Oh. Another sketchbook." She tried to muster some enthusiasm. "Thank you."

Father tried to hide a frown. "Yes. Well. I saw that you'd used up your old one. So . . . yes. There you are. Have a good day."

This was about all the attention Gwendolyn could stand. She said a hurried thank you, dashed out the door, and didn't stop dashing until she was safely aboard the monorail.

The train wound its way out from the Middling, away from the School she'd said she was going to. Flopping onto a seat, she opened her bag and put on Starling's goggles, using them to hold back her bushy red curls. To answer Father's question—she certainly *did* feel older. This had nothing to do with the number of birthdays she'd had, of course. She wasn't exactly sure what *older* was supposed to feel like, but to her it felt like tired, and angry, and more tired. She hardly recognized herself anymore, and she didn't like it—but like her parents, she didn't know what to do about it.

She leaned her head against the window, and watched the buildings slide by.

The City was a dull, grey place, full of boxy buildings and forbidding skyscrapers. It owed much of that dullness to the Lambents, thousands of clear, crystal balls each the size of a marble. When working properly, the Lambents would emit a white light, filling the Cityzens with a wonderful feeling of calm, draining them of their worries and concerns. It also drained them of any troublesome ideas or questions that might alter the City in any way.

But the Lambents were *not* working properly. Gwendolyn had seen to that on her previous adventure. The trouble started when her daydreams had gotten a bit out of control, which involved making a certain classmate grow honest-to-goodness rabbit ears and infesting her bedroom with an all-too-real imaginary monster.

These changes did not go unnoticed in the highly unimaginative City, and Gwendolyn found herself subject to the attentions of the Faceless Gentlemen—Mister Five and Mister Six—whose job was to make sure the City stayed as dull and unchanged as possible. So naturally, they attempted to erase all her changes, along with our girl herself.

She had narrowly escaped them with the sudden appearance of Sparrow and Starling, two world-hopping explorers who helped Gwendolyn travel into her favorite book, *Kolonius Thrash and the Perilous Pirates*, and its fantastic world of Tohk.

Unfortunately, the Faceless Gentlemen had followed them, and unleashed a ravenous shadow monster, the Abscess. After a rollicking adventure involving perilous escapes, ingenious traps, and a thrilling airship battle with dastardly pirates, Gwendolyn had blasted the Abscess with the legendary Pistola Luminant, blowing the darkness to pieces.

But she had not stopped there. She returned home and blasted every Lambent in the City to smithereens, freeing the Cityzens from its hypnotic influence. She had expended the rest of her power restoring what the Abscess had erased. For a full account of these Marvelous Adventures, see the previous volume, but for those who are just joining us, we must make them feel welcome.

Needless to say, Gwendolyn's life had been much simpler before all that. Her biggest challenges had been boredom, and getting teased at the School. In hindsight, boredom was a very fine problem to have, because it meant that nothing truly bad was happening to you. She knew now that there was so much worse than boredom.

The mono was dirtier than usual. Grime, trash, and even some graffiti had accumulated, and no one seemed interested in cleaning it. At least she was alone. No one ever came this far but her. Finally she reached the Edge, the farthest part of the City, the part that no one else knew existed. The part that she had found three weeks ago. The only place in the City where she could be really, truly alone. She got out and walked past the automated factories that belched smoke into the sky.

Gwendolyn trudged her familiar path to a familiar building,

entered through the broken window, climbed up to the roof, and sat in her usual spot. She dangled her legs over the side and stared at it.

The Wall. It needed no other name. It stretched at least a hundred stories high, and as far as she could see in both directions. Where everything came to an end, but where her adventures had all begun. Where she'd been chased into that abandoned old apartment, where she found the book and the gem. And then there were Sparrow and Starling.

It hurt to think about them, but an old familiar hurt, like poking a sore in your mouth with your tongue. But sometimes you bite the sore by mistake, and feel a fresh throb of pain, and a blaze of anger, as Gwendolyn did now. She grabbed an empty bottle from a pile she had gathered for precisely this purpose. She flung it at the Wall, but it fell short, hitting the ground with a satisfying smash. "Happy birthday to me," she mumbled.

She'd spent a day traveling all over different parts of the City, but no matter which way she went, the Wall was there, waiting. No way out.

So Gwendolyn sat and stared and sulked and sketched, filling the pages in her new sketchbook, though inside she just felt empty.

She found her favorite picture of her friends again. Sparrow, winking up at her. Starling, trying to be serious, but with a hint of a smile at the corner of her mouth. Gwendolyn's relationship with them was . . . complicated. It turned out that her friends were not from another world at all, but had instead leapt fully formed from her imagination. But Gwendolyn's imagination had a habit of becoming real, and Sparrow and Starling were now as real as it got.

Maybe it had all been just a dream. But it hadn't *felt* like a dream. She may have imagined Sparrow and Starling, but the things she imagined became *real*, and she knew they were real now, were really still out there somewhere. Sparrow and Starling, probably stuck in Tohk where she left them, probably having adventures with Kolonius Thrash, the Figment lacking the power to bring them here, its energy spent in saving the world.

She could never have imagined all of Tohk by herself. It was just as real as her own world, which made losing it all the more awful. It would have been better if it *had* all been in her imagination. But it was all as real as the ache in her chest. She wondered if they even missed her.

After a few hours, her drawing was interrupted by another smash of glass. Not one from her. She ran to the opposite side of the roof and looked down.

A group of boys wandered the street below, prying up cobblestones and throwing them through factory windows. There was no doubt in her mind that they were trouble.

Well, Gwendolyn could use a bit of trouble.

She rushed down to the street and darted around the corner, planting herself directly in the boys' path. "Hello, children," she said, bold as you please. "What brings you out this far?"

"'Ello yourself," one of them snapped back. There were three, all taller and older than her. They were the sort of dirty and shabby that one only saw in the Outskirts. The Lambents would normally have kept the boys glued to their couches at home, hypnotizing them into dull-witted lumps, but it had been more than a fortnight since the Lambents had broken. They must have gone to play outside for once in their pasty lives, wandering farther out until they reached the Edge.

"Lookit that dress. What's a fancy thing like her doin' so far out 'ere? Whaddya think, boys?" said the tallest boy.

"I think she's got a right pretty dress on. Must be a Central. And what's with that hair?" said the boy to his right.

Gwendolyn was used to that sort of thing. After all, she was the only redhead in the City. And her red dress just made her stand out all the more.

"'Ey, you. Got any food, oddling?" the first one said, pointing to her bag.

She snorted dismissively. "Didn't your mothers teach you to wash before eating?"

"Fancy thing's got a mouth on 'er," said the lead boy. His hair was long and greasy and pale.

"Lookit that bag of hers. I'd say she's holdin' out on us," said the one on her left, his face a cratered map of fresh pimples and old pitted scars. He drew out a knife, which would have been altogether too dark and frightening for a story of this sort, but it was a small vegetable paring knife he had obviously taken from his mother's kitchen, and Gwendolyn had to stifle a laugh. It was nowhere near as frightening as a gang of pirates armed with proper swords. The boy edged around behind her, and gave her a little push.

"Yeah, holdin' out on us," said Long Hair. "Whaddya think, Travis?"

Travis, the mouth breather on her right, grunted.

"Right," said Long Hair. "Get it."

Pimples grabbed her arm with his free hand while Travis yanked her bag off, tearing the sleeve of her dress.

Gwendolyn just stared at them. "You tore my dress," she said. Anger flickered through her numbness. It felt good. Feeling anything felt good.

Long Hair leaned in close. "I don't bleedin' care, you red-headed freak. Now run on home to mummy."

"I like this dress. It's my favorite." She clenched her fists. "And I'll be needing my bag back."

"Ooo, listen to her," Long Hair said, turning to his cronies. "It's her favorit—"

Gwendolyn grabbed a handful of greasy hair and yanked. The boy shrieked.

Pimples lunged at her. She twirled out of the way but still caught a nasty cut on her cheek. She kicked him in a place a polite girl would not. He sucked in a sharp breath and dropped the knife, clutching himself with both hands.

Travis got an arm around her neck, his breath heavy in her ear. She bit him, hard enough to break the skin—just like a zombie would, though she won't discover what they are 'til chapter three.

Travis yelped and let go. Gwendolyn snatched up the knife and waved it at them. "Run away now, boys."

"Get outta here, she's feral!" Long Hair yelled. Two of them sprinted down the street, while Pimples hobbled gingerly after them. She scooped up a loose cobblestone and threw it after them. Soon all three were out of sight.

Gwendolyn stood there, panting. Her chest burned. She dropped the knife and stepped back, shocked at herself. Who was she? Fighting, and threatening people with knives?

The world spun around her, and Gwendolyn collapsed to the pavement and wrapped her arms around her knees. Her whole body shook, suddenly weak and fragile. Her breath came in rapid gasps. Her vision grew dark around the edges.

She forced herself to take one deep breath, and another. And another. Eventually, the adrenaline subsided. The anger faded. The numbing blanket wrapped itself around her again, and all she felt was tired.

Gwendolyn Gray forced herself to stand. "So," she said, looking at the grey buildings all around, "this is the City I helped save."

And after saving the world, Gwendolyn might have expected some kind of "happily ever after." But she'd never heard of any "happily ever afters," and things seemed to be worse than ever. It was not the end to her story that she'd expected.

But this is no story, she thought.

She was quite wrong, of course. We're all in a story. Just rarely the one we expect.

Gwendolyn picked up her bag from where Travis had dropped it, and inspected the rip in her dress. The seam on the sleeve had split. Something warm ran down her cheek, and she probed the cut. It stung. She used the hem of her dress to dab at it. No one would notice the blood against the red fabric.

She headed home, using the hazy spire of Central Tower to guide her. She was in no hurry, so she walked instead of taking the mono, strolling right down the very middle of the street, as if daring the City to get in her way.

CHAPTER TWO

Another Unpleasant Homecoming

It took Gwendolyn most of the day to walk back to the Middling. The lamps were coming on as she reached her street. She looked very out of place in the relative nicety of the Middling, with her torn red dress, wild hair, and cut cheek. But no one saw her as she rode the elevator back up to whatever her parents had in store.

A lot of yelling was what they had in store.

"Gone! Who knows where? I called the School and they said you haven't been there in days!" Father railed, his mustache quivering.

"Fighting, by the looks of it. Where did you get that cut on your face? It's awful!" Mother shouted, her voice getting higher with each syllable. "This has to stop! Scratching the Forthright girl, sulking around, the constant disrespect! We raised you better than that! You're not behaving like our daughter!"

Father chimed in, his voice cold and steady. "We have certain rules in this house, young lady, rules you will abide by. You're a part of this family and you will *act* like a part of this family. Until you leave this house, you will do as we say."

Gwendolyn said nothing. What could they do to her? Ground her? Keep her from her friends? They were already gone. She was already miserable.

Eventually they ran out of steam. "Well?" Mother said, tapping her foot. "Do you have anything to say for yourself?"

Gwendolyn didn't.

"Of course not." Mother took a steadying breath. "Gwendolyn, we know you have been going through a rough time. I know you haven't been sleeping well since the Lambents burst, and I can only assume that has exacerbated this attitude."

Father slumped into his desk chair, looking defeated. "We tried today, Bless. We didn't want to argue—it is your birthday after all. But . . . this is entirely too much."

"Go to your room," Mother said. "You'll be seeing a lot of it. And you are *absolutely* going to the School tomorrow, even if I have to drag you by the heels. Go."

Gwendolyn went, her parents' voices trailing behind her.

"Well, she's certainly a teenager now," Father said.

"Can't even see her freckles under all that dirt—" Mother replied.

Gwendolyn slammed her door, and she was alone again, the way she liked it. Just because Mother didn't have a job, or any friends, didn't mean she had to spend all her free time nagging

Gwendolyn. She threw herself facedown on the bed, exhausted by the prospect of yet another sleepless night.

~~~

Which brings us to that fateful day where our story begins. Gwendolyn stood looking up at the School, though Mother hadn't needed to drag her at all. Some days Gwendolyn felt so angry she might explode, but others she didn't have the energy to swat a fly. She felt like a zombie herself, though the analogy would be lost on her until later that day. She didn't know what was wrong with her.

Mother was worried as well, particularly when Gwendolyn did not put up her usual fight about wearing her School uniform. This gave her mother pause, and she was wise enough to suggest Gwendolyn wear something else instead in an attempt to improve her daughter's dark mood. Gwendolyn's red dress was in a disastrous state, so Marie presented her with the green puffed-sleeve dress instead, even though it was getting a bit short on her. Gwendolyn said nothing as she dressed and stayed just as silent when Mother put a large bandage on her cheek.

"I'm sorry we argued, Bless," Mother said. Gwendolyn could hear her working up to her usual "I-understand-what-you're-going-through-but-I'm-worried-about-you" speech.

"Gwendolyn, I understand what you're going through, but I'm worried about you. I feel like I'm losing my little girl. You've been angry all the time, snapping at us for the smallest thing, and that's whenever you'll come out of your room to talk to us at all. If you'd just tell us what's bothering you, we can help."

"I couldn't even begin to explain it to you," Gwendolyn said, in the tone of teenagers everywhere. Then she cringed. It had come out harsher than she'd meant.

"Fine." Mother pulled away. "You're a teenager now, no one in the world could *possibly* understand you, least of all your own mother, who went through the exact same things. Thank heavens the School's getting a new shipment of Lambents in today—"

"What?" Gwendolyn's head whipped around so fast some vertebrae in her neck popped.

"That's what I've heard, anyway. Ours should come through the mail tube soon. Maybe it will finally get back to normal around here."

"Why didn't you tell me?" Gwendolyn demanded, immediately jerked out of her stupor.

Mother's eyes narrowed. "Well, if you would actually *talk* to me, you would know these things, so watch your tone. I've had quite enough of this new attitude."

Gwendolyn glared at her. "Good. You won't have to deal with it anymore, and if you like, never again. I'll vanish, and you won't have a freak for a daughter. You can get one of the normal ones if you like." And Gwendolyn Gray ran away.

There was no "Gwendolyn, wait! Stop!" this time. Just Mother, staring after her. Gwendolyn was up the stairs and through the door in an instant. Had she turned around, she would have seen the pained look that crossed Mother's face. She would have seen the way Mother's shoulders slumped as she headed for home. And Gwendolyn would have felt absolutely terrible and would have apologized immediately. But she had no idea just how long it would be before she could say she was sorry.

All she could think of was the Lambents. They couldn't be back, they just couldn't. She'd blasted them all into glittering dust. Yes, the City had been going downhill without them, but the return of the Lambents could *not* be a change for the good. Anything to do with those Faceless Gentlemen was bound to make things worse.

She walked through hallways full of zombies, but only of the ordinary variety: bleary-eyed students groaning and shuffling to their various classes. The youngest students entered rooms on the first floor, while the rest of the students headed for the wide bank of elevators at the end of the hall, the oldest students headed for the highest floor.

Gwendolyn had been so excited at the possibilities without the Lambents. She'd come every day for a week just to see what would happen. But every day, the fires of her excitement had burned lower and lower until they were now just the bitter ash of disappointment. A new normal had developed. A worse one. Saving the world was not all it was cracked up to be.

After a long and crowded trip up the elevator, she emerged onto the twelfth floor, and walked down to her classroom. It was a bare grey space, with thirty desks all in rows. Not even twenty were full. Cecilia Forthright and her goons were all here, because why not? This was where *they* ruled, bossing and bullying and receiving constant praise from the ignorant teachers.

Cecilia looked up from a whispered conversation, glared at Gwendolyn, and quickly looked away. Gwendolyn smirked at that.

She'd put Cecilia in her place on Gwendolyn's first day back, and she imagined she only looked wilder and more dangerous since. Cecilia was one problem she didn't have anymore.

Ian Haldrake was there. Jessica Tawny as well. Gwendolyn was mildly pleased to see them, and Missy Cartblatt too, still very much unvanished and un-rabbit-eared. Tommy Ungeroot was sitting at his desk. They had all been getting along recently, at least during those times Gwendolyn bothered to show up. Missy and Ian and Jessica had largely ignored her before, save for the odd disgusted look when Gwendolyn did anything out of the ordinary. Which, to be fair, was often. But now things were different, and her relationship with her Schoolmates was one of the few things that had improved in recent weeks. Even Tommy had been much less irritating than usual. If she had to go to the School, at least the four of them were there.

Tommy brightened at the sight of her. He had stringy blond hair, a bulbous nose, and the disheveled appearance of a lack of adult supervision, though with the number of siblings he had, it was no surprise his mother had little time to spare. The Ungeroots were scattered across the School like dandelion seeds.

"Hello, Tommy," she said, taking her seat behind him.

"Hey, Freckles!" He wouldn't quit calling her that, no matter how many times she told him to stop.

"Why are you here? I was sure you would jump at the chance to skip." But come to think of it, he'd been here every day she had. The School was excruciatingly boring at the best of times, and this was certainly *not* the best of times, if you please, and thank you very much. But Gwendolyn had bigger worries on her mind. Boredom was another problem she didn't have anymore.

"Yeah, I was, uh . . . I was hoping I'd see you. I mean hear you. I mean, I wanted to hear the rest of the story."

She blinked. "Yes, well . . . here I am." She was suddenly very self-conscious of the bandage on her cheek.

"What 'append to your face?"

She shrank down in her seat but was spared the need to answer by the arrival of their teacher, Mr. Percival. The balding little man waddled to his desk and flopped down into his chair. "All right, which of you actually turned up today? Not much point in calling roll. Coleridge, pass out the Lists."

Gwendolyn groaned. She'd forgotten about the Lists. With no Lambents to hypnotize their students, the teachers had resorted to handing out Lists of facts, figures, and formulas for them to memorize. They read them silently, then stood and recited them. Then another List was handed out, and another. At least with the Lambents she'd been able to draw under her desk.

But a new shipment of Lambents . . . that was bad news indeed. The Lists were tedious, but the Lambents were trouble. Fortunately, it seemed Mother had been wrong. Gwendolyn sighed, and suffered through the morning's recitations until it was time for the teachers' recess, and the students were sent to the courtyard. It was a patch of bare grey ground under a patch of pale grey sky, surrounded on all sides by towering grey walls.

Gwendolyn sat in her usual spot under the scraggly old tree that had somehow clawed its way up from the cracked earth. She leaned against the bark and closed her eyes, relaxing and completely unchased by zombies. At least for the next few minutes, anyway.

"Wake up, oddling. Did you bring it?"

She smiled the tiniest smile without opening her eyes. "I'm sure I don't know what you're talking about."

Someone kicked her foot. "Yes, you do. Where's the book, Red?" said the voice.

She opened one eye. "What book?"

"Kick her until she remembers, Ian," said a girl's voice.

"Oh, *that* book." Gwendolyn sat up, smiling even wider. Ian, Jessica, Missy, and Tommy were standing over her. "Hang on a minute." She opened her bag and pulled out a bright-red book decorated with golden gears. "Did you want to borrow it?"

Ian rolled his eyes. "You know we don't understand half of it. You read it. And don't skimp on the explanations."

Jessica nodded. "*And* do the voices."

"Yes," said Missy. "I like the voices."

"After all," Ian said, "it's not like we came to the School to read Lists with Percival."

Tommy nodded. "Too right."

Gwendolyn had started out reading the book to Tommy on her return three weeks ago, explaining things like airships and robots to him. Before long, the other three had joined, and the five of them read together under the tree every day for that first week back. Suddenly, she couldn't remember why she'd started skipping School in the first place. "All right. Sit down."

They did. "You never said what 'append to your face," Tommy

said. He had freckles, like her, and front teeth that were a little too large.

Missy gasped a little, and touched her own cheek in sympathy. "Don't it hurt?"

Gwendolyn shrugged bravely. She told them of her fight with the boys, making herself look a bit more noble than she'd actually been. "But enough about that," she finished, basking slightly in the looks of amazement and admiration from her friends. She opened the red book stenciled with golden gears, *Kolonius Thrash and the Perilous Pirates*. "Where did we leave off?"

"Kolonius was on the Storm Train!" Missy said, louder than was usual for the pale, shy girl. She brushed her stringy blonde hair out of her eyes.

"Right. And what was the Storm Train?" Gwendolyn asked.

Jessica actually raised her hand. "It's an elevated train, like the monorail. It runs through the Stormlands, an area of Tohk with electrical storms that never stop. Too dangerous for airships. The train is the only way across." She was dark in all the ways that Missy was pale—dark skin, dark eyes, dark hair done up in intricate braids.

"And Thrash is searching for the assassin who's trying to take out the Duchess of Carbony," said Ian. He was thin faced, with stylish hair that was long on top and closely shaved on the sides. "And a duchess is someone who is . . . in charge of . . . stuff."

"Correct all around," Gwendolyn said. She turned the pages and began to read. Soon they were all lost in the wonderful words. She was swept back into the world she'd left and felt a mite more like herself again. The voices tumbled out of her.

Kolonius, bossy and arrogant as only a seventeen-year-old can be. Brunswick, with his gruff voice and swashbuckling slang. Massive Carsair, native of the Stormlands with the accent to match.

Gwendolyn had to stop frequently to explain foreign concepts to the others, but before long they were all up and acting out the parts. Ian, tall and wiry and always dramatic, made a dashing enough Kolonius. Jessica was absolutely hilarious as Brunswick. Tommy was a decently evil assassin, and Missy . . . well, she was a rather shy and reluctant duchess.

"'And Kolonius thrust with his spiral blade, but the assassin was too quick.' No, Ian, hold the stick a little lower, like this. 'And she rolled away, scoring a nasty cut on the boy captain's calf.' Good, Tommy, now jump back up. 'Lightning flashed all around. Kolonius lost his footing on the top of the train. He managed to catch hold of one of the lightning rods, and—'"

But at that moment, the School buzzer sounded, signaling a return to classes. A collective groan went up from the yard as students filed back inside.

The five of them headed toward the doors, Jessica taking a turn to duel Ian with sticks, Missy asking them to be careful. Gwendolyn smiled at them. It was all a bit childish—the way they clamored for her to read and played their game of pretend. But children in the City were never allowed to *act* like children, and it should come as no surprise that these four would try to make up for lost time, so let us allow them their childhood while it lasts.

Tommy hung back. "Will you be here tomorrow?"

"Yes. Perhaps," Gwendolyn replied. But she wasn't sure anymore. She looked down at the book, and her green dress.

And she remembered why she'd stopped coming.

It felt a bit like eating an entire birthday cake by yourself. In the beginning and most of the middle, it is fun and exciting and delicious, but when it's all over, you feel sick and wish you had never done it at all. Reading the book was wonderful at first, but in the end, it just reminded her of a world she could no longer go back to, and her insides broke all over again. She knelt down and pretended to tie her shoe, letting her friends get ahead of her.

Friends. She'd always thought of them as classmates before, but they were more than that now, weren't they? Was she betraying Sparrow and Starling by moving on? By not looking for them? By playing silly pretendings at the School? Should she invite her School friends home for games like Father said? Maybe a proper birthday party was exactly what she needed.

"Gwendolyn, are you coming?" Jessica called.

"Try and catch me," Gwendolyn said, snatching up her bag and sprinting for the door, trying to act more cheerful than she felt. But she couldn't make it last. Things that should have made her happy just didn't . . . stick. Another reason she had stopped coming. She was not a little girl anymore—all this waving sticks and playing pretend was ridiculous, and having a party to celebrate surviving another year was a pointless waste of energy. By the time they reached the classroom, gloom had settled on her again like a heavy blanket.

But that was to be the least of her problems at the moment.

As soon as she'd reached her desk, Mr. Percival burst through the door holding a large box.

"Good news, everyone!" he said, his reedy voice unusually cheerful. He set the box on the desk and opened it to reveal nearly three dozen glass beads, nestled in protective foam. "No more Lists. The new Lambents are ready!"

There was a cheer from the room, but the blood drained from Gwendolyn's face. *No,* she thought. *It can't be. Not again.*

Her mind reeled as Mr. Percival placed a bead into the special cradle on each desk. Things couldn't go back to how they were, there was no way. She had destroyed all the Lambents; who had made more of them? Would things be better with everything back the way it was? But no! Ian and Jessica were proof of how good things could be if only—

"Gwen, are you all right?" Tommy asked.

But the Lambents flared to life, and everyone went silent. The glass beads bathed the room in dancing light and ghostly shadows. The students went into a slack-jawed trance.

Gwendolyn did not remember the Lambents being this bright. She tried to shut her eyes, but the light burned right through her eyelids. It grew brighter still, and started flickering. The pulsing intensified, a blinding strobe that filled the room. With a jolt, she thought of the Figment, and her eyes shot open. If the Lambents were working again, then maybe the Figment would work too—

Suddenly, the children all turned and stared directly at Gwendolyn. She nearly fell out of her chair, but instead she froze with fear.

The students' eyes were gone. Out of their sockets blazed a cold white light. Gwendolyn shrank back as every person in the room stared at her with glowing eyes and blank faces.

Moving as one, the students all cocked their heads to the side. Carter Shrewsbury opened his mouth. But the voice that came out was not the usual one that hurled insults at her. Instead, a high-pitched and terrifyingly familiar monotone came from his unmoving lips, as if he were no more than a gramophone speaker.

"Hello again, Miss Gray."

Gwendolyn's eyes widened, and she shrank back farther in her chair, as her heart tried to sink further into her chest. Like a nightmare come to life, Missy Cartblatt's jaw fell open, and the voice continued unbroken from its new source.

"Did you believe—"

The voice jumped over to Ian.

"—you could be rid of us—"

The voice jumped again, this time coming from her white-eyed teacher.

"—so easily?"

The children stood in one smooth motion, as if they were puppets hanging from the same strings. Slowly, ever so slowly, they started toward Gwendolyn.

"Did you truly think—"

"—you could possibly—"

"—escape us?"

CHAPTER THREE

And Then There Were Zombies

And now we come to the point where we entered this tale, with our poor Gwendolyn surrounded by mindless, shambling zombies. They did not hunger for brains, nor were they the rotting undead, but that would have been almost comforting compared to the bone-chilling voices of Mister Five and Mister Six.

"We don't know how—" said Jannette Tice-Nichols.

"—you managed to escape—" said Karl Scrump.

"—from that silly book of yours," said Cecilia Forthright.

"But it will not matter," said Jessica.

More than a little terror seized Gwendolyn then. She had suspected something nasty at the return of the Lambents, but this was something even her nightmares had not prepared her for.

Tommy Ungeroot lunged at her and caught hold of her wrist. His face was slack, but his grip was like iron.

Suddenly, Tommy blinked, eyes clearing. For a moment, her friend was back.

"Tommy?" she said. She pulled free, but he was gone again, his eyes shining white, face slack.

"Run!" someone shouted, and Gwendolyn saw Missy's dark eyes for a second, then the glowing white took over again. Gwendolyn didn't question the command but climbed on top of her desk, above the sea of students. Their arms reached toward her, and they blundered into desks and chairs to get at her.

She leapt to the next desk, and the next. Then Cecilia Forthright got in her way, so Gwendolyn aimed a kick at her head, which we can all agree was probably deserved, but Gwendolyn missed and slipped. She fell hard, hit her head on the edge of a desk, then scrambled dizzily under the desks until she reached the door and burst into the hallway. The expressionless voice called after her.

"You will not—"

"—evade us—"

"—again. We will—"

"—find you."

The last few days, Gwendolyn had been desperate for something to penetrate the numbness inside her. Bone-rattling terror was not exactly what she'd had in mind.

She sprinted toward the elevators, feet pounding on the tiles, heart pounding in her chest, classroom doors whipping past her. She reached the end just as a shambling Cecilia came into the hall, and Gwendolyn jabbed the call button.

The elevator ascended at an agonizingly slow pace as Cecilia drew closer and closer, feet shuffling, arms outstretched. This empty-eyed version of her was more frightening than the one that used to torment Gwendolyn. Trailing Cecilia, the rest of Gwendolyn's class filed into the hall.

Finally, one of the elevators chimed, and Gwendolyn threw herself inside and hit the button for the ground floor. "Looks like I'm skipping School again. Sorry, Mother," she mumbled.

The elevator was eerily calm. Her head throbbed where she had hit it. The numbers ticked down from twelve, and Gwendolyn prepared to run. She had no plan, but had been on enough adventures to know that you run *away* from the danger first, *then* come up with a plan . . . and then usually run back *toward* the danger again.

The door opened with a chime, and she exploded out of it. She hadn't gone three steps when every door along the empty corridor burst open. Hundreds of small children poured out, all the youngest students on the first floor. Tiny hands reached for her, tiny eyes glowed at her, tiny faces drooled slack jawed at her. They shuffled toward her, an unstoppable wave, their movements stiff and unnatural as they jostled down the hall.

The voice of the Mister Men jumped from child to child.

"It is no—"

"—use. We are—"

"—everywhere."

With another chime, the elevators all opened, and her older classmates poured out, trapping her. Her panic reached new heights, and for your own sake, please don't imagine what it would be like if your own glowing-eyed classmates were chasing you down the halls of your school.

Gwendolyn tried to run again, but her shoes slipped on the tile and she fell. Familiar faces closed in around her. "No," she moaned. "Please." She skittered toward the wall on hands and knees as the children clawed at her skirt.

With a last desperate thought, she reached into her bag, and thrust the Figment at them. To her grateful surprise, it flashed a feeble blue, the power of concentrated imagination returning as the Lambents drained everyone else's. The eyes of the children closest to her turned blue as well, flickering in time with the gem she held. She sprang up and ran, the Figment's weak light carving a path for her. She trampled a group of eight-year-olds to reach the door, and tumbled out of the School and onto the street.

The street was empty, an oddity for the City at any time of day, and a chilly mist made it impossible to see more than a few feet. She tried to think, but fear fogged her mind the way the mist fogged everything else. So she sprinted blindly across the road, searching for some escape among the City's endless grid of alleys and cross streets.

She looked back to see if any zombies had followed when she collided with two men and fell to the ground, just as she had the first time. Once again, she noticed their gleaming black shoes, their perfectly pressed grey suits, their bowler hats above those faces that were not faces at all. She stared up at them.

The Faceless Gentlemen. Though that was how she thought of them, it was not entirely accurate. They did have faces, of some sort or another. But whatever Gwendolyn was seeing, her eyes refused to report the images to her mind, and they left a blank spot in her memory.

The Faceless Gentlemen loomed menacingly out of the fog. It is no easy thing to loom menacingly—most people can only manage a sort of aggressive lean—but the men had certainly learned the trick of it. Slowly, ever so slowly, they looked down at the little girl sprawled in the street. Her thoughts turned to frightened gibberish.

"Well, Mister Five, it seems our quarry has come to us."

"Indeed it has, Mister Six, indeed it has. Much has changed. A girl such as this cannot merely be erased."

"Her power must not go to waste. The Collector wishes to see her."

While they were blathering, she got her feet under her and readied the Figment. Then she leapt at them and thrust the Figment in their faceless faces, but Mister Six whipped off his bowler hat, the inside flashed like a Lambent, and the Figment's glow went out completely.

"Surely the girl did not believe that would work, Mister Five."

"Clearly, she did not, and so it does not. Isn't that just the thing, Mister Six," said Mister Five.

Gwendolyn ran backward out of the alley until Misters Five and Six vanished into the mist. She turned to run, only to slam into something else. She looked up and saw two faceless men in bowler hats. Two *more* men.

"She is such a little thing, Mister Three," said one of the men. "Hardly worth all this fuss."

"Yet she has caused much fuss of her own, Mister Four," said Mister Three. "The City must be restored."

Gwendolyn didn't wait around to listen but pushed past and ran back toward the School. It wasn't a great option, but maybe she could get past the zombie horde, past the School, and to the nearest monorail stop, which she should have done in the first place.

But two *more* men loomed out of the mist and blocked her way.

"It seems we shall have the honor of her capture, Mister Nine."

"So it seems, Mister Ten. This girl has violated the Whyte Proposal, and it is time to face the consequences."

Gwendolyn gaped. She couldn't run anymore, even if she wanted to. What would Sparrow and Starling do?

Sparrow and Starling. A smug smile curled her lip. The Lambents were back, and the Mister Men right along with them. But the Figment was back as well. And the Mister Men weren't the only ones with friends.

"Once upon a time," she shouted, remembering her magic words, "there was a little girl who sang a song, and it always brought her help. *Sparrow and Starling, darrow and darling, come to the aid of your–"*

But Mister Nine opened his mouth wide, ever so wide. Gwendolyn heard a sound of rushing air as he sucked in a rattling breath. The song turned sour and cold in her throat, and a golden mist rose from her mouth. The golden mist mingled with the fog for a moment, then was sucked into the man's gaping maw.

What are you— she started to say, but nothing came out. She clutched her throat. *What did you—* she tried again, but still, nothing. She was completely unable to speak.

"Now, now, now," Mister Nine said, each word dripping steadily like a leaky faucet. "We won't be having any of *that.*"

Misters Five and Six approached from behind, closing the trap. The four men herded her back toward the School. The massive doors opened, and glowing-eyed children oozed down the steps. At both ends of this street, more faceless men appeared, gliding toward her through the mist. Completely surrounded on all sides.

"Mister Nine, if you would be so kind as to grab her head, and point it this way?"

"I shall endeavor to do so without removing it completely, Mister Six," Mister Nine said, appearing behind her. She punched and kicked, but every blow was deflected by the effortless wave of a white-gloved hand. Mister Nine placed an iron hand on each of her shoulders and spun her around to face Mister Six.

This was it. There was nothing left. She looked around, desperate, eyes whirling, seeing nothing but fog and concrete and asphalt.

And then, she noticed something. Something that kindled a flicker of hope that thawed the icy fear. Floating above Mister Six's head, dancing and twirling through the mist, was a tiny, emerald leaf.

And Gwendolyn Gray had an idea.

She pictured the City transforming, just as she had on that long-ago morning when the leaf had first come to her. She imagined it as vividly as she could. And once again, the City bowed to her wishes. Grass carpeted the sidewalk. Bark coated the buildings as they became enormous trees. Light pierced the clouds, golden rays burning away the mist.

The Faceless Gentlemen looked around, distracted for the merest of moments, and Gwendolyn darted out of Mister Nine's grip. There was a ripping noise, and she was free.

Gwendolyn waved her hands, and branches erupted from the trees and slammed into the Mister Men. A thicket of brambles sprang up in front of the School, keeping the zombie children at bay. She ran, heavy bushes springing up to hide her as she darted through the group of men guarding what used to be a street. A smile broke out across her freckled face. It felt good to smile. It felt good to run. It felt good to *feel*.

She sprinted through the warm, sunny forest. She leapt over fallen logs and ducked hanging vines. She tried imagining two children leaping from the brush like before, arriving just in the nick of time, but Sparrow and Starling failed to appear.

But Gwendolyn had other tricks up her sleeve. The trees thinned, and she reached a familiar river, its banks coated in pink flowers. With a gesture, a wind sprang up and scattered the petals across the water, forming a bridge of pink blossoms that hovered in midair.

She raced across it. Another wave of her hand sent the petals drifting lazily into the water, coloring the river pink as they were washed away. The Mister Men appeared on the opposite bank.

They paused for a moment, surveying this new obstacle, and Gwendolyn hollered at them through cupped hands. *If you want to collect me, I'm afraid you'll have to catch me first!*

Or at least, she tried to. But nothing came out. Her smile faltered a little.

She was only mildly surprised when the four men started to fly. They lifted off the ground, feet hovering several inches above the forest floor, and they floated out over the river. The noise of the water grew louder, a deafening roar like an on-coming train.

Gwendolyn's smile became a smirk. She raised her arms high, then brought them down in a cutting motion.

Suddenly the forest was gone. The four men now stood on a set of monorail tracks. They looked to their left just in time to see an actual oncoming train. It slammed into them with tremendous force. The monorail slowed and came to a stop as usual, the computerized conductor failing to notice the men it had just flattened. But once the train had passed, there was no sign of them. Gone as quick as they came.

Gwendolyn nodded with grim satisfaction, and climbed aboard. The monorail went about its business, whisking her away to relative safety.

Gwendolyn investigated her dress and found gashes from each of the Faceless Gentlemen's steel-like fingers. Some of her white slip showed through the holes, but thankfully she was decent. She collapsed in a heap on one of the seats.

Thoughts raced through her mind. The Lambents were back, and so were the Mister Men. The power was back as well, there for her to tap into. What had they done to her voice? She tried to speak, but nothing came out, not even a whisper. *At least Mother will be pleased*, she thought bitterly, trying not to be scared.

What did the men want from her? They had said they wanted her power, the same way they drained the power from everyone else in the City. She supposed it was the only thing that kept them from erasing her altogether.

And that leaf . . . it had appeared again. The same one she'd imagined on her way to the School that fateful morning. The first thing she'd brought to life. And it had appeared several times since then, always when she needed it most. What was it? Where did it come from?

No time for that now. She had to go somewhere, but nowhere in the City was safe.

So she'd have to go nowhere *in* the City. The Figment was still clutched tight in her fist, its blue flicker growing stronger again. Her initials, two swirling *G*'s looped inside one another, had once again appeared on its faceted surface. There was only one way to get out of the City, and now it just might work.

She rode the train until it reached the Hall of Records, a place Gwendolyn knew better than anyone else after the hours she'd spent reading in it. She got off the mono and glanced around, but the City was deserted here too. No doubt everyone was clinging to their Lambents again. Order restored. Everything the same, except the one girl who was different. Gwendolyn swiped a sweaty red curl away from her face at the thought.

You may have been to a library before, but the Hall of Records was less like a library and more like a government archive. There were no stories inside, and the thought that any-one might actually read for *enjoyment* was a foreign concept in the City. Books were like vegetables—some were forced upon children because it was supposed to be "good for them," but no one expected the adults to put themselves through such misery.

Fluorescent lights buzzed. Gwendolyn walked up to a seg-mented wall of metal panels, each two feet wide with a small button on it. She pressed the button on the shelf she wanted, and the metal panels split apart, the gap in the middle widening to reveal two long shelves of books and files. There was very little of interest in the Hall of Records, but on her last adventure, she had found something very interesting indeed. At the end of this particular row of shelves was a blank stretch of wall. A wall that had once contained a portal to other worlds. A portal she had visited over the past few weeks, but it could not help her without the Figment's power.

Perhaps it could help her now.

Gwendolyn was halfway down the row of shelves when she heard the inevitable footsteps. Unsurprised, she turned to see six Mister Men standing just before the entrance to the row, shoulder to shoulder, all identical. Except perhaps for two: Mister Five and Mister Six. She had no trouble picking them out from the rest. They felt . . . different, somehow. Darker, in a way she could not explain.

"Come, Miss Gray. You will not be able to escape us again," said Mister Five.

"No indeed. We have all been here before. That way is sealed. It cannot help you this time," said Mister Six.

And the shelves began to close.

The walls of books drew closer together, threatening to smash her in between. She tried to shout, but again, no sound came from her throat. Instead she pointed at the floor, and *imagined*.

Thorny branches thicker than her wrist sprang from the floor and grew up in front of the men, blocking the row, forcing the shelves to stay open.

The Faceless Gentlemen tried forcing their way through, turning vines to dust with each touch of a white-gloved hand, but the branches were growing too fast, and the men were soon tangled in the thorny barricade. More vines grew to replace the ones that dissolved.

Gwendolyn felt a small moment of triumph, but there was no time to gloat. She faced the wall and held the Figment to her eye. Suddenly, there was a door where no door had been before. A plain grey door, glittering with golden light around the edges. She tried to run toward it but tripped and fell on her face, smashing her nose against the tile.

A thorny branch had wrapped around her ankle. She pulled free but gasped in pain at the scratches she earned. The briars were out of control, and she tried to picture them stopping, but they kept growing.

At least the Mister Men seemed to be stuck as well. But she was pricked and scratched repeatedly as she inched forward. The thicket was now up to her waist. Thank goodness she was so small.

With a final pull, she reached the door, used the Figment to see the knob—

But it was locked. Sealed, the Mister Men had said. And they were halfway down the row, battling the wild spread of thicket that threatened to drown them altogether.

She pounded at the door, screaming silently, willing it open, *imagining* it open.

And suddenly, it was. The door opened a crack and out flew a tiny metal . . . thing. She recognized the clockwork technology of Tohk. The Figment twinkled a blue thought at her, and the word *faerie* popped into her head. It was a tiny clockwork faerie, so small it would fit comfortably in her palm. It fluttered down and landed on her shoulder. A voice came out of it from somewhere, a recording of a woman's voice, strangely accented and as unfamiliar to Gwendolyn as it would be to you, dear reader.

"Well, come on," the voice said. "I've been waiting for you."

Gwendolyn didn't need to be told twice. The door was only open a crack, and she pulled, trying to force back the thicket enough to slip through.

Behind her, she saw Faceless Gentlemen trapped in snarls of thorny briars. Some had even been lifted off the ground by vines that climbed toward the ceiling. She grinned, and slipped through the crack in the doorway.

CHAPTER FOUR

The Library of All Wonder

Gwendolyn had expected to be floating in the nothingness of the In-Between. On her previous trips, she had been pulled at by waves of light and darkness, caught in some struggle between powerful forces.

But none of that happened. Instead, she stepped through as easily as any normal doorway. She was in a stone tunnel, strung with cozy yellow bulbs. The clockwork faerie zipped off, and Gwendolyn lost sight of it. She looked behind her, expecting to see nothing but a dead end, cut off from her home, just like before.

But the door was still open. Mister Five and Mister Six stood on the other side, still in the Hall of Records.

She tensed, then flung herself at the door, about to slam it and find some way to lock it, but the men made no move to stop her. In fact, it seemed they couldn't see her at all. They were searching for something. Mister Five put his hand out, trying to reach through the doorway, but seemed to meet a solid barrier.

How odd, she thought. What was he doing? Then she realized—he must have been placing his hand against the bare wall on the other side. He could not see the doorway without the Figment.

Mister Five reached back and struck the barrier. His hand bounced off of an invisible wall. They could not get through.

She waved her hand inches from the man's invisible face. He did not react. She pulled one of the dangling scraps of cloth from her dress, wadded it into a ball, and threw it through the doorway. The men's heads whipped around to follow it. Then they turned back and stared blankly at the door.

She smiled a mean little smile. *Let them stare*, she thought. *They can stand there and rot for all I care.*

Then she turned, and her smile went from mean and little to wide and wonderful. She was back. She was not sure where she was, but she was out of the City, and that was all that mattered. Somehow, someway, she would find Sparrow and Starling again.

Gwendolyn walked to the end of the tunnel, wiping away a bit of blood that had trickled from her nose after its rather harsh encounter with the ground. She emerged into the most breathtaking place she had ever seen. And given her adventures thus far, that was truly saying something.

There was a courtyard, so large she could hardly see the ceiling. A tile mosaic stretched across the floor, showing knights, cowboys, pirates, vampires, dancing animals, and horrific monsters. Even someone riding what looked like a flying throw rug.

No, not a rug; a *carpet*. The tiles shifted and moved, each one a tiny pixel, making the pictures come alive.

Gwendolyn backed away to take in the enormous picture and bumped against something hard. A bookshelf stretched above her, loaded with heavy volumes. It made her dizzy just looking at it. Around her were more shelves, thousands of them, perhaps millions.

They were not in neat, claustrophobic rows like the Hall of Records but arranged at odd angles here and there, with no rhyme or reason. Some were several stories high, some small enough that they only came up to her waist. The taller ones each had a sliding ladder that moved itself back and forth across the shelf. Gwendolyn dashed over to one, and the ladder held itself still as she climbed to the top and looked out.

There were forests of shelves and books, stretching away as far as she could see. There were twisting stairways, soaring landings and lofts, and cavernous tunnels. Light flooded in from tall, thin windows, and where no light reached, yellow bulbs buzzed. It was an entire city of books.

The air was full of buttery sunbeams, dancing dust motes, and the sort of smell that brings an instant improvement in mood: the smell of *books*. Old books and new books, ink and parchment and paper and binding. It is a very specific sort of smell, one you may recognize if you are a specific sort of person.

Books flew through the air, zooming magically like flocks of birds with paper wings. They flapped their covers and made peculiar rustling sounds as they migrated and sorted and rearranged themselves, new arrivals constantly streaming in through the open windows and finding shelves to nest on.

Watching a flock of books flying in a V formation led her eyes back to the entrance hall. Above it were large golden letters, several feet high.

The Library of All Wonder
Imagination Can Take You Anywhere

It certainly can, Gwendolyn thought.

And then she noticed something she had missed in all her initial wonder at her surroundings. Though the light coming through the windows was yellow and sunny, there was no sun outside. Through the windows shimmered the indescribable blankness of the In-Between, filled with colors that she could not quite make out, dazzling not-light that made her eyes swim until she had to look away.

So, this place was in the In-Between, somehow. That settled part of the question of her location. She wasn't *anywhere.* But who had brought her here? She wasn't worried—she got no ominous feelings from this place. No awful person would own this many books. And why would they pull Gwendolyn *out* of danger just to harm her?

Questions could wait. She was itching to dive into those shelves, a feeling I'm sure you've had when something amazing lies ahead but your parents won't let you go until you've got your jacket on. A glow of happiness filled her for the first time in weeks, and she felt something like her usual self again. Gwendolyn Gray, out on an adventure. It felt like greeting an old friend after the depression she'd been mired in. I'm sure it comes as a relief for you as well. It can be difficult to watch someone we love struggle when we are unable to help them. Let us take our happiness where we can, as it may be in scant supply later.

She clambered down the ladder and grabbed a book at random. It was a book of famous horses, and for a moment she was disappointed at the same sort of dull encyclopedia she could find in her own world. But looking closer, she saw that some of these horses had *wings*. Or tails of fire. Or a single gleaming horn.

She grabbed another, and another, and soon she couldn't even see where she was going over the towering pile of books in her arms. Something snagged her foot and she fell, sending books skittering across the tile. She looked back to see what had tripped her.

A brass plaque was set into the floor of the courtyard, and Gwendolyn crawled over to get a better look. It read:

The Library of All Wonder

Herein are all the stories ever writ,

engraved, or typed, or scrawled, in print or script.

As well as those ne'er writ but only dreamed,

imagined, pondered, wondered, never seen.

From all the worlds that are or e'er might be,

all come to life in this, the world between.

Take what you will, find stories old or new,

for yours will surely come to rest here too.

All the stories ever writ . . . Gwendolyn thought, trying to puzzle out the meaning of the poem. Well, there was time for that later. She gathered up her books, and then she spotted a little book cart, which she dumped her books onto. *Thank you, little cart,* she tried to say, then clenched her fists in frustration as nothing came out. She frowned. Her voice hadn't come back. Would it ever? What if she could never talk again? What if . . .

No, she told herself. No time for thoughts like that. Magic words like *what if* could cut both ways, and she reminded herself that her bad ideas could become just as real as her good ones.

She patted the cart in silent gratitude. Gwendolyn was quite surprised when the wooden cart bumped itself up against her, playfully.

Her mouth formed a silent *Oh!*, though she supposed she should hardly be surprised if there were wonderful things in the Library of All Wonder. The cart turned another circle, then squeaked away through the twisting labyrinth of shelves. Gwendolyn shrugged and followed it.

It led her up several flights of stairs, its wheels whirring as they extended and retracted to get it up each step. It led Gwendolyn to an open loft filled with an incredible variety of chairs, couches, and pillows.

She smiled and plopped into a cushy leather armchair, pulling her feet up under her and wriggling with pleasure. She smoothed out her skirt and felt a pang of sadness. It was in little more than tatters now. Her precious puffed-sleeve dress, given to her by the pretty dressmaker in Copernium. The rips in the fabric hurt more than the scratches on her arms and legs. She would have to do something about the Mister Men. And find Sparrow and Starling. And learn who had brought her here.

But that all seemed awfully tiring, and the chair was so awfully comfortable. She needed rest, and these books needed to be read.

The cart wheeled itself within arm's reach. The clockwork faerie flitted down from somewhere and landed on Gwendolyn's shoulder, curling her tiny metal legs under her in just the same pose as Gwendolyn. It looked up at her, jeweled green eyes twinkling in its metal face.

Gwendolyn grinned and gave the little thing a pat on the head. Then she dove into the books, marveling at the largest variety of fascinating stories she had ever seen. There were heroes saving damsels in distress, damsels saving heroes in distress, tales of many futures and of pasts that never existed, books of songs and rhymes and riddles. One book had pictures of beautiful women with tails like fish, and Gwendolyn dearly wished she could meet one.

She was drawn to a book about a boy who never grew up. *That* sounded wonderful; growing up had not been a pleasant experience thus far. She would love to be his Darling, to fly away with him and tell him stories as she did to her own lost boys and girls, Tommy and Missy and Ian and Jessica. But if *Gwendolyn* ever got captured by pirates, she certainly wouldn't wait around for some crowing *boy* to save her—she would jolly well do something about it. Though she rather liked the name "Wendy."

The clockwork faerie flitted up to examine the stack of

books, emitting a noise somewhere between a click and a chirp, and accidentally knocked one to the floor. It fell with its back cover open, and Gwendolyn spotted a familiar golden sticker in the back of it.

A sudden thought nearly knocked her out of her chair. Gwendolyn lunged for her bag, sending the tiny faerie into a tizzy. She flipped to the back cover of *Kolonius Thrash*. There it was, the sticker she and Tommy had found and puzzled over.

Kolonius Thrash and the Perilous Pirates
by Stanley Kirby
328A5H
If found, please return to
The Library of All Wonder

She smacked her forehead, scolding herself for being so distracted that she hadn't immediately made the connection. This was where it had come from. Sure enough, each of the books from her cart had a similar sticker with a different code.

Another clue to add to the exhausting pile. It was getting late, she supposed, though in the In-Between it was impossible to tell. She was enormously tired. The School, the return of the Lambents *and* her powers, armies of zombie children, numerous Mister Men, this beautiful library . . . she wanted nothing more than to curl up in a pile of pillows and close her eyes for a year or two.

But one must tidy up one's mess before bed. She trudged back to the library entrance and the door where Mister Five and Mister Six stood frozen on the other side. It would be utter foolishness to leave it open while she slept.

She was about to close it when she noticed something peculiar. On this side, the plain grey door was surrounded by a solid gold frame made of golden branches that sprouted pages instead of leaves. Across the top, in script that curled around the golden branches, were two words: *Egressai Infinitus.*

Gwendolyn didn't know what to make of it. Perhaps this was the reason the portal hadn't closed behind her, letting her look back into the Hall of Records. But she was far too tired for anymore mysteries just now, if you please and thank you very much. She slammed the door, hoping to smack the Mister Men in the face, and turned to head back to the loft.

But a noise from behind her made her pause. Turning, she saw the plain grey door slip sideways out of the golden frame and disappear. Another door slid into place, and another, dozens of them, spinning faster and faster through the golden frame like a merry-go-round. Eventually, the doors slowed, and a new door settled into the frame with a dull *thud.*

This door was made of rough tree bark. A brass plaque in the middle read *M-S-N-D-W-S*. But that was all she noticed before the door flew open and knocked her flat on her back.

A woman stood on the other side, silhouetted in golden light. Gwendolyn sprawled on the floor, looking up at her.

The first thing Gwendolyn noticed was a magnificent pair of clockwork wings that sprouted from the woman's back, glinting with a rainbow of metallic colors. She wore an emerald green bodice over a satin blouse, along with high-heeled boots and tweed knickerbockers. Her short bob of snow-white hair was held back by a pair of goggles, and around her neck was a glowing red jewel on a silver necklace.

All in all, she cut quite a dashing figure.

The woman put her hands on her hips. Her metal wings twitched in annoyance. "Finally. There you are. I've been trying to get through for hours. What sort of unlicked cub leaves the door open all bleeding day?"

CHAPTER FIVE

The Inventress of Faeoria

"What's the matter, dolly? Cat got your tongue?"

Gwendolyn stared up at the stranger, then nodded.

"What, really?"

Gwendolyn gave an exaggerated shrug.

The woman's face scrunched in thought. She was older, but with an unlined visage that made it impossible to tell her age. She could have been Gwendolyn's young aunt, or as old as her mother, or any number of years older. But she had the air of someone who knew exactly what she was doing, if you please and thank you very much. "Hadn't planned on you being mute. That'll make things a skosh more difficult . . ."

Gwendolyn had no idea what was going on, but she was never without ideas entirely. She dug out her sketchbook and pencil.

The mystery woman nodded. "Good girl. Can't be playing charades every time you need to use the washroom, can we?"

Gwendolyn flipped open the sketchbook and scrawled three quick words.

Who are you?

"Sprout, we're not going to have an entire conversation through the doorway. I've been expecting you, so come in, get proper comfortable, and we can blither on as long as you like. Or at least *I* can, but you're welcome to scribble. Hop to it!" Then she turned and walked away.

Gallivanting off with strangers is exactly the sort of things your parents warn you about. But Gwendolyn had a strange, warm feeling about this woman. And she wouldn't find Sparrow and Starling by standing still, after all. She took a deep breath and stepped across the threshold.

Beyond was a hallway where the floors, walls, and ceiling were all made of a rich yellow wood. The hallway was like a spiral staircase with no steps, smooth floors sloping downward. Doors lined the inner wall of the spiral, and arched windows lined the other. The windows held no glass, and sweet evening air wafted through them. Gwendolyn went to one and peeked outside.

She was in a forest that made her own imaginary woods look small and ugly by comparison. The trees were larger than the skyscrapers she was used to. Branches intertwined to form covered walkways and stairways and byways, entire streets and neighborhoods suspended in the treetops.

Gwendolyn looked down and saw that she was *inside* one of the trees. The sun was setting, rays of crimson light trickled through the forest, and night was just beginning to wake. Flickering motes of light danced in the growing darkness between the trees, like fireworks that did not fade, infesting every shadow.

"Yes, the first glance is breathtaking, but don't lollygag," came the woman's voice from down the spiraling hall. "We've much to do, so pick up your jaw and shake a sock."

Gwendolyn turned away from the window. The voice was definitely the one that had come from the clockwork faerie. This woman had rescued Gwendolyn from the Faceless Gentlemen. But who was she, and what was this place? As there was only one way to find out, Gwendolyn headed down the spiral.

The hallway opened up into an enormous laboratory carved from the heart of the tree. A rough wooden column rose from the center of the lab like a tree trunk. At the top, branches sprouted into an enormous model of a solar system. The branches moved, the orbs on their ends revolving to mimic the movement of some unknown planets. More branches stretched all over the lab, shaped like shelves or racks, some of them holding long rows of bottles with glowing liquid, others dangling with glittering tools. They moved as well, bringing whatever was needed into arm's reach.

She spotted the woman again, goggles lowered, tapping one of a cluster of tubes that had colored liquids running through them. Then Gwendolyn realized they weren't tubes at all, but translucent vines. "Hmm," the woman said. "Distillation margins are a bit low. Have to make the pixies stir the algae pots again."

There were wooden tables and benches cluttered with strange items. Everywhere she walked there were beakers bubbling, potions simmering, strange devices made of wood and stone and gold.

The woman appeared and grabbed her hand, making

Gwendolyn jump. "Distracted again. Stars and sprockets, we'll have work to do with this one. No time to gawk yet, though it is all a bit *flash*, if I'm forced to brag." She beamed, leading Gwendolyn away. "Ah, here we are."

The woman pulled Gwendolyn into a cozy sitting room. A fire of lavender flames crackled under an ornately carved mantle. Books lined the walls, and there was a desk cluttered with papers and maps. Two armchairs seemed to have grown themselves right out of the floor. In the corner stood a large instrument with two rows of black and white keys, which the Figment could have told Gwendolyn was a *harpsichord*, had it not been in her bag.

The woman rolled her shoulders, and the clockwork wings folded themselves up and out of sight. She unclipped some sort of harness and hung the whole winged contraption on a coatrack. Then she plopped herself into a chair.

Still a bit reluctant, Gwendolyn settled herself into the other.

"No need for questions yet," the woman said, crossing one leg over. "Have a gape, let it percolate. You'll be peckish, I don't doubt."

She clapped her hands, and dozens of clockwork creatures buzzed and flew and crawled around them, carrying cups and saucers and kettles, until an entire tea service was set before them. Gwendolyn noticed that the coffee table was actually a toadstool, and the cup in front of her was a sturdy flower that had blossomed into a proper little teacup. It seemed just the place where one might have a tea party with a badger.

Any wonderings she had were banished by the seductive

aroma of vanilla and jasmine. It was the most tempting thing Gwendolyn had ever smelled.

She looked suspiciously at the brew, but the woman was already sipping her own with a contented sigh. Gwendolyn couldn't resist. She was terribly thirsty. The tea took care of that, quenching her thirst with a single magical sip. It made her feel snug and lovely, right down to her toes, as though it were smoothing over cracks in her spirit. She was instantly awake and alert, her exhaustion gone. Truly, there is nothing like a good cup of tea, though "good" doesn't begin to describe this exquisite concoction.

"Turkish delight?" The woman offered a tray of colorful cubes dusted in white sugar. "No, where's my sense, one must have bread before cake. Real food first." And instead she handed Gwendolyn a scone stuffed with bacon and cheese and chives, which the girl devoured.

The food was mind-bogglingly good, especially compared to the unimaginative cuisine of the City. Come to think of it, it had been a long time since Gwendolyn had felt like eating at all. But her old appetites seemed to be returning along with much of her old self.

She would have kept eating and drinking until she burst, but the woman set her cup down and leaned forward, hands folded. "So then. I believe you were fizzing with questions, my silent friend."

Gwendolyn froze mid-reach, stretching for a frosted cube of Turkish delight with one hand, her tea in the other, and a second scone stuffed in her mouth. With great reluctance and a look of longing at a stacked assortment of dainty teacakes, she put the food down and picked up her sketchbook. She drew a line under what she had already written.

Who are you?

"Ah, yes, always was rubbish at introductions." The woman leaned forward for an awkward handshake. "Cyria Kytain. Maker and traveler."

Gwendolyn shook hands, her now-empty mouth open in shock. She began scribbling furiously.

Cyrio Kytain? Tohk? Famous inventor?

"Yes, that's the one. Cyri-a, dear, not Cyrio."

Gwendolyn didn't understand. Cyrio Kytain was a legendary figure in Tohk, founder of Copernium. He had vanished hundreds of years earlier, and his abandoned laboratory in the Crystal Coves had been proof of that. Gwendolyn kept scribbling.

Grandfather? Great-great?

"My granddad? What about him?" the woman said with a puzzled smile. "What a delightfully random conversation."

Gwendolyn gritted her teeth. This would be so much easier if she could *speak*. She wrote more slowly.

Are you related to the famous inventor from Tohk? Is he your ancestor?

"What? Oh-ho, I see your puzzlement. *I* am the famous inventor, the *only* Cyria Kytain. And like to be the last. Never had any children as far as I can recall, though if there are ones I don't know about, I'd jolly well like to know how they snuck past without my notice . . ."

You invented the Pistola Luminant?

The woman smiled, violet eyes sparkling. "That old thing. Yes, quite proud of it."

More scribbling. *But you're a woman.*

Her smile turned mischievous. "Last anyone bothered to check."

Gwendolyn had to turn the page. Her mind was working faster than her hand could keep up.

Everyone says that Kytain was a man.

Kytain's smile vanished. "Well, they would, wouldn't they? It's those writers. You do anything smart or strong or important, and they all just *assume* you're a *man*. Lack of diversity in publishing, this is where it gets you. Of course, the tales of my many wives may have had something to do with it . . ." She trailed off, a wistful look shadowing her handsome features.

Gwendolyn scribbled down a thought that was bursting to get out. *Where in Tohk are we?*

The sound of Gwendolyn's pen snapped the woman out of her thoughts. "What? Oh." And she laughed a bold and brassy laugh. "Nowhere in Tohk at all. You've got the wrong world, I'm afraid. What a poor host I am. Welcome to Faeoria."

A question bubbled up inside Gwendolyn, a question she was nearly too afraid to ask, and equally afraid to know the answer to. But she scribbled it down nonetheless.

Is this all inside my head?

Kytain laughed again, louder and longer, until she was nearly out of breath. Eventually, she settled back down. "Well, for one so silent, you've no shortage of arrogance. You think all this is yours?" Kytain gestured to the room around them, to the world itself. "Think you've got the smarts to conjure whole worlds at will, eh? Maybe you think Tohk is yours as well, eh? No, sprout, I'm afraid you're really here, whether you like it or not. This world is every bit as real as yours, and Tohk as well."

Gwendolyn sighed with relief. She hadn't wanted to believe it was all just some wonderful dream, but hearing it out loud seemed to relax muscles she hadn't known she'd clenched.

She started writing again, but the woman put a hand on her paper. "Stop that, you've had your go. I've queries for you as well. Tell me smart, who are you? No, bother that, no names. Not here. Even the trees have ears."

"I heard that," came a low voice from all around them, vibrating the very walls.

Gwendolyn jumped up in surprise. She knocked over her cup, but two clockwork birds snatched it up before it could spill.

"Precisely my point, you great nosy thing!" Kytain shouted. "We're inside your bloody self, after all . . ." she mumbled. "Pardon the interruption, sprout."

Gwendolyn glanced around nervously, then eased back into the chair.

"Pressing on," Kytain said. "What's your story? Blast, never mind, we'll be here all night. I'll be blunt. Why can't you talk?"

That one Gwendolyn could answer. *The Faceless Gentlemen took my voice.*

Kytain raised an eyebrow. "What a horrifying sentence. I'm positively tingling to hear all about it. You know of *me*, though. You've visited Tohk, I take it?"

Gwendolyn wrote. *Yes.*

"The place you come from. Do you like it?"

She scribbled *No.*

Kytain took a sip of tea. "Not surprising, from what I'm told. Stand out a bit, do you?"

Tap. Tap. Tap. *Yes. Yes. Yes.*

"Well, everyone stands out here. So, let's take your vitals. Are you an orphan or a twin?"

Gwendolyn tapped. *No.*

"Any relatives who died in mysterious accidents?"

No.

"Strange scars, birthmarks, or tattoos?"

No.

"Boy you're being forced to marry?"

Furious tapping. *No. No. No. No. No.*

Kytain shivered. "My thoughts exactly. Prophetic dreams?"

Well . . . there were her nightmares. *Maybe . . .*

"Thought so." Kytain stared at her, her gaze looking deeper than any normal one. Gwendolyn was going to ask about the strange questions, but Kytain seemed to read her mind and said, "I'm trying to see what kind of story you're in."

Gwendolyn wanted to say that she wasn't in a story, but Kytain was well ahead of her. "We're all in a story, dearie, and rest assured that your story is every bit as real as mine. Now it's just a matter of genre. I nabbed you from the Dystopic regions. Nasty places, though I suppose home is home . . ." She held Gwendolyn's gaze for a moment longer, then nodded and went back to her chair. "That hair of yours is a dead giveaway. You redheads do crop up in those parts. Though with all your hopping around, who knows what sort of story arc you're bound for. Never saw myself as the mystical mentor figure, but if needs must . . ."

Gwendolyn hadn't understood a word of that. She took another sip of tea, trying to clear those purple eyes from her mind. Then she wrote *Why?*

Kytain raised an eyebrow. "Why what?"

Gwendolyn wrote three more questions. *Am I here? Did you help me? Were you expecting me?* She drew three lines, connecting each question to the word *Why?*

"In order: because I have things to teach you, because you needed it, and because she told me you were coming. Though she skimped a bit on the *who* of it all . . ."

Who? Teach me what? I don't understand.

"And you won't, not 'til you can converse a little more effectively. But we'll get your voice fixed up, and this monologue can become a proper dialogue."

None of this was making sense. I'm sure you can imagine how frustrating it was to have so much to say but no way to be heard. Gwendolyn had more questions than she could write and didn't know where to start. So Gwendolyn sat and thought, listening to the crackle of the purple fire, trying to decide what she wanted most. But as soon as she'd thought those words, the answer was obvious.

Can you help me get back to Tohk?

Kytain scoffed. "You just got here, you can't leave yet."

Gwendolyn wrote furiously. *If you're really the great inventor Kytain, you can help me get back to Tohk.*

"Oh, balderdash, what for? It's not *your* home," Kytain snapped. Gwendolyn had clearly touched a nerve. She pressed on.

I need to find my friends.

Kytain softened. "I see . . . We might be able to finagle a visit eventually. But sending you now, untrained, would be dangerous to stupidity."

Training for what?

"Why, to change your world, of course."

That stunned Gwendolyn. She recovered, turned a page, and wrote *I already tried that.*

Kytain laughed again, though Gwendolyn didn't appreciate it as much this time. "*Saving* the world is one thing, dolly. *Changing* the world is an entirely different story."

Gwendolyn thought about that, then shook her head.

I don't care. I need to find my friends.

"You will, when you're ready."

She growled silently. She couldn't argue if she couldn't *talk*. This lack of voice was incredibly frustrating and more than a little scary. And who was this woman to tell her what she could and couldn't do? She flipped back a page and tapped it repeatedly.

No. No. No.

"I said, not yet."

Gwendolyn's heart beat faster. What if her voice never came back? What if she was stuck like this, scribbling down her thoughts, never fully able to express herself? She felt the bitter pinch of anxiety, and her breathing was fast and shallow.

I need to get back to Tohk. I need to find my friends. She held the sketchbook right under Kytain's nose, practically banging on the page.

"Don't shove that in my face, little thing. I saved your life."

This lady wouldn't *listen*, and Gwendolyn couldn't convince her with these stupid *scribbles*.

I. Don't. Care. I need to find my friends.

"No. And that's final," she said in the same tone Gwendolyn's mother always used.

Gwendolyn screamed in silent frustration, and flung the sketchbook across the room. It hit the desk and smashed a collection of ink bottles, ruining the papers and maps.

Gwendolyn hadn't meant to break anything, and it only made her feel worse. She leapt from her chair, stormed out of the room, and sprinted straight through the impressive laboratory. She ran all the way up the spiraling hall to the door at the top of the tree, the one she'd first come in.

It was closed again. She would go back into the Library of All Wonder and figure out how to use that Egressai Infinitus thing to get back to Tohk. She flung open the door, but the Library of All Wonder was gone.

She was stuck. Again.

CHAPTER FIVE-AND-A-HALF

Unbreakable Rules

Yes, this is chapter five-and-a-half; you've read that correctly. Time moves in unpredictable ways in the realm of the Fae folk, as Gwendolyn will soon learn. But for now, she simply stood, staring through the doorway. A warm summer night greeted her, dancing motes of light flickering through the trees of the forest outside. Definitely not the Library she'd come from.

She slammed the door and opened it, but there was still no library. She slammed it again. And again. Her heart was pounding—she had to get *out*, she couldn't *breathe*. But the forest seemed to laugh at her. She put her back against the wall and slumped to the ground.

Sitting there at the top of the tree, Gwendolyn Gray began to sob. She knew she was overreacting, but the tears came anyway, and she didn't know why, and she didn't know how to make them stop, and even her crying made no sound, which made it all the worse. It was a wet and messy cry, full of panting and anger.

By now, you have noticed that something is askew inside

our precious Gwendolyn, beyond the already daunting trials of teenage hormones. But Gwendolyn couldn't begin to explain it any more than you could explain the workings of the clockwork faerie that fluttered up and rested on Gwendolyn's shoulder.

Kytain came around the corner and stood with her hands on her hips. "Well? Got it all out?" she said, though she seemed more uncomfortable than stern.

Gwendolyn wanted to throw something at the inventress, but she was suddenly too tired to even lift her head. So she rested it on her knees and looked down at the floor between her feet.

Cyria Kytain sat down beside her. The inventress leaned her head on top of Gwendolyn's. It wasn't a hug, which Gwendolyn would never have accepted, but it *did* feel nice. Eventually, Gwendolyn relaxed against Kytain, and they just sat together until the girl's breathing returned to normal.

Kytain was the first to break the silence. "So, this." She held out Gwendolyn's sketchbook, open to an ink-splattered picture of Sparrow and Starling. "Those friends of yours, I presume?"

Gwendolyn gave a soggy little nod.

"I see. Well, come on. You'll feel better after some sleep. Then we'll see to fixing your voice, and you can tell me all about these two. I *am* quite clever you know, and I can help if you'll let me." Kytain stood up and held out a hand.

Gwendolyn looked up, eyes red and puffy. She took Kytain's hand and the inventress pulled her up and led her down the hall. The clockwork faerie landed on her head and made a nest in her wild hair, sitting cross-legged with wings spread like some strange hair bow.

Kytain indicated a blank stretch of wall. "This will do. Tree, would you be so kind?"

The voice returned, slow and deep and everywhere. "Only if the quickling promises not to slam me anymore."

Kytain looked at Gwendolyn. "Well? Do you?"

Gwendolyn nodded.

"She promises!" Kytain hollered.

"No need to shout, I'm right here." The wood twisted and creaked, and a little door appeared.

Gwendolyn opened it. Inside was a cozy little bedroom, all the furnishings perfectly proportioned for Gwendolyn's small frame. There were flickering candles on a mirrored vanity, and the scent of cinnamon filled the room.

Kytain entered and banged her head on the low ceiling. "Ow! Sarcastic overgrown stump. You did that on purpose," she said, rubbing her head. She turned to Gwendolyn. "You can catch your winks here, free of charge," Kytain said, head tilted. The clockwork faerie zipped up and around, inspecting everything.

Gwendolyn gave Kytain a fierce look that said, *I'll stay here for now, but only for one night and only because I'm very tired and then I'll be gone and nothing you can do will stop me.* It was a very specific sort of look.

Kytain rolled her eyes. "Stars and sprockets, you couldn't pay me to be thirteen again for all the gold in Archicon. To bed, little bunny."

The bed *did* look terribly soft. Gwendolyn pulled back a blanket grown from fresh cotton, sat down, and took off her shoes. There are few things more satisfying than removing a tight pair of shoes after a long day of too much running.

Kytain tossed the sketchbook to the faerie, who caught it and fluttered it over to a little bedside table. "Now, it is essential that you do not leave this tree. If you do, your very life will be in danger."

Gwendolyn shrugged.

Kytain massaged her brow. "Please. Take this seriously. This is the realm of the faeries, and they are not the cute playful things you find in stories. Stay put."

Gwendolyn shrugged again, too exhausted to argue.

"Fine. Sleep. I'll wake you . . . whenever they decide to bring the sun up. Dawn is rather unreliable." Kytain looked around the room, clearly clueless as to the proper way to put a child to bed. She settled for an awkward pat on Gwendolyn's frizzy head. "Yes. Well. Good night." And she ducked out the door.

Gwendolyn stretched and yawned. The faerie landed on the bedside table and stretched and yawned as well. Gwendolyn lay back and sighed. The faerie lay back and sighed.

Flickering motes of light danced in the night outside her window. So, she was trapped on another strange and beautiful world. But it was much less fun alone. Thoughts of Sparrow and Starling rolled around until she finally closed her eyes.

"Sweet dreams," bellowed the tree.

Gwendolyn jumped with a silent shriek and fell out of bed.

~~~

Her sleep did not last long, and she woke up in a cold sweat. Even here, she couldn't escape the nightmares of the blackened, lightning-struck wastelands. And now there were glowing-eyed zombie children in the mix.

The room was still dark. Nighttime noises drifted through the window, all foreign to a City girl like her: buzzing insects, creaking branches, the growl of a distant predator. And then, something else.

"Hey."

She perked up. That was definitely a voice.

"Hey. Down here!"

A familiar voice that made her rush to the window.

And there he was. Standing on a wooden platform below was a boy just her age with a red shirt, leather jacket, and yellow scarf. His checkered cap was perched jauntily on his brown hair, and his hands were shoved into his pockets.

"Hello, girlie," Sparrow said.

Gwendolyn felt something akin to the electric thrill you may have enjoyed upon receiving a gift you had not expected, and opening it to find exactly what you always wanted. She was speechless as all the things she wanted to say tried to get out at once. Then she remembered that she couldn't speak anyway, and waved her arms wildly.

"Come down here," he said, grinning his wolfish grin.

At this point, Gwendolyn could have paused to consider Kytain's warning. She could have ignored it by convincing herself that Sparrow might have stumbled upon this world on his own, and no one here knew about Sparrow, so he must be real. All reasonable thoughts. But in truth, she thought none of these things. All she could think of was *Sparrow*, who was *right there*, which left no room for thoughts of *wait* and *beware*.

She stripped the bed of its covers and tied them together into a makeshift rope. Whatever they were made of was nice and stretchy. She tied one end to the bedpost and tossed the other end out the window.

But as she went to climb out the window, it shrank until it was too small for her to fit. "Stay inside, little quickling," the tree said. "Desire creates the space for disappointment."

She didn't know what *that* was supposed to mean, but she had come too far to let some talking piece of wood get in her way. She looked at the window and *imagined*, picturing the wood stretching, and it obeyed her with a horrible grinding sound.

She was out the window in a flash, sliding down the bed-sheets until her feet hit a wooden walkway that wrapped around the tree.

It was a perfect summer night, just the thing for a reunion of lost friends. Sparrow was already heading down a walkway to another tree. "This way," he said. Then he disappeared into the darkness.

Gwendolyn started to run, but there was a fluttering sound, and someone grabbed her and spun her round. It was Cyria Kytain, looking furious, metal wings flared.

"What have you done?"

Gwendolyn gestured to where Sparrow had been.

"Are you deaf as well as mute?" Kytain shouted. "I told you not to leave the tree! Blast these narrative conventions, why can't heroes ever follow the rules? You saw something you wanted, yes? Perhaps someone you loved?"

Gwendolyn nodded.

Kytain shook her head. "By the suns, girl, you seemed cleverer than this. You were tricked. *Easily.*"

Gwendolyn pouted in defiance. If no one here knew about Sparrow, how could she have been tricked?

"It's basic desire magic—you see what you *want* to see, and even the spell's caster won't know exactly what you saw. It was that boy you're stuck on, wasn't it? Teenagers. I'll wager he didn't call you by name?"

Gwendolyn froze. No, he hadn't. She had a sudden sinking feeling.

"Then you've been hoodwinked, bamboozled, sent on a trip for biscuits, and—"

Thunder rumbled through the cloudless sky. A bolt of angry red lightning split the air.

Kytain's eyes narrowed. "—And we don't have much time. They know you're here, and are not best pleased. Well, little Miss Silent-but-Moody, I hope you snatched a wink or two, because you're in for a long night in more ways than one."

The inventress tried to pull her along, but Gwendolyn kept her feet planted. She crossed her arms and tapped her foot in an I'm-not-moving-until-you-explain kind of way. It was a very specific sort of tapping.

Kytain sighed and ran a hand through her snow-white hair, then gestured to the sky. "Stars and sprockets, girl, you've been summoned to the court. I'll prepare you on the way." She looked down at the frizzy, filthy Gwendolyn. "Nothing to be done about you now, ragamuffin. You didn't even think to put on your shoes before scampering off to do the one thing I told you not to. But time is not our friend. Get a wiggle on!" And Kytain hustled her away from the laboratory tree, deeper into the forest.

~~~

Mere words cannot do justice to the vast and magnificent splendor of the Fae lands. I've no small skill with words, but even my best will be but the palest reflection of the wonders Gwendolyn saw as they traveled through the tree-top city.

Kytain pulled her along soaring walkways grown from branches and up staircases that spiraled around enormous tree trunks, none of which had any sort of guardrails. Gwendolyn supposed if you had wings on, you might be quite comfortable with the sheer drops all around, but that hardly stopped her own palms from sweating. She felt much better once they turned onto the wide avenue of the high street.

Buildings lined either side, with more buildings rising up in tiers behind those, though we can hardly call them "buildings" since none of them had been "built" but rather grown right from the trees around them. She could see other platforms in the distance, whole suspended neighborhoods, all golden and glittering. It was a sparkling city in the treetops.

Gwendolyn had seen some fairly spectacular sights on her adventures thus far, but nothing could have prepared her for this. The buildings resembled some of the old-fashioned houses you might see in your world—stately manors with mansard roofs, dormer windows, columned porticos, and other features that would take an architectural degree to describe—but Gwendolyn had never seen such gorgeously peculiar buildings. They looked a bit like brightly colored dollhouses, grown to life size.

There were fountains and gazebos and gardens that invited you to take pleasant afternoon strolls, and warm light poured from every opening, enticing and cozy. Flickering strings of lights lined every rooftop and doorway, wrapped around every column. You might call them Christmas lights, though Gwendolyn knew of no such thing as Christmas, and the colors were of shades that would put any holiday decorator to shame. There is good reason such things are known as "faerie lights" in certain parts of certain worlds.

"That's where we're headed," Kytain said, pointing past the breathtaking display.

At the end of the street was a building that reeked of authority—perhaps a cathedral, a palace, or a castle, but something altogether wilder and more beautiful. Soaring arches, pointed spires, and menacing gargoyles loomed over her.

The heart of the cathedral was a tower that stretched so high Gwendolyn thought it should have clouds around it. But the top of the tower ceased to be building and instead burst into thick leafy branches, capped with a stained-glass dome. A tree with a castle for a trunk, or a castle that decided it would be a tree when it grew up. She got dizzy just looking at it.

"The court of the Fae, seat of the Willow Throne," Kytain said. She looked down at Gwendolyn. "Time you learned who you're dealing with."

Gwendolyn prepared herself to pay attention. *By now I might have learned to look before leaping,* she scolded herself, and vowed not to make any more missteps.

Kytain knelt down to look Gwendolyn in the eye. "First, tell no one your name. Names have a certain power, so don't utter even a single syllable."

Gwendolyn glared and pointed angrily at her throat.

"Right. Suppose that's not much of a problem at the moment. Second, accept no gifts, bargains, or favors. There are always strings attached. The Fae cannot lie outright, but truth always makes the best tricks, and tricksy they are in spades. Third, no food or drink, not a drop of water on a leaf, not an acorn from the ground, unless I give it to you myself."

Gwendolyn nodded. Like most children, she sometimes struggled to remember rules, but these seemed like especially important ones. *No names, no gifts, no food, faeries can't lie,* she repeated to herself.

"Logic is our best weapon. Faeries hate it, don't use it, and barely understand it. We can make allowances for your silence, but you must be all reverence and curtsies. We mortals are their playthings, so mind your manners, or you'll end up losing more than just your voice. If you're lucky enough to still be human-shaped at all, that is. They're not overly fond of humans."

Gwendolyn gestured to indicate the inventor herself.

"Well, they find *me* amusing, so long as I keep them supplied with interesting new ideas. I've convinced them that courtly etiquette is the height of fashion, and they think it quite a fun game. They're rather taken with the notion of clothes. When

I arrived, they were all running around starkers with naught but a leaf or two between them. Quite a sight, I'll tell you . . . But we're nearly there. Best be silent."

Gwendolyn shot her another glare.

"Yes, fine, *I'll* be silent. Come. We're late."

They reached the palace doors, and the crimson lightning flashed again.

CHAPTER FIVE-AND-TWO-THIRDS

Broken Rules

One endless trek up elaborate winding staircases later, they reached the top of the tower. The stairway opened onto a room so large that Gwendolyn froze in sheer agoraphobic shock.

The throne room had no walls. The whole of Faeoria could be seen through the arched openings around the edge. Stately columns grew from the floor, and the higher they grew, the more tree-like they became. The tops of them sprouted into leafy branches that intertwined to form a domed canopy. What she had taken for a stained-glass dome on the outside was actually thousands of paper-thin leaves, brightly colored and translucent, coloring the floor with shards of rainbow light.

In the center of the throne room sprouted an enormous willow tree. Each of its branches was heavily laden not with fruit, but with glowing gemstones: rubies, emeralds, diamonds, and sapphires, all pulsing with life.

Kytain moved with steady grace, and barefoot Gwendolyn padded awkwardly behind. The willow fronds pulled back at their approach, lifting like curtains to reveal two wooden thrones, and two magnificent beings upon them.

Gwendolyn gasped soundlessly at the sight of them.

On the left was a woman of exquisite beauty. Piercing blue eyes glared from a regal face, with high cheekbones and sharp features. She had hair of gold, not pale blonde like many of the Cityzens, but a rich buttery yellow, set in elaborate cascading braids and capped with a crown of twigs and bluebells. She was slender as a birch tree, and had she been standing, she would have towered over both girl and inventress alike.

Her dress was sewn from blue and yellow butterfly wings. But after a moment, Gwendolyn realized it wasn't sewn together at all. The woman was entirely clothed in *living* butterflies, forming a fluttering gown. From her bare shoulders sprouted six oversized dragonfly wings that draped casually over the arms of the throne. She sat prettily, back straight and ankles crossed.

On the right sat a man, if you could call him that. He looked every bit as strong and wild as his companion was regal and lovely, his skin a rich dark bronze while hers was rosy and pale. A set of antlers sprouted from his head and formed a magnificent crown, laced with gold and peacock feathers. His beard was full of moss, and his chest was covered with fine black fur, which also coated his legs and hoofed feet. He wore no clothing, save for two enormous eagle's wings that he wrapped around himself like a cloak. He sprawled lazily on his throne.

"So," he said. "She is here. Your respect for our rules has not improved, inventress."

Gwendolyn gulped.

Kytain sank to one knee and bowed, and Gwendolyn followed suit. "My lord Oberon, my lady Titania, I follow the edicts of the Fae to the very letter."

He scowled. "You have brought a mortal from the otherlands here into our realm."

Kytain held up a finger in correction. "Ah, but I only brought her into my workshop. And after all, she's only a little thing . . ."

Gwendolyn shot her a scowl.

The lady on her throne shrugged her milk-white shoulders, sending a ripple through her shimmering wings. "Little or not, here she is. And this is not your workshop."

Kytain nodded. "Correct. We are here at your royal summons."

King Oberon bristled. "We only summoned her here because she *left* your workshop. We felt it the moment she set foot upon our land. I should add her to my throne for such trespassing."

Gwendolyn looked at the thrones. Each was carved into shapes of people and animals, pitiful creatures with pained faces, bent at wrong angles to form the shape of a chair. And she had the horrible realization that these were not carvings at all, but living beings, trapped in torment.

"Any monstrous . . . thing . . . could have come through your doors into my realm," Oberon rumbled. "Nothing is to cross the threshold of your workshop. That was the bargain we made when you began tampering with portals."

Gwendolyn caught a glimpse of someone peeking from behind Oberon's throne. An unruly mop of black hair partially obscured a bronze-skinned face, with seductively dainty features and a knowing smirk.

"But my lord," Kytain said, "you *ordered* the girl to leave my workshop. We didn't dare disobey."

Oberon straightened in his chair, looming larger. "I ordered no such thing. Do not speak such lies in my presence."

"Sire, is that not Robin Goodfellow there? Your bonded servant?" Kytain gestured to the simpering figure behind the throne.

Oberon cast the barest glance at the slender creature. The faerie was dressed in tight black knickers and a short jacket, with a bright orange shirt unbuttoned almost to the navel. He was older than Gwendolyn, looking somewhere in his early twenties, though she suspected that this creature was far older indeed.

"Of what consequence is Robin in this?" Oberon rumbled.

"Well, it was Robin who summoned her from my tree, albeit in a clever disguise. If *your* servant summoned her from my workshop, it must have been on *your* command."

Titania raised an eyebrow, the slightest smile playing at her glittering blue lips. "And so?"

Kytain looked triumphant. "So, either the king ordered Robin to bring her here, and we have only obeyed his command, or Oberon's own servant disobeys his rules by luring the girl out. Is Robin no longer under your control? Perhaps the king grows tired, and Robin acts as Robin pleases, directly disobeying—"

"My powers are as strong as ever. What angers me is . . . is . . . that it took you so long to arrive. I expect all my summonses to be obeyed promptly," Oberon snapped.

Gwendolyn saw the trap, realizing what Kytain was up to. Oberon couldn't appear weak, but he couldn't directly lie about it.

Kytain rose and clapped her gloved hands together. "Well, the girl is here now, for your inspection."

"And yet, dear sweet Cyria," Titania said, the slightest frost forming on her words, "the girl *is* here against our will, and we all know good and well my husband did not order it, despite his attempts to protect his pride. You have sparred well, but a price must be paid. Let us have the measure of her."

Kytain's victorious look turned to one of defeat. "As you wish." One metal wing swept Gwendolyn forward. Gwendolyn looked back at Kytain, but the inventress wouldn't meet her eye.

"Look this way, cherry child," Titania said. Her tone was so sweet that Gwendolyn felt dizzy, as though nothing would be more pleasant than to obey that lovely voice. She found her gaze locked by Titania's blue eyes and Oberon's hazel.

They bored into her. She felt their gaze on her very heart.

"I like her," Titania sang. "Though she be but little, she is fierce."

Gwendolyn didn't see how she was fierce; she'd done nothing but stand silently since they'd come in. But those eyes clearly saw more than what lay on the surface. She suddenly felt very aware of how beautiful they were, and how ragged and ugly she must seem in comparison.

"I see spirit. And danger," Oberon said.

"Is your strength so easily rattled?" said Titania.

Gwendolyn expected another outburst, but Oberon only smirked. "My pride has been pricked enough for one day. Prudence would do me better. What would you have, lady of my heart?"

"I would have this girl, lord of sweet words. She would serve me well, would she not?"

Oberon steepled his fingers. "Perhaps, but she is mischievous, and we already have one more trickster than I'd like. Can we not just kill her? These mortals break so easily."

The queen rolled her eyes. "I have a solution for all. Puck Robin!"

The faerie popped up behind Gwendolyn, making her jump. "Yesss?" he crooned, voice smooth as silk. "Robin is here, but Puck's away, Robin's a fellow good today."

"Yes, yes," Titania waved a dismissive hand. "My lord, Robin has offended, and this must be mended."

Oberon frowned. "What do you suggest we do with her? Or *him*, or . . . oh, *tiach-fala*! Robin, I cannot keep track of which you are each day."

"He's a *he* today, dearest, and watch your language in front of our guests. My proposal is this: to pay for her trespassing, the girl shall serve me, and for that time, Robin Goodfellow shall serve precious Cyria."

"What?" both Kytain and Robin shouted at once.

Oberon smiled. "A fine chance to see if the inventress's new toy works. Madame Kytain, if you please?"

With a scowl, Kytain reached into a pouch and brought out a bracelet and a necklace. They were made of braided gold and twigs, studded with softly glowing jewels.

Oberon waved his hand, and they floated to him. "Yes. Finely wrought, as always. But do they work?"

He flung the necklace at Robin. The twigs broke apart, then reformed around the faerie's throat, forming a glowing choker. Oberon tossed the bracelet back to Kytain, who slipped it on.

"Now, give him a command. Something . . . ridiculous," Oberon said.

"If I must. Though I'll say it again: this tool disturbs me. I only made it because you ordered it. Do a jig, Robin Goodfellow."

Robin crossed his arms, and stamped his foot. "No, I'll never, I won't, I shan't. And make me, mortal toad, you can't."

Kytain held up her bracelet, and the tiny jewels glowed brighter. Robin's necklace glowed as well, and he began a jerky dance.

"Enough," Kytain said. The choker dimmed, and Robin sank to the ground.

He sprang up immediately and lunged at Kytain, his nails growing into long claws. "You make me jump, you make me twitch, I'll have your tongue, you rotten—" but the choker flared to life again, and he froze, claws inches from Kytain's throat.

"Hmm," muttered Titania. "It protects the wearer without conscious command."

"I thought that might be useful," Kytain said. Though Robin's claws were still dangerously close to her throat, she seemed completely unruffled. "Go lick your wounded pride, Robin Goodfellow, and don't muss up the lab."

Robin shot Kytain a murderous glare, then clapped his hands and vanished with a loud *crack*.

Gwendolyn, who had done her best to stay out of the way, now felt like she had been silent long enough. She coughed.

Titania gave her a kind smile, and Gwendolyn went dizzy again, smiling in return. "We have not forgotten you," the queen said. "Such poor form, to enter without so much as a greeting. But a sweet face forgives much. Shall we have an introduction, pretty thing?"

Kytain spoke up. "The girl apologizes, my queen, but she is under some enchantment that robs her of speech. Otherwise, she would sing praises of your beauty. Might you be able to assist her?"

"Our help?" said Oberon. "Without payment or bargain?"

Kytain shrugged. "A servant who cannot speak cannot show proper courtesy to your guests. I don't wish her to shame your house."

"We have plenty of shame from the one that *can* talk—" Oberon groaned.

"I would have the girl speak. Silence is dull." Titania held up a hand, and a branch of the willow tree descended. She plucked a sapphire the size of her palm. With another gesture, it floated toward Gwendolyn, but Kytain intercepted it.

"Is this food? Does it invoke the Binding of the Shea?" She shot Titania a murderous glare.

"No, dear inventress," Titania said, returning the glare with a seductive smile. "The girl shall remain unbound, though still in my service. You have my word."

Kytain handed Gwendolyn the blue gem, which looked a lot like the Figment. "It seems to be on the up and honest. They can't lie directly, and I suppose it's not technically food. Have a nibble."

Gwendolyn frowned, but did so. The jewel was not hard, as she'd expected. She bit through firm skin and into soft flesh, blue juices spilling down her chin. The taste was indescribable for those who have never eaten the jewel fruit of the Willow Court, but the words *sweet* and *bright* are as close as I can manage.

"Well? Speak," commanded Oberon.

Gwendolyn opened her mouth, but out came a chorus of birdsong, all tweets and whistles.

Titania's smile grew. "Oops. I beg your pardons. Here," and the willow extended another branch. The queen plucked a luscious ruby and sent it gliding to Gwendolyn.

She gave it a bite. It tasted earthier, but just as tender and juicy. She tried to speak again, but this time a lion's roar erupted from her throat.

"Marvelous!" Titania laughed, like the tinkling of crystal bells.

"My queen . . ." Oberon said.

"Very well. Enough fun. Here, child, this shall restore you." This time she presented a berry-sized emerald, which Gwendolyn ate like a grape.

Tentatively, she tried to speak. "Th . . . thank you, umm, Mrs. Queen," she said in a shy voice. "Thank you ever so much!" she blurted, louder than she'd meant to. But it felt so good to hear her own voice again. Though that lion's roar had been impressive . . . "I am pleased to make your royal acquaintance. You *are* the most beautiful woman I have ever seen—" she said, blushing at her honesty. "But what do you mean by service?"

"It is a bargain, dear. And a generous one. For as long as you stay here, you will do my bidding."

"You won't . . . you won't make me hurt anyone, will you?"

Titania's eyes flashed. "I could." Then her face softened. "But I won't. Come, crimson child. Kneel."

Gwendolyn looked at Kytain, who nodded. It wasn't as if she had much choice. She lowered herself to one knee, unsure what these strange creatures had in store, and not at all certain she would like it.

Titania stood, butterflies fluttering and reforming to suit her movements. Her skin glowed with a golden light that flickered around the throne room with each step. She approached Gwendolyn, who saw that the queen's feet were as bare as her own. "Little one. Do you agree to this bargain?"

Gwendolyn was silent, by choice this time. She looked back at Kytain. She'd broken enough rules for one night. But Kytain made no movement. So Gwendolyn looked solemnly back at Titania.

"Yes. I accept."

CHAPTER FIVE-AND-THREE-QUARTERS

A Feast Interrupted

Titania smiled and approached the kneeling girl. "Hold out your hand, sweetling."

Gwendolyn did.

Titania drew a fingernail across Gwendolyn's palm, and a line of blood appeared. Gwendolyn winced.

The queen brought a drop of Gwendolyn's blood to her lips, kissed it, and nodded. "The bargain is sealed." She waved a hand over Gwendolyn's, and the wound sealed itself. Titania, now with a stripe of red on the blue of her lower lip, placed a finger under Gwendolyn's chin and brought her face up.

"You are my bonded servant. Though I'm afraid that we cannot present you in this . . . state," and she gestured to the whole of Gwendolyn.

Blushing, Gwendolyn looked at what remained of the faithful dress from Copernium. It barely covered everything it was supposed to. Not to mention the filthy bandage on her cheek. "I—I'm sorry, I don't have anything else."

Titania's face glowed like the spring sun melting snow. "Charming girl."

She made a lifting motion, and Gwendolyn was jerked off the ground. She floated in midair. At a gesture from the queen, she spun around like a puppet on strings. A finger ran along her spine, making her shiver. Then, just like her palm, all her clothes split in a neat line.

Mortified, Gwendolyn tried to clutch at them, but the rags fell apart in her hands.

Yet rather than finding herself floating there in her altogether, there was another layer of clothing underneath, as though she'd been wearing it the whole time.

She was clad in a flowing green tunic of silken leaves. The sleeves draped so long they almost reached the floor, and there was a jagged skirt of overlapping green and brown strips. Long brown leaves unfurled from her shoulders like a pair of decorative fake wings.

Gwendolyn drifted gently downward, and as her feet touched the floor she found she could move again. She stepped out of the pile of rags to find a pair of soft leather boots laced up to her knees. The boots formed a stirrup around the arch of her foot but had cutaways that left her toes and heels bare.

"Look here, treasure." Titania cupped her hands, cradling a pool of water. Gwendolyn looked into it, and some enchanted faerie girl stared back at her. Her hair was in a long braid, woven with blossoms of baby's breath. Green designs swirled around her eyes, her cheeks glittered with sparkles of red and violet, and her lips were glossy pink. The bandage on her cheek was gone, along with the cut.

Was this really her? This girl was . . . beautiful. She touched her hair, her cheeks, making sure it was all real. Niceness and beauty so rarely come to our Gwendolyn, so we must savor each bit of loveliness as we can, amidst all the horrors and dangers. Let us be happy for her, just as she felt happiness swelling inside herself.

"Look, Cyria! See how skilled I have become with clothing?" Titania crooned.

"Fetchingly done, milady," Kytain said.

"Now you are fit for court." Titania clapped twice, scattering the water in her hands into shimmering droplets. "Lords and ladies of the Fae, show yourselves! I know you are there, my mischievous darlings, but let us pretend that you have not been so rude as to eavesdrop, and have only now arrived at my calling. Come!"

There was a moment of silence. Then, hundreds of people stepped out from behind the columns, where Gwendolyn had certainly seen no people before. The Willow Court was suddenly packed with courtiers. Her knees buckled with the shock, much as if she had been shoved through a curtain to find herself alone onstage, and Gwendolyn had no idea what part she was to play.

Each being radiated a different color light and sported an enormous variety of wings. Bird wings, bat wings, insect wings. A pixie to Gwendolyn's left had wings of bright pink petals, and she glowed the same shade. She gave Gwendolyn a flirtatious wave. Two spidery women next to her were whispering behind cupped hands, shooting glances like amused and judgmental daggers. It was a very specific sort of glance.

Most were clad in things familiar to Gwendolyn: billowing skirts, corsets, top hats. It was the same style of clothing she had seen in Tohk, with a bit of woodland flair. Kytain's influence, clearly. Though it seemed the inventress's own taste had evolved in the past five hundred years, and even among the fabulous faeries, she was quite the trendsetter.

Titania knelt behind Gwendolyn and whispered in her ear. "How shall I introduce you, my strawberry darling? What name would you have?"

Gwendolyn was determined to follow at least *one* of Kytain's rules. "Um . . . name me as you see fit, your majesty."

"Clever." And Gwendolyn could feel the warmth of the queen's smile even from behind. "I am so pleased I didn't kill you." Titania turned her attention to the onlookers. "My creatures of the Fae! Pixies, sprites, devas, and sidhe. My precious nymphs and dryads, my elves and oni and djinn. We welcome another foreigner into our realm this night. Treat her with all the kindness due a guest at our table. Allow me to introduce—" she fingered a curl of Gwendolyn's fiery hair—"my sweet Rosecap!"

The applause was deafening.

Kytain leaned in and whispered, "You're in the thick of it now, Rosie."

Gwendolyn tried to swallow, but her throat was suddenly dry.

Oberon stood, and silence fell. "Let there be a feast!" He waved his hand, and chairs and banquet tables grew out of the floor. Birds darted in through the maze of columns, bringing plates and goblets and food.

Oh, the food! Such a glorious banquet was set on that table, the likes of which have never been seen outside the lands of the Fae. I will not even attempt to describe the wondrous morsels presented there, for to read of those magnificent dishes without being able to taste them is far more cruel than I am willing to be.

Gwendolyn knew that cruelty all too well, for she was able to see and smell and salivate over the spread, but a stern look from Kytain reminded her that she could have none of it. She had no idea how she would resist the temptation throughout an entire feast.

She needn't have worried. The queen wasted no time in ordering Gwendolyn about, and she was kept too busy serving to eat, which seemed an odd way to treat someone who'd just been announced as a guest. But she was beckoned here there, carrying various dishes along the impossibly long table. A mug of something white and frothy to the faerie in the feather corset; a plate of steaming meats smothered in gravy to the elf in the jacket made of mushroom skin rather than leather. A bowl of exotic fruits with sparkling sugar to the lady in the batwing cape, who nearly took a bite of Gwendolyn's hand instead. To a dryad in a mossy robe, a tray of . . . ah, but now I am teasing you just as I said I wouldn't.

The inventress sat a few seats down from the thrones, and Gwendolyn dropped a goblet of cherry fizzwine when she saw Kytain shoveling down food as fast as any of them.

"You rotten hypocrite!" Gwendolyn blurted.

Kytain smiled and dabbed a bit of lingonberry sauce from the corner of her mouth. "It's too late for me, girl. I paid the price for this food long ago, and the taste doesn't begin to make it a square bargain. But these leek and onion popovers come close. Now hand me that giggle-water over there."

"Fine," Gwendolyn said, reaching for a pitcher. "But when does it end?"

"Dawn will come when the faeries grow bored of the night. One time the festivities lasted seven years, though faerie time is fairly fluid."

Gwendolyn gaped. "I can't keep this up for seven years! I've got to find my friends—"

"You know, I do recall you mentioning that once or twice. You're going to make me regret getting your voice back, aren't you? But you're stuck in service for now. The faeries hate manual labor, and since they can do everything by magic, making others work *for* them is quite the mark of status, from unnecessary servants to handcrafted goods."

Gwendolyn grumbled, but the queen was already calling her.

"Rosecap? There you are, my berry babe. Pass me that diamondfruit marmalade. I've just made a wager with the Lady Fen, here." She gestured to a woman dressed in lime green, from her green hair to the glittering green paint on her toes. "She says you mortals are clumsy things, and cannot dance a whit, but I say you seem nimble and clever footed. Give us a dance from your world!"

Gwendolyn both paled and blushed at the same time, which is no easy feat. "My . . . my lady, I don't know how."

Titania waved dismissively. "*Alletheon*! Ridiculous! You are my servant, and all my servants can dance. I much fancy Lady Fen's greengold earrings, and I'd just as rather not lose my favorite golden wingwraps."

"A dance! A dance!" chanted the pink-petal faerie, clapping. "Let us have a—"

But a thunderous sound from above drowned out all the chatter. An enormous *boom*, followed by a whistling whine that split the air. Suddenly, a black fireball smashed through the leafy dome. Before anyone had time to do much more than gasp, the black comet crashed into the banquet table. Food and dishes went flying in every direction, and faeries scattered back from the table in alarm, some of them fluttering into the air.

A figure crouched in the center of the scorched table then stood, six feet if he was an inch. He was clad entirely in black. His black longcoat had two rows of gleaming buttons running up to a high-necked collar. He wore a black fedora, and his face was hidden by a strange mask with goggles and a cylindrical breathing canister. He wore one black glove, the other hand bare and pale.

He stomped his way down the length of the table, trampling the feastings under heavy boots. He stopped a few paces from the thrones.

"That girl," he said, his voice gravelly and distorted through the mask. "Give her to me." He pointed at Gwendolyn, and she saw a black seven-pointed star tattooed on the back of his hand. She took a step back in surprise, looking from Kytain to the queen for any explanation. She was used to being chased by villains, but this was a new one to her, and she already had quite the collection to begin with.

Titania raised an eyebrow. "Thou art a mad-brained rudesby, villain. I will not suffer such at my feast. Robin?"

Without a sound, the sprite appeared with a knife in hand, and he stabbed the man in the back.

Or at least, he tried to. But the man whirled, and a seven-pointed shield sprang out of the back of his hand. The knife struck it and flew out of Robin's hand.

Six of the shield points vanished, and the seventh point formed a shimmering black sword. The man slashed at Robin, but the faerie flowed around each swipe of the sword without ever moving his feet. Robin flipped onto his hands and swung his legs in a whirlwind kick, knocking the man's mask off and sending it soaring down the table, where it landed in a bowl of strawberry glimmer pudding.

The stranger's blade vanished, and he rubbed his jaw. Then he held out his hand, flicked a finger, and a wave of black energy sent Robin skittering down the length of the table and right onto the floor.

The faerie sat up and groaned. "What right and most foul day I've had, with tricks undone and fortunes bad."

The man turned back to the king and queen and adjusted his hat. He was not particularly handsome, with skin so pale it was almost sickly, though nothing about him seemed weak. His jaw was shadowed with stubble, and he looked rather bored. The tattoo on his hand glowed again.

"You know this mark. You don't want this fight. Give me the girl."

Oberon's eagle wings unfurled menacingly. "Do not presume to tell us what we want. We know of you, Blackstar. You'd be best served to return to your own dark kingdom, or you will make a fine addition to *my* throne."

If the stranger noticed the twisted bodies that composed the two chairs, he gave no indication. "A power greater than you owns her world, and owns her. Give her back. Nothing unpleasant has to happen."

Gwendolyn stepped forward. "No one gets to 'own' me, you—" but Titania held out an arm to block her. The queen's butterflies fluttered in agitation.

"*You* are unpleasant, shadow rogue. The girl holds the protection of my house."

"One does not walk into Faeoria and make demands," Oberon growled.

"I walk where I want," the Blackstar said. "But we'll do it your way. A bargain."

A murmur of excitement rippled through the court as the curious faeries returned to the table. A hungry twinkle appeared in Oberon's eye. "A bargain, you say? What terms?"

The Blackstar crossed his arms. "A duel. I win, I take the girl."

"And if we win?" Oberon asked.

The stranger held out his hand, palm up. An image shimmered in the air over it, a nighttime village of thatched roof cottages. Behind them, a castle stood on a mountaintop, silhouetted by lightning. "This world. My master will give it to you. Should be an entertaining one."

Oberon stroked his beard. "A duel could prove quite amusing. It has been a unicorn's age since last we saw decent violence. What says my lady?"

Titania put a finger to her blood-stained lip. "Who would you challenge?"

"The girl can fight for herself," the black-clad villain said.

The eyes of the court turned toward Gwendolyn. Her face flushed. "You don't frighten me." She wasn't entirely lying. He was much less terrifying than the Abscess, or the Mister Men.

Kytain stood up. "Rosie, don't—"

But Titania held up a hand. "I *am* curious as to the girl's abilities. Such a victory would bring great honor to our court."

Kytain put a protective hand on Gwendolyn's shoulder. "Your grace, the girl is not ready—"

"Yes I am," Gwendolyn blurted.

"No, you're not." Kytain gave her shoulder a hard squeeze and hissed in Gwendolyn's ear. "Just because you *can* talk doesn't mean you *should*."

"Does Rosecap refuse the challenge?" Oberon said. "Does she besmirch our house with cowardice?"

Titania turned a frosty stare on Gwendolyn. "I said I would not make you harm another, but I never said I would not harm *you*."

"No, I'll fight him!" Gwendolyn insisted. She would not give in to this overgrown bully. "But . . . I have some conditions."

Titania warmed. "Yes, my pet? You would bargain for something more?"

"If I win, *you* get a world. But *I* would like my freedom."

Titania nodded. "Acceptable. The bargain is made. Shall we begin?"

Kytain stepped forward. "Milady, look to tradition. Shouldn't the champion be given time to prepare?"

The pink-petal faerie stood up. "'Tis right! 'Tis tradition!" she squeaked.

Rumbles of "Good form!" echoed down the length of the table.

"Right again, dear Cyria," Titania said. "I believe three is the correct number by such traditions. Warmonger, darken our door again in three years' time."

"No," the Blackstar said, seeming to loom larger from his place atop the table. "Three years might be three millennia here, and I have my own world to take care of. Three days."

Titania considered. "Nay, three months."

"*Days*. Then I fight her, or fight you."

"Very well," Oberon agreed. "I am impatient myself. Three days, and done."

The Blackstar frowned. "How long are those days?"

"Shall we say, forty of your hours each?" Titania said. "Twenty light, and twenty dark. You may return at the fourth rising of the sun."

"With sixty minutes in an hour, and sixty seconds in a minute. Just like these." The Blackstar patted out several seconds on his leg. "Then the girl is mine."

"*If* you can defeat her. I gather your master has not had much success in the matter to date," Titania said.

He waved a hand, his tattoo glowed, and his mask reappeared on his face. "I know who I'm dealing with," he growled, his voice distorted.

The queen stood. "As do we. But before you go, I believe payment is in order."

"Payment? What payment?"

Titania glared. She grew taller, and more terrible. Her yellow hair went white, and her eyes and lips turned black. Her butterflies became a dress of black moths.

"You ruined my *party*."

Titania flung her arms out. A murder of crows flew from her hands, razor-sharp beaks gleaming.

The Blackstar was quick. His shield came to life, but the deadly birds shattered it like glass. He flipped backward along the table, dodging as many as he could. He dropped his shield and crouched. Shadows gathered around him like the light that glowed from the faeries. Then he burst upward like an ebony comet and was gone.

CHAPTER SIX

Long Tales

Oberon stood, eagle wings flared. "This night is done! I weary of it." He waved his hand, and the feastings burst into a shower of green sparks. The courtiers scattered and flew out between the columns and into the night.

"Sire, if I might implore," Kytain said, "let it last a little while longer. The girl is tired. I have told you of the mortal need for sleep, if you recall."

"Bah! I cannot be expected to remember all your ramblings. I want my duel."

Titania cocked an eyebrow. "You grow dangerously tiresome, sweet Cyria. You have denied us the pleasure of your company of late, and you are not as amusing a playmate as you once were. Do not test our patience."

"My lieges, you agreed on the length of three days, but not when this one would end. It would be quite a trick if this night were to last, and we could have . . . a head start."

Oberon raised a furry eyebrow. "Hmm. I *do* enjoy a good

cheat. Very well. The night will linger a little longer. Go! I am bored already."

"The manyest of thanks," Kytain replied, then grabbed Gwendolyn's arm and hustled her out of the throne room. "The night's not a complete ruination, then. At least you'll have some rest."

"But I'm not tired," Gwendolyn protested. "I just slept, after all."

Kytain snorted. "You *just* slept? Child, it's been nearly a day since Robin lured you out."

Gwendolyn gaped. "What?"

"At least eighteen hours, I'd hazard. Time is bloody useless here . . ." Kytain looked over at Gwendolyn, then frowned, a frown that had nothing to do with the time and everything to do with the girl.

"What? What is it?" Gwendolyn asked.

"Well . . . excuse me for saying so, but you're practically *glowing*."

Gwendolyn *did* feel quite excited and was about to laugh when she noticed her hands. A literal golden gleam was coming from somewhere beneath her skin.

Turning into a night-light would come as quite a shock to most of us, but after the day so far, Gwendolyn didn't have any shocks left to give. "Is that bad? It seems quite nice. I wouldn't mind glowing like a fairy does. They're so lovely."

"That's . . . we'll need to keep an eye on it." Kytain led her out of the palace and onto the main street. "And it's faerie, with an E. Two *E*'s."

"How does that change the way you say it?"

Kytain shrugged. "They're very particular about it. Remember, don't get too dazzled by the Fae folk, or it'll cost you in the end."

"What do you mean? I thought the faeries liked me."

"They *do* like you, my molly—they go mad for a bricky girl like you. But they only love you 'til you bore them. You're hardly the first. I've only just convinced them to stop snatching children from their beds and replacing them with trolls and suchlike. Living forever is quite tedious, so games, bargains, and tricks are like catnip to them."

"What's catnip?"

"Ah, I forgot that you're a Dystopian. Never mind. But that pretty frock will not come cheap, and this duel will be no cat-flap, so make sure your worry's up and running."

But Gwendolyn found it hard to worry much as she strolled down a beautiful lane in a beautiful dress on a beautiful night. *It's a wonder what a proper set of clothes can do for your mood,* she thought.

The street was now full of faerie passersby, buzzing with conversation and sizing up the mortal girl in their midst, but she was no stranger to crowds gawping at her.

"I'll be careful," Gwendolyn assured Kytain. "You just worry about training me. I don't know who that bully is, but I'm not going to be pushed around by strange men anymore."

Kytain snorted a laugh. "I knew I liked you."

Gwendolyn looked around at all the quaint manor houses with their colorful strings of lights. "In three days, I'll win that duel, and be on my way to find Sparrow and Starling."

"Best not say their names, then." Kytain slowed and stopped at a cute little gazebo that overlooked the twinkling forest. Her metal wings glittered, and her hair was the color of moonlight. "You really care for them, don't you?" But her eyes were sad and far away. "Are they from my world?"

Gwendolyn thought about that. She had created them, but now she realized how much she had been inspired by *Kolonius Thrash* to do so. Much of who they were would not have been in her head without reading that book first. "Near enough, I suppose."

Kytain nodded. "I miss it, you know. Tohk. Two suns blazing in the sky. The rings of the moon. Regular nights and days. What I wouldn't give to see the Spiced Seas again, or the Violet Veldt. See how far Copernium has come along."

"How old *are* you, Cyria?" Gwendolyn asked.

"Oy, mind your own potatoes! Asking a lady her age . . . Well, between faerie time, faerie food, and faerie dust, age grows rather meaningless, and the years become a bit fluid. Not sure if I've been gone five years, and the time's been stretched in some odd way, or if I'm five hundred years older and stayed magically fabulous."

"Faerie dust?"

Kytain gestured to the colored specks of light that floated through the air. "That. It's all around. The very air is full of energy."

Our clever Gwendolyn quickly absorbed all this, and stitched some other clues together. "You can't leave, can you? You ate their food. Now you're 'bound,' or something."

"Wasn't *my* fault. I'd been here for a while, experimenting with their magic, living off what food I could bring through the doorway. But I got a bit careless around the Fae. They dazzled me, just as they're dazzling you. Suffice to say, I had a little something I shouldn't have with the queen one night. But that bit of delicious came with a price."

"And you haven't been back to Tohk since," Gwendolyn said.

"Or anywhere. I can't even go into the Library. Literally, there's a barrier that prevents me from crossing the threshold of the Egressai Infinitus. But how I'd love the thrill of adventure again, exploring strange new worlds and new civilizations . . . ah, well, I'm rambling."

"You lost someone too, didn't you?" The inventress hadn't said anything, but Gwendolyn was a clever noticer, and she recognized the faraway look in the woman's eyes.

Cyria Kytain sighed. "Well, to be technical, I lost everyone. But yes, one more than most. Oh, she was a choice bit of calico, that one. Don't suppose I'm like to see her again, especially not five centuries later."

Gwendolyn hugged her. She didn't know why, but she had long since stopped asking herself *why* she did anything. Maybe it was because Cyria looked so much like Sparrow then, gazing into the distance and thinking of home. The woman's wings made the hug awkward, but Gwendolyn managed.

At first, Cyria stiffened and gave her an awkward pat on the head. But then she relaxed and hugged her back. As they walked to the workshop tree, Cyria Kytain kept an arm around the red-and-green girl's shoulders.

~~~

Oberon was true to his word, for when she woke the next morning, Gwendolyn felt as though she'd slept for days. Her first untroubled sleep in weeks, and she almost felt like a completely new girl. The sun was beginning to peek through the window.

A window that had grown wooden bars.

Gwendolyn got out of bed and touched them. "I'm sorry," she said aloud. "Forcing my way through wasn't very polite."

The tree did not respond.

Gwendolyn caught her reflection in the mirror, and indulged in a rare moment of vanity. Titania's makeover was a good one. The draped-sleeve green tunic and cutaway boots were so comfortable she hadn't even thought to take them off for bed. Her hair was perfect, her cheeks still glistened with red and violet sparkles, and the green designs on her eyes had not so much as smudged. Her mother would be so proud. Cecilia Forthright would be so jealous.

Her glow seemed to have faded, which was very comforting. Glowing skin seemed far more disturbing in the cold light of day, away from Faeoria's glittering dreamscapes. But she had no time to dwell on it. She had a battle to fight.

Gwendolyn found Cyria in the sitting room, plunking out a charming tune on the harpsichord.

"Good morning, you drowsy damsel. Come and sit. We have much to say to one another, now that the conversation will be a little less one sided." She stood up from the harpsichord and adjusted a pair of high-waisted trousers. The harpsichord kept on playing by itself. Cyria was wearing a billowing silken blouse this morning, daffodil yellow, complete with suspenders and a black cravat tied at her throat.

"Time is short," she said, as she took a seat by the fire.

"Is it?" Gwendolyn asked, sitting cross-legged in the other chair. "Three days, twenty hours each of day and night. That's one hundred and twenty hours total. About five *real* days."

"Rose, that Blackstar fellow is well out of your league, and you have much to do after that even *if* you survive. If you don't find some humility soon, it will be the very literal end of you."

Gwendolyn fidgeted in her seat. "All right. I'll try."

"A wise magical mentor would lecture you on the difference between 'trying' and 'doing,' but I doubt you'd listen. Eat."

Breakfast was laid out, and Gwendolyn picked up a frosted pastry dusted with silver sugar. It oozed custardy cream and bright blue jam.

"Now, I want all the cards on the table. Speaking of . . ." Cyria waved a hand at the ink-stained desk and ruined documents in the corner. "*Riag!*"

The ink stains vanished. The desk was clean again, and the papers were all blank.

"*Rofirthar!*"

All the work Gwendolyn had ruined suddenly reappeared, scribbling itself into place, good as new.

"What was that?" spluttered Gwendolyn through a mouthful of caramelized pears.

"Restoration spell. Terribly useful."

Gwendolyn swallowed, excited by the idea of actual magic spells. "When do I start these lessons?"

"Later. First, I want *your* story, Miss Rose." Cyria snuggled down, ready for a long tale.

Gwendolyn didn't say anything at first. Where did she start? The last four weeks had been a series of fantastic dreams and horrifying nightmares, and had she known what a roller coaster was, she'd have felt like she'd been on one. So she began her tale the best way she knew how.

"Once upon a time—"

"Powerful magic, that," Cyria said.

"Yes, but it won't work if you interrupt me. *Ahem.* 'Once upon a time, in the City of No Stories . . .'"

And Gwendolyn told her everything. As we have been alongside her for all of it, I will not bore you with repetition.

Cyria listened politely, nodding and asking as occasion warranted. When Gwendolyn finished, the inventress sat silently for a long moment. "That explains a great deal. Well, the Blackstar is certainly linked to your Mister Men. It seems to me that both are working for the same side. And learning to defeat him here will be the key to defeating them there."

"What?" Gwendolyn said, astonished.

"Oh yes. This Collector fellow your Faceless Men keep rambling about? The Collector likely controls your world, as the Blackstar controls his own black land. And these Mister Men act as drones, of a sort. They keep everything nice and tidy."

"How do you know so much if I've only just told you?" Gwendolyn asked.

"Yours is not the only world where such things happen. These faceless drones aren't equipped to handle more . . . *complex* problems, such as yourself. You have a powerful imagination, so someone must be sent with an equally strong imagination. A counterpart. Your dark opposite. One of my *favorite* narrative conventions, incidentally—"

"So the Blackstar is working for the Collector?" That was a scary thought. Someone with as much imagination as her, but evil.

Cyria frowned. "Well, these are all just speculations, but not so much working *for* as working *with*. I'd bet my gorgeous heels these blackguards are all in cahoots. The two are probably colleagues, working for some higher nastiness. There are other powers meddling here. Powers of light and dark, powers beyond any one world."

That clicked with her. "When I went from the City into Tohk, there was a blackness in the In-Between. It took the Figment from me. And on my way back again, after blasting the Abscess, I saw that man."

"Exactly. And so your training begins." Cyria steepled her fingers. "Tell me more."

"What do you mean?" Gwendolyn said.

"Follow the clues. Find the patterns."

Gwendolyn thought. "Powers beyond my world. The lady. The voice I heard in the In-Between. The light that fought back the darkness. That's this mysterious *she* you mentioned. She was battling the dark man. You said she has helped me before. How?"

A small smile appeared as Cyria sipped her tea. "Think, clever flower."

Gwendolyn tried to sort through the mess of memories from the past weeks, looking for a pattern. Then, like driftwood surfacing after a storm, one idea floated to the surface.

"The leaf."

"What about it?"

"It was always there exactly when I needed it. When I was in trouble. I . . . I think it helped me. But how?"

"I have a guess," Cyria said. "Do you? What did it bring you?"

Gwendolyn was silent for a long moment. Then, ironically, it came to her: "Inspiration. An idea. Every time I saw the leaf, it brought me an idea."

"Quite perceptive."

"But . . . then that means . . ." Gwendolyn was struggling a bit now.

"Bring it back around."

"This lady . . . she sent me those ideas, she sent you to find me. And now I'm here, and she wants you to teach me, and then—"

"And then you'll have the training and experience to change your world. You've blown up your little Lambents, but as you can see, blowing things up doesn't fix things in the long run. Destruction doesn't change much. It's creation you need. You took away the Lambents, which appeared to be draining everyone dry. But all that destruction created was a void. If you want to change things for good, you need to replace it with something else. Give people something to believe in. She told me you'd be a changer, and now I think I see how."

Cyria paused for a sip of tea. "Your Collector sees it too. It's why he's so determined to get rid of you. His Mister Men have failed repeatedly. Now the Blackstar is here to correct their mistakes. The Blackstar, the Faceless Gentlemen, and the Collector. All out for you. Quite the rogue's gallery. Well, I had to train you anyway. We'll just have to do it a bit faster than I'd like. Then you can set about changing this world of yours."

This was getting too big. Gwendolyn felt a strange clutching sensation in her chest. It might have been fear. She'd never asked to be a hero. This was not the journey she wanted.

"No," Gwendolyn said.

"What?" Cyria asked, puzzled.

"I tried helping the City once, and I've been having the most awful time of my life ever since. I don't think the City wants to be fixed. Last time, everything just got worse. And . . . I think *I* got worse."

"Changing the world isn't easy, love, or else everyone would be doing it."

Gwendolyn's head was spinning, which I'm sure we can understand given the week she'd had. "I don't know. Maybe after I find my friends, we could try to help the City. But I'm not getting stuck there again just to see everything go back to normal. The normal can keep to its own self, if you please and thank you very much. I'll be staying in the fantastic." She gestured to the sparkling neon fire, the furniture that grew from the tree, the harpsichord playing to itself in the corner.

Cyria stared at her with those piercing purple eyes, as if she suspected something but was not ready to reveal it. "Hmm. Well, that conversation can wait. For now, our goals are the same. You can't leave until you defeat that greasy gatecrashing gutterguzzler, and for that, you must learn." She stood up, took her wing harness from the coatrack, and slipped it on. The she grabbed a bell-shaped cloche hat and set it at a jaunty angle. "Come. You'll be late for your next lesson."

CHAPTER SIX-AND-SO-ON

The Easy Lessons

Cyria led Gwendolyn out of the laboratory tree. "Hang on to your knickers," she said, then scooped the little girl up in her arms. With the beat of a metal wing, Cyria swept them up into the air without so much as an if-you-don't-mind. Gwendolyn gasped at the sudden rush of wind. Being a bit used to falling off of things, she marveled at how much nicer it was to fly, and she took a moment to admire the streets suspended in the trees below. The air around them was full of flying faerie gentry, just as many as on the streets below, all hustling and fluttering and gossiping.

They rose even higher, away from the dense morning air traffic, and landed on a wooden platform high up in the canopy. There was little shade from the bright sun, and a redheaded girl who'd only seen a sun once or twice in her life was liable to burn quite easily. But the faerie light was kind enough to spare her.

Cyria looked around. "It would appear your teacher has not

arrived. Very well." She held up the wooden bracelet. "Robin Goodfellooow . . ." she crooned.

There was a whirl of leaves, and Robin stood in the center of the platform, arms folded, jeweled choker glowing. "This cursed device leaves my head throbbin', and today you'll know me as Puck Robin."

"Yes, fine," growled Cyria. "It is time for Rosecap's first lesson. And if you lay so much as a hand on her, I'll leave you with more than a throbbing head." Cyria turned to Gwendolyn. "Do what she says. Puck Robin is quite skilled, even if she is an insufferable brat."

"You can't leave alrea—wait, *she*?"

The inventress gestured toward Robin. "Use your peepers. Details, details."

The faerie did look different today. The black mop of hair was the same, but the olive-skinned features were softer, the jaw not as firm. And though it wasn't polite to stare, Gwendolyn thought the shape under that black suit was a bit different as well. A definitely feminine shape.

"Oh. Well then," Gwendolyn said. "People come and go so quickly here."

"As do I. I'll not spend my day in Ms. Thing's company, and there's work needs doing. Ta-ta." And Cyria leapt off the platform.

Gwendolyn suddenly felt very alone. "So, Robin Goodfellow, yes? I'm ready to learn."

"Then first to learn is naming true, *Puck* Robin's mine when I'm as you. A fellow good is fine to be, but fellow not as you can see." The faerie turned a dainty twirl, then curtsied low.

Gwendolyn suspected that she was in for a long day, figuratively as well as literally. "All right, but would plain 'Robin' do? It seems simpler."

Robin glided up to her. "*Plain*'s not a thing I've ever been, but time is short so let's begin."

Gwendolyn frowned. "All this rhyming seems a terrible bother."

"Why use your words, why speak at all? 'Tis but my fancy, little doll. You clomp and bumble, all a-fright. My task is to put you to rights. Your body now is mine to teach, to move, to dance, to tap your feet."

Gwendolyn put her hands on her hips. "Dancing? That's silly! I don't know if you heard, but I'll be fighting for my life in three days—"

Robin slipped behind her and smacked the back of her head with two fingers, all before Gwendolyn could so much as blink.

She stumbled forward, rubbing the spot. Our girl may have been stubborn, but she was far from stupid. "Very well. Dancing." Eagerness blossomed on her face. "Show me."

Robin flowed through the air like she could swim in it. "Look down, dear Rose, these lines beneath, these spheres and patterns at your feet. These are the worlds, the realm entire, the suns, their paths, the Fae empire."

She looked down. A kaleidoscope of lines and circles was painted on the wood. It looked like the spinning planets that hung in Cyria's workshop. "And I'm supposed to dance on the stars. Right? I think . . . I think I understand."

Robin gave her a sideways glance. "She thinks she thinks,

but does she know? We'll see when she gets on her toes." Robin placed her right foot on a painted sphere, and it lit up. One of the connecting lines lit up as well, and she slid her foot across it. Another sphere lit up, and she slid her feet together, then clapped her hands. "Move along the floor just so. Follow the pattern, find the flow."

Gwendolyn did, and moved her foot along a glowing line.

THWAK.

"Ow!" Gwendolyn cried, rubbing her head from Robin's smack.

"Stand straight, don't bend."

Gwendolyn growled, and tried again. "That didn't rhyme—"

THWAK. Robin hit the top of her knee. "Don't overextend."

Gwendolyn nodded, fought down a burst of anger, and did her best to mimic the faerie's movements.

The dance was a series of poses, with flowing movements connecting one stance to another. Gwendolyn was surprised to find that she had some skill. There was no dancing in the City, so she'd had no chance to try herself before. With the glowing pattern of stars and constellations to guide her, it was almost easy.

Robin kept a running commentary. "Universe moves, and so do you. The planets move, and so do you. Your enemy moves, and so do you. Your teacher moves, and so do you."

SMACK.

"No, not like that. Keep that leg flat."

Around the platform they went, following the glowing lines, their arms carving patterns in the air. Gwendolyn knew she could never do this well, this quickly, on her own. Everything about Faeoria was making her stronger, more flexible. It felt fantastic. She wanted more.

After hours of training, her body did not ache or complain. She was working on a particularly difficult pose, a low lunge with her arms spread wide. Then she swept her arms up, brought her feet together, and leapt into a perfect backflip. "I can do it!"

She ran through the sequence again, but harder, faster. She leapt and twisted, her long sleeves and leaf-wings whirling. "First there's the twisty one, then you bend, then the reaching-pulling one, jump into that one-footed part, roll, back up, then turn—"

"That will be all for you today. Our time is up, so on your way," Robin said.

"What?" Gwendolyn said. "No! Show me more!" She somersaulted and came up into a handstand.

"I'd say you're done, look at your hands." Puck pointed at them.

Still in her handstand, Gwendolyn looked down. Her skin was glowing, and green stems were growing out of the platform and curling around her fingers. "Oh. Oh my." She lost her focus and fell flat on her back.

"Now learn to grow them on command. My lady liege will teach you next, so for Titania do your best." She extended a hand to pull Gwendolyn up.

Gwendolyn reached to take it.

THWAK! Robin hit her right between the eyes with two fingers.

"Ow, what was that for, you lunatic?" Gwendolyn stood, but

Robin got a foot behind her leg and knocked her flat on her back again.

"Never let your defenses down," Robin said.

"Argh!" Gwendolyn groaned. "And what then? Push your opponent to the ground?"

"No . . ." Robin bent down to whisper in her ear. "Always cheat." She winked, twirled, and vanished on the spot.

~~~

Gwendolyn was left to her own devices to find her way through the boroughs of Faeoria and down to the castle. To judge by the sun, she'd had eight hours of practice. Even still, she had picked up the faerie dance so *quickly*. This definitely wasn't the natural result of hard work and effort. This world was changing her, pushing her to her limits. Everything felt so fluid and dream-like, and she wasn't even tired.

The throne room was just as it had been the day before. She walked through the columns, staring up at the dome they grew into, marveling at the rainbows of light from the stained-glass leaves.

There, under the jewel fruit willow, stood a golden-glowing Titania. Gone was the butterfly dress, and instead the queen seemed relatively casual, with a corset of tree bark pulled tight over a lace tunic, and a long skirt made of feathers from various birds. Between the slits in the dress Gwendolyn saw tall, striped stockings that left her feet mostly bare. The queen's hair was a glossy chestnut brown today. Her lower lip still had a vertical stripe of red, stained with Gwendolyn's blood.

"Welcome, Rosecap. Time to continue your service and win me a new realm to rule."

Gwendolyn swallowed. "Uh, where is Oberon? I mean, Lord Oberon?" she said, remembering her manners.

"The king is off on his hunt. He commands the more . . . unsavory beings of our realm, and last night's events left him quite perturbed. But enough of him. You must learn to harness the power of the spirit. Otherwise known as *magic*."

"Magic?"

"Yes. The power is strong on our world, in the very air we breathe. I daresay you have noticed a change in *you* already."

Gwendolyn nodded.

"Good. Let us determine where your talents lie."

She showed Gwendolyn to a table, covered in a variety of objects. A stone. Ingots of copper, gold, and iron. A feather, a clump of fur, a snakeskin, a cluster of bones. Bottles of colored gasses. Bowls of water, soil, and seeds, as well as a bowl of blood, one of fire, and one of what looked like liquid sunlight.

"You will see similar tests on other worlds, sortings and choosings when younglings come of age. Echoes in the ether."

Gwendolyn eyed the table warily, looking at the blood and bones. "What do I do?"

"Bid them rise." Titania waved her arms, and all the objects rose, hovered for a moment, then settled down again.

"All right. I'll try." Gwendolyn waved her hands as Titania had done. Nothing happened.

"Ah. I forget how difficult it is for your kind. Many mortals find words helpful to focus their ideas. Do you know any magic words, Rosecap?"

"Umm . . ." She tried to think of what Cyria had said that morning. "I know *riag*, and *rofirthar*."

"Yes, but those are not *your* words. Magic is different for each, just as every creator has their own style."

Now *that* made a sort of sense. Gwendolyn stepped back from the table, held out her hand, and tried to imagine the objects rising. "*I wonder* . . . could you all rise for me? *Please?*" she said, throwing in another sort of magic word for good measure.

Most of the objects did not move, but the liquid sunlight floated upward into a ball. The feather leapt jerkily into the air, then fell back down. The seeds in the bowl shot up into a cluster of stems, blossoms exploding like confetti. Likewise, excitement blossomed inside Gwendolyn. Excitement, and a hunger for more.

Titania smiled. "Interesting. But can you make it *stop*?"

"Just watch me," Gwendolyn said. "*I wonder* . . ." and she pictured the plants retreating back into their seeds and the ball of light settling into its bowl.

But they did not obey. The bowl of seeds broke, and roots spread across the table, scattering the other objects, sending bottles smashing to the floor. The ball of light grew brighter and brighter, then exploded in a blinding flash.

"Enough!" called Titania. At her word, the light faded, the plants withered, and the table reset itself as it had been.

Gwendolyn's excitement withered as quickly as the plants did, replaced with a nervous disappointment, something you may have felt when you have given a very wrong answer in front of a very stern teacher. "What . . . what does that mean?"

Titania smiled. "Many things, my poppy-headed girl. You show a fondness for the green and gold magics. Light and life are the very basics of creation, and quite potent. Your choice of words is intriguing as well. You seem drawn to the magic of stories, another form of creation. Light, life, and stories. Green and gold and words. A combination with much potential. But potential for what?"

Gwendolyn was excited again, bouncing on her toes in anticipation. "Anything. I'm ready."

"Anything? As you wish. Show me anything."

Gwendolyn thought for a moment. A blank canvas is frightening for any creator. But her brief flight with Cyria that morning had been exciting and inspiring. She focused on the leaf-wings attached to her back. *What if?* she thought. She tried to imagine what she wanted. "*What if* I could fly?"

The wings sprang obediently to life. Gwendolyn rose into the air, hair fluttering in the wind that the wings stirred up. She hovered a few inches off the ground, looking down at the queen with the sort of nervous joy that might vanish if you thought about it too hard. It was a very specific sort of joy.

The queen smiled. "Yes? And what else?"

With a whoop, Gwendolyn soared higher into the air. She danced through the throne room just as Robin had shown her, twisting and twirling, but now swooping and diving as well, no longer slave to the rules of gravity. She soared all the way up to the dome overhead, running a hand along the stained-glass leaves. Then she dove, faster and faster, darting between columns—

Too fast. She clipped one of the columns with her shoulder and went spinning into another. She crashed against it, then plummeted to the floor with a sickening crunch.

Gwendolyn gasped, more in terror at the sound than in actual pain. She tried to push herself up, but then the pain *did* come, a sickening wave of it. She rolled over on her back, clenching her teeth to keep from crying out, and looked down. Her right arm had a strange bend in it, as if she had a new elbow halfway down her forearm. The sight of it made her stomach lurch, and she splattered the flagstones with her once-delicious breakfast.

Then Titania was standing over her. "Dear, dear. A most amusing display. Until the end, that is. I forget how fragile you mortals are. Does that hurt terribly?"

"No," Gwendolyn hissed through clenched teeth, tasting bile mingled with a little blood. "Only . . . a little."

Titania smiled a wicked smile. "If you're to remain in my service, you must learn to be a better liar." She knelt down and grabbed Gwendolyn's arm, right at the break.

Gwendolyn screamed.

But then the pain vanished. From Titania's grip, wooden patterns spread across her skin. The patterns thickened until her arm was entirely transformed into actual wood. The wooden arm straightened itself with a cracking and splintering that she could not feel. Then the wood flaked away like old bark. Sensation returned and her arm was normal once more.

"Thank you! I mean . . . many thanks, my lady." She flexed.

It was good as new. She leapt up from the floor, flooded with energy again. "What's next? Can we keep going?"

Titania gave her a measured glance. "Power you have, but it is useless without control. Let the lesson begin."

For the next several hours, Titania made Gwendolyn create things out of thin air with her imagination. Gwendolyn felt as though she'd tapped into an ocean of energy, and it felt fantastic.

"Now, focus. A small blade of light. Slice this neatly in half," Titania said. She conjured a sapling from the floor.

But Gwendolyn could do better than that. She wanted to do *more*, something *impressive*. She took a few running steps, leapt into a twirl, and let loose a blast of light. A bright, sharp line arced across the throne room and splashed against the tree and Titania as well. The tree split neatly in two. Gwendolyn smiled, and punched the air with a whoop.

But Titania said nothing. A small green line appeared on her cheek, oozing a droplet of emerald blood. "That is *not* what I asked. You are my servant, child, you—"

"I did what you said! I cut the tree in two, and even caught you by surprise. Imagine what I can do to the Black—"

Titania's wings whirred and she rose from the floor. "Do *not* interrupt me, mortal." Her words could have frozen an erupting volcano. She wiped the line of blood away with a pale finger, and the scratch disappeared. "You have much to learn—"

But Gwendolyn couldn't contain herself. "But look what I can do! See, flowers!" She stretched out her arm, and a field of flowers coated the floor. "Birds!" And thousands of sparrows, starlings, and robins flitted through the air around them. "Light!"

There was an explosion of brightness, like a second sun, and the world vanished into white.

"Enough!" roared Titania. The light vanished. The queen waved a hand and vines sprang from the columns. They snared Gwendolyn, lifting her off the floor until she was level with the flying faerie queen. Smaller vines wrapped around her mouth and throat.

"You are *mine*, body and soul. Were it not for the world I stand to gain, you would spend your remaining years in the kind of torture and agony that even your imagination could not conceive of. Learn some humility by tomorrow, or all you will learn is pain."

The vines wrapped themselves around Gwendolyn's face, and the world went black.

All in all, not the *best* first day of school.

CHAPTER SIX-AND-SOME-SUCH

Dangerous Gaieties

When light and breath returned, Gwendolyn found herself on the ground outside the palace. She took a moment to reflect. Perhaps mouthing off to the queen was not the best tactic. What had gotten into her?

Then she noticed the package in her lap, and the note.

Dearest Rosecap,
You may have this chance to redeem yourself as my servant. Deliver this parcel to the Lady Fen. Otherwise, please select which body parts you would least mind parting with.

Lovingly Yours,
Her Majesty, Queen Titania

Well, Gwendolyn reasoned, *there's no sense sitting here scolding myself. It appears I have a job to do.* She was determined not to mess this up as well.

The trouble was . . . she had no idea where the Lady Fen

lived. Nor did she feel like embarrassing herself by running to Cyria Kytain for help with a simple delivery. She'd already been in enough trouble, and she was anxious to show that she could handle things on her own. So she set off to find her way as best she could.

She wandered aimlessly for a while, until she ran out of houses and entered what was apparently a park, a grassy meadow suspended high in the treetops. Dapper faeries lounged and picnicked and chatted. Some of them were hurling a small wooden ball at a set of pins. Others were gathered around a gazebo where a quartet of winged musicians played stringed instruments, albeit not very well.

A carousel turned in lazy circles, where delighted faeries rode horses that looked much too real and none too pleased to have a pole stuck through them. There was even a pond where ladies with parasols were rowed around by men in striped coats and straw hats. The whole thing had the air of some elaborate game.

Part of the park was dedicated to booths and stalls, and had the air of a carnival. There were not just faeries here, but also fauns, satyrs, leprechauns, blue-skinned djinn, red-skinned oni, and green-skinned dryads—most of which Gwendolyn did not know the names of, but they all looked rather impressive. She wished she had the Figment to explain it to her, but it was back in the tree, in her bag.

She saw a booth with a puppet show, in which two characters committed increasingly extraordinary acts of magical violence against each other. A group of winged and mustachioed men were seated at a table in the grass playing cards and arguing quite a bit because every one of them was magically changing his cards as soon as they were drawn.

There was a juggler tossing swords, but he didn't quite seem to grasp the point of it; all the swords kept floating away on their own. Gwendolyn was quite fascinated by a horned fire-eater with flaming hair. No one else seemed to be watching him though. For all they noticed, he might have just been having lunch.

"I must say, this all seems rather ludicrous," said a voice. Gwendolyn turned and saw a hare, sitting on a table next to a silk top hat. "What is it I'm supposed to be doing again?" the hare said.

A woman in a black suit crouched down next to him. "I've seen mortals do it before, it's their sort of magic, the absolute height of fashion. They call it abra-ca-rabbit, or something. You just sit in the hat, and then I pull you out of it."

"That's all?" The hare frowned, and poked the hat with a paw. "If you say so, but I really don't understand the purpose of it . . ."

"None of us do, darling. They're just mortals."

Gwendolyn chuckled. "To think, all of this was started by Cyria Kytain," she said aloud. "I suppose . . ." She didn't like her next thought, but it had to be said. "I suppose one person really can change a world."

The whole thing reminded her of Copernium, and it would have saddened her to think of exploring it without her friends, but I'm afraid it was all so wonderful that thoughts of Sparrow and Starling never even entered her head. The barking voice of an auctioneer distracted her from any such thoughts, and she came to a large crowd.

"Yes, a prime specimen of a mortal two-cycle," called the auctioneer, showing off a bicycle with an extra-large front wheel. "A most tricksy contraption. No mere trinket, ladies and gentlebeings, this takes *true* skill to operate."

Two ladies in puffy red dresses chatted in front of her. "I don't understand what's wrong with flying. You've got two perfectly good wings, Lafina."

"*Anyone* can do that, Sebella. You just don't appreciate the finer things. Someone had to *make* this. With their *hands.* Isn't that just the most darling thing you've ever heard?"

"I'm going to appreciate it quite a bit when you make an absolute fool of yourself."

Gwendolyn was about to ask them for directions, when there was a blast of trumpets. Suddenly, dozens of black horses burst into the square. Their manes were wild, their tails were made of fire, and their eyes blazed with the same. Gwendolyn recognized them as the Night Mares she had read about in the library.

The riders were a terrifying bunch, wilder faeries with wings from reptiles or birds of prey. There were also dwarfs, goblins, and trolls, all whooping in a frenzy. There were centaurs too, running alongside the Night Mares and brandishing bows and arrows.

At the head of them rode the familiar figure of King Oberon, his hooved feet spurring his giant mount onward, his crown of antlers held high. A team of enormous hounds dashed in front of him, shouting, "Here! Here!" The party wheeled around, scattering the market-goers, cheering and whooping. A hobgoblin swung a sword half-heartedly at Gwendolyn as the group passed, and she had to throw herself to the ground to get out of the way, dropping her package.

The hounds fanned out around the market. "Lost," they barked. "Lost, lost." They circled, trying to pick up the scent again.

Oberon scowled. "It can't have gotten far. Come! Find the trail!"

The creatures whooped, their steeds whirled, and the Wild Hunt thundered out of the bazaar. Slowly, the market-goers resumed their various activities.

Gwendolyn straightened and looked around. "Well, one thing I will say. Faeoria certainly does keep you on your toes." Gwendolyn went to the ladies who had been admiring the bicycle, both now sprawled on the ground. "Here, let me help you." She extended a hand.

One of the ladies took it. "Thank you . . . Rosecap," the lady said with a giggle and a glance at her sister.

"You're welcome, *Lafina*." She remembered what Cyria had said about names having power, and tried to put a little magic into her voice. "I don't suppose you could give me directions to the Lady Fen's?"

Lafina and Sebella glanced at each other and giggled again.

"Did she just try to spell me, sister?" Lafina said.

"I believe she did, sister," Sebella said.

"What an adorable little mortal." Lafina gestured to the right. "That way. Fourteen houses down, green mansion with a domed roof. You can't miss it."

Gwendolyn gathered up her package. "Thank you." She started to leave.

"I'll collect my favor later," the faerie called after her.

"I helped you up, so it was *you* who repaid *me*," Gwendolyn called over her shoulder, allowing herself a smug smile as she headed in the direction the faerie had indicated.

Soon she found the green mansion. Her smile faded, and she had a sudden feeling of dread, one you might also feel when standing at the door of an unfamiliar house. After all, even for those who have faced monsters and pirates, entering a party full of strangers can be utterly terrifying.

Nevertheless, she rang the bell. The door opened with an ominous creak, the insides too dark to make out. Gwendolyn looked down to see a figure with pointed ears, white hair, and jet-black skin. He barely came up to her knee and was impeccably dressed in a tiny tuxedo.

"Yeeesss?" he droned.

Gwendolyn fidgeted. "Umm . . . I have a delivery for Lady Fen."

The creature shook his head. "I'm afraid the lady is engaged at the moment. You may leave it with me."

Gwendolyn didn't trust this chap as far as she could throw him. And not even that far, since she could probably throw him quite a good distance. "I don't think I should. I—"

"Rosecap?" squeaked a voice. A girl appeared wearing a glittering gown. Gwendolyn recognized the pink-petal faerie from the feast. "Rosecap! It's you! Come in, come in! Move aside, Krift, she's my dearest friend."

"I am?" Gwendolyn said in surprise.

"Of course! Don't stand outside, 'tis much more fun in here. Krift, please. Lady Fen will be so pleased!"

The little figure nodded. "As you wish, Madame Drizelda."

"I wish, I wish." The pink faerie grabbed Gwendolyn's arm and nearly yanked it off as she pulled her inside. The faerie was strong for someone so petite. She was only an inch taller than Gwendolyn herself and looked no more than fourteen, though Gwendolyn knew she was no such age. "And please, call me Drizzy!"

Inside was an entry hall, with lots of dark wood and gold filigree and wainscoting and other decorations with fancy names. Light flickered from candelabras, competing with the pink glow of Gwendolyn's escort. "Those night hobs can be so stuffy. Oh, no, no, no, honeybee, you can't go in dressed like that!" the faerie gasped in her high-pitched voice. The girl herself was dressed in an elaborate pink ball gown whose overall impression was that of a rather seductive cupcake.

"What's wrong with what I'm wearing?"

"Nothing, nothing. But this is a *ball*." She wiggled her painted fingernails at Gwendolyn. "Bibbidi, bobbidi . . . I forget the rest. Poof."

Gwendolyn's dress flipped itself inside-out and she was suddenly wrapped in an emerald ball gown with swirling silver needlework, layers of petticoats, and a neckline she wasn't entirely comfortable with. It left her freckled shoulders bare and made her feel strangely cold and exposed, though she was swathed in yards of fabric. The skirt was so wide it didn't even touch her legs, and she wondered how she would get through doorways. Her leaf-wings had become hanging strips of silver lace, and she even found a bow on top of her head, which absolutely disgusted her.

"I . . . thank you?" She winced, remembering her manners. She tugged at the uncomfortably tight bodice. "Is this really necessary?"

"Quite! Quite! Oh, you look positively delicious!" And the faerie kissed her on both cheeks.

Gwendolyn was about to protest, but she couldn't get a word out before the bubbly faerie flung open a pair of large double doors and dragged her into an enormous ballroom.

It was as grand a room as you could imagine. It was lit by torches that did not glow but burst in a dazzling array of neon colors, fizzing and shimmering like fireworks. Music filled the room, jaunty strings and pounding drums that would make even the sourest of listeners tap their toes.

Fog drifted across the floor, swirled by countless dancing feet. Hanging from the ceiling were strips of colored cloth that drifted around the room as if to some dance of their own. In between the maze of hanging banners darted dozens of dancers. Glowing, winged, and elegantly dressed, they swirled dreamily through the misty ballroom shadows and flickering neon lights, their bare feet all elaborately painted.

Gwendolyn clutched her package to her chest in apprehension. She had only an instant to take all of this in before her guide dragged her over to a woman dressed all in green, with a tiny green top hat pinned rakishly to her green hair.

"Lady Fen! Lady Fen! Look who's arrived!" clamored the dainty young faerie.

"Calm yourself, Drizelda. A bit of decorum, please," purred Lady Fen.

The pink faerie whipped back toward Gwendolyn. "Oh, yes, I'm Drizzy. Nice to meet you, nice, nice."

"Uh, you said so already. N-nice to meet you both," Gwendolyn said, feeling a bit "drizzy" herself. She turned to the Lady Fen "I'm Gw—er, we met at the feast last night."

Lady Fen nodded. She looked pleasant enough, but her expression was as unreadable as a painting. "Oh, yes. Rosecap, I believe we're calling you? You're the talk of the town, you know."

"I am?" Gwendolyn said. "I suppose it was a rather dramatic evening. Though this ball is quite exciting as well!" And it was. The color and energy were infectious, and her anxiety was drowned out by the pounding music. "Oh! I have something for you from the queen." She held out the package.

The Lady Fen unwrapped it, revealing two intricate strands of linked gold chains, dripping with jewels. "The queen is true to her word. Spectacular. And entirely handcrafted."

"Are those the queen's golden wingwraps?" Gwendolyn asked.

"A good memory. She lost our wager, after all. And how thoughtful to send you here in person. Now my ball is the most fashionable function in Faeoria. Spectacular," she repeated. She said it less like she was welcoming an honored guest and more like the way she had praised her new wingwraps.

But Gwendolyn had a sudden idea. A way to put herself

back in the queen's good graces. "At the feast, you wagered that I couldn't dance," she said.

"And you did not. So . . ." the Lady Fen whipped the golden ornaments onto her own emerald wings.

"So unless your wager had some sort of expiration date, I am here, and I suppose one dance wouldn't hurt anything."

Drizzy actually bounced up and down. "Yes! Yes! A dance!"

Lady Fen's green lips curled upward. "The pleasure of your company may be worth the loss of a small wager. Shall we?"

"We certainly shall," said Gwendolyn, growing bolder with every passing moment. She had been taught to dance, after all, so she might as well practice. That would still be training, wouldn't it?

The faeries took her by either hand and led her in a dance, twisting and twirling in a circle with the other guests as the colored hangings shifted, constantly rearranging the dance floor.

"This is all so marvelous, isn't it?" Gwendolyn said to the faerie next to her as they all took turns switching partners. She felt light headed, all lovely and weightless and dreamy. "Where I come from it's all so dreary and dull, but everything here is soft and pretty and fun. I know I should probably be worried, but who could be worried when there is so much to see, and everything you see is wild and wonderful and—" the words poured out in a steady stream to whoever happened to be her partner at the time.

Her lace wings whirled as she was handed from one faerie guest to another. "It would be so lovely to have wings like yours, real wings," she babbled to random revelers. "It must be incredible to fly, and very practical as well, since my adventures typically involve a lot of falling." She found herself next to the Lady Fen again, pressing their palms together as they circled one another.

"Would you like a pair?" the Lady Fen asked. "It could be done. For a price . . ."

"Oh yes!" Gwendolyn blurted. "But what kind would I choose? I'm not sure what would suit me; there's the butterfly wings, and the bird wings, and those flower wings like Drizzy has, but not those dragon wings, I think—"

"Rosecap!" boomed a voice over the noise of the party. A hand grabbed her shoulder and spun her around. Cyria Kytain wore a furious expression that was becoming all too familiar. "What in the blazes of all the suns do you think you're doing?"

"Nothing!" she said.

"I would hardly call this nothing. We're leaving, this in-stant!" Cyria shot a fiery look at Lady Fen, who returned it with a smug shrug. Then Gwendolyn was pulled out of the ball just as quickly as she had been dragged in. "Been looking all over for you. Had me so worried I was like to cast a kitten. I go to the throne room to find that you'd gone who-knows-where, had me searching for ages—"

"Ages? I've only just gotten here, it was just one dance, and—" but Gwendolyn stopped when she saw the sky outside. It was dark, and stars winked mockingly at her.

"Oh." Gwendolyn smacked her forehead. "Faerie time."

"Well, you're learning *something*. Just because the hours are ticking at a regular pace doesn't mean you'll keep track of them. Your first night is nearly half done! And just look at you!"

Gwendolyn looked down at the ball gown Drizzy had created. "I don't see what's wrong with it. I wasn't too fond of it at first either, but it is rather—"

"Not the dress!" Cyria snatched her arm. "This! You're glowing again!"

And indeed, Gwendolyn saw that she was right.

CHAPTER SIX-AND-DONE

Egress

"I don't see what the problem is," Gwendolyn said as she twirled around the workshop a little while later, dancing to music she could no longer hear. Her ball gown had crumbled and blown away like dead leaves, and she was left wearing Titania's dress again. She admired her skin's golden gleam. "It's quite lovely. And it doesn't seem to bother the faeries. And I'll never struggle to find my shoes without turning on the light."

Like many children who have had an exciting day far from home and full of fun, Gwendolyn was having trouble coming down again. And like many adults, Cyria was unused to having an overstimulated child bouncing around, and was more than a little irritated.

The inventress sat at a worktable, furiously trying to tinker her frustrations away. "You haven't touched your food," Cyria said. A plate of delectables sat cooling on the worktable. "Eat. You've had a day longer than most."

"I'm not hungry." Gwendolyn looked around the bustling laboratory, at the translucent vines pumping bubbling liquids, the spinning orrery of planets, the tree branches that moved to bring tools into arm's reach. "What are you working on?" Gwendolyn reached over Cyria's shoulder to touch a set of ticking gears.

A metal wing swatted her hand away. "Mechanical life, if you must pry," Cyria said. "An artificial being who can think for itself. I've come close, but haven't quite cracked it."

"Like my friend here?" Gwendolyn held out a hand, and the clockwork faerie landed in it. "Or those automatons at the Crystal Coves?"

"Early tests. But never you mind," Cyria grumbled without looking up. "It is time for *my* lesson, and you've frittered away a good chunk of your first day."

"So? It's going swimmingly. Look what I can do!" And she did a backflip.

Cyria did not look-what-she-could-do. "What about your kerfuffle with the queen?"

"I got her wingwraps back, didn't I? That should fix things." Gwendolyn inspected a row of colored bottles on a passing branch. "Why doesn't Robin have wings? And why doesn't anyone wear shoes? Are there any mermaids here? I'd love to meet one. And why—"

"One pointless question after another. Robin doesn't have wings because she's being punished, and for more than just tricking you. That little chippie's always in trouble of some sort or another. As for shoes, faeries are creatures of nature—they can't bear to separate themselves from the earth and don't trust those who do."

Gwendolyn flipped herself into a handstand, marveling at how *easy* everything was here. "What about you? You wear shoes."

"That's different. I'm *me*."

Gwendolyn waggled her feet in the air, watching her glow make flickering patterns on the wall. "Do you ever glow?"

"No. Now stop pestering me. You have to focus, or you'll get hurt."

She rolled down from her handstand. "Yes, I know, that Robin lady can really sting."

"What?" For the first time, Cyria dropped her work and turned around.

"Puck Robin. She kept hitting me whenever I fumbled a pose."

"That rotten—PUCK ROBIN!" Cyria roared. Her bracelet flared to life.

There was a *crack*, and the faerie appeared. "Yes, oh sweet mistress of the night? Ask what you will, it is your right." She gave a sarcastic little bow.

"You were not to harm Rosecap! How have you disobeyed?"

Puck Robin smiled. "Not could I, would I, disobey. A hand you said I must not lay." She held up two fingers. "I used just these, and nothing more. I laid no hand, as two's not four."

"Five," Gwendolyn corrected, holding up her glowing hand with a smirk.

Robin glowered. "The rhyming's not as easy as it looks, minnow."

"Enough!" shouted Cyria. "Do not touch her, at all. No physical contact."

Robin's choker flashed for a moment. "I shall do whatever you ask, you enormous pain in my—"

"Oh, clam up, sauce-box." Cyria waved, and the bracelet flashed.

Robin clutched at her throat, mouthing words, all of which were horrible if Gwendolyn had to guess.

Cyria turned back to her work. "Meddlesome creature. Should tell you to go drown in the lake. Shame I'm such a tenderhearted thing."

"Please don't force her to be silent," Gwendolyn said. "It is very upsetting, I can tell you."

Cyria rolled her eyes. "Fine. Speak as you will, just get out of my sight."

Robin wandered away, examining the laboratory, looking dangerously bored.

"Now then, Rose, I've been thinking about your world," Cyria said. "And examining this little shiny of yours. You call it the Figment?" She produced the blue gem from a pocket.

"You went through my bag!" Gwendolyn tried to snatch it back.

Cyria held it out of reach. "'Course I did, keep up. This is some spiffy tech. Yet apparently very old. Seems to be an information storage device. Probably a sort of educational tool, beaming information directly into your head."

Gwendolyn thought about the words that would jump into

her head when she looked through it, and how she'd wake feeling strangely full after nights spent with it on her nightstand. "That makes sense. Lately I've known a lot of things I probably shouldn't."

"Not unlike these gems I've been storing faerie magic in." She held up the crimson jewel that hung from her own neck. She waved her hand over a collection of tools, parts, and bits of leather. *"Deyan forthare."*

Pieces jumped up and assembled themselves around the Figment. When they stopped, Cyria picked it up, stepped behind Gwendolyn, and fastened it around her neck. The Figment hung from a leather cord, encased in an elaborate silver frame. It even seemed smaller than before, about as big as her thumb and finger circled together. "That should be a tad more convenient."

"It's beautiful," Gwendolyn said. "But . . . you said it holds information, not magic."

"Stars and sprockets, haven't you been paying attention? Information is ideas, and ideas are magic. What do they teach in those schools?" She resumed her tinkerings. "And put that down."

Gwendolyn dropped the parts she was fidgeting with. "I know enough."

"Anyone who claims they know enough obviously knows very little. Hand me that spanner." She pointed.

Gwendolyn didn't know what a spanner was, but snatched the indicated tool from a passing branch and plunked it down. "Fine. Teach me, O wise inventress."

Cyria waggled the spanner at her. "Better. Now, magic—"

"Why are you building things by hand if you can just wave your arms around and do it by magic?" Gwendolyn interrupted.

"That is *actually* an intelligent question, and a good lead-in to my lesson." She straightened up and cleared her throat, much like Mr. Percival did before launching into a lecture. "Magic always has a cost. All that energy has to come from somewhere, so using parts at hand is more efficient than creating things out of thin air. Even writers and artists need fuel to create, and magic is creation, so the creative process is important. The best ideas usually come in the middle, when you're getting your hands dirty—be careful with that!"

Gwendolyn nearly dropped a jar of glowing green liquid she'd been shaking. She put it back on the shelf. "But I can already create things! I know what I'm doing!"

"Oh, do you? What about those scratches you had on you when you arrived, eh?"

Gwendolyn's expression fell, remembering her experience with the runaway thorns in the Hall of Records. She knew better than to mouth off like that. She couldn't understand why she couldn't settle down and pay attention. But that thought was lost as Robin appeared next to Cyria and began making faces, *technically* staying out of her sight.

The inventress didn't notice, hunched over her inventions. "Control. You must learn control! Ideas *spread*. Bad ideas faster than most."

But Gwendolyn wasn't listening. Robin was leading her through a series of tumbling tricks, both of them giggling silently.

"There are few things harder than trying to control an idea that's gotten away from you. That's why it's so important for you to learn to empty your mind. Will you *stop* doing cartwheels, you rumbumptious fopdoodles! And stop egging her on, you jumped-up jackanape," Cyria called over her shoulder without looking.

Robin pouted. "Fine, but the girl's more fun this way . . ." and she wandered deeper into the lab.

Gwendolyn fidgeted a glowing toe against the floor. "Calm, calm, calm. Everyone keeps telling me to calm down and control myself. I *can* control it. Watch." She waved her hand over a collection of parts on the bench. "*Deyan forthare.*"

The pieces floated up and swirled around like they had for Cyria. But they went too fast, whirling madly, until they all smashed into each other. A faerie gem burst in an explosion of orange light. Flying shards shattered some bottles on a nearby shelf.

"Oops."

Cyria turned around, her lips pressed together in a bloodless line. "*Riag.*" She waved, and everything pieced itself together again. "Quit bulling around, this is important! I know you're not all jolly on stopping those men yet, but have you forgotten about your friends?"

Gwendolyn froze. A flood of guilt washed over her. She *had* forgotten, hadn't thought of Sparrow and Starling all day.

"I feared this. Faeoria is befuddling you. The Neverlands can make you forget."

But at that moment, a large and expensive-sounding crash came from the other side of the lab.

Cyria whirled. "Puck! What has that ossified twit done now? I can't fix *all* of it by magic, you know!" She stood up. "Park it, Rose. We're not finished." Then she stormed off.

"Now seize your chance to sneak away," Puck whispered into Gwendolyn's ear, making her jump.

"Ah! Stop doing that!" Gwendolyn said. "What are you talking about?"

"Go find your friends on other worlds. Give that magical door a whirl."

Gwendolyn frowned. She was excitable, not gullible. "Cyria said to stay."

"These boring tasks you've now begun, with friends would be a lot more fun. Be there and back before she knows. But if you're scared, away I'll go . . ."

"No, wait." Gwendolyn considered. It wasn't the *worst* idea in the world. Why waste time with Cyria's lectures when she could cut right to the chase and get what she wanted? "But I can't get back into the library on my own. It's vanished."

"A clever girl could figure out what that key around her neck's about." Puck knocked over a wooden contraption topped with a globe of swirling liquid. It crashed to the ground with a satisfying smash. "Go now, be gone, you don't have long."

Gwendolyn didn't hesitate. She bolted out of the lab, and up to the top of the tree. She reached the door at the top and flung it open, but there was still no library, only the Faeorian forest outside.

A key around my neck, she thought. Of course. The Figment. She lifted the necklace to her eye, and sure enough, the door she saw through the Figment was different from the normal one. It was no longer made from a solid piece of the tree, but was an ornate, paneled thing, its wood a much darker shade than the hallway around it.

She opened it, and the Library of All Wonder stood on the other side once more.

Without stopping to think, she stepped through, her glowing skin lighting up the dim entry hall. She shut the door behind her and examined the ornate golden doorframe again, with *Egressai Infinitus* stenciled at the top.

Cyria certainly likes her fancy names, Gwendolyn thought. But she hadn't the faintest clue how to make the doors spin like Cyria had, or how to actually find Sparrow and Starling. "I'm not sure how well this plan was thought through," she mumbled.

She examined the doorframe and the surrounding walls, and found something peculiar she hadn't noticed before. There was a wheel covered in letters and numbers, like her mother's telephone dial. At the center of the wheel was a slot, just the right size and shape for the jewel in Cyria's necklace.

Gwendolyn looked back at the door. There was a brass plaque on it labeled *M-S-N-D-W-S*.

She looked between the door and the control panel.

A phone number? No, she realized. *An address.* She took off her new necklace. *A door, and a key.*

She stuck the Figment in the center of the wheel, where it clicked into place. Then she memorized the letters on the door. "No sense leaving if I can't come back," she said aloud. "Here goes nothing."

She turned the dialing wheel to the number 7. It turned, clicked, then whirred back.

The Figment glowed a brighter blue. She spun the wheel again, dialing at random until she had entered *7-8-9-A-B-C*. As the last letter clicked in, the wooden door to Faeoria disappeared, and more doors spun through the golden frame like a carousel.

Eventually, the doors slowed to a stop with a soft *click*. A new door stood before her. It was a slab of pink stone with a dull brass plaque in the center. *7-8-9-A-B-C*.

Gwendolyn opened it to find a crimson desert and a sky choked with dust. In the distance, she could make out glass domes and strange ships that blasted upward with great columns of fire.

"Oh. Now *that's* interesting." But a sudden blast of dry air hit her face, stinging her with grit, and she slammed the door shut, rubbing her eyes.

She glanced at the dial again. She knew she had to hurry. But . . .

"There are so many other combinations. It would be a shame not to at least try a few of them." She spun the dial again. "One more," she reasoned. "I hardly got a look at that one."

One more brought her a snowy forest of trees no higher than her shoulders.

Another "one more" led to an ancient kingdom of ruins, with three large planets in the sky overhead.

Just one more showed her a pleasant little town, a street lined with houses and apple trees.

The problem with looking for *just one more* is that you're always looking for something better than what you have. Of course, this sort of thing usually ends only when things get worse.

Gwendolyn dialed for what she swore was *really* the last time, and found a door made of old, blackened beams. She grabbed the rough stone handle and flung it open.

There was a deafening roar. Hot breath rolled over her in a wave. The doorway was filled with an enormous mouth of gnashing teeth.

She threw her back against the door, but it would not stay closed. A gigantic scaly snout tried to push its way through, roaring and snapping. Thinking quickly, she imagined some of her exploding colored spheres and hurled them around the door and into the thundering lizard's jaws. There was a flash of light, and the pushing against the door stopped. It slammed shut under Gwendolyn's weight.

Gwendolyn slid to the floor, panting. She forced herself to breathe slower, in and out, calming her racing heart. For the first time in days, she breathed air with no taint of faerie dust, no extra rush of energy to distort the world around her. After a few breaths, she was able to find a sense of peace. The glow from her skin flickered and dimmed.

What am I doing? she thought. This wasn't like her. She *liked* Cyria, even if the inventress was acting a bit dull and grown-up-like at the moment. Gwendolyn had been so worked up that she hadn't been thinking clearly.

And then she realized what her glowing skin meant. It was an indication of wildness, of too much energy. Of being dangerously out of control.

She thought about how she was shirking her training. Breaking her bargain. Of how the Fae would surely come for revenge, possibly taking their anger out on Cyria for Gwendolyn's oath-breaking. She had made a promise in blood, and that was surely not something lightly broken.

What would Starling think about that? Would Sparrow see her differently, knowing she had behaved so cowardly, so selfishly?

There are times where knowing the right choice is easy, but the choosing itself is difficult. Gwendolyn was having such a moment. But she forced herself to dial *M-S-N-D-W-S*.

Cyria stood on the other side of the door, looking weary and disappointed.

"Well?" she said. "Did you at least learn something?"

Gwendolyn coughed. "You've created a way to steer between worlds, and the library collects them all. Each book in the library has a code in the back to dial up a portal. I think I saw a doorway like this back in your laboratory in Tohk. That's what those metal men were guarding, wasn't it?"

"Yes, my first design. A bit rough, but it was enough to start my journey." She sighed. "At least you're not *entirely* thick. Come." Cyria stalked away.

Gwendolyn followed, head down. "Cyria, I promise, I won't do anything like this again."

"Three times," Cyria muttered. "Three times, you have done exactly what you shouldn't. I'm not even going to pretend to know what to do with you." She stopped at the small doorway to Gwendolyn's room. "Bed. Now. And stay there this time."

And for once, Gwendolyn did exactly as she was told.

PART TWO: BLACK

CHAPTER SEVEN

The Hard Lessons

After a few short hours of tossing and turning, the sun rose on Gwendolyn's second day. She recharged herself with breakfast and tea, preparing for another forty-hour day of training and lectures. Cyria barely said two words to her before whisking her away to lessons with Robin.

Gwendolyn didn't blame Robin for her own poor choices the previous evening—she understood that mischief was in the faerie's nature. She blamed herself for listening.

Robin stood with their hands behind their back. Gwendolyn was not entirely certain what form the faerie was in today, whether male, female, or something in between. "With dance you have acquired some skill, but dance alone will rarely kill. Prepare the girl is what I'm told, and weapons make a warrior bold. Not ranger nor a fighter be, you're more a caster, I can see. But you face a most grave peril . . ."

They produced a small knife in a leather sheath. Robin bent

and helped strap it high up on Gwendolyn's thigh, hidden by her slitted skirt but still easily accessible. "A girl cannot be too careful," they said with a wink.

Gwendolyn blushed. She drew the knife, examining its curved talon-like shape. "So we're not dancing today?" She slashed the air a couple of times. She liked the feel of it.

"Oh, we shall dance, we two indeed. You have the blade, but skill you need. You move, and flow, and learn to fight. Your magic grows, soon burning bright." They drew their own knife. "Come at the Robin, Rosie girl. We'll see if I can trim those curls."

Gwendolyn felt more confident than yesterday, which already seemed ages ago. She waggled her knife. "You can try. Shall we dance?" And she lunged.

Robin stepped easily out of the way and brought their knife hilt down on Gwendolyn's wrist. Her hand went numb, and she dropped her knife. Robin merely cocked an eyebrow.

But Gwendolyn remembered her lessons. She rolled, sprang up, and used her foot to slide her knife back to her. She kicked it up into the air and caught it. Then she struck one of the poses Robin had taught her, which now formed a perfect defensive position. She waved Robin forward with her free hand and smiled.

Robin smiled back, their gentle features ambiguously seductive, their tanned skin glowing softly. Then, like a striking snake, they came at her, twirled around her knife arm, and stabbed at Gwendolyn's eye.

Gwendolyn jerked backward, tripped, and fell.

Robin stared down at her, lip curled in contempt. "Bravado fades like morning mist, with the least palpable of hits."

They were right. Her attitude was gone. She jumped up and tried again, slashing once, twice, three times. But the faerie dodged, dodged again, deflected the third, then darted in and pricked her wrist.

Gwendolyn dropped her knife again. A drop of blood fell from her wrist and splattered the painted orbital chart with a new, crimson star.

"Ow! I thought Cyria ordered you not to touch—oh, I see," Gwendolyn said. "You're not touching me, the *knife* is touching me, right?"

Robin smiled again.

"You're such a child," Gwendolyn snapped.

Robin put her through her paces, endless hours of dancing and twirling and thrusting and dodging. Endless hours of pricks and falls and pain and failure. All the changes Faeoria had wrought in Gwendolyn made little difference. She couldn't lay a finger on Robin, and true to the faerie's word, Robin never laid one on her. Technically. Gwendolyn's frustration turned to anger, then humiliation, and eventually, despair.

She tried one last trick, spinning and cartwheeling behind the faerie, then lunging at Robin's back.

The faerie reached behind and caught Gwendolyn's blade in their free hand, without even looking. Then they kicked backward, hitting Gwendolyn full in the chest and sending her skidding back across the platform.

Robin turned and threw their knife at Gwendolyn, where it stuck in the floor a hair's width away from her left ear, neatly shearing off a crimson curl. Robin folded their arms dismissively. "You've seemed to learn all that you can. Or say perhaps all that you can't."

"No!" shouted Gwendolyn, leaping to her feet. "I'm not through with you yet!" she roared and went at Robin with her own knife, but the faerie just wasn't *there* anymore. Gwendolyn's knife was gone too. She looked up and saw them both in the air above, Robin performing a graceful flip and holding Gwendolyn's blade.

Bare feet landed softly behind her, and she felt the knife bite into her, a nick in each shoulder, the small of her back, and the back of each knee. She fell to all fours with shaking arms. They were no worse than a prick from a sewing needle, but she had to bite her lip to keep from crying out, though she couldn't hold back a small whimper.

"Titania no doubt waits for thee. You don't dare disappoint thy queen." Robin tossed the knife on the ground next to Gwendolyn.

Still trembling and forcing back tears, she picked herself up. She sheathed her knife and began limping her way down to the palace.

~~~

All the boundless energy of the day before had drained away, leaving her feeling like an empty cup. What didn't help were the eyes of the Fae folk as she hobbled down the main street, eyes that were not entirely friendly. Every move she made was being watched and no doubt gossiped about in all the Faeorian parlors and shops.

Robin had beaten her so *easily*. But Robin had been beaten by the Blackstar in seconds. What chance did she stand? She could not hope to defeat him with her tiny knife.

"It'll just have to be magic, then," she said, trying to sound determined.

Titania met her in the throne room. The queen was clad from neck to ankle in form-fitting armor made of overlapping leather leaves. The leaves were an autumnal red, decorated with green and gold filigree. The armor left her pale arms bare, and her waist-length hair was ebony black, tied in a braid with a sharp golden spike at the end. Her dragonfly wings twitched, and she tapped a bare foot in impatience. She looked positively warlike.

Gwendolyn gulped.

The table of objects was laid out again, and the queen gave Gwendolyn the same test as the day before, with the same result. The light and the seeds responded to her, but she quickly lost control. This time, the plants lunged for Titania, and the ball of light set the table on fire.

Titania waved, and the fire burned away the plants. Then the fire retreated obediently into its bowl. "So. You have learned nothing, Rosecap. And time grows short. Shorter even than you."

"That was unnecessary," grumbled Gwendolyn.

"Silence. I tire of you—"

Gwendolyn glowered at her. "Then you needn't bother teaching me. I'm not afraid," she lied. "I know I can—"

Titania whirled, and her long braid whipped across Gwendolyn's face, the spike at the end cutting across her cheek in the same spot as her cut from the Outskirts, which could not have been a coincidence. "Do *not* interrupt me again. You lack control over your magic and your mouth, and either could be your end."

"Give me another chance. I can control it!" she shouted, clutching her bleeding cheek.

Titania smirked. "Very well. Retrieving my wingwraps from Lady Fen has at least earned you one last attempt." Titania waved her hand, and a hurricane engulfed Gwendolyn. Her hair whipped her face, and she could neither speak nor breathe.

"Stop me. End my wind, little Rose. If you cannot even do that, perhaps your life is not worth sparing until this duel."

Gwendolyn had to think of something. The wind spun her around, faster and faster, until her feet left the floor. So she embraced that feeling—she imagined she was as light as the feather on the table, and she went even higher. She fluttered across the throne room, and the long brown leaves attached to her dress sprang to life, slowing her until she made a gentle landing.

Cyria had been right. These faeries did change quickly. Gone was the sweet and regal lady who had greeted her that first night. In her place was a fierce warrior queen with ice in her eyes. The sinking feeling returned. She was in over her head. *Deeply.*

"A minor feat," Titania said. "You merely *escaped* my spell. You must do better. Or perish. At this point, I'm not sure I care which." She raised her pale arms. Gwendolyn felt an intense wave of cold. The stained-glass leaves frosted over, and a giant icicle formed over the queen's head. Larger and larger it grew, until it broke with a loud *crack*. It fell toward Titania, but in the moment before she was impaled, she waved her hand, and the icicle vanished into shimmering mist.

"Control. Now, dear Rosecap, let us see how well you dance."

She raised her arms again, and more icicles formed. There was a series of loud cracks, and icicles plummeted toward Gwendolyn like a hard and very pointy rain.

She threw herself to the side just as the first spike smashed into the floor. Shards stung her face. She tried to imagine them vanishing, but the icicles remained very real, and she barely managed to dodge another two.

The dread in her stomach exploded into full-fledged panic. The Blackstar was the least of her problems. It seemed Titania would kill her first. She fell backward, out of the way of another spike, and rolled to dodge yet another.

Gwendolyn snarled, a sudden defiance roaring up inside. *I will not be killed by an icicle!* she thought. She rolled onto her back and pointed her palms skyward. *"What if . . ."* she said, and bright beams of light shot from her hands. It blinded her for a moment, but she felt a warm rain fall. When she opened her eyes, the ice was gone.

"You can deflect," Titania said. "But you must learn to dispel." The queen gestured toward the table, and all the objects rose. A large stone broke apart, and the pieces zipped at her like bullets. Gwendolyn was quick enough to create a wall of wood to stop them, but the bowl of fire erupted in a geyser of flames and burned her wall away.

The wind returned, picked up the earth from its bowl, and turned into a blistering sandstorm. Gwendolyn was driven back to the edge of the throne room, and one foot slipped over the side. She was foolish enough to cast a glance down the outside of the palace, and she had a vivid image of falling and hitting who-knows-how-many spires and gargoyles in the process.

"Stop it!" Gwendolyn yelled. She managed to conjure vines that wrapped around her ankles, keeping her from sliding over the edge. But her mind was racing, and the vines continued growing up her legs.

Titania waved at the table again, and gemstones elongated into a dozen sharp knives, which flew at her face. Gwendolyn waved her arms frantically, trying to deflect them, and while some obeyed her and flew off course, others did not. She caught a gash on her right arm.

"Stop it!" Gwendolyn yelled again. She drew her own knife and sliced herself free of the vines she had created. She tried to run away from the edge but was driven to all fours by the force of the wind. The bowl of blood on the table overflowed and spread across the floor, and suddenly she was kneeling in a pool of it. It burned where it touched her.

Titania did not stop. The feather turned into a flock of razor-beaked crows. The clump of fur became a pack of snarling wolves. Bones clattered to the ground and assembled themselves into a gang of walking skeletons. The snake skin grew into a thirty-foot serpent with dripping fangs. All of them moved toward Gwendolyn, sprawled on her hands and knees.

She held out a hand, which was red and wet with burning blood, and tried to make them vanish. "Dispel," she said, but nothing happened. "*I wonder . . . What if you vanished? If only* you would vanish! Dispel, *please!*" The words were choked by wind and earth. Her eyes blurred with tears, and not just from the sandstorm.

"You must learn control, Rosecap. Or you are of no use to me," Titania said, hovering above the fray, wings whirring.

Panic overwhelmed Gwendolyn, keeping her from focusing enough to create anything. The crows darted in to slash and peck and pull at her hair. The pooling blood continued to burn her hands and knees, but the wind kept her from standing. The wolves, snake, and skeletons were almost upon her.

"I can't!" she screamed into the hurricane. "Please! It's too much! I can't . . . stop it!"

Darkness crowded the edge of her vision. Images flashed into her mind. A blackened, cratered landscape with thundering clouds and deadly heat. A room full of children with glowing eyes. Men with bowler hats and no faces.

Then the image shifted. She saw her parents, staring into the Lambent, but they were screaming, writhing in pain. Her mother was crying. The Abscess's black tentacles reached for her parents—

"No!" she screeched. A burst of light radiated from her in all directions. The monsters were blasted to pieces. The table cracked in half. Gwendolyn rolled to the side, and over the edge.

Falling. The architecture of the palace rushed up to greet her in its pointy embrace. She tried to fly, but she couldn't focus. Her leaf-wings fluttered just enough to get her away from the side of the palace. She tumbled through the air, missing the street and gliding away from the Faeorian cities, and all the long way to the ground below.

Gwendolyn landed on the forest floor with a soft *thump* rather than the much louder and wetter sound she would have made without her wings. She ran, too upset to take in her surroundings as she set foot on solid earth for the first time in days. Leaves crunched under her semi-booted feet, strange animals skittered through the undergrowth, and even the dancing lights of the faerie dust made a path for her.

She ran like there were monsters chasing her. Which, to be fair, there had been. Legs pumping, chest burning, breaths coming in sobbing gasps, she tried to escape the darkness that pursued her.

But no kind of monster, that. This darkness was inside her, and she couldn't outrun it. It had lain dormant during her time in Faeoria, but now it came roaring back with a vengeance. It pressed on her shoulders like heavy hands, and she just wanted it to stop, wanted *all* of it to stop. It was just too much.

She tripped on a root and skidded along the leafy ground, the soft soil, the loose stones. Her knee was now bleeding, but so was her hand, her shoulder, and her cheek, and her palms were still blistered from the burning blood, so she hardly noticed. She limped and stumbled along and slammed her back against a hollow tree, unable to run any farther. She couldn't breathe. She couldn't *breathe*. What was wrong with her?

Someplace dark, that was what she needed. Someplace alone. With a cry of desperate anger, she spun to face the hollow tree and made a ripping motion with her hands. A hole in the tree trunk split open, forming a space inside just large enough for her, with a bench to sit on. She threw herself on it, curled into a ball, and slammed her hands together with a loud clap. The tree sealed itself completely.

The darkness embraced her. Blackness. Emptiness. All the feelings she had tried to leave behind in the City broke upon her in waves. She didn't know how she could feel so angry and lonely and sad and afraid and yet so utterly, completely numb all at the same time. How could a person feel nothing and everything all at once? Was she broken?

She lay on the rough wooden bench in the darkened heart of the tree. She was so tired. Could she just stay here forever? Never have to do anything, never have to leave?

Thought fragments flashed through her mind, too quick to grab hold of. Sparrow. Starling. Her parents. The Mister Men. Tommy. Missy. Ian. Jessica. Kolonius. Copernium. Cyria. The Blackstar. The duel. Her training. Her failure. All her failures. They whirled like a hurricane, overwhelming her.

As she sat in the dark, she heard her heart beating in her ears, could feel the pounding through her whole body. She tried to focus on that. Just the feeling of her heartbeat, the sound of her breathing. It seemed like the loudest thing in the world inside that closed space. And slowly, the whirling thoughts died down, and she was left with what she wanted. To be alone, in the dark, with nothing to do or say or think. Eventually she fell into a messy sort of half-sleep, and the world disappeared for a time.

CHAPTER SEVEN-AND-ALMOST

The Way of the Worlds

Moments like this are the hardest to share with you. Monsters and dangers are all well and good, but it breaks my heart to show you the struggles that Gwendolyn holds inside, struggles that many of us must face. And it is even more painful to tell you that there will be many more hardships to come, and this day will have been one of the least of them. But lest you lose hope, let me assure you that there will also be light along the way, and dancing, and more than a little love.

But for now, I must allow our story to unfold, which resumes with a soft nudge against Gwendolyn's shoulder, bringing her back to the world. She opened her eyes to find a pair of twinkling jeweled ones staring back at her. By the light of its glowing eyes, she saw the little clockwork faerie hovering inches from her face. It cocked its head at her curiously.

Then it made a loud screeching sound. Gwendolyn practically jumped out of her skin.

"What, in the tree?" said a voice from outside.

Cyria. Just hearing her voice sent a spike of tension through the space under Gwendolyn's ribs, the dread that comes with facing up to a monumental mistake. Another one.

She scrunched her eyes shut, not ready to face . . . everything. Anything.

The faerie made another screeching sound. There was a knocking noise from outside.

"Hello, Rosecap? Do you mind if I come in? Just to chat. You can even, er, stay in the tree, but if you wouldn't mind just opening it up a smidge . . ."

Gwendolyn sat up, brushing dirt from herself. Clearly, she would not be left alone. She twirled a finger, trying to open a small hole in the trunk, but nothing happened. She called out in a tiny, raspy voice. "I . . . I can't. Can you do it? Just a little?"

A hole opened in the trunk. Afternoon sunlight came through the crack. "Hello there," Cyria's eye appeared at the hole. "Sorry about the faerie. Little blighters have minds of their own. Though I suppose that's what I was aiming for . . . *Ahem.* Are you all right in there, bunny? Well, of course you're not all right, obviously, anyone could see you're feeling a bit grummy, but . . . do you want to . . . to talk about it? Or something? I'm not terribly good at this. I may have mentioned, I haven't had children before and—"

"I'm fine," Gwendolyn said, as much to stop Cyria's babbling as anything else. "Please go away now."

"Hmm. Well, I'm afraid I can't. I told Titania I'd handle the situation. Erm . . . what exactly is the situation?"

"Is this the part where I tell you everything, and you say

you understand completely, and that everything will be fine?" Gwendolyn said sarcastically.

"Heavens no, love. Who would say such a silly thing? No one will ever completely understand you, just as no one will ever fit into your skin. And if someone told me that everything would be fine, I'd smack them for lying. But I can listen, or talk a bit. I daresay I've some experience with talking to a tree—"

"It's . . . it's all right." Though that may have been the biggest lie she had ever told.

The tree opened with a rush of fresh forest air. Cyria looked inside, her white hair disheveled, her expression worried. She collapsed her wings and squeezed onto the bench next to Gwendolyn, disturbing the little faerie. It chirped, and continued to hover nearby, clearly reluctant to leave Gwendolyn.

"So . . ." the inventress said.

"What's wrong with me, Cyria?" Gwendolyn blurted.

"Can you be a tad more specific?"

"This," she gestured to the tree. "It's like something in me snapped. I was training with Titania, and suddenly it was all too much. I had to get away."

Cyria fidgeted with one of her metal feathers. "Is this the first time you've felt this way?"

She thought about it for a minute. "No. I suppose I've felt this way since leaving Tohk. Like nothing will ever matter again, and I'd rather just lie down and never get back up."

"Ah," Cyria said. "Like that."

"But not only that. Here in Faeoria, I've been just the opposite.

I get out of control. Like . . . like I was running nonstop, and just couldn't get enough."

"Of what?"

"Of everything. It's like I'm two completely different people now, and I don't recognize either of them. What is wrong with me?"

"Well . . . I won't say *nothing*, love, because it's plainly *something*. But you're not alone. No one returns from their adventures the same as when they left. Facing death and monsters and coming out the other side doesn't always make you stronger. Tragedy leaves its mark. Not a physical one, necessarily, but spirits are fragile things, and it would take a lot less than what you've seen to send someone into the darkness."

"So you've felt this too?" Gwendolyn asked.

"I can't say, as I'm not you, and I can't feel what you do. But it seems familiar enough. I've certainly had my struggles with the black dog. That feeling beyond feeling, beyond sadness. Though this other side, this manic energy of yours, that's new to me. I told you that magic has a cost—your cost might be losing control. Perhaps Faeoria is changing you, making you more like them. Impulsive, reckless. Combined with a lack of sleep, an intense case of time lag, a heaping dose of pressure, and a dash of mortal danger, it's no wonder you've suffered a bit of a breakdown."

"But you can fix me? I don't want to feel this way anymore. I'm tired, Cyria. I'm just so tired. I'm . . . I'm broken."

Cyria put a hand on Gwendolyn's bloody knee. "You're not broken, Rose. You're changed. Your mind, your emotions—they likely work differently now. Your wiring's been shifted. Trees don't grow in straight lines, and neither do people. You can never tell what direction they'll go, but they're always growing upward, never backward. We all have our own burdens to bear, and while you can't just move on from your pain, you can choose how you go on with it. Shoulder your load, and live your life as best you can."

"So I'm stuck this way? A freak. A piece that doesn't fit. I don't fit in the City. I don't fit in Tohk, not really. And I don't fit here."

Cyria smiled weakly at that. "Listen, lass, I've only known you a short time, but I can tell you true: You are not a freak. You are wonderful, and beautiful, and kind, and clever. I've never met anyone else like you, my bricky little molly, and I never will. And anyone who tells you different? You give them a sock on the jaw from me."

She lifted her hand and saw the blood from Gwendolyn's knee, but she didn't say a word about it, just wiped her hand on her sleeve. Then she held it out to Gwendolyn. "Come on. Let's ankle ourselves back to the lab. That is, unless you'd like to spend the night out here?"

Given what she'd seen of Faeoria, the idea of being on the forest floor after dark was more than a little frightening. She took Cyria's hand, and they walked back to the laboratory tree.

~~~

Cyria gave Gwendolyn a cup of bright red tea that tasted of cinnamon and cardamom and warm fires. She muttered and waved her hands over Gwendolyn's numerous wounds. They healed immediately, and Gwendolyn felt more than a little better.

"I only know a trifle of healing magic, but that should do you," Cyria said. "At least on the outside. As for the rest . . . in Tohk there are chemicals, certain medicines that are quite effective if used properly. They could help you balance yourself out, to a degree. But here we must make do with other methods. Now look at this."

Cyria led her to a section of the workshop Gwendolyn had not been to before. There was a series of hanging tapestries there, a few dozen, all being worked on by mechanical creatures. Metal spiders were spinning multicolored threads while birds and squirrels wove them together.

"This is my map room," Cyria said. She tapped one tapestry. "Recognize this?"

Gwendolyn's heart skipped a beat. "Yes."

It was a picture of Copernium. The fantastic buildings, domes, and spires, the two suns in the orange sky, all rendered in woven thread with loving detail. She ached looking at it. "Is . . . is this what you wanted to show me?"

Cyria stood back and looked wistfully at the tapestry of Tohk. "If you're going to go traipsing about from world to world, you might as well understand something about them. It's my life's work. It's what I started in Tohk, what eventually led me to leave it. Through the Fae's magic, I built the Library, which grows on its own now. It's more than a little alive. Every world gets neatly catalogued with its own little book and its own little door. But some worlds I like to map in more detail, especially since I can no longer visit them. Now, how about *this* one?"

Cyria stopped in front of a tapestry that showed big blocky skyscrapers, grey clouds, and a monorail that weaved in between them. Looking closer, Gwendolyn saw that the monorail was actually moving. The sight gave her a jolt of an entirely different kind.

"That's my world. The City."

"Exactly. Once I located it, I had my busy bees create this. Advanced Fae magic, sort of a picture of the spirit of a place. Shows you how things *really* are. Note the seeming lack of color. You come from a type of world I've classified as Dystopics. Dreary places with far too many rules and silly ideas."

"And that one?" Gwendolyn pointed to the tapestry next to hers. While her world was grey, this one was nearly black. Blocky vehicles on rolling treads belched smoke into the air. Brutal-looking concrete structures loomed in the background.

"The Blackstar's world, I believe," Cyria said. "Nasty place. Seems even darker than yours."

"I'm not sure I understand. Is this supposed to help me?" Gwendolyn still struggled to care, or even to stand up straight. She was too tired for a lecture just now.

"I'm trying to make a point, dolly, stay with me." She gestured to the tapestries around her. One down from the Blackstar's was a tapestry with turreted castles lit by flickering lights. Next to Tohk was a portrait of gleaming silver cities that floated through the sky as people in colorful clothes flew between them on rocket packs. "All the worlds are different kinds of stories."

"What? Isn't it all just . . . life?" Gwendolyn asked.

Cyria gave her a sly look. "Oh? When you ask someone to tell you about their life, they tell you a *story*, a series of tales and events. When you take all those little strands of story and twist them together, you make a thread, a lifeline. Weave together all those lifelines—those lives—and you make a world, which looks a bit like a tapestry, each little colored strand another person in the grand picture of everything."

Cyria fingered the edge of the City's tapestry. "And every once in a while, I notice a thread that's different from the rest. Like this one . . ." She tapped the picture of the City.

Gwendolyn had to look very close to see it. A single red thread ran through the grey center.

"We call these heroes. Or villains. Or sometimes just people. But they buck against the shape of things, twisting and pulling and changing the strands around them. That red thread? I'd say that's you, Rosecap."

Gwendolyn ran a finger along it.

"You're a *changer*, Rose. Look closer. You've already started."

Looking even closer, Gwendolyn saw four threads that had started to take on a bit of color of their own.

"Any notioning as to who that might be?"

Gwendolyn touched them. "My friends. At the School. I've started reading to them, and they're . . . I guess they're changing." But there was still so much grey. "So it's like I said. See? I don't belong. And I'm making it worse for them too."

"Well, *belong* is a strong word. Clever people never truly belong, do they? There are always those who will tell you to sit down, hush up, don't cause a fuss, get your head out of the clouds, and why can't you behave like everyone else? But I've always thought that behaving like everyone else sounds painfully dull. Why be ordinary when you can be *extra?*"

"If I'm extraordinary, it's just meant a lot of trouble."

Cyria put her hands on her hips. "Rose, do you remember the story of the girl who acted just like everyone else?"

Gwendolyn frowned. "No."

"Of course not, nobody does. Acting like everyone else means never getting noticed, never doing anything important. Your thread may match the color of some other world, but not because you fit into them any better. None of us are born to fit in. Just look at the trouble I had in Tohk! Before being a 'legendary inventor' I had to spend quite a few years as 'that daft young chippie down the way whose house is always exploding.' We each must find our own way in the world. And I think you're meant to save yours."

Gwendolyn's frown deepened. "We've already been over this. It doesn't *want* to be saved. The City is the way it's always been, and just the way it wants to be. How can I fix it when nothing seems to be broken?"

"I'm not so sure . . ." Cyria pointed to the bottom of the tapestry. The threads there were black, writhing and twisting like the fronds of a sea anemone. "Something is wrong with your world. Something has been ripped from it, or done to it. You say you're not normal, but I'd say it's your *world* that isn't normal, and hasn't been for some time."

Cyria was right, there clearly *was* something wrong with

the tapestry. But Gwendolyn's thread still seemed awfully small compared to all that black. "So I've got the spark."

Cyria's eyebrows went up. "Ah. Where did you hear about that?"

"Someone in Tohk said I had it. And then again in your lab, your mechanical men said they recognized it in me. What is it?"

"Just some of my early research into destiny and 'chosen ones.' I was fascinated by the notion that some people were born extra special, fated for more than the ordinary person."

"So I was born different?"

"Stars and sprockets, dolly, haven't you been listening? *Everyone* is born different. One of the perks of living so long is that you learn that there is no such thing as an ordinary person. But only a few *embrace* that different and live loud enough that others can't help but notice. That is the spark. The spark of change. After all, creativity is just a matter of asking the right questions."

Gwendolyn thought about her magic words. "*What if? I wonder?*"

Cyria tapped the side of her nose. "On the button. You ask the right questions long enough, you become the sort of person who asks questions. Dream enough, you become a dreamer. We become what we do. Which is why your spark is stronger than most. It takes a lot of strength to be yourself, especially in a world like yours."

Gwendolyn sighed. "I appreciate you trying to help, Cyria, but I'm not sure what I'm supposed to do."

Cyria flung up her arms in agitation. "Not sure? Not sure?

You have a power, Rosie girl, and you must learn to use it! If not for your world, then for yourself! To stop those who are trying to take it from you, or corrupt you. Just look at the Blackstar." She gestured to the smoky, oily tapestry next to the City. "His power is the same as yours, but turned to dark purposes. You've got a fight on your hands, whether you accept it or not. But . . . well, I suppose you shouldn't have to do it alone."

Gwendolyn froze. "You mean . . ."

Cyria sighed, and led her out of the lab. "I may have been a bit hasty with you. I'm meant to teach you these things, but there's nothing saying you can't have company in your lessons. After you defeat the Blackstar, I'll show you how to use the Egressai Infinitus to find those friends of yours. You can finish your training with the two of them in tow."

Gwendolyn's heart gave a momentary lurch before crashing down again. "That's *if* I defeat the Blackstar. And that looks increasingly unlikely. If it's anything like what happened with Titania . . . I couldn't touch her, couldn't stop her, couldn't even control my own powers, how am I ever going to—"

"Nope, none of that sort of talk. You're spiraling, and exhausted." They reached Gwendolyn's room. "So clam up, and in you go. Lay down and bat a lash."

Gwendolyn went inside. And in truth, she had never been so happy to see a bed in all her life.

CHAPTER EIGHT

Nothing and Everything

Eventually, she must have fallen asleep, because the nightmares came.

Walking skeletons and pools of acid blood. Her parents again, no longer screaming, but blank faced and dull, shining in the draining light of the Lambent.

And then the black wastelands. The heart of her nightmares since she had first started this journey. The landscape reflecting the darkness that threatened to overwhelm her.

The clouds twisted and churned like an angry soup. The clouds became tentacles, as they always did, reaching toward her. The Abscess. The tentacles grabbed at her, pulled at her, but at the very last moment, Gwendolyn woke up.

This time, however, something woke up with her.

Gwendolyn felt a horrible squirming and threw back the covers to find a cluster of black shadows writhing around her legs like snakes.

She screamed, of course.

The shadows grew up her legs. She kicked and twisted, but it was as though the shadows were pulling her out of Faeoria itself, feet first. Which was exactly what they were doing. But something in her was fighting back. Gwendolyn felt a horrible burning inside, a hot tugging that resisted the shadows' grasp. Though she did not know it, her very blood was anchoring her to the faerie world. Titania's powerful magic bound her to Faeoria, and it strained against the shadow's pull.

"Inventress!" boomed the tree.

Moments later Cyria burst into the room, clad in velvet pajamas and a silk robe, her short white hair sticking out in all directions. She was stunned, but only for a moment. She dashed to Gwendolyn's bedside and pointed her necklace at the shadows. Her red gem shone like a star. She waved her free hand over the tentacles and began muttering something in the Fae tongue. The shadows shrieked and pulled back from Gwendolyn's legs, then dropped to the floor with a wet *thud*. Cyria moved the light closer, and the shadows dried up like a puddle in the sun.

Gwendolyn sat up, shivering and gripping her knees. "What . . . what was that?"

Cyria frowned. "You know what that was."

Gwendolyn bit her lower lip. "But . . . how did it get here?"

"You're not going to like this, but I think it came through your mind. Your . . . condition must have left you open to such an attack." Cyria glared down at the spot where the shadows had been. "It would seem the faeries aren't the only ones who can cheat."

Gwendolyn pressed her palms against her temples as if to

hold back any more attacks from within. "What am I going to do, Cyria? What—" but her voice choked off in a rasping sob.

Cyria placed a hand on her shoulder. "Dawn is nearly here. It's time you met your final teacher."

"More lessons? Cyria, I can't. Not again." But her curiosity, buried deep in a cave somewhere inside her, gave a little twitch. "What sort of lessons?"

"Oh, nothing, really."

Gwendolyn glared up at her with eyes reddened by tears. "Tell me, or I won't go."

"I just told you. He will teach you nothing."

~~~

As Gwendolyn's third and final day of training began, Cyria led her down to the forest floor. Morning mist clung to the ground. Pale fingers of light crept around the trees, colored motes of faerie dust dancing seductively in the shadows between.

"I have helped you fill your mind," Cyria said, "but you must also learn to empty it. And there is no teacher better than this." She gestured to the workshop tree.

Gwendolyn looked around. "Where? I don't see anyone."

"Look again." The inventress pointed higher up.

She did, and Gwendolyn thought she could see something resembling a face in the patterns of the bark.

"Oh, no," she groaned.

"Oh yes," Cyria said. "Sit there, and be good." She pointed to a stump in front of the tree.

Gwendolyn looked at Cyria, then at the stump. She went and

sat cross-legged on it. It was hardly comfortable, but she tried to be quiet and still.

Nothing happened.

She turned back to Cyria. "Is this a kind of self-taught lesson?"

"No," Cyria replied. "Hello! Your pupil is here. Wake up, you dozy dogwood."

The face on the tree shifted, and the parts of the bark that looked like eyes might have opened. "No," rumbled a voice that shook the ground. "She assaulted me."

Gwendolyn winced.

Cyria shrugged. "Well, surely a mighty tree like yourself won't be troubled by such a little thing. And this *is* on the queen's orders."

"Hrm. Very well," said the tree. "I will teach the quickling."

Gwendolyn turned to Cyria to bid her goodbye, but the inventress was already gone. Gwendolyn reluctantly looked back at the tree. "I *am* very sorry. How do we start?"

"Sit . . . breathe . . ."

"What? That's all?"

"Emptiness is peace. Quiet body, quiet mind."

Gwendolyn crossed her arms. This was not going to be easy. But she would try, if Cyria thought it would help. So she sat. And sat. Once she had settled a bit, she started to notice how the sunbeams trickled through the golden woods. She noticed the sounds of wind and insect and animal. It really was peaceful.

"I think it's working," she said. "How long is this supposed to take?"

"Longer than that," said the tree. "Close your eyes. Listen to your breath. Feel the flow."

She closed. She listened. She felt. She opened one eye. "How is this going to help me, mister . . . what do I call you?"

The leaves on the tree shivered. "Wind and rain, do the questions ever end? Allow your thoughts to pass through you. Stray thoughts lead to more . . . rabbit incidents."

Gwendolyn pictured the rabbit ears that had grown out of Missy Cartblatt's head. "How do you know about that?"

"It is difficult *not* to hear what is said inside of you."

"Oh," she said. "I hadn't thought of that."

"You have yet to glimpse even the merest wave in the ocean of things you have not thought of. Calm yourself, little river. Let your mud settle and your water become clear."

Gwendolyn took a deep breath in, closed her eyes, then exhaled. And then her eyes shot open again. "But you didn't tell me your name. Who are you?"

There was a cracking and breaking sound, which Gwendolyn took to be the arboreal version of a curse. "I am nothing, quickling. I am everything."

"That's stupid, that doesn't mean anything." She clapped her hands over her mouth in horror. "I'm sorry! I didn't mean that. I just . . . I don't understand. What do I call you?"

"*Tree* will be enough. It is what I am, as much as I am wood, and I am soil, and I am light, and I am rain, and I am little girls sleeping in my branches. We are all intertwined. We are all one. Now, back to your breathing."

Gwendolyn took exactly one deep breath. "You're very talkative, for a tree."

"Such irony is a profound display of ignorance. But knowing when to speak means knowing when to listen. When we define the noise, we create the silence. Now be *still*, you flitting fledgling."

"All right, no need to get your branches bothered . . ." Gwendolyn grumbled, then resettled herself on the hard stump.

"To the mind that is still, the whole universe surrenders," Tree continued. "Those who control others may be powerful, but those who have mastered themselves are mightier still."

His babbling was not making this any easier. She was bored, uncomfortable, and a bit hungry. Sitting quietly for long stretches of time is a struggle for any thirteen-year-old, particularly Gwendolyn Gray.

"To be full, one must learn to be empty. Fill your bowl to the brim, and it will spill."

Any time she tried to escape into her imagination, as she normally did when forced to sit through School, Tree reminded her to "let your thoughts go," and "come back to the moment." When she grew restless, he would tell her when to breathe, how long, how fast.

Hours passed that were some of the most frustrating she had ever known. But eventually, calm crept up on her. The discomfort was there, but less important. There was stillness and silence, and when thoughts came, she was able to recognize them and let them go without getting sucked in.

Gwendolyn was a clever noticer, and as she noticed her

thoughts, she noticed something deeper as well. She felt lighter. She felt *better*. No squeezing anxiety, no dark depression, no manic energy. She felt . . . balanced. Centered.

"Good," Tree rumbled. "It has only taken half a day, and you have found a taste of peace. Can you use it? That is the question. To be, or not to be. It is always both. Create something, quickling. Something small."

Gwendolyn could do that. She had the perfect idea. She held out her hand. "*Once upon a time . . .*" she whispered. And into her hand fluttered a tiny, emerald leaf.

"A wise choice. To be? Yes. Now, not to be. Dispel the magic. Empty your mind."

She took a deep breath in, and let it out, picturing all her thoughts floating away with the air as it left her.

And the leaf vanished.

"I did it!" she cried. She jumped up, ready to dash off and tell Cyria, but Tree stopped her.

"Proof of concept, not competence. Sit. Again."

Tree made her practice the rest of the afternoon, creating things and making them vanish. An acorn. A rock. A butterfly. A flower. On and on, one after the next, in and out like her breath.

Many more hours had passed, but there was a peculiar feeling of timelessness, one that will be familiar to any of you who have spent time wandering in nature. But eventually the sun dipped low on the horizon.

Gwendolyn heard leaves crunch behind her, and she turned to see Cyria landing softly, wings extended.

"Oh, thank heavens," Gwendolyn said. She leapt off the

stump, then tripped and fell on her face. Her legs were completely numb.

Cyria barked a laugh.

Gwendolyn scrambled back to her feet, smiling at herself. "Am I done?" She was starving, and her back ached, but her mind felt clearer than it had in . . . well, possibly ever.

"For today," said Cyria. "How did she fare?"

"Abysmally. But less so by the end," said Tree.

"It'll do. Come, Rose, let's go fill your belly, then pop you straight into bed."

After another meal of food so delicious that it would be disgustingly unfair to describe to you, Gwendolyn was whisked away to her bedroom. Cyria gave her a cup of purple liquid with steam that rose in perfect little spirals.

"There. A little noodle-juice to make you sleep. No attacks tonight," the inventress said.

"Noodle juice?" Gwendolyn frowned distastefully at the cup.

"Not *made* from noodles, *for* your noodle. For your head. *Tea*—oh, just drink it."

"Well, if you'd speak more plainly, you wouldn't have to explain so much. And after last night, I don't think I can ever sleep again." She took a sip.

Slumber swept her up in its comforting embrace, and she was asleep before her head hit the pillow.

The clockwork faerie caught the cup before it could spill, set it on the nightstand, then made a nest for itself in Gwendolyn's hair and closed its own jeweled eyes.

But despite the soothing tea, Gwendolyn woke a while later to the sound of voices in the hall.

"She is *my* servant, inventress. Do not stand in my way."

"My queen, I've taught you about the mortal need for sleep—"

"I am not my husband, you need not remind me. A world is at stake, and I will not lose. She must train."

"She must *rest*. She is sick."

"Sick? That is easily cured. I can heal any—"

"Not *this*, you can't. It is not a sickness of the body. It is a sickness of the spirit. At first, I believed it to be caused by your world, but now I fear it is not something from Faeoria, but something within the girl herself. The energy of the Neverlands is merely worsening a problem that lies within her already. And your cheating has not been helping."

"What? You accuse me of deception?" Titania demanded.

"Yes, I do. You've been mucking about with Rosecap's personal timeline. You can't alter the length of the days, so you've been altering the girl herself, slowing the speed at which she experiences each day. All you have to do is look at her. Look how much she's grown. How long does each hour feel to her? How long has she been here?"

"I have no way of knowing. You mortals are the ones so concerned with *time*. Though I suppose if I had a limited number of seconds to walk these worlds, I too might grow obsessed with keeping track of each one—"

"You don't need to hear this," whispered Tree. Extra layers of wood sealed the door, blocking out the voices.

"Thank you, Tree . . ." Gwendolyn mumbled groggily. She took another sip of tea, then dropped back into oblivion. It was to be her last bit of peace for quite some time.

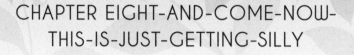

CHAPTER EIGHT-AND-COME-NOW-THIS-IS-JUST-GETTING-SILLY

The Duel

Morning came, but Gwendolyn was not allowed to wait for it, and she woke as unhappy as any of us who must begin our jobs before the sun begins hers.

Gwendolyn was marched through the pre-dawn gloom and up to the throne room. The thrones beneath the jewel fruit willow were as terrifying as ever, with the twisted bodies of the monarchs' enemies trapped in their prison. Oberon and Titania were in their places, and the entire faerie court had turned out for the occasion. Their combined glows flickered with anticipation.

No one said a word. The air was sweet but chilly, the sort of chilly that is not actually all that cold, but still gives you a shiver. At least, this was how Gwendolyn explained her shaking limbs. She spotted the Lady Fen and Drizzy, who gave her a comforting wave. Gwendolyn forced a small grin and waved back.

The first rays of the sun crept through the columns and reached Titania, illuminating a dress that seemed to be made of running water that flowed around her body in the shape of a dress. Currents created frills and ruffles like rippling turquoise silk. Lotus petals floated and swirled across its surface, the only bit of modesty the dress allowed.

The stripe of Gwendolyn's blood was still bright on the queen's lower lip, which pouted impatiently. She raised her voice to the sky. "Hear us, Blackstar. You have leave to enter our realm. Come and fight."

"I don't need your permission," said a gravelly voice. A masked figure stepped out from behind Drizzy, who gave a little yelp of surprise. "Do we still have a deal?"

Oberon nodded. "Does your master still offer his prize?"

The Blackstar held out his hand, and the image of the misty world shimmered into view again. "And when I win, I take the girl." His expression was unreadable behind the contraption on his face, which the Figment informed her was a *gas mask*.

"*If* you win I shall relinquish my claim on her, yes," Titania said. "The duel shall be to first blood only. No outsider shall be allowed the privilege to kill in our lands. That pleasure is reserved for my husband and me."

"Fine." The Blackstar clenched his fist, and his seven-pointed star tattoo glowed. A long blade that seemed to be made of pure shadow extended from the back of his hand, a flat and deadly spike of pure black energy. "Let's go."

Gwendolyn drew her dagger, struck a ready pose, and waited for some sort of signal to begin.

But there was none. The Blackstar walked right up to her,

casual as Father on his way to work, and drove the blade at her chest.

Three days ago, her surprise would have been her end. But Faeoria had worked strange magic on her, and she had improved much more than her three instructors could have taught her. Instinctively she flowed around the blade, then darted in with her knife.

The Blackstar grabbed her wrist and slashed at her arm. Gwendolyn fell backward, breaking his grip and landing up-side-down on her hands in a bridge pose. He kicked at her head, but she did a neat back-walkover and readied herself again.

It was as if Robin's dance had been burned into her muscles. She could almost see the glowing patterns of the dance floor, showing her where to move. She spread her arms in a gesture of welcome.

The Blackstar only grunted. He walked straight toward her again. Gwendolyn jumped at him with a twirling leap, knife extended, but the Blackstar merely caught her by the waist and tossed her aside.

She hit the ground and the breath was knocked from her lungs. She barely had time to get up before he was on her again, his attacks brutal and efficient. Gwendolyn danced around each strike, Robin's teaching clearly effective, but was unable to land a hit herself. The Blackstar took a slash at her, but she ducked, then sprang upward and drove both fists into his jaw.

"A hit!" Drizzy yelled, jumping and clapping. "A very pal-pable hit!"

The Blackstar's gas mask was askew, and he tore it off.

Gwendolyn dodged his next blow with a flip that she thought was quite impressive, landing soundlessly. But the Blackstar slammed his fists into the ground and the floor rippled like water.

Gwendolyn was knocked off her feet, but only for a moment. She sprang back up, finding herself in front of the thrones again.

"Don't let up, Rose," Cyria called.

"My little flower has learned her lessons well after all, my husband. I find my humor most improved by such an excellent bout," Titania said.

"Mildly amusing, my life and love. Though it is nothing if she loses."

The Blackstar's sword shrank into his hand. He threw back the flaps of his coat and drew two objects from sheaths under his arms. The Figment around Gwendolyn's neck flashed a word into her mind.

Guns.

She had seen pistols before, of course, but these were ugly, blunt, and black. Gwendolyn waved her arms, and the air shimmered and thickened into a wall of rainbow glass, just in time to block his fire. The glass cracked with each bullet, but it held.

The Blackstar darted sideways, guns spitting smoke and lead. He tried to get around the shield, but Gwendolyn spread the wall into a circular barrier.

"*If only* this glass would hold . . ." Gwendolyn whispered, adding layer after layer.

Then the bullets stopped. Through the glass, Gwendolyn saw the Blackstar holster his weapons. His tattoo glowed, and a ball of energy solidified in his hand, creating a cylinder with a long handle at the end. The Blackstar hurled it at her wall, and the Figment glowed helpfully.

Grenade.

An explosion of darkness shattered the glass into glimmering dust. Gwendolyn threw her arms up, but glimpsed another grenade sailing toward her. She formed a globe of rainbow glass around the grenade, then hurled the ball out of the throne room. All they heard was a distant thump.

The Blackstar flung more grenades at her, but Gwendolyn conjured a wind that blew them backward and knocked the fedora from his head. The grenades exploded, but he just held out a hand and sucked the black fireballs into his palm. He held out another hand and summoned his hat and mask back as well, taking a moment to put them back into place. Then he stretched out both hands and started muttering some spell under his breath.

Out of the floor grew an entire line of men in black uniforms, with short curved swords and the same frightening masks. They advanced on her, swords at the ready. Then clouds of yellow smoke poured out of the Blackstar's downturned palms.

From the masks on the villains, Gwendolyn could guess that this was not some harmless fog. She *imagined*, and another wind sprang up behind her to push the cloud away, but it was so strong that it knocked her forward onto her hands and knees. The men came closer.

She focused on her hands, touching the wooden flagstones. "*I wonder . . .*"

Vines grew up around the men's legs, holding them fast.

The vines kept growing, covering the men entirely, until they were a line of vaguely human-shaped shrubs.

But the Blackstar wasn't finished. He threw his hands to the sky, and black mist poured out. The dome above filled with dark clouds.

"Welcome to my world," the Blackstar said.

It began to rain. Fat, tar-like droplets hit the floor. Living in the City, Gwendolyn had plenty of experience with rain. She simply imagined a cheerful yellow umbrella for herself and skipped merrily toward the Blackstar, trying to seem confident. Heavy drops hit the umbrella and stuck fast, but Gwendolyn was quite dry.

Then she saw that the droplets on the ground around her were moving. They rose up, growing larger and reaching toward her. Each sticky drop had a tiny mouth with gnashing teeth. They were spreading, forming a sticky black bog full of biting little mouths. The droplets on her umbrella began to chew their way through.

She flung it away from her in revulsion, but the pool of tar had already reached her feet. The tiny mouths bit at her ankles.

But none of the teeth could break through her faerie boots. Even her bare toes and heels seemed magically protected. Gwendolyn threw an amazed look at Titania, who replied with the smallest of nods.

Unable to bite through her boots, the tar started spreading up her legs, toward the unprotected skin on her thighs. She quivered with disgust, and with it came a bright bolt of fear.

She would lose.

There was nothing she could do. He would take her to the Collector, and she'd never see Sparrow or Starling or Tommy or Missy or Ian or Jessica or Cyria or her parents ever again. She'd be erased, be turned into nothingness, everything going black . . . Her thoughts whirled out of control.

Then she thought of Tree, and one of his sayings popped into her head. *To the mind that is still, the whole universe surrenders.*

She stopped struggling. She focused on her breathing, allowing her racing thoughts to drift away like flowing water, and slowed her breaths. The tar on her legs slowed its climb as well.

Emptiness is peace.

She looked down at the tar and waved at it, thinking only of her breath. In, and out. The biting mouths stilled, and the black goop hardened to grey.

Those who control others may be powerful, but those who have mastered themselves are mightier still. To be full, one must learn to be empty.

Gwendolyn held out her arms, and instead of trying to fill herself with ideas, she did the opposite. She let her thoughts float away like a balloon, emptying herself until she was nothing more than another piece of the world. She exhaled slowly.

The shadow bog crumbled into dust and blew away. The throne room returned to normal, with nothing but the Blackstar in front of her and the faerie court surrounding them. She breathed a sigh of relief.

And then she felt a sudden slice of pain across her shoulders. She cried out and whirled around. The Blackstar was behind her, a black knife protruding from his tattoo.

"No!" Cyria cried.

Gwendolyn whirled back around, and saw another Blackstar on the other side of the throne room. This one shimmered like a mirage, and vanished.

The real Blackstar turned to face the thrones. "It's over. Give her to me."

"No it isn't. I can still fight!" Gwendolyn balled her hands into fists.

"Notice, little one," Oberon said. "Blood has been drawn."

She put a hand to her back and it came away wet and red. The duel was well and truly lost. But this is only the middle of the tale, and there is much still to come, though I cannot guarantee the ending will be any happier.

"Let's go." The Blackstar grabbed her arm.

"No!" She struggled, but she couldn't pull away. Despair roared up like a wave, and she tried to cast a spell, to imagine something, but nothing would come through the fear.

The Blackstar hauled her around and turned to leave, but Cyria dropped down on clockwork wings and planted herself in their path. "I'm afraid I can't allow you to be traipsing off with my assistant. She is occasionally useful."

"Out of my way." He turned to Titania. "We had a deal, witch."

"We did indeed, villain. And I shall keep my end. Rosecap, I release you from my service." She dipped a hand into her watery dress, then used the wet finger to wipe away the blood on her lip. She blew Gwendolyn a kiss, and red sparks fizzled through the air. "Though I shan't pretend I am pleased with you, lovey. You have cost me a new world, and such debts must be paid."

"Don't care," said the Blackstar. He began to gather a cloud of blackness around them as he had done on his last exit from Faeoria.

"However . . ." said Titania in a voice dripping with sweetness and death, "I said nothing about *helping* you leave with the girl. She is yours, *if* you can take her."

"And *I* don't recall making deals with any monochromatic brigands," growled Cyria. Before Gwendolyn knew what was happening, the air was full of tiny clockwork figures. Birds, faeries, and insects darted around them, and metal animals scurried along the ground.

The Blackstar flailed about, trying to swat them away. The dark energy he had been gathering vanished. He held out a hand to dispel the clockwork creatures, but these were no imaginary constructs. They were made of good solid metal that Cyria had toiled to build by hand.

Gwendolyn stomped on his foot with all her tiny strength. He hissed, and his grip loosened enough to pull free. She dashed toward Cyria.

"Rose, down!" Cyria yelled.

Gwendolyn threw herself flat on her belly and looked back. The Blackstar's guns were drawn.

Cyria held out her necklace and blew on it. A stream of red smoke shot through the air. The Blackstar fired, but the smoke absorbed the bullets. It swirled around the Blackstar's guns and solidified, encasing his hands in thick red crystal. More smoke swirled at his feet, hardening and cementing them inside glittering red boots.

"Hop it, sprite!" Cyria shouted at her. The inventress grabbed Gwendolyn's hand and leapt over the edge of the throne room, pulling the girl along for the ride. Gwendolyn's leaf-wings whirred alongside Cyria's clockwork ones, and they glided away from the Willow Court.

~~~

The door to the laboratory burst open, and Cyria rushed in, yanking Gwendolyn along.

"Tree! Seal yourself! Buy us time! And hope to glory it's enough," Cyria said. She ran about, pressing buttons, pulling levers, and flipping switches. Gwendolyn marveled as machinery everywhere sprang to life. The branch-shelves whirled around, ready to club any intruders.

"Cyria, what are you doing? We have to go back and stop him!" Gwendolyn said.

But Cyria was busy tapping a row of mushrooms that lit up as she pressed them. "No. You have to go, period. And I'm afraid I'll be staying here like always." She grabbed two vines and connected the loose ends of them, which sent out a shower of green sparks. There was an electrical hum, and a dozen mechanical men sprang out of giant seed pods—like the servants in the Crystal Coves, but made from wood instead of metal. Beams of light shot out from faerie jewels scattered around the lab, creating a crisscrossing web of neon lines.

Cyria grabbed Gwendolyn and pulled her up the hallway. Wooden bulkheads sealed the way behind them, solid barriers that thumped into place every few feet. They reached the door at the top of the tree. Cyria flung it open, and there was the Library of All Wonder once more.

"Quickly, inside. Actually, wait—" Cyria put two fingers to her lips and whistled.

A hole opened in the wall of the tree beside them, and the clockwork faerie flew through it, struggling to carry Gwendolyn's satchel.

Cyria grabbed it and pulled out the sketchbook and pencil. She scribbled something down, tore it out, and shoved the scrap into Gwendolyn's hand. "Take it. And this as well." She slipped the jeweled control bracelet off her wrist and slapped it onto Gwendolyn's, where it re-formed to fit her. Lastly, she took Starling's goggles out of Gwendolyn's bag, and placed them tenderly on Gwendolyn's head, pushing back the bushy red mane.

"That's better. You can't fight if you can't see." The inventress stared at her for a moment, a strange look in her eye. She gave the girl a quick hug, then pushed her away. "Go get help. Find those friends of yours, and by jolly, I hope they're a pair of hard-boiled scrappers."

"No! I'm not leaving you! Together we can *fight*—"

She was interrupted by a cacophony of crashes from below.

Tree's voice rumbled from the walls. "I don't know who you were expecting, but I believe he's here."

"Tree, are you all right?" Gwendolyn shouted. "Please, stop him!"

"I'm . . . trying my best, quickling." His voice sounded strained. "He's as strong as you are, and *far* more rude."

"We can't win," Cyria said, slinging the satchel over

Gwendolyn's shoulder. "He was holding back because he wasn't allowed to kill you. He's not like to be as cuddly now. Go!"

But Gwendolyn grabbed Cyria's hands again. "Fine. I'll lead him away, and then use the doorway to come back for you, and—"

"*No*, Rose. You've cost the faeries an entire world, and that Blackstar fellow will be nothing compared to Oberon's and Titania's wrath. Under *no circumstances* are you to return here!" A series of tremendous explosions rocked the tree. Cyria looked back. "That'll be the planets in the orrery going off. Time's up, sprout."

The whole tree shuddered, and there was a splintering crash. Then another. One after the next, an ominous drumbeat of cracking wood. Then the barrier behind them shattered, showering them in sawdust. The Blackstar stood there, gun in one hand, a severed wooden robot head impaled on a sword in the other. He let the sword vanish and the head thumped to the floor, leaking glowing green fluid and magical sparks.

"So," Cyria said. "It's like this, is it?" She planted herself in front of Gwendolyn. "Well, we all know what happens to the magical mentor in the end. I was afraid of this when I took the gig." She looked back at Gwendolyn, a strange sparkle in her eye. "Though I never could have predicted *you*, my bricky girl." And a sad little smile appeared at the corner of her mouth, like a hidden kiss.

The Blackstar pointed a gun at them. "The girl. I won't ask again."

Cyria didn't budge. Her wings expanded, and she pulled an improbably long wrench out of an impossibly small pocket. She tapped the heavy thing against her other hand. "Get in, Rose, and close the door behind you. That slip'll get you home when you need it."

"No!" Gwendolyn shouted. Her hands balled into fists and started to glow. "Let's stop him."

She put everything she had into a single ball of light, and sent it sizzling toward the Blackstar. But it was larger than she expected. Its edge caught Cyria on the shoulder, and the whole thing exploded in a blinding flash.

Gwendolyn couldn't see. She heard a thump, and a woman's voice cry out, and the Blackstar's steel grip closed around her arm. Then her vision cleared, and she saw Cyria slumped against the wall, eyes closed, jaw slack, a small line of blood trickling from the corner of her mouth. The inventress was utterly still.

"No!" Gwendolyn screamed.

But the Blackstar hauled her through the library door and slammed it shut behind them.

CHAPTER NINE

The Most Unpleasant Homecoming Yet

They stood in the entrance corridor, with the Library of All Wonder just beyond. The Blackstar dragged Gwendolyn, kicking and flailing, out into the library, and stared around in what seemed like amazement, though it was impossible to tell through his mask.

The forest of shelves stretched before them, inviting and warm, filled with every story from every world. Outside the windows, swirling colors danced in their hypnotic patterns. Books continued to stream in through them, shelving themselves.

The Blackstar looked at the windows. "The In-Between? This place is in the In-Between?"

Gwendolyn noticed his distraction and tried to stomp on his foot again, but he jerked it away and threw her into a bookshelf. Hard. Spots danced in her vision, and she slumped to the floor.

He knelt down until they were face to face. "Stay still. I don't enjoy hurting little girls." He waved a hand in front of his face, and his mask dissolved in a puff of greasy smoke. He was utterly unremarkable—just a man, with deep-set lines in his face that spoke more to worry than age. His cheeks were covered in dark stubble, and he looked more tired than anything else.

He took a book off a shelf. He flipped through it, tossed it over his shoulder, then rifled through another. And another.

"I don't understand you," he said, flipping through a large leather-bound volume.

"That's fine. I wouldn't want you to be confused, so I'll just be on my way," she said, and started to get up.

The Blackstar snapped his fingers, and iron manacles sprang from the floor and snapped themselves around her ankles. "It didn't have to be like this, kid. You're like me. You could make whatever you want, take whatever you want. You could be free."

"I could be free right now. Just let me go." Gwendolyn strained against the manacles, trying to stand, but she couldn't budge.

"You had your chance. You gave up your power, your freedom, trapped yourself. For what? To help your little City?" He tossed the book on the floor, took off his hat, and ran his hand through greasy black hair. "Stupid girl."

Fire leapt within her. "You don't get to call me that."

"You blew out your power trying to stop the Collector. You gave up everything you had to destroy those little Lambents and just made things worse for yourself. And for everyone else, too. Stupid."

Gwendolyn stared at him blankly. "What are you talking about?"

He examined the back cover of a book, looking at the code printed there. "If you'd just looked out for yourself, you'd have all been better off. Your City was happy. You could have been happy. Anyone who serves others makes themself a slave. The only way to be free is to be your own master. If everyone takes care of themselves, everyone can be free. Sacrificing your own interests for others just makes everyone weak."

Gwendolyn rolled her eyes. "That is the most absurd thing I've ever heard. I'm not asking you to be my slave or something, just let me go. You said I'm like you, so help me!" She jangled the manacles.

The Blackstar crouched down and scratched at the stubble on his cheek. "Why? It doesn't help *me*. I take you to the Collector, I get what I want. I let you go, and I don't. It's that simple."

"I—" She didn't have an immediate answer for that. But she wasn't going to fight her way out of this one. After the duel, she wasn't sure how much fight she had left. Maybe she could talk her way out. "I can do something for you. Help you get whatever it is you want. I'll owe you."

"Cute. But you can't do anything for me. You're just a little girl."

Gwendolyn spit in his face. "I'm not *just* anything."

All right, so maybe talking her way out wasn't her strong suit.

He wiped the spit from his face. He snapped his fingers, and the manacles disappeared. Gwendolyn tried to bolt, but he grabbed a handful of her hair and yanked her to her feet. She kicked his shin, but he didn't even flinch. "Stop fighting. It won't do you any good. Now, to find the way out of here."

"I could help you with that," she snapped.

His lip curled in the hint of a smile. "No thanks. I'll help myself." He slicked his hair back into place, the long hair on top pulling all the way back to meet the short hair at the nape of his neck. He donned his hat, waved his hand in front of his face, and his gas mask reappeared.

The Blackstar marched Gwendolyn back to the golden door-frame of the Egressai Infinitus. Gwendolyn kept struggling, but it was useless. He touched the plaque on the back of the door, with the address of Faeoria, and eyed the dialing console. "Clever. Dialing up the worlds. And each book with a code in the back," he said, his voice distorted by the mask again. The Blackstar turned back to Gwendolyn. "Ah. And that woman said this would get you home." He pried the piece of paper out of her hand, which Gwendolyn had almost forgotten she was holding. "It was her last request. I guess we should honor it. Time to go home."

That brought another burst of anger, but it was quickly smothered when she remembered that this had all been her fault. She hadn't listened to Cyria, couldn't control her own power, and it had gotten the inventress killed. The thought nearly sucked all the fight out of her.

The Blackstar spun the dialing circle to *M-A-G-G-8-6*, but nothing happened. Then he touched the empty slot in the center of the dial. "Missing a piece." He looked back over to Gwendolyn.

Automatically, she glanced down at the Figment around her neck, then quickly tried to hide her look.

But the Blackstar was as clever a noticer as Gwendolyn. He snatched the necklace away, the leather cord rubbing Gwendolyn's neck painfully, and stuck the Figment in the slot. He dialed again, and the grey door to Gwendolyn's world slid into place. He reached for the knob, opened the door, and tossed her through.

She stumbled and fell onto cold tile, but she saw what might be her only chance. She caught her balance, whirled around, and tried to *imagine*. She was almost completely spent, but she remembered what Cyria had said about how it was easier to use what was at hand, and she remembered how Cyria's mechanical creations had worked better than Gwendolyn's constructs. *"Once upon a time . . ."*

Concrete bricks pulled themselves out of the walls and flew at the Blackstar, driving him backward through the door.

". . . there was a girl . . ."

One after another, huge grey blocks slammed into the Blackstar.

". . . who was utterly sick . . ."

The shadow rogue tried throwing up shields, but these blocks were not imaginary, and hit all the harder for it.

". . . of you and your *nonsense.*"

She clapped her hands together and the entire wall collapsed with a horrendous crash.

Gwendolyn took a step back, panting. "Help yourself out of *that*. You greasy gatecrashing gutterguzzler," she said, trying out one of Cyria's better insults.

She turned and looked around. The end of the row of shelves

was just a pile of rubble now, and another room full of shelves was visible through the hole. The doorway was gone, and the Blackstar was nowhere to be seen.

And so was the Figment, she realized. It was still on the other side. *Everything* was on the other side. So was the Blackstar, but that wasn't much comfort.

She slumped down against the shelves. Would she ever end up in the right place, with all the right people? She tried to slow her breathing before the despair could creep up and overwhelm her. It was making a valiant effort. She could feel the beginning of a massive panic attack, and it was all she could do not to curl up on the ground.

Only one thought pierced her mental fog. *Get help*, Cyria had said. There was only one thing left she hadn't tried, something she would never even consider for a moment if the situation hadn't been so dire.

It was time to talk to her parents.

She staggered her way onto the monorail, too tired to care what people thought of the outrageously dressed girl covered in grey dust. There was barely enough energy in her to worry about the Mister Men. Surely it wouldn't be long before they came for her, or Blackstar found another way in, or this Collector person got to her. And now the faeries would be out for her too. She snorted the bitter laugh of someone whose list of enemies had grown quite long while their list of allies had grown worryingly short. It was a very specific sort of laugh.

Eventually she made it back home, stumbling into the apartment building. The door marked 6E was locked, which was unusual, and she was about to knock when she noticed something strange. The door handle did not seem to be in the right place. Or . . . was she *taller* now? Her time in Faeoria had changed her more than she'd thought.

She knocked, hoping her appearance wouldn't startle her parents too badly. Her mother answered the door.

"Hello? Yes?" Mother said.

Gwendolyn felt her heart melt. Here was her mother, neat and tidy, not a hair out of place.

"I'm home," Gwendolyn said, not sure what else to say after her absence. How long had she been gone? "I—"

"I'm sorry? Can I help you?" Mother said.

Gwendolyn supposed she must be rather unrecognizable by now, taller and dressed in faerie clothes. "Mother, it's me. I'm sorry I skipped School, it was an emergency, I'll never do it again—"

"Are you lost, dear?" She took Gwendolyn's hands. "Where are your parents? Do they live around here?"

Gwendolyn jerked her hands away as if burned. She was about to reply when she heard her father's voice. "What is it, love? Is something the matter? Who is at the door?"

Gwendolyn's mother turned back. "There's a girl here, Dan. I think she's lost."

"Well, bring her inside. The authorities can sort the matter out, or perhaps the Home for Unclaimed Children. I'm sure the Childkeeper will know what to do. What's the girl's name?" he said.

"What is your name, sweetheart?" her mother asked. Her

tone was gentle, but the words were delivered without any hint of motherly affection, and they hit Gwendolyn like a sledgehammer.

"Er . . . Gwendolyn." It sounded strange to hear her true name after so long.

Her mother winced, as if she had a sudden headache. Then her expression cleared. "Gwendolyn. That's a pretty name. Come inside. I'm sure your parents are worried sick."

"I'm not at all certain they are . . ." Gwendolyn whispered in numb shock.

"I'm sorry?"

"Nothing. I really should be—"

"I insist." Gwendolyn's mother took her by the hand again and pulled her inside. "We'll make some calls and have you home before supper."

A Lambént was out on the table, flickering. Gwendolyn pulled away before it could see her. "No, thank you. I'm sorry, I have to go!" She twisted away and ran back down the hall.

"Wait! Come back! Don't I know you from some—" her mother called, but Gwendolyn was halfway to the elevators now, one arm flung across her eyes in a useless attempt to stop the tears. Once the elevator door was closed, she pressed the emergency stop button and collapsed in a heap in the corner.

They don't even know who I am, she thought miserably. *I've been erased.*

The emptiness opened inside her, worse than ever. And why not? She was nothing now. Her parents did not know her. She had no home, no friends, no family. She might as well be one of the faceless men.

I can't stay here. They'll find me. The thought burst through her depression, sharp and strong. But where could she go? Nowhere in the City was safe. The way out of the City was gone. And she had no one left to turn to for help.

No. There was one place she could go. But it was a thought even more unpleasant than talking to her parents.

She would have to go back to the School.

Gwendolyn didn't know where she found the energy, but she managed to drag herself out of the elevator, out to the monorail, and into the School.

She crept in the front doors, as stealthily as a girl in a bright green dress could. But with the Lambents back, all the students were tucked safely in their classrooms, and she made it to the twelfth floor without incident. She stood on tip-toe to peek through the narrow horizontal slit of a window in the classroom door.

The students were all deep in their Lambent trance. She spotted two of her last hopes: Ian and Jessica. They were slack jawed and silent. Ian was drooling.

She didn't know how they could help. She had no plan. But she was running on fumes and out of ideas, and if she couldn't get the help from the friends she missed desperately, she'd settle for the friends she had.

But where were Tommy and Missy? They were gone. Even their desks were gone. Just like her parents' memories were gone. These dots connected into a bright and frightening line: the two children had been erased.

Somewhere deep inside, a growing heat burned up all the

sadness. She clenched her hands into fists, but it didn't stop their shaking. *Why don't they just leave. Me. Alone?!*

Her friends. Her parents. Her life. Gwendolyn was seeing red. Then she realized it was because her skin was glowing.

The School buzzer sounded, signaling the end of class. The students shot out of their desks. Gwendolyn threw herself behind the door as it swung open and breathed, trying to extinguish the glow and still her trembling hands. *You're swinging back and forth again,* she told herself. *You don't have time for this.*

Ian and Jessica came out, and Gwendolyn called their names. The two of them turned, and their eyes went wide with fear.

Gwendolyn supposed that was a normal enough reaction to her wild appearance. She hoped she'd stopped glowing, at least. "Where are Tommy and Missy?" she asked.

"Look, I-I don't know w-who you are, but leave us alone, all right?" Ian stammered. He grabbed Jessica by the arm and hustled her down the hallway.

Gwendolyn's expression became one of grim unsurprise. No doubt they had no memory of Tommy or Missy, just as they had no memory of Gwendolyn.

That was it, then. She would get them back, and her parents' memories. No more running. No more getting chased, no more waiting to be attacked. It was time the Mister Men ran from *her* for a change. She was *not* the same girl they had ambushed on the street all those weeks ago.

But where could she find them? They always seemed to be around when she *didn't* want them. That's the problem with the sorts of villains you got those days. So unreliable.

As Gwendolyn stood on the front steps of the School, she nearly tumbled down them with the force of a sudden realization. The answer was staring her right in the face. Literally. It was obvious: The Mister Men were at the center of everything. The absolute center.

She stared up at the Central Tower. The tallest building in the City, the gleaming domed skyscraper at its very heart.

She had never been there before, had spent most of her time *avoiding* the center. But there was no question that the Tower was the end of this particular journey, though she could not realize how enormously true that statement would prove to be. The ride there wasn't long, and she spent it trying to breathe and balance her excess energy with her lurking depression.

Now, you might think that a teenager who hurls herself into the clutches of her enemies must be a terribly foolish girl indeed. But if so, you've clearly not met many teenagers, particularly emotionally unstable ones with little sleep, a score to settle, and nothing to lose. It is a uniquely dangerous combination. Though dangerous to *whom* remains to be seen.

Unlike every other building in the City, the Central Tower was round, not square. A sleek shining cylinder, all the way up to its gleaming mirrored dome. All Gwendolyn knew about it was that the City Council supposedly had their offices there, keeping everything well maintained and exactly the same.

Without any better ideas, Gwendolyn strolled right through the front doors.

The lobby had soaring ceilings, white marble floors, and a long reception desk in front of a bank of elevators. Gwendolyn walked right past the receptionists, who didn't even glance up from the ledgers they were scribbling in, and boarded an elevator.

After a moment's pause, she shrugged and pressed a floor at random. The elevator whisked her up to the thirty-second floor, and the doors opened to reveal a sprawling office area. It was the size of several City blocks, with no walls to break up the space. Hundreds of desks were lined up in neat rows, all too much like the School for Gwendolyn's taste.

Which was, of course, the point. The School was designed to churn out drones who would sit quietly in rows and work all day without complaining. And here they were, hundreds of people all hunched over their desks, with not a sound save the clacking of typewriter keys. No one even noticed the sound of the elevator.

Gwendolyn pressed a button for the eighty-sixth floor. This was a much nicer area, all private offices with glass walls. The people looked the same as on the other floor—intent on their typewriters, tapping away. She wondered how these fancy glass boxes were any different from the rows downstairs.

Finally, she pressed a button for the top floor. The counter on the wall ticked upward—*148, 149, 150*. It chimed to a stop, but nothing happened.

Gwendolyn put her hands on her hips. "Well? I'm here. That's what you wanted, isn't it? Am I just going to stand here all day, or are you going to—"

The elevator door opened to a blinding flash of light, and Gwendolyn collapsed.

CHAPTER TEN

The ORB

Gwendolyn awoke in darkness.

She felt smooth, cold floors beneath her, and a wall against her back. Her eyes adjusted, and she jumped to see a girl, staring dazedly at her through a tangle of red curls.

Gwendolyn recovered and reached to touch the mirror in front of her. The ruins of elaborate designs streaked her face; her tears had proved too much for even Titania's magic makeup. At least she still had Robin's knife strapped to her thigh.

She stood up. Jagged, irregular mirrors surrounded her on all sides. It was a tiny mirror-chamber, with Gwendolyns as far as the eye could see. Even the floor and ceiling were mirrored.

Seeing her body reflected to infinity forced her to admit that it *was* different. A little taller. But also softer, somehow. And . . . other things. She didn't seem to be a clumsy collection of elbows, knees, and feet anymore. Exactly what had Faeoria done to her? How much time had she spent there? Or did the magic of that world make everything in it more beautiful?

Then she noticed that not all her reflections were the same. Some Gwendolyns wore her School uniform. Some wore the red dress she had accidentally made, and some wore the puffed-sleeve green one from Tohk. One of them had straight blonde hair, which looked just awful on her. Another had no hair at all.

But this was no time for self-reflection. A voice rang through the chamber, a cold low monotone rumble. "Well, Mister One. The girl is no longer running, is she?"

Slowly, ever so slowly, two faceless men in bowler hats stepped out of the crowd of reflected Gwendolyns. Unlike her own image, these men were not reflected to infinity. In all of the mirrors, there were only exactly two.

"Running was futile, Mister Two. The Bureau was always her inevitable destination. Provided with the proper . . . motivations."

"No need for the outsider and his uncivilized methods. And now her contaminations have been scrubbed clean from the City—"

"Shut it," Gwendolyn snapped. "Where am I?"

The two men cocked their heads.

"You are inside the Origination Regulation Bureau," Mister Two said. "We control all that is new."

"You have violated the Whyte Proposal," said Mister One. "And for that, there are . . . consequences."

Gwendolyn made a show of rolling her eyes. "Can we *possibly* get on with—"

The chamber shuddered and split apart. The mirrors moved, all attached to mechanical arms, and Gwendolyn was suddenly stranded on a single mirrored platform. Other platforms rose to meet her, clicking together to form a floor of irregular mirrored panels. More panels joined to form new walls. Her tiny chamber was now an enormous faceted silver dome.

"Perhaps now she will be more receptive, Mister One," said a voice from behind her.

"Perhaps, Mister Two," said a voice from over her other shoulder. Something hard was slipped around her wrists, binding them behind her back. Her knife was torn away from her leg, strap and all. "There. The Collector will see you now, Gwendolyn Gray."

Slowly, ever so slowly, a column of glass rose from the middle of the dome. It was the size of a tree trunk, but faceted like rough-cut crystal. The column rose until it connected to the roof of the dome with a *thud*.

Around the base of the spire was a ring of clear glowing beads. *Lambents,* Gwendolyn thought. But all her thoughts fled as she noticed the person floating in the glowing spire, suspended thirty feet above.

It was a little boy. No more than eight, with withered limbs so small she could have wrapped her fingers around them. His long platinum hair floated as though he were underwater. Tubes ran into his arms and legs and back, pumping colored liquids into him.

"Hello, Gwendolyn," he said, though he never opened his mouth. "I'm so happy you're finally here."

That voice. Childish, but with the weight of years behind it. She had heard it before.

"So. You're the Collector," she said. The dome was fairly

sizzling with energy, making the hair on her arms stand up. She'd have to be careful. She had to stay balanced.

"Yes," the Collector said, his voice vibrating from the crystal. It was impossible to tell where he was looking, since his eyes were glowing white. "It's funny that I know so much about you, and you know so little about me." He laughed, a disturbingly high-pitched giggle.

"I don't care who you are. Where are Tommy and Missy?"

"Your friends, yes. I'd forgotten that you'd finally made some. Of course, they forgot too, didn't they?"

Gwendolyn's fists clenched, bound behind her back. "I'm not in the mood for games, whoever you are."

"Oh, she's not in the mood for games. That's too bad. I love games. The first one is a guessing game. Who do you *think* I am? A clever girl like you must have all sorts of inklings."

She glared at the glowing spire. "You're the Collector. I don't know why you've been attacking me, but it ends now."

"A good guess," came the boy's voice. "I *am* a collector. But I am the protector as well, keeping us safe, keeping the monsters out."

"Out?" she blurted. "The only monster here is you."

"Wrong, wrong, wrongity-wrong. I am the emptiness that protects us from the new. I am the hole where we keep all the bad things, locked away in the nothingness. I think you called it the Abscess? That's a neat name. But why don't you call me Mister Zero. Get it? Because—"

"Yes, yes, nothingness, emptiness, zero. You're *some* sort of hole, all right." She rolled her eyes. Sarcasm kept the fear at bay. "What do you want? I've never done anything to you."

"A lonely little girl with a big imagination. What greater threat could there be, Gwendolyn?"

She hated the way he said her name, in a disturbing little sing-song tone. "You attacked *me* first. I stopped you before, and I'll do it again."

"Oh, Gwendolyn, but your power is gone now, blocked by fear, and pain, and sad things."

Gwendolyn paused mid-retort. That . . . was more accurate than she'd like.

"Yes." Dark shapes flickered across the surface of the mirrors. "Fear is a great weapon, especially against imagination. Depression is even better. They stop up your mind like a cork. That's why your powers are so *sometimesy*. Sometimes-here, sometimes-not. But I can pluck out all those pesky feelings and leave you feeling blissfully happy."

"The Lambents," Gwendolyn said. "But emptiness and happiness aren't the same thing."

"Aren't they though? Empty of cares and worries. The Lambents protect everyone from those nasty ideas."

"There is nothing wrong with my ideas!" She strained against her bindings, testing them, but they held firm. "You're the problem. You use the Lambents to steal everyone's imagination."

"Oh, but you couldn't be more wrong! The Lambents aren't the problem, they're the solution, keeping everything nice and tidy. I hold in all the thoughts that nobody wants to think. Do you know how hard that is?"

Gwendolyn scoffed. "Origination Regulation Bureau." She looked at the round room they were in. "The ORB. Keeping anything from changing, regulating anything new. Then I come along and start changing things left and right."

"Indeed, you've made quite a spectacle of yourself, with your bunny ears, and your forests. Contaminating everything."

"And what's wrong with that? I don't see anyone else complaining. You're just a selfish little boy. You want all the power for yourself, and you're throwing a fit because I'm mucking about with your *collection*." She stood as straight as she could. "You use the Lambents to control everyone, but people don't want to be controlled. People want to be free!"

Mister Zero giggled again, a soft, tinny laugh. "Oh, Gwendolyn. You're so *funny*. What do you know about people? How could you know what they want, when they've never wanted *you*? They don't want to be free. Freedom is scary, full of work and struggle and fighting to keep it. People want to be *comfortable*. Happy is better than free. I am not some storybook villain. I am the hero."

Gwendolyn thought of Kolonius. "I know heroes," she said proudly. "They don't act like you. Heroes don't just take, they sacrifice themselves for others."

"Which is what I do. I sacrificed myself to the City. I saved it. Everyone wanted it this way. I didn't conquer anything. I was *chosen*. They *elected* me."

"No one would choose to brainwash themselves and let other people control them," Gwendolyn said. "People aren't like that."

"Aren't they, though? No one is forcing them to look at the

Lambent every day. I don't steal. They *give*. Just as I gave up my life for the greater good."

Gwendolyn stamped her foot. "What greater good? What are you talking about?"

The little boy in the glowing pillar sighed. "Gwendolyn, in all your wonderings and dreamings, have you ever asked yourself what was *outside* the City?"

This boy had a talent for saying things that stopped her anger in its tracks. She had spent much time thinking that very thought. "What does that have to do with anything?"

"You've spent enough time staring at the Wall," Mister Zero said. "Let's take a walk outside, shall we?"

There was a flash of light from the Lambents at the base of the pillar, and the dome of the ORB vanished. Gwendolyn found herself surrounded by a perfectly projected image, and a terrifyingly familiar one at that. She stood in a projection of blackened rock and craggy mountains and churning black clouds.

"I know this place," Gwendolyn said. The land of her nightmares.

"Yes," said Mister Zero softly, though she could not see him. His spire had disappeared with the rest of the ORB. "These are the Wastelands of What Has Come Before. This is what's outside the Wall."

"What?" Gwendolyn looked again at the cratered ground and angry skies. "What do you mean?"

"I mean that if you climbed over the Wall, and if you could walk through it without dying from the poisoned air, this is all you would see. This is all that's left of our world. The City, and this."

"So why doesn't anyone know about it?"

"They don't want to. People don't want to remember the terrible things they've done. The Lambents help them forget. It is my job to remember how dangerous imagination is. It is a very lonely job. Having you here is the most fun I've had in years. Are you sure you don't want to play a game?"

"No!" Gwendolyn shouted at the boy she could not see. "Imagination isn't dangerous, it's wonderful! I don't believe that people would give it up without a fight."

"Oh, there was a fight. There's always a fight," Mister Zero said.

There was a flash from the Lambents, and the scene around them changed, like a movie on rewind. The clouds rolled back to reveal a bright blue sky. A city rose, but this one was bustling with activity and color, shining with neon and chrome, full of people dressed in fantastic colors and patterns. There were gardens and parks with trees, grass, and flowers.

"Once upon a time, this is how the world looked. People, all over the planet, millions of them in farms and villages and yes, great big cities like this one. It was an age of wonder. There was plenty of everything for everyone. Information and ideas could be shared instantly."

Gwendolyn saw people looking into colored gems identical to the Figment. Information storage devices, Gwendolyn guessed, just as Cyria said.

"But it couldn't last."

Suddenly, there was an explosion from a building above her. The images sped up, and scenes of chaos flickered by faster than she could follow.

"Wait! Stop!" Gwendolyn cried. "What happened?"

"The same thing that always happens. War."

"But why?" Images of fighting and dying flickered all around her, images that I will spare you the details of. "What are they fighting about?"

"Ideas, of course. Some people wanted change, and others didn't. The why of it all didn't matter. These people had great imagination, on both sides. So they invented new weapons, new ways to destroy, until the weapons became so destructive that using them was unthinkable, un-*imaginable*. But they imagined it, and they did it, and blah blah blah, you've got your basic run-of-the-mill apocalypse."

There was a blinding flash of white that burned Gwendolyn's eyes. When it cleared, she was back in the Wastelands.

"It isn't a very *original* story, but that was the day the world ended. In the end, the right side won. The side that knew that everything was better the way it used to be, and that progress was always dangerous. The few thousand survivors decided to start over. They had the resources to rebuild one city, to partially clear a piece of sky and generate a small amount of food and water."

Out of the Wastelands grew a place she knew quite well: a City the color of ash, full of stone and cement and clouds.

"The survivors had to ensure that it would never happen again. The balance was so delicate. Too many changes, and the

City would fall apart. So a plan was made to keep everything exactly the same."

"The Lambents?" Gwendolyn asked.

"Yes. The Whyte Proposal was passed. The Whyte Proposal states that things must stay the way they are. Peaceful, and calm, and permanent. Or the last of us might not survive."

"So you turned the Figments, which shared ideas, into the Lambents, which take away ideas. All to keep everything exactly the same. No more imagination."

"They were tired, Gwendolyn. So tired. The vote was held. The Lambents sweep away dangerous thoughts, putting a stop to all wars, forever. No invention means no new weapons. No ideas means nothing to fight over. No memories of what we lost means no questions about where it all went. Everything is the way it is, and the 'good old days' will be all of our days. Everyone is happy."

"I'm not happy," Gwendolyn murmured.

With a flash, Gwendolyn was back in the mirrored dome of the ORB with the unmoving child in the spire. "I wasn't happy either. Not at first. I tried to hide my collection."

Mister One waved a hand, and produced her copy of *Kolonius Thrash and the Perilous Pirates* from thin air. Mister Two produced a glowing blue jewel in a silver casing. Somehow, they'd gotten them from the Library. The Blackstar, no doubt.

"Those are mine! Give them back!" she yelled.

"No. They're mine. Did you think I wouldn't find you in my *favorite* story? And the . . . Figment, you call it? Adorable. One of the old devices, full of all the stories and information from before the Fall. I'd say that lately you've probably known lots of things you couldn't know."

Gwendolyn thought of knights and unicorns and genies, things she'd never learned in the School.

"Now my collection is complete again. Because that's what the City needed: someone who would *collect* the power but never use it. An adult would want to take control and do things their own way, but children know the truth: change is scary. So here I am. Forgotten, but very busy."

Gwendolyn let it all sink in. "Mister Zero," she said quietly, "how old are you?"

"Golly, Gwendolyn, what a rude question to ask. But since we're friends now, I can tell you. I have been in the ORB for over five hundred years."

"Five hundred . . ." Gwendolyn stammered. She looked at the tubes that pumped glowing, multicolored liquids into him. She looked at his long white hair, and thought of Cyria, kept magically young. "Imagination is power. And I don't look into the Lambents. I was born different. A stray thread."

"Different?" Mister Zero giggled his boyish giggle. "Gwendolyn, you don't really think you're the only one, do you? The only dreamer? The first one to fight back? Did you think you were *special?*" And he laughed some more, higher and higher until it hurt her ears.

Gwendolyn's heart sank. She *had* thought she was special. We have all had a thought like that, a thought that we have never thought out loud, but once we have thought about it, it seems so obviously silly that we wonder why we ever thought it at all.

It is a very specific sort of thought. And at Mister Zero's words, the thought of her specialness began to shrivel like a flower in want of water.

"No, Gwendolyn. You aren't special. The Lambents are very helpful. If revolutions happen, and no one remembers them, it's like they never happened at all. Imagination is too dangerous to take chances with."

Gwendolyn glared. "And you erase those sorts of people. Like my friends."

"You are so smart! It's why you've been such a troublemaker. Destroying the Lambents almost killed everyone, by the way."

"I . . ." His words hit her like the bricks she'd hurled at the Blackstar. "What do you mean, I nearly killed everyone?"

"No Lambents, no power. Ideas have power, and the Lambents take that power and put it to good use, nice and safe. While you're busy using it to create imaginary fuzzball creatures and fancy new dresses, I'm using it to create clean air, food, and electricity. But you switched it all off. I had to draw on some deep reserves to hold it all together, and I didn't have time to deal with you."

"I don't believe you," she said, but she wasn't very convincing.

"By the time I fixed it, you had contaminated more people. Your four friends. Two of them were not so far gone, and we could simply erase your changes from their minds. But the other two had to be cut out. Collected. The Lambents can only do so much. People tend to break if you push things too far, add too many changes, and your two friends were waking up too much to be sent back to sleep. Fortunately, you never really shared anything with your parents. So we neatly erased you from their minds as well. I don't want to cause any more damage than I have to."

"Except for me. You have no problem coming after me."

A long, sad sigh filled the dome. His voice vibrated from the spire again, though his body remained frozen, save for his long floating hair. "I am very tired. I need someone new. Someone like me."

"I'm nothing like you!" Gwendolyn blurted.

Mister Zero giggled. "Oh, *so* much like me. You're the only one of your kind that ever escaped, you know. As you may have noticed, I'm not trying to *collect* you anymore. If I did, why would I bother explaining all of this? I'm not some monologuing villain like that pirate Drekk."

"What . . . what *do* you want?" Gwendolyn said.

"I thought you'd never ask," the boy replied. "I want to die, Gwendolyn."

CHAPTER ELEVEN

Blood and Feathers

That was the last thing Gwendolyn expected to hear. "I thought . . . I thought you wanted to collect me. Or erase me, or something."

"No, no, no. I need someone like you to take my place. Then I can stop, knowing that the City is cared for. Five hundred years is such a long time."

"I don't understand," Gwendolyn said.

"Just think. It's not as if anyone wants you here."

The mirrors around her were suddenly filled with images of children from the School. Shouts and taunts echoed through the ORB.

"Weirdy."

"Oddling."

"Look at that hair."

"Talking to your stuff again? You look plain mad."

"That tree's not going to be your friend either, Weird-o-lyn!"

The mirrors showed Gwendolyn's every trip and shove, every

mean word, every hateful glance from passersby on the street. Gwendolyn's face burned. As much as we might try to pretend that such things do not bother us, the truth is that the wounds of childhood never truly heal, just as the scars on a tree remain etched in its bark as it grows.

"Children are so mean," Mister Zero said. "No one missed me. Would anyone miss you?"

Gwendolyn gave him a defiant look. "My parents would have. If you hadn't gotten to them first."

"Would they?"

Her parents appeared, fifty-foot images that towered over her like angry giants.

"Scratching the Forthright girl, sulking around, the constant disrespect! We raised you better than that!" Mother shouted. "You're not our daughter!"

"We have certain rules in this house, young lady, rules you do not abide by," boomed Father. "You're not a part of this family. You don't belong in this house."

Gwendolyn's heart sank into her boots. She recognized the fight from her birthday.

"You see?" Mister Zero said. "I'm sorry, Gwendolyn. I know how it feels to have parents who don't want you. Out there, you're unwanted. But in here, you can be important. Never worrying about fitting in or growing up."

Suddenly, Gwendolyn did not feel like the bold warrior who had marched into the Central Tower. She just felt . . . empty.

But then Gwendolyn noticed something. Something that shattered Mister Zero's illusions like glass.

"My parents never said that," she muttered.

"What was that?" the boy asked.

Gwendolyn lifted her head. "My parents never said that. Not exactly. You've changed it. You're trying to trick me. You're mean, and horrible. If you think I would ever be like you, then all that power has addled your tiny little brain."

Flecks of black appeared around the floating boy. "You're hurting my feelings. You know you don't mean that."

But anger was rising inside her, anger at what he'd done, anger at herself for letting his words get inside her. "What you're doing is wrong. I'm going to stop you and make you sorry you ever hurt me or my friends."

Thin black threads swirled inside the spire. Images from her entire life in the City appeared on the mirrors, every memory of her that he had erased from everyone else's minds. "Well, Gwendolyn, if you won't stay and play, then you'll just stay. I'm not a liar. No one will miss you. After all, no one even remembers you."

Gwendolyn's mind, freed from all his words and tricks, scrambled about in search of an escape. What could she do? Her wrists were bound behind her back, and Misters One and Two still stood on either side of her. She needed an idea. She needed to shut everything out and focus past the fear that threatened to block her thoughts.

And she found something. A tiny notion, but it might be enough. There was a small *snick*. The bindings on her wrist parted. Then something small and metal flitted up onto her shoulder.

"What are you doing? I can feel your energy, Gwendolyn. Stop it!" Mister Zero shouted.

But she didn't stop. In a move born of Robin's training, she spun and kicked Mister Two in the knee, and he stumbled. Gwendolyn snatched the Figment from his gloved hand, then dashed away just in time to escape the grasping fingers of Mister One. She ran across the dome, looking desperately for any sort of exit.

"Stop her!" shrieked Mister Zero like the whining child he was. "Bring her back! She's mine!"

Suddenly, the mirrors around her shifted. The floor split apart into individual mirrors again, pulled by mechanical arms. The dome became a chaotic maze of whirling glass platforms, each mirror still showing some picture from her life.

Without a floor, the dome had become a sphere. An ORB. Her piece of floor was now a solitary platform, and it tilted to try and throw her off. She looked down and saw the hydraulics and pistons below, waiting to crush her when she fell. The mirror kept tilting, and she slid farther and farther. So instead of falling, she leapt, landing on a different platform, a mirror that showed an image of her School teacher from the previous year.

A grim little smile crept across her face. Now *this* was a game she could play, and she spotted a way to win it. A single image, nearly impossible to notice among all the shining memories around her. But of course, Gwendolyn was a clever noticer.

It was the image of a plain grey door at the end of a row of bookshelves. The memory of the day she first discovered the portal. The real door was no longer there, destroyed when she'd brought down the wall. But a *memory* of the door ... she didn't know whether this would work, but she *imagined* that it might, and that would have to be enough.

Behind her, mirrors rose up to form a path for the Mister Men. They walked calmly toward her, stepping on the images of her life.

She jumped again, and landed on a mirror showing her reading to Tommy Ungeroot. Jumped again, and almost slid off her mother's face as she braided a younger Gwendolyn's hair. She twirled and leapt, and it was no different than dancing in the treetops with Robin. She saw a path to where she needed to go, just like the paths painted on the training floor.

The universe moves and so do you, she thought. *Your enemy moves, and so do you.*

The Mister Men were within arm's reach. She ducked the groping hand of Mister One, and rolled off the platform, dropping to land on another that was passing below, whisking her toward her destination—the mirror with the door. She was nearly there. It was only twenty feet below. She pointed the Figment at the image of the door and it swung open.

"You're not going anywhere, Gwendolyn," said the boy in the spire at the center of the mad kaleidoscope of spinning mirrors. "You belong here. You belong to me."

Gwendolyn shot him a smirk. "You don't want me, Mister Zero. I'm afraid I just don't fit in here." And with that, she leapt for the image of the door, diving headfirst, the Figment glowing like a beacon.

The boy shouted, his voice an inhuman roar. Shadow

tentacles burst from the glowing surface of the spire. One of them knocked the Figment from her hand.

Gwendolyn reached the mirror, but instead of smashing into a solid pane of glass, she vanished inside.

~~~

She opened her eyes to find herself in the entryway of the Library of All Wonder, though the stone hallway was unusually dark. Some distant part of her noticed that the yellow lightbulbs were all shattered. Gwendolyn had wits enough to close the Egressai Infinitus behind her this time.

Something small and glittering fluttered out from under her hair. The clockwork faerie that had snipped her restraints.

"So. A stowaway," she whispered. "Thank you. You're quite a helpful little thing, aren't you?"

The faerie whistled and puffed a bit of steam. It was tiny, but it had been the biggest idea Gwendolyn could muster. She hobbled out of the entryway and into the Library. But what she saw almost made her forget her exhaustion.

The Library of All Wonder had been destroyed.

The shelves were bare. Most had been toppled. The magnificent mosaic in the courtyard was faded and cracked, its tiles no longer moving. Decaying books littered the floor like fallen leaves. And she saw that every single book was blank.

Mister Zero had been at work here, adding to his "collection." The Blackstar must have shown him in.

"It's gone," Gwendolyn moaned. "It's . . . it's all gone. Everything." She thought of how her parents' minds were now as blank as these books. Her life was as ruined as the Library. All her worlds, her friends, her stories, her family. She had nothing. She *was* nothing.

What was the last thing she'd said to her parents, when they had still remembered her? Mother had tried to hug her on the steps of the School, but Gwendolyn had pulled away. Mother said she was sick of Gwendolyn's attitude.

"Good," Gwendolyn had snapped. *"You won't have to deal with it anymore, and if you like, never again. I'll vanish, and you won't have a freak for a daughter. You can get one of the normal ones if you like."*

She hadn't said anything at all to Father. Not even goodbye.

It felt as though someone were removing her organs without anesthesia. Somehow, she trudged her way to the loft where, once upon a time, she had spent a pleasant afternoon reading. She crawled into the red leather armchair, now aged and cracked, and curled her legs beneath her.

The emptiness ate at her. The despair was so much worse than it had been in the forest when she'd run from Titania. Now she had nowhere to run to. Her breath came fast and shallow, and her body rocked with barely contained sobs.

The only thing left inside her was a loop of thoughts, replaying a list of everything and everyone she had lost, all because she wasn't good enough, or strong enough, or smart enough.

Overcome with the desire to leave the world and its troubles behind, she closed her eyes. The clockwork faerie landed on her shoulder and curled up in her hair as Gwendolyn cried herself to sleep.

~~~

Sleep is a marvelous thing. There are few problems that can't be improved by good exercise, good food, and a good night's sleep. Gwendolyn had more than she liked of the first, and none at all of the second. As for the third, when she awoke a while later, she felt a bit better, though for the first time in her life she was completely out of ideas.

She turned to her clockwork friend. "What next?" she asked.

The faerie shrugged.

Gwendolyn sighed. "I don't know either."

The Figment was gone. Her satchel was gone, along with her sketchbook and her copy of *Kolonius Thrash and the Perilous Pirates*. Everything was gone, in every sense of the word, save for the clothes on her back and the little faerie.

With nothing better to do, she wandered the ruins of Cyria's magical library. Where there had once been clear pathways, she now had to clamber over fallen shelves and mounds of books.

She picked one up from the ground, its cover grey, its pages blank, even the sticker in the back erased. Without the codes or the Figment to power the doorway, she wasn't going anywhere.

A faint squeaking sound jerked her from her thoughts. The little wooden cart was wheeling itself in a tiny circle, helplessly trapped by the wreckage.

"Hello!" called Gwendolyn. "It's good to see you again." At this point, she was grateful for any familiar face, even if it didn't have one. She rushed over to it.

"I'm sorry," she said. "I never meant for any of this to happen."

The cart stopped turning circles and bumped gently up against her. On the top shelf sat a single, solitary book.

"Is that for me?" Gwendolyn asked, reaching for it. It was not grey like the rest, but was the only speck of color left in the entire Library, save for Gwendolyn herself. It had an emerald green cover that precisely matched her eyes. It was decorated with swirling red designs the same fiery shade as her hair. But what shocked her was not the color of the book, but the title.

The Marvelous Adventures
of
GWENDOLYN GRAY

Too amazed for words, she traced a finger over each curling letter. There was her name, plain as day. And on the spine, her initials, the two curling *G*'s, just like on the Figment. She shivered with excitement and just a bit of unease. Many of us have felt the urge to dive into a new book, but never as strongly as Gwendolyn did at that moment. She turned to the first page. It was blank.

Of course, she thought. But something small and delicate had been pressed between the empty pages.

"A feather," she said. Not being an ornithologist, she could not tell you what kind, but now I can tell you that it was, in fact, a sparrow's feather.

"Hmm ..." Gwendolyn said.

"Hmm ..." the little faerie buzzed.

The cart just sat there.

Gwendolyn scratched the feather absentmindedly against the blank paper. She doodled invisible initials, two interlocking *G*'s. For some reason, she thought of how Titania had slit open her palm to draw a drop of blood.

She jabbed the point of the feather against her finger. It hurt. A crimson droplet welled up. The faerie puffed in alarm, but Gwendolyn ignored it. She dipped the feather into the blood, pressed it to the page, and began to write.

CHAPTER ONE

Things That Begin . . .

Yes, that sounded nice. She pressed the feather to her finger again and used her magic words.

Once upon a time, in the City of No Stories, Gwendolyn Gray ran away.

She did always seem to be running, didn't she? She placed the period, and the paper absorbed the droplet of blood, drinking it up like rain on dry earth. Words began scribbling themselves onto the page, so fast that Gwendolyn could hardly follow them.

"Mother, must I go to the School today? What if I came with you? We could explore the City together!" she said. "What if we found a secret passageway and met some sort of friendly animal, like a badger—a real badger, not just the kind we see in books at the School? Oh, and what if he took us home for tea! I think it would be just wonderful to have tea with a badger. I wonder what type of tea badgers drink? Though I suppose it would be awfully hard to hold a cup with such long claws—"

She was babbling again. Gwendolyn couldn't help but smile at the girl whose biggest problems were the size of Cecilia

Forthright. But the words kept coming, and the pages turned themselves as if caught in a playful breeze. Whole chapters appeared by magic, though writing is never so easy. To a reader, finding a page full of words seems like magic, when they cannot see the sweat and struggle that went into setting the words down.

Gwendolyn skimmed, awed to see her trials, triumphs, and even her own secret thoughts all jotted down in plain ink.

At last, the book came to its final page, where Tommy Ungeroot sat under a tree reading to Gwendolyn. The book scribbled its final line—

And So Ends

The Marvelous Adventures of
GWENDOLYN GRAY

—and the back cover flipped closed.

Gwendolyn tapped a finger against her lips, the way Father did when he was thinking hard, as she absorbed this incredible occurrence with her usual speed.

"It really isn't as strange as all that, I suppose," she told the faerie. "This Library claims to be the place where all stories end up. So why not mine?" But why did it stop there? Seeing a definite end to her story was a little unnerving. The whole *thing* was a little unnerving. Tenderly, she placed the book upon the nearest shelf, perhaps the only story left in the entire Library. *Her* story. Just like Cyria had said. The faerie fluttered up and touched the spine, then chirped.

"Yes," Gwendolyn said, "it does seem awfully lonely on the shelf all by itself."

As if on cue, she heard a fluttering sound and looked up.

Another book soared through an open window, its pages fluttering like wings. It came to rest next to her story, its cover a dark red.

"Curiouser and curiouser . . ." Gwendolyn said, picking up this new volume.

The Fantastical Exploits of
GWENDOLYN GRAY

Inside, neat little sentences and paragraphs described everything that had happened since she had destroyed the Lambents, and her time in Faeoria. But this book was only half full. She came to a page where sentences appeared slowly, one at a time. She read about herself, sitting and reading a book.

"Where is this coming from?" Gwendolyn said aloud.

"Where is this coming from?" Gwendolyn said aloud, she read.

"Where is this coming from?" Gwendolyn said aloud, she read, she read.

Fortunately, before this sort of thing got really out of hand, Gwendolyn dropped the book. "I'd better behave myself," she told her faerie friend. "I'd hate for anyone to see me pick my nose or say something naughty. Best put it away. It seems terribly vain to spend one's time reading about oneself," she reasoned, though in truth she was troubled by the books that knew her every thought. She put the book on the shelf next to the first, sneezing at the dust it kicked up.

"Who is writing all this?" she wondered, wiping her nose on her sleeve. "Though . . . perhaps *I'm* the one writing it. Everything I do adds another line to the book." Her thoughts clicked together, this idea combining with others to create even more. Something about the way the words had appeared on the page was familiar.

She sat cross-legged on the dirty floor, and the faerie fluttered down to her knee. Gwendolyn stroked its metal hair absently, trying to remember a word, something Cyria had said. The inventress had waved her hand over a blank page, and all the words had returned. A restoration spell, she'd said. Was this any different?

Gwendolyn looked toward the nearest heap of books, waved a hand, and said, "*Rofirthar!*"

Color flowed across the books, titles scribbling themselves onto their covers. The books jumped obediently back upon the shelf and arranged themselves next to her own.

She looked at another pile, and waved her hand.

"*Rofirthar!*"

Color and words appeared on them as well, and they jumped onto the shelf to join the rest.

Gwendolyn smiled. She waved her hand, and two whole shelves righted themselves. The little faerie flew up in surprise, chittering and squeaking.

"It's all right," Gwendolyn said. "Or at least, there's a chance it might be."

She sprang to her feet, then looked at the floor, imagining flowing patterns stenciled on it. And she began to dance. She danced, and the Library of All Wonder danced with her. Books and shelves flew about, cheerfully arranging themselves as before. She imagined music for herself, a glorious symphony that swept her up along with everything around her. She twirled faster and faster and she let herself get carried away and she knew her skin was glowing, but she didn't care because it felt so *good*.

Finally, she stopped. Her skin shone a glittering gold. Then she examined her handiwork.

It wasn't perfect. The Library was infinitely large, so of course she couldn't put it all back herself. But there was a path of words and color where she had danced, and it was spreading. Books trickled through the windows once more, nesting themselves on shelves. The tile mosaic was restored, its pictures moving again. The Library was coming back to life.

Gwendolyn's heart swelled until she thought it might burst. If only she could show this to Sparrow and Starling. But she didn't have the Figment, or *Kolonius Thrash and the Perilous Pirates* with its dialing code.

But . . . her own story had more than one volume, didn't it? She turned to the cart, then gestured to the shelves. "Can you take me to *Kolonius Thrash*?"

The book cart twirled and wheeled away. Gwendolyn followed it down miles of jumbled shelves, where books were still busy reorganizing themselves. Eventually they reached a group of books with red leather covers and golden titles.

Gwendolyn caressed the spines. *Kolonius Thrash and the Deadly Dirigible. Kolonius Thrash and the Spiced Seas.* And one that made her heart flutter. *Kolonius Thrash and the Castaway Kids.* She snatched that one up, flung it open—and there they were.

Sparrow and Starling, their names on the page in black and white. Her two little castaways, lost in a world that wasn't their own. She flipped through and even found an illustration of them, zip-lining down from the *Lucrative Endeavour* on motorized pneumo handles. But pictures weren't what she wanted. She flipped to the back of the book and found the code printed there. A wide smile spread across her face, and it hurt somewhat to stretch muscles that had been so little used of late.

Gwendolyn knew what she must do. She sprinted to the Egressai Infinitus and placed the book on the floor, open to the back sticker. Then she pressed her hand to the empty power slot and allowed her thoughts to run wild, building the excitement within her to a fevered pitch. The gems in the faerie bracelet on her wrist started to flash. Her skin glowed even brighter. She tried to *push* that glow, that energy, into the empty slot where the Figment should go, hoping she could power the door herself. With her other hand she dialed the code.

Softly, almost prayerfully, she sang.

Sparrow and Starling, Darrow and darling
Return from the worlds beyond.
Come to me here, there's nothing to fear,
Our story is not yet done
Hey ho, here we go,
Our story is not yet done.

Nothing happened. "Come on," she pleaded with the door, hoping against hope. "Please work." If she could bring back thousands of books and stories, then surely, she could bring back two little friends? Couldn't she have this one nice thing for herself?

The doors began to spin slowly, delicately. A new door came

to a stop in the golden frame, a door made entirely of inter-locking gears.

Gwendolyn reached for the knob, and turned it. The gears on the door clicked and whirred, and the door sprang open. Out tumbled a couple of disheveled figures, knocking her over, and the three of them wound up hopelessly tangled on the floor. After much groaning, they all regained their feet, and two children stood before her, blinking and confused.

"Gwendolyn!" they shouted in unison.

CHAPTER TWELVE

Returns and Returns

And there they were. Sparrow, in his crimson jacket and yellow scarf. Starling, in her turquoise blouse and orange vest, her black hair with the blue stripe that always fell into her face.

The three of them sprang into a crushing embrace, and even the faerie joined in, standing on Gwendolyn's shoulder and pressing itself to Starling's head.

Gwendolyn thought her heart might explode, either from delight, or from the strength of their grip. Wrapped in the safety of her friends' arms, she felt better than she had in weeks. Tension seeped out of her, and she relaxed so completely that the glow faded from her skin.

Eventually they parted enough to look each other over, and Gwendolyn drank in the sight of her friends like a woman dying of thirst. "Sparrow! Starling! You're . . . you . . . I . . ." but she couldn't think of what to say. Instead, heart fluttering like a bird, she tumbled back into Sparrow's arms and gave him a shy and delicate kiss. And not on the cheek, either.

Sparrow wrapped her up even tighter, and she felt her feet leave the floor. If you have ever had a dream where you were flying, you know it is wondrous, and fragile. You can soar through the clouds, but as soon as you think *Oh! I'm flying,* you will surely fall. That was how Gwendolyn felt now. There was softness, and tenderness, and though it lasted only a moment, it was a moment that would remain etched on Gwendolyn's heart for the rest of her life.

The clockwork faerie on Gwendolyn's shoulder hid itself under her hair in embarrassment. Starling glanced around, whistling to herself.

"Hey, girlie," Sparrow said when his lips were free for speaking. He smelled of sawdust and sunshine. Gwendolyn stumbled back again, and there was a twinkle in her eye that had surely not been there before.

"I . . . I missed you . . . your . . . hat," she said with a bashful smile. "You must have lost it somewhere." A giggle escaped her, a strange girlish sound that she had no idea she could make.

Sparrow's face reddened. "Thanks. Uh . . . are you taller than me now? Last time we . . . you know . . . you weren't so—"

"No time for that," Starling jumped in. "Gwendolyn, you've got to come with us, we need your help!"

"What?" Gwendolyn said, coming back to earth with a crash. "You need *my* help? I need *your* help!"

"Kolonius has been captured," Starling said. "Drekk's got him. It's good to see you, and I'm glad you're okay, but if we don't hurry, Drekk . . . will . . . will . . ." she trailed off, gaping at the Library of All Wonder. "What *is* this place?"

"And what happened to you?" Sparrow said, eying Gwendolyn up and down with admiration. "You look . . . umm . . ." He gulped. "Different. I mean, uh, your *clothes* look different."

"Oh, this." Gwendolyn looked down at the faerie clothes, which Sparrow seemed to be inspecting so closely. She wiped at her smeared makeup with a sleeve. "I must look a fright." She tried to run her fingers through her tangled hair, and touched the goggles on her head. She'd forgotten she was wearing them. "Oh, here, Starling. These are yours." She felt a quick stab of grief at the memory of Cyria placing them on her head.

"Hey! I missed these. Never had time to make a new pair. Thanks." She used them to pull back her own hair, looking more herself again. "Now, what's going on here? What's this?" she brushed Gwendolyn's hair back to examine the clockwork faerie on her shoulder.

"I can explain everything. And you have your share of explaining to do too. We'll need a plan. Do you have a plan?"

"Of course we have a pl—" Sparrow said, but his sister thumped him in the chest. "Okay, no plan. Not yet, anyway."

"Fine. We'll make it up as we go, as usual. We'll rescue Kolonius from Tylerium Drekk, then find a way to fix my parents and save my friends."

"But we're fine," said Sparrow.

"My *other* friends. No time for chit-chat! There's lots of rescuing to do today." She had no idea where this new attitude had come from, but with Sparrow and Starling by her side, she felt like she could take on the world. Multiple worlds. With her bare hands.

Without further explanation, Gwendolyn stepped through the Egressai Infinitus. Sparrow shrugged at his sister, and followed. Starling took a last longing look at the Library of All Wonder, then stepped through as well.

~~~

Orange light embraced Gwendolyn, and she found herself standing where she had longed to be these past few weeks. The land of Tohk, the home of Kolonius Thrash, the first and favorite of the worlds she'd traveled to. More specifically, they were in the Mainspring Marketplace, the central hub of the city of Copernium. The citizens bustled around her, and it was here, it was all here. She was back.

Every last detail was perfect. The domes and spires and gardens, the two suns grinning in the orange sky where dirigibles and airships floated effortlessly. And the *people*. Fantastically dressed, zipping about on pneumo lines or winged bicycles. Barkers called out their wares as the market-goers browsed, and it was all so fantastically *alive*.

Gwendolyn closed her eyes and breathed it in. Cyria had founded this city as a haven for inventors and artists. From what Gwendolyn had heard, the inventress had fled soon after, trying to escape her admirers and find somewhere to do her inventing in peace. Which, now that Gwendolyn had met her, sounded *exactly* like Cyria.

Thinking of Cyria, Gwendolyn looked back at the doorway of the Egressai Infinitus. "Huh," she said.

"What?" Sparrow asked, as he usually did when Gwendolyn noticed the things he didn't.

"The doorway. Look where it comes out." The doorway was set into the wall of an impressive columned building, but Gwendolyn was looking at the words carved in stone at the top.

Cyrio Kytain Memorial Lending Library.

Gwendolyn smiled. "Clever Cyria. The Library of All Wonder connects to libraries on other worlds. Just like in the Hall of Records in the City. And that name . . ." Her smile widened. She hadn't done so much smiling in a long time. "Cyri-*o*. She'd have some things to say about that." And then she remembered. Cyria was gone.

"Again, *so* confused," Sparrow said.

Gwendolyn turned back to them. "Never mind. Kolonius needs rescuing from that pirate. Do you know where Drekk is?"

"Yes," said Starling. "The *Lucrative Endeavour* and the rest of Kolonius's crew will be leaving Archicon as soon as repairs are complete. But it will be a couple days."

"Repairs?"

"We ran into a bit of trouble," Starling mumbled.

"And do you have a way to get us to Archicon and the *Endeavour*?" Gwendolyn asked.

"We were *on* the *Endeavour*," Starling said. "So, no, I hadn't exactly planned an impromptu inter-dimensional reunion yanking us back to Copernium."

"Right," Gwendolyn said, blushing slightly. "And since Kolonius is still alive, I presume there's something Drekk wants?"

Sparrow fidgeted. "We *may* have taken something from

him. Some things. He wants them back in exchange for Captain Grumpy."

Gwendolyn nodded. "Any chance we can just give them back?"

"No," Starling said firmly. "We can't."

"Fine, you can tell me the rest later. But first we'll need a ship. Stand back." Gwendolyn stretched out her arms, and imagined a small wooden ship with propellers on the sides. But nothing happened, save for a strange sucking feeling that left her instantly more tired.

Sparrow frowned. "What are you doing?"

"I'm trying to create one of the *Endeavour*'s longboats. But I forgot how hard it is to use magic here. I'm . . . practically normal."

Sparrow shivered. "Don't say such horrible things."

Gwendolyn grinned, and she remembered again why she liked him so much.

Starling, always the practical one, said, "Then we need a ship, and a plan. Tylerium Drekk won't just hand over Kolonius because we said 'please.'"

"Right," Gwendolyn said, toying absently with the faerie bracelet around her wrist. Then she looked down, realizing what she was doing. "Unless . . ."

"Unless what?" Sparrow asked.

"Unless he *had* to do whatever we asked. Come on! Let's find somewhere private." Gwendolyn dashed off into the marketplace, and the other two hustled to keep up.

She ducked through the crowds of people. The curious little

faerie zipped about, examining everything, not at all out of place among the clockwork technology of Tohk. They passed a fashion stall, staffed by a dressmaker named Iona who eyed Gwendolyn's faerie ensemble with a mix of fascination and envy. It put a fresh spring in Gwendolyn's stride to see this woman who had given her the precious puffed-sleeve dress and who had showed Gwendolyn a little kindness when she had needed it most.

A little too much spring. She was so busy looking at the dressmaker that she ran right into someone and fell sprawled in the street.

"Hello, there. Are you all right?" An older girl stuck out a hand to help her out.

"Yes, I'm fine, are you all right?" Gwendolyn said.

"I'm as fine as you are." The girl looked a little older than Starling, and she wore a rather random assortment of clothing that would have been considered odd even by Copernium's standards. She had a flat checked cap like the one Sparrow had lost, and a battered satchel was slung over one shoulder. The girl looked Gwendolyn up and down, and Gwendolyn assumed she was taking in Gwendolyn's own odd clothing.

"Well, I promise I'll watch where I'm going in the future," Gwendolyn said, anxious not to draw too much attention to herself.

"No, you won't." The girl gestured to Sparrow and Starling. "But the two of them will take care of you, and if you take care of them, you should do just fine." And the girl vanished into the crowds of the marketplace.

"Who was that?" Sparrow said.

"I've no idea," said Gwendolyn, frowning in puzzlement. "Did she look familiar to you?"

"Don't get distracted," Starling said. "Time is running out."

"Right," Gwendolyn said, shaking her head to clear her mind. They had a lot to do. She led them down a secluded alley.

"Where are we going?" Sparrow asked. "Do you know what you're doing?"

"Mostly. Well, I know the beginning. We'll figure it out as we go. Just watch." She held up the glowing jeweled bracelet. "Puck Robin, or Robin Goodfellow, whichever you wish, please appear!"

"Puck Robin's here, my little dears. I felt a burning in my ears," said Robin, stooping over Sparrow's shoulder.

"Gah!" Sparrow screamed, whirling around. The clockwork faerie hid itself under Gwendolyn's hair.

Puck Robin, for she was a she just now. Sparrow looked small next to the willowy faerie. She was dressed in her usual black suit and plunging orange tunic, and her brown skin and soft features were as seductive and ambiguous as ever. "This boy was not expecting me, but I am as surprised as he. This curse Kytain will not remove, I'll dance as you will make me move."

"Cyria! She's not dead?" Gwendolyn's heart leapt. "Is she all right? Did Titania punish her for helping me?"

"Inventress does as best she can, and she remains in faerie land. The queen is soft on Kytain yet, so she still has some uses left. Titania's moods are like the waves, they ebb and flow from day to day."

"Who is this . . . person?" Starling said, eyeing the barefoot faerie.

"She's—a friend. Sort of. I'll explain later. Puck Robin, we could use your trickery. Do you have any experience with pirates?"

Puck Robin raised a delicate eyebrow, and her lips curled into a grin.

Gwendolyn explained what she had in mind. Sparrow and Starling were completely lost. But Puck leaned against the wall, arms folded, listening carefully.

"And what's in this crusade for me? Or dost be done by slavery?" She tugged at her glowing collar.

"It is your choice. I won't force you," said Gwendolyn. "And if I tried, you'd just weasel out of it somehow. But if you do this, I'll give you your freedom."

"If you should die, released I'll be. So let's sweeten the deal for me."

Gwendolyn bit her lip in hesitation. She'd been afraid of something like this. "I—I'll owe you a favor."

Robin's cocky expression flickered. "Not lightly offer favors so. I'll not come cheap, so you should know."

"I understand, but all the same. That's my offer."

Puck Robin stuck out a hand. "My honor staked, I give my word. Puck comes when your command is heard. Then someday to your door I'll come, and you'll serve *me*, my little one." The faerie smiled, radiating mischief and wicked glee.

Gwendolyn began to regret the bargain, but there really was no choice. She shook the proffered hand, and an electric tingle shot up her arm. Robin smiled again, then disappeared in a flash of light.

"That was . . . odd. Even by our standards," said Starling.

"Oh yes," Puck said, leaning over Sparrow's shoulder.

Sparrow screamed and whirled. "Stop doing that!" he yelled.

But Gwendolyn was distracted by the object Puck Robin held. A gleaming golden pistol, gracefully crafted with three long bulbs on top. "That's the Pistola Luminant!"

Robin nodded. "As I left you, she caught my ear, and bade me bring this to you here."

Gwendolyn gaped. "But . . . I lost it when I destroyed the Abscess and fell through the In-Between. Who told you to bring it? Cyria? Titania?"

"Not queen, nor inventress, not those," Robin said, handing the pistol to Gwendolyn. "One who knows you, but you'll not know. The Lady of the In-Between, the Lady you've but heard, not seen. She says take this, you'll need it soon. You'll meet when times are ripe, and soon."

"You just used 'soon' twice," Starling said.

Puck Robin scowled. "Bloody mortals." She clapped her hands, and vanished again.

"Are you going to explain all of the . . . *that* to us at some point?" Sparrow asked.

"Maybe when I understand it myself," Gwendolyn said, examining the pistol. "But now, we need to rescue Kolonius. Where do we start?"

"With some food," Sparrow said. "I'm—"

"We know," said Starling. "*Starving*," she whined, mimicking Sparrow's voice to perfection. "But Kolonius needs our help, so we don't have time to fill your bottomless pit!"

"Right," Sparrow said. "But we need a ship, and a plan, and since we don't have the first one, our best chance of saving Captain Boyfriend is to compare notes and come up with the other one. And I always think better on a full stomach. Come on, let's hit that little café over there." Then he walked away without waiting for an answer.

"Kolonius isn't my *boyfriend*," Starling grumbled.

~~~

Minutes later, the three of them sat at a small outdoor table outside one of Copernium's most fashionable eateries. Waiters waltzed around taking orders, all in black bow ties, red suspenders, and crisp white aprons.

A railing surrounded the outdoor tables, and the top of the railing was lined with miniature train tracks. Tiny train cars trundled along the tracks, delivering delicious treats to the patrons sitting in the warm suns-shine.

Gwendolyn had a difficult time sitting still. She felt the urge to run around looking at all the marvelousness that was Tohk, reveling in the joy of finally being back in her favorite place with her favorite people.

But she managed to contain her excitement while they ordered, then filled in her friends on everything that had happened. She told them all about Faeoria, and the Collector, and her quest to save the City. The Cityzens may have been horrible to her, but at least now she knew the reason. Though she supposed some of them were probably horrible no matter what. But that didn't mean she shouldn't try to help them.

"It's one thing to *say* I'm going to help them, though," Gwendolyn said. "It's quite another thing to do."

"So how do we do it?" Starling said. She took a fizzy concoction with swirling orange and white foam from the tiny train that arrived. Sparrow reached over her, snatched his plate, and attacked a heaping helping of some sort of red meat drowned in a butter-and-herb sauce.

Gwendolyn took her own plate of grilled fish with yellow sea spices and a slice of charred lemon. "Well, I had an idea. It's probably stupid—"

"Gwen, next time you call yourself stupid, I'm going to thump you," Sparrow spluttered with his mouth full.

She grinned a bashful grin, and looked away. "All right. Well, there's this." She plunked the Pistola Luminant down on the table.

"What?" Sparrow said. "Blast the creepy kid, the day is saved, and we all go home? I guess it worked last time. Sorta."

"But we can't just *destroy* the ORB and the Lambents," Gwendolyn said. "We have to *reverse* them somehow. Give everyone back their imagination. So we'll need the Figment too."

Starling lit up. "Oh! I see. We need to connect the Figment to the Pistola Luminant. Then we can use it as a transmitter for all the stories and information stored in the Figment. Then the Lambents will fill everyone's heads with what the Collector took, and more. We'll need to install a crystalline insertion matrix into the Pistola Luminant, of course, and alter the photonic relay coil—"

"Yes," Gwendolyn said, cutting her off. "Do you think you could do . . . those things you just said?"

"I don't think so. I'm good with gadgets, but that's a little out of my league. We need someone skilled in imagination energy science, as well as light projection technology."

"Oh sure," Sparrow groaned. "Let me just look one up in the phone book, huh? I'll search under crystallic institution whatsit technicians. Besides, you said Mister Zero has the Figment."

"That's the hard part. We'll have to break in and take it back. And to do that, I think we'll need a lot more than just three children," Gwendolyn said.

Sparrow grinned. "He's only one children. How hard could it be?"

Starling rolled her eyes. "We'd need an army to get past all those Mister Men. How many are there, anyway?"

"I don't know. I don't suppose you've run across any spare armies in your recent travels?" Gwendolyn asked.

"Not exactly," Starling said. "I suppose it's our turn to fill you in."

And Gwendolyn finally got the chance to eat while Sparrow and Starling told of their adventures.

There can be a certain awkwardness when you reunite with those you have not seen in some time. But not here, not between these three. Theirs was the best sort of friendship, the kind that can be picked up right where it left off, no matter how long you have been apart. To Gwendolyn, it felt as though no time had passed at all.

But time had passed indeed. It passed at different rates on different worlds, and that was even before taking into account Faeoria's tenuous relationship with it. Three months had passed from Sparrow's and Starling's perspective. Their adventure makes for a thrilling story, one much too long to recount here, and I won't ruin it by telling it poorly. It is, as they say, a tale for another time.

"So, here's our growing to-do list," Starling said. "Find a ship, rescue Kolonius, find someone to alter the Pistola Luminant, get an army together to storm the ORB, get the Figment back, blast your city full of imagination again, fix your parents' memories, and bring back everyone who was erased."

"See? Simple," Gwendolyn said. "You two seem to have been up to quite a lot while I've been away."

"Yeah, I'm not entirely sure how that's even possible," Sparrow said. "You kind of . . . created us. Does that make you, like, our god or something?"

Starling made a face. "I hope not."

Gwendolyn's freckled nose scrunched up as she considered that. "I don't think so. My parents created me, but they've never been able to control me. Here I am, running around as I please and . . ." she trailed off as her thoughts veered in the painful direction of Mother and Father.

"I'm not calling you 'mom,' if that's what you mean," Sparrow said, jerking her out of it.

She smiled. "I'll thank you not to." She looked across the street at *Professor Zangetsky's Imagination Engineerium and Clockwork Phantasmagoria*, a sort of holographic theater they had attended on their last visit. "I suppose it's like Professor Zangetsky said. If you're not careful, your ideas can take on a life of their own, and run away from you."

"Though in this case we've been trying to run *toward* you," Sparrow said. "We tried finding a portal to get back to your world, but we could never be sure if it would take us back, or throw us to some random world where you'd never find us again."

"We didn't think she'd be *able* to find us again," Starling reminded him. "She didn't have enough energy left to steer her way through the In-Between."

"*You* didn't think she could find us again. I knew better." He puffed out his chest and wiggled his eyebrows at her.

The corner of Gwendolyn's mouth twitched upward just as her shoulders crept up to her ears, and she looked away. Her eyes came to rest on the sign for Professor Zangetsky's theater again. She thought about his *Clockwork Phantasmagoria* show and the stories he shared with his incredible projector. Several thoughts clicked together all at once.

"Oh!" Gwendolyn cried out.

"What?" Starling asked.

"I have a plan! A real plan, not like a Sparrow plan."

"Hurtful," he said.

"I think I've got a way to save Kolonius, and the City. To fix *everything*. Come on!"

"Where are you going?" asked Starling as Gwendolyn got up.

"To the theater!" Gwendolyn said, dashing across the street.

Sparrow let out a whoop, and ran after her.

Starling gave an exasperated sigh and reached into one of her many pockets. "Children. They're complete children." And she followed, but only after she'd left enough money to cover their bill.

CHAPTER THIRTEEN

Reluctant Assistance

"W-what? What do you mean, you need my help?" Professor Zangetsky stammered when they burst into the workshop of his hologram theater and explained the situation.

Professor Zangetsky was clad in his leather laboratory smock. A pair of oversized goggles combined with his flyaway brown hair gave the impression of a startled squirrel. And like most grown-ups, he was not keen on leaving his comfortable little life and going off on wild adventures. "No, no, I couldn't possibly, I've got a show in three minutes!"

"Don't count on it. Your place is empty," Sparrow said.

"See, you don't want the help of some washed-up old story-teller. Go ask Max O'Millions, he's got all my other customers."

"You've spent your life studying Kytain's research," Gwendolyn said. "You're the only one who understands it enough to help us," Gwendolyn implored, but it was no use. He continued to resist until Starling plunked the Pistola Luminant down on his worktable.

The professor's eyes grew even larger. "Is that what I think it is?"

"Yes," Gwendolyn said. "I need you to make some alterations to it. I'd have Kytain do it herself, but she's a bit . . . indisposed at the moment. So we'll need you to come along. We're in a bit of a rush, so you'll have to work on the run."

"Kytain?" Professor Zangetsky leapt up from his worktable. "You've met him? Impossible, he'd be hundreds of years old, and . . . did you say *her*self?"

Gwendolyn smiled.

That was all it took. The chance to work on the legendary pistol and hear firsthand stories of Kytain was too much for the professor. He hastily gathered up a bag full of tools and stumbled along after them.

"Great," Starling said as the four left the theater together. "Now, where are we going to get a ship so we can *finally* go rescue Kolonius?"

"A ship? I've got a ship," the professor said. "Haven't used it in years, mind, but a bit of patching on the hull, some engine grease . . . oh, and we'll have to figure out where I parked it, I don't entirely recall . . ."

So that was how, a full day later, Gwendolyn found herself on a small air-yacht of questionable construction, flying over the Violet Veldt and headed toward a meeting with the most feared pirate in Tohk. She stood at the prow, fiery hair streaming in the breeze, her jagged skirt fluttering, the clockwork faerie striking a heroic pose on her shoulder.

The ship seemed to be thrown together more from random parts than any coherent plan. Gwendolyn hoped her own plan was a better one, though there were still a lot of random parts *she* had to throw together.

After leaving Tohk, they had sailed to Archicon, where the *Lucrative Endeavour* was docked. Burly Brunswick, Kolonius's first mate, had been overjoyed to see Gwendolyn. The big man with his big orange mustache had wrapped her up in a big bear hug that was bound to leave big bruises later.

But his smile turned to a frown when Gwendolyn explained that they couldn't wait for repairs on the *Endeavour* to be completed, and it would be better if it were just the three of them and the professor. But Brunswick insisted that they at least take Carsair along, the biggest and strongest of his crew, with instructions to "babysit the young'uns."

That was how the fifth member of their party came to be standing at the tiller, steady as a stone. Carsair was a woman well past seven feet tall, with short hair that was dyed a bright teal, rather than the pink it had been on their last meeting. Her sleeveless tunic revealed tattooed arms that were so heavily muscled Gwendolyn wondered whether sleeves were ever even an option for her. All in all, it was a look that Gwendolyn found stunningly gorgeous in a way that none of the Fae could match. It was a very specific sort of look.

Professor Zangetsky glanced from Carsair to Gwendolyn. "I-I-I'm still not sure about all this . . . Tylerium Drekk, well, he's not exactly the sort of fellow you visit for Sunday tea. He's dangerous!"

"Dangerous? No. It is pleasure cruise," Carsair said in her thick Stormlands accent.

"Gwendolyn knows what she's doing," said Sparrow. "Right?"

Gwendolyn didn't answer. She just stared out over the purple grasslands.

"Hey. You okay, Gwen?" Sparrow said, coming close enough that the others wouldn't overhear.

"Yes . . . just thinking."

"A dangerous pastime."

"I know." She forced a chuckle. "Especially for me, if I'm not careful."

"You seem nervous," Sparrow said.

She sighed. "I am. But even so . . . this is what I wanted. On an airship, with you, headed toward adventure. Is it strange that this feels almost natural? More natural than anything else in the past few weeks?"

"Yeah. Still, it'd be nice if we weren't always running. Toward stuff, away from stuff. Can't we ever get a real moment alone?"

Their gazes mingled until they both blushed and looked away. Gwendolyn wondered whether this sort of thing would ever stop being awkward. Many adults are still wondering the same thing.

"What, um, what would we do instead? If we weren't running away?" She couldn't remember swallowing all these butterflies.

Sparrow shrugged. "I dunno." He scrunched up his nose in uncertainty. "Go to a dance, maybe? Isn't that a thing people do?"

Gwendolyn bit her lip to keep from laughing at his sheepish expression. She reached out and gave his hand a little squeeze. He squeezed back harder. She squeezed back harder still, and giggled. "Well, we could dance right now, couldn't we?"

"What?" Sparrow said, terrified. "There's no room, there's no music, and—"

But Gwendolyn took a step back and began to dance. She put her hands on her hips and turned a jaunty little jig, with lots of leaping and stomping, but all the while staying in the same spot. Sparrow was frozen, his face a priceless mask of shock and awe. Gwendolyn laughed, grabbed his arm, and spun him around.

"Oy! Girl!" yelled Carsair. "Stop shaking ship!"

They stopped. Starling gave them a well-practiced eye roll, and went back to fidgeting with the ship's machinery. Gwendolyn and Sparrow turned back around to avoid the others, both of them struggling not to laugh as the little faerie mimicked Gwendolyn's dance.

Sparrow looked over at Gwendolyn, then cocked his head. "That's weird . . ."

"What?" she said.

"Are you . . . glowing?"

"Maybe." She winked at him. "Do you like it?"

Sparrow looked askance. "I guess. It's not something you see every day, that's for sure."

Gwendolyn held out a hand and admired the golden gleam. "Well, I think it's splendid. Someday, perhaps I'll take you to Faeoria to meet the Fae folk. They all glow like this, and they're positively splendid." Which was a fairly generous description that glossed over the darker parts of Gwendolyn's stay there, many of which Gwendolyn hadn't been ready to share with her friends. But she was here, in the fresh air and sunshine, bound for adventure with her two kindred spirits. And if her skin was glowing the tiniest bit, what did that matter? Just now she felt pretty nearly perfectly happy. She couldn't feel exactly perfectly happy because, well . . .

"What color would you call this?" Sparrow said, pointing out to a patch of grass that was a shocking neon somewhere between ultramarine and heliotrope.

The interruption neatly steered Gwendolyn away from unpleasant thoughts. "I don't rightly know," Gwendolyn said. "Oh, it is wonderful here, isn't it?" She leaned out over the railing, letting the wind whip her hair around, right into Sparrow's face.

He laughed and brushed it away. "Yeah . . . You know, I've been thinking too—"

"I suppose there's a first time for everything." She elbowed him playfully.

"I'll try not to make a habit of it." He lowered his voice so the others couldn't hear. "But I was thinking about us."

"Us?"

"Yeah. Not like, you-me-and-Starling us. Just you-and-me us."

"Oh. *That* us." The fluttery thing that lived in her stomach woke up and stretched its wings. "What about . . . us?"

"We haven't really had a chance to talk about *it*."

"By *it*, do you mean how I brought you to life with my imagination, but somehow you're also really real, and then I lost you forever, but it wasn't really the forever kind of forever, and you've been having all sorts of adventures on your own, but now we're heading toward danger again and haven't had a chance to talk about where we go from here? That *it*?"

"Oh." Sparrow blushed. "That's a big *it*. I just meant that . . . we kissed. Like, twice."

It was Gwendolyn's turn to blush. "Oh. *That* it."

"I mean, I *liked* that part, the kissing. But now that you mention all that . . ." and he seemed relieved to change the subject, "where *do* we go from here? What's the plan? You'll be amazing, the day will be saved, but then . . . are you staying? Or are you coming with m—us?"

Gwendolyn hadn't cast the merest thought in that direction. "I don't truly know. Where might you be going?"

Sparrow gave her an incredulous look. "Home. You said that door in the Library can dial up any world. So we'll find ours."

Gwendolyn chuckled a little. "Oh, right. It is about time, isn't it? We'll get you home. Or I'll just make you one."

Sparrow recoiled as if he'd been flicked on the nose. "What do you mean by that?"

"Well, I created you. I've not gotten around to picturing your home and parents, but I suppose I could make them however you like." She was rambling, intoxicated with the idea, her skin glowing a little brighter. "Tall, short, pleasant, strict . . . Though why you'd *want* strict parents is beyond me—"

"Wait, you can't just make us new parents—"

"Why not? It's not as if they're real. I can do it like *that*." She snapped her fingers, creating a brief flash of light.

Sparrow jerked backward. "So *I'm* not real either?"

Gwendolyn turned, a little exasperated. "No, weren't you listening? That isn't what I said at all."

"Oh, I heard you. Are you just going to change *me* if there's something you don't like? Or make a new Sparrow if you get bored with the old one?"

Gwendolyn frowned. "Stop it. That wasn't what I meant to say."

"No, I bet it wasn't." He took a step back. "We don't always mean to say what we really think. Sometimes it just slips out."

"That's not fair," Gwendolyn said.

"Look, I know it might all seem like pretend to you, but it's real to me. I remember my parents, even if you haven't bothered to think about them. My memories, my life, it's all real, and I don't care where they came from. I'm nobody's imaginary friend. Who says someone didn't imagine *you*?"

Gwendolyn was not the sort of girl to just stand around and get yelled at. "Well, it's not as if you've been trying very hard to find them. Or me, for that matter. You two were more than happy to dash about with Kolonius, having adventures, leaving me to rot."

Sparrow looked away. "We had to help, we couldn't just go stumbling blindly through portals—"

"*I* needed your help. While you were off playing pirates, I was having a perfectly wretched time."

"Focus, munchkins," Starling called out. "Look."

Hovering in the distance was Tylerium Drekk's ship, the *Swift Retribution*, with its tall masts, wide sails, and deadly cannons.

Propellers sprang up from the deck on long poles, holding the ship aloft.

Sparrow stuck his hands in his jacket pockets. "Whatever, Gwendolyn." And he strode off and sulked on the other side of the ship.

Gwendolyn scoffed, and busied herself fiddling with her new bag. Starling had gotten her a replacement satchel in Archicon, since Gwendolyn couldn't very well go around with a giant legendary pistol stuck in her belt. Gwendolyn motioned to the clockwork faerie. "Well? In you go." The toy obeyed, zipping in next to the Pistola Luminant.

They pulled alongside the *Swift Retribution*. Brunswick had radioed ahead to arrange a parlay, so they were expected. A row of mangy-looking pirates was arrayed to greet them.

"I'll just be staying here, yes?" Professor Zangetsky said. "With the big lady?"

"Big lady could crush little squirrel-man if little squirrel-man not watch his words," Carsair said. She extended a collapsible metal gangplank, which attached to the pirate ship with a magnetic *clunk*.

"He's right, Carsair, it would be best if you stayed with the professor for now," Gwendolyn said. "You know the plan."

"I know the plan. I do not like the plan," she rumbled.

"Let's just get this over with," Sparrow said. And the three children stepped onto the pirate ship.

Muscles tensed. Hands moved toward blades. Dirty fingers tightened on triggers. But none of the pirates made a move toward them.

"I don't see why we've gotta be lettin' these brats on board, Bucket," said a weaselly looking one as they passed. "They's nothing but trouble. I say we slice 'em some gills and see if they can swim."

"We's bein' over land right now, you jabbery ninky-poop," said an oversized mouth breather next to him. "Now shut up, Muffins, a'fore Cap'n hears you. He's already in one o' his ear-pullin' moods. I won't be hearin' nothin' on this side for a fork-night."

Gwendolyn, Sparrow, and Starling strode along the line of pirates to the wheelhouse, where the pirate captain waited. Tylerium Drekk was as impeccably dressed as always, clad in an electric blue coat and a red silk shirt, his blond curls fluttering in the breeze. In one hand, he held a stylish red cane with a jeweled handle. In the other was a pistol aimed at Kolonius Thrash's head. The boy captain was on his knees, wrists shackled to a ring set into the deck.

"Well, if it isn't the pretty poppet, all dressed up just for us," drawled Tylerium Drekk in his honeyed voice. "Finally ready to leave the nursery, are we? You seem to be positively glowing. It will make you quite an easy target for my men."

"What are you doing, Starling? Get out of here!" Kolonius said. His white shirt was torn, his feet bare, and his dreadlocks were a matted mess. His eyepatch was gone, showing an empty socket set off by a long scar. The sight was a sobering one.

"Now, now, cabin boy. This meeting was their idea, and it is rude to interrupt our guests. They were just about to give me back my two treasures. Where are they?" Drekk said.

Starling started to retort, but Gwendolyn held up a hand. To Gwendolyn's surprise, the older girl obeyed. Gwendolyn took a deep breath and stood up straighter. If her friends expected her to be in charge, she had better act like it. "I've been meaning to ask you, Mr. Drekk," she said, trying to sound bold. "Shouldn't you have a hook? All good pirates I've read about have a hook, or a peg leg, or something."

Drekk snorted. "Those aren't good pirates, they're inept ones. It's my enemies who tend to lose things." And he tapped his pistol against Kolonius's scarred cheek. "I love a good banter as much as the next chap, but my time is more valuable than you can afford, and my former cabin boy here has precious little of it left. Where. Are. They?"

"We didn't bring them," Gwendolyn said.

"That's right, you can't have them!" chirped Sparrow.

Drekk's face darkened. He nodded at his crew, and the pirates closed in, forming a circle. Two men stood behind Drekk, one whose face was hidden by a feathered hat, the other bald and shiny as a polished doorknob.

"Did you hear that, Letchford? They say I can't have them," Drekk said to the bald one. "Then what, pray tell, are we doing here, dolly?"

"You are going to give us Kolonius. And then you are going to help us steal something, if you please, and thank you very much."

Drekk barked a laugh, and his crew joined in. He stopped suddenly, and his crew went instantly silent. "And why would an upstanding gentleman such as myself be inclined to do these things?"

"You'll help us because I said please," Gwendolyn said.

The crew roared with laughter again. Kolonius shook his head in disbelief.

Drekk held up a hand for silence. "And what if I refuse so polite an offer?"

Gwendolyn leaned forward. "Then I'll say it again. Without the *please*."

The pirates were nearly dying of laughter now, several of them rolling on the deck, holding their sides in exaggerated merriment, their antics making the others laugh all the harder. Drekk did not even try to stop them, and a corner of his mouth crept up into a serpent's smile.

"You know, I am so dreadfully curious, I think I'll risk it. I appreciate a good bluff—you've got more spine than half my crew. But bold as you are, I am afraid I must decline. Give me what is mine, or I kill the boy. Maybe both of them," he gestured, indicating Sparrow and Kolonius.

Gwendolyn shrugged. "I warned you. Robin? I release you."

CHAPTER FOURTEEN

Jumping at Shadows

Gwendolyn held up her faerie bracelet, and the jewels in it flashed.

"By the pricking of my thumbs, something wicked this way comes." The pirate behind Drekk whipped off his hat and cloak, and Robin Goodfellow stood there, an expression of mischievous glee on his handsome features. "Oh. It's *me*." Robin kicked the bald pirate's legs out from under him, sending him into the air, then slammed him to the ground with a blow to his middle.

Then Robin tore the magical collar from his neck and slapped it on Drekk's instead, where it tightened to form a glowing choker.

The other pirates drew their weapons, but Robin went through them like a wind. He danced beautifully, bobbing and weaving and dodging every blow. Sparrow and Starling flicked open collapsible swords, but Gwendolyn turned to Drekk. "Tell your men to stand down. And drop your pistol," she commanded. Her bracelet glowed.

Drekk's pistol clattered to the deck. "Stand down!" he barked, then he clutched his throat, a look of shock on his face. He recovered, pressed a button on the side of his cane, and a thin sword sprang out of the cane and into the air. Drekk caught it and lunged at Gwendolyn, but he missed. He tried thrust after thrust, but each time, his arm steered the sword away at the last moment. Finally, he stopped, panting and glaring at her.

"Don't look at me like that," Gwendolyn said.

His face twisted into a handsome smile. Despite his beatific expression, he swung his rapier at Sparrow instead.

"No, you're not to harm them, either."

The sword froze.

Gwendolyn smirked. "None of my friends or associates are to be harmed by you or your men. Tell them. And you can stop smiling, it's quite disturbing."

"Do as she says!" Drekk said, his voice hoarse and reluctant.

The remaining conscious pirates looked at each other, shrugged, and put away their weapons. They eyed Robin, none of them terribly eager to fight this barefoot devil in their midst.

Sparrow let out a low whistle. "Wow. It actually worked."

"We'll be taking Kolonius now." Gwendolyn opened her bag. "Go ahead," she whispered.

The clockwork faerie zipped out, fluttered to Kolonius, and opened his shackles. He stood, groaning, and rubbed his wrists. "Thanks, Red," he said.

"Don't mention it."

"What have you done to me, you freckled witch?" Drekk snarled. He clutched at the choker, but it would not budge.

"I've merely made you a bit more cooperative is all. As I said, I'll be needing your help, and that of your crew." She hoped no one could see how her hands shook as she said it.

"And if I refuse?"

She shrugged. "Fine. Go jump off the ship for all I care."

Immediately, Drekk walked to the edge of the deck, choker glowing. Some of his crew tried to hold him back, but he easily swatted them aside, and none of them tried very *hard*, anyway. He climbed the railing and stood, poised to jump.

"Stop," Gwendolyn ordered.

He did, his blue coat flapping in the wind.

"Feeling more . . . *helpful*, yet?"

"A complete change of heart," he said. "I'm a new man, all over rainbows and puppy dogs."

"Glad to hear it," Gwendolyn said. "You may step down."

"Oh, thank you *ever* so," Drekk grumbled.

"Need you any more assistance?" Robin asked, lounging casually against the mainmast. "Or could this fellow be dismissed?"

"You have done quite well, friend Robin. You have your freedom, and I owe you a favor, as promised. I suppose this is goodbye."

He gave her a wink. "I am a merry wanderer of the night. One never knows, I turn up where I might." And with a twirl of black and orange, he was gone.

"That was ten syllables, not eight!" Starling called to the wind.

They all stood around awkwardly for a moment, the pirates, the reunited friends, and the redheaded girl at the center of it all. None of them were quite sure what to do next, and none were anxious to make the first move.

"So, you've got your army," Starling whispered to her. "With Kolonius's crew, do you think that will be enough?"

"It will have to do," Gwendolyn whispered back.

"Well chaps, it's been fun, but we really must dash," said Sparrow in a terrible imitation of Drekk's accent.

"Already?" came a voice from above. The Blackstar stood on the crow's nest, coat flapping behind him, the lenses of his mask glinting in the sun. "Fine. It was getting boring anyway."

He dropped to the deck with a *thud*. When he straightened, he towered over even Tylerium Drekk. "Let's go, kid," he said to Gwendolyn. "Home. To stay. If those faceless things can handle you."

"Who's this?" Starling asked.

"Trouble," Gwendolyn replied.

"Surprise, surprise. You seem to drag it with you," Kolonius growled.

"Don't I know it," she said.

"Is that the Blackstar guy?" Sparrow asked.

"Yes." Gwendolyn drew the Pistola Luminant from her bag. "Weapons please, everyone."

The pirates looked to their captain. He shrugged. "Do as she says." He picked up his own pistol and pointed it at the Blackstar. "At least I'll get to kill *someone* today."

The Blackstar's own guns appeared, brutal blocky things next to the pirates' ornate flintlocks. "You know, it'd be nice if someone came quietly for once."

His shadow stretched long in front of him. Then it multiplied by five. Out of each shadow rose a man-shaped figure in a black trench coat and gas mask. All five of them held strange, two-handed guns, and although Gwendolyn had no Figment to tell her that they were *machine guns*, she knew danger when she saw it.

She had to shut this down, and fast, but her powers were weaker here. Using what was on hand was easier, but what did she have? She noticed how the orange sunlight glinted off the ugly metal barrels pointed toward them. And she had an idea. After all, light *was* one of her specialties. She imagined, and the light on the barrels grew brighter, until it looked as though a glowing ball of orange light surrounded each gun.

"*What if* . . ." she whispered.

The balls of light exploded. Bits of metal flew everywhere. At once, the crowd burst into action. The pirates fired at the shadow intruders, but the bullets thudding into their coats did not seem to bother them, and the Blackstar used his shadow shield to protect himself.

"Kolonius, catch," called Starling. She tossed him one of her collapsible swords, and he flicked it open.

The Blackstar's constructs charged, shadow blades extending from the front of their useless guns. The pirates and her friends rushed to meet them, sword against bayonet.

Carsair bounded onto the deck, swinging her long-handled sledgehammer with indiscriminate glee, not seeming to care if she hit the Blackstar's men or Drekk's. "Yes! Now this is very good cruise!"

Gwendolyn tried to focus enough energy to power the Pistola Luminant. It glowed to life, and she fired a bolt of lightning straight at the Blackstar. But he caught it in his palm, condensing it into a flickering ball, and threw it back at her. Only the reflexes Robin had drilled into her saved her life. The ball exploded, leaving a splintered hole in the deck.

"So *that's* not going to work . . ." she mumbled. "Kolonius, catch this too!" She tossed the Pistola Luminant to him. He turned away from his fight long enough to snag it out of the air, then pistol-whipped a shadow man with it. It had no effect.

"All right, now what?" he said.

One of the shadow men had lost an arm, but the stump looked more like solid rubber than flesh and bone. None of them gave signs of slowing. The Blackstar joined the fight directly, lazily slicing through any pirate that got in his way.

"Starling! Find us a portal. Carsair!" Gwendolyn shouted. "Get Kolonius to the *Endeavour*, and give the Pistola Luminant to the professor!"

"And leave all the fun to glowing girl and bird children?" Carsair bellowed. "You are outnumbered!"

"Not for long . . ." Gwendolyn said. After all, if the Blackstar could bring his minions to life, she could do it too. She closed her eyes, shutting out the battle around her, and pictured what she wanted. She'd done this on accident once before. How hard could it be to do it on purpose?

And she had it. The picture was firmly cemented in her mind. Her eyes flew open, and she threw out her hands. "*Once upon a time . . .*"

There was a loud *pop*, and a small creature covered in orange fur appeared on the deck. It had purple antennae, flappy feet, and a big goofy grin. "Meep!" it squealed.

"Criminy! What is that?" Kolonius shouted, ducking a blow from a shadow man.

"Criminy!" Gwendolyn called.

"That's what I said!" Kolonius replied.

"No, that's his *name*."

"Meep!" called the furball, who started waddling in circles around the battle.

"That doesn't tell us what it is or how it's going to help us," he said, his sword locked against an attacking bayonet.

"He's a Falderal. I accidentally imagined him in my bedroom one night. But I've learned a thing or two since then. Which means I can do this." She waved her hands and there were a dozen more popping sounds. A whole rainbow of colorful Falderals appeared and ran around the deck, meeping and bouncing, adding to the general chaos.

"Meep! Meep! Meep! Meep!"

Gwendolyn staggered, hit with a sudden wave of exhaustion. Her arms were trembling.

"More of them? Aren't you tired of playing god yet? Stop messing around and do something useful!" Sparrow spat.

Drekk battled the Blackstar, and the man in black was forced to exert himself to fend off the pirate's rapier and cane. Even so, Gwendolyn could have sworn the Blackstar was smiling.

"They're cute," the Blackstar said. "But it won't help."

"Oh? Well, *I wonder* what would happen if . . ." And Gwendolyn snapped her fingers.

Suddenly the Falderals turned toward the Blackstar, and rows of sharp teeth sprang out of their wide floppy grins.

"Ah!" screamed Muffins.

"Meep!" screamed the fanged Falderals. The furry creatures threw themselves on the shadow men, bouncing around the villains like demented rubber balls, biting anything within reach. They gnawed and chewed, and pieces of shadow fell to the deck like bits of old tire. Carsair bludgeoned a path back to the rickety yacht where the professor was cowering, and Kolonius followed.

"Keep fighting, Drekk! Just hold him off for a moment!" Gwendolyn said.

"It's not as if the gentleman's giving me much of a choice in the matter." He slashed at the Blackstar's throat, but the taller man ducked and swept Drekk's legs out from under him.

"You know I can hear everything you're saying, right?" the Blackstar said.

"Oh, do shut up," Gwendolyn muttered. She gathered as much energy as she could, drawing on the glow that surrounded her, and drove him back with exploding spheres of sunshine. But her glow only got brighter.

"Ow!" Sparrow shrieked as a green Falderal bit him on the ankle. "Gwendolyn, control these things!"

"Oh, lighten up, they're here to help," she said. "Starling, where's my portal?"

Starling used the distraction of the Falderals to group up

with Gwendolyn again, and Sparrow hobbled his way over. "I've got bad news . . ." the older girl said.

Sparrow groaned. "No portal?"

"Nope."

"No portal, no problem," Gwendolyn said. She grabbed their hands and pulled them to the edge of the deck. It was a long, long way down.

"What are you doing?" Sparrow said.

"No idea!"

"Do you have a plan?" Starling asked.

"Not really!" Gwendolyn said.

"I know I pushed you off a building once, but this is no time for payback!" Sparrow said.

"It's okay, I've done this before. Drekk, I'll be back for your help soon."

"Oh goody," Drekk sneered, never taking his eyes off his opponent.

The Blackstar held up his glowing tattoo. "Be smart, kid. There's nowhere to run. Nowhere to hide. So spare me the trouble of killing all your people. The more you try to help them, the more they'll just get hurt. And then I'll find you anyway." His tone was terrifyingly casual, as though he were asking Sparrow where he'd bought his scarf.

Gwendolyn grabbed Sparrow and Starling by the hands. "You might find us, but can you catch us?" And she jumped, taking the others with her.

For the second time in her life, she fell through the orange skies of Tohk. Wind tore at her hair and clothes, and she held tight to her friends' hands. The clockwork faerie was yanking on the back of her tunic, uselessly trying to hold them all aloft.

"Gwendolyn! Are you trying to kill us?" Sparrow called over the wind.

"We need a portal!" she shouted.

"But . . . but there isn't one!" Starling stammered.

"Not yet! Trust me, I can do this!" Adrenaline coursed through her veins, pushing her excitement to feverish heights. It felt *amazing*. She was glowing brighter than ever before, shining like a third sun. She let out a loud whoop of joy.

"She's crazy!" Sparrow shouted.

Images of the glittering nothingness of the In-Between filled her mind. She pictured the very world shattering apart, just like when she'd blasted her way out of Tohk with the Pistola Luminant.

And then Gwendolyn spotted it. A shimmer in the air below them, like heat haze, but still a long way in front of them. "Look!"

"We're not going to make it!" shouted Sparrow.

"Not our only problem!" Starling shouted back. The Blackstar was above them, the folds of his coat spread like wings.

"He can fly," Sparrow said. "Of *course* he can fly. That is not a happy thought."

"We'll make it . . ." Gwendolyn said. She closed her eyes. She could do this. She focused on the leaf-wings attached to her shoulders, and she willed them to life. The leaves buzzed and blurred like a hummingbird's, and she knew that if she thought about it too hard, they would stop working. She could feel her strength draining. But she summoned every feeling she'd ever had of wanting to *leave*, to *get out*, to be somewhere *else*.

What if . . . she thought. *What if . . .*

"*What if* this actually works?" she said. And then, just as it seemed they would be meeting the ground with a rather permanent first impression, they surged forward and vanished into the shimmering hole in the air.

~~~

Gwendolyn was instantly wrapped in darkness and burning cold, and she immediately knew that something was very, very wrong. Without the safe passage of the Egressai Infinitus, they were adrift in the currents of reality, and she was expecting to be wrapped in the shimmering not-quite-colors of the space between worlds.

But the In-Between was full of shadows that grabbed at her, pulled at her, tore at her from all directions. It was in her mouth, her nose, her ears. She was choking on it.

From somewhere there was a brief flash of white light. But then she heard the sound of a woman screaming in pain, and the light disappeared. A man laughed, the dark man, his voice booming like thunder in the shadowy storm around her.

There was nothing to fight back the darkness, no words of comfort from the mysterious lady. The Abscess was here, and it was going to take Gwendolyn. She was smothering, drowning. She would be torn apart and her friends along with her.

She couldn't let that happen. Gwendolyn fought the blackness, and she glowed ever brighter, bursting with energy. She thought of warmth, and light, and love. The strain was incredible.

Every ounce of her was full of fire and pain and screaming as she struggled against the darkness . . .

And then she fainted, and knew no more.

PART THREE: BLUE

CHAPTER FIFTEEN

Out of the Darkness . . .

Gwendolyn was not long in the blessed relief of unconsciousness. When she awoke, she was lying down. Her muscles ached, and she shivered uncontrollably. Someone was cradling her head. Above her, she saw something that should have been comforting, yet only filled her with dread.

It was Cyria Kytain.

"Well, sprout," she said, Gwendolyn's head cradled gently in her hands. "Whatever ill wind blew you back, I hope it was worth the whirlwind that's waiting to reap you here."

"Cyria?" Gwendolyn choked out, a burst of confusion knifing through the anxiety. She tried to slow her breathing, but all she could manage were short, jerky gasps. She could see Starling overhead as well, and an upside-down Sparrow. Some distant part of her recognized the woodlands of Faeoria.

She tried to stand, but the world spun around her, and she fell down again. Oberon and Titania would kill her for coming back after her defeat at the duel. Sparrow and Starling were in danger now too. Black feelings wrapped her in a smothering cocoon, and she couldn't stop shaking. Every last ounce of strength and energy and confidence had been ripped from her in the In-Between and she felt herself falling, down, down into the dark. "No. We can't be here," she whimpered.

"Gwendolyn!" Sparrow said, though his words seemed so far away. But his other words rang loud and clear. *I'm nobody's imaginary friend,* he'd said. She'd hurt him. She'd been careless again, let her energy run out of control, and now they were all going to die. Everything was spinning, crashing down around her piece by piece.

"I can't stop it, Cyria, I can't—" She was hysterical, gripping her knees and rocking back and forth. She couldn't slow down, couldn't get control. "Make it stop," she sobbed.

"Just breathe, bunny." Cyria stroked her hair.

"I can't," was all Gwendolyn could say. She was shaking so hard her teeth were chattering.

"What's wrong with her?" Sparrow asked.

"I—I don't know," Starling said with a tremble in her voice.

"I do," said Cyria.

"And who the heck are you?" Sparrow shouted.

"I'm here to help." A metal wing nudged Sparrow out of the way and Cyria scooped Gwendolyn into her arms. "I take it you're the friends she was so anxious to find. Let's get Rose somewhere comfortable, and we'll sort everything out."

"Rose?" Sparrow said. "You don't even know her name. Why should we trust you?"

"I'm just putting her to bed. You can come along if you like."

"No, I don't know where we are, or who you are, but—"

"Cyria . . . please . . ." Gwendolyn said weakly. All the arguing was more than she could bear. She felt like an exposed nerve, and the presence of the other three was rubbing her raw.

Starling turned to Sparrow. "Let her help."

Sparrow crossed his arms. "Fine. But I'm watching you, lady."

But Cyria was already carrying Gwendolyn away. The next thing Gwendolyn knew, she was laid gently in bed, and Cyria was closing the door.

"There. What she needs now is time and rest," Gwendolyn heard Cyria say.

"Will that help?" came Starling's voice from the other side of the door.

"If anything will. She's sick, and—"

"What do you mean? She seemed fine," said Sparrow. "She was literally glowing, and then she just . . . crashed."

"What?" Cyria said, alarmed. "She was glowing? Are you sure?"

"Yes, but what does that have to do with any—"

"And was she acting strangely? Overconfident, reckless? Throwing her magic around?"

"Yes," Starling said from the hall. "She wasn't herself."

"No, she wasn't. That's the mania. I was worried about this. She has a condition, and too much magic only makes it worse. She'll become like the faeries if she's not careful. Or worse, get sucked into a darkness even she can't get out of. The farther she's pushed in one direction, the farther she'll snap back the other way. But come, conversations in hallways are quite tedious. Let us chat over tea instead. Cracking goggles, by the way."

"Oh. Thanks," Starling replied. "You too, I guess."

The voices faded, and Gwendolyn was alone in her room. Her *only* room, as surely her room in the City had been erased. Along with her clothes, and her pictures, and her parents' memories. Her chest tightened again, her breath came in ragged gasps, and she tried to sink deeper into the bed, to curl up so small that she simply vanished. The shivering returned, violent and unstoppable.

"I feel you, little quickling," rumbled Tree, wrapping her in gentle woody tones. "You are loved. You are you. Remember what I taught you."

Gwendolyn snorted in spite of herself. "You taught me nothing."

The room seemed to smile at her. "You finally understand something. Do not hold tight. Loosen. Open like a flower."

She didn't want to, but she did. She forced herself to lie spread eagle, palms up, as open as she could make herself. It hurt, not physically, but somewhere deep inside. It was too vulnerable, like something would attack her heart at any moment.

"Feel your feelings. They are large. You are larger. They are water. You are the river. Feel them swell, and rage, and let them flow out of you."

She tried her best to do what Tree said, but she just started crying in great heaving sobs.

"Yes. That is the beginning. Feel, and breathe, and be. Just be."

She cried. And she cried. And she cried. For her parents, for Tommy and Missy, for herself. It was indeed like a dam had burst inside her, and she cried until she was empty and asleep.

~~~

She found herself standing in the Wastelands again, surrounded by the cratered remains of the world outside the City. This time, she turned around and saw the Wall looming above. A harsh wind tore at her, bringing the sound of Mister Zero's voice as his words wormed their way into her sleeping mind.

"You'll come back to me, you know. You don't have anywhere else to go."

Gwendolyn shivered.

"There's no one else you can turn to, no one else you can trust."

"You can't scare me, Mister Zero," she said.

"I'm not trying to scare you. I'm trying to help you," the wind replied.

"The only one you want to help is yourself," she spat.

Lightning flashed. "Now Gwendolyn, you know that's not true. I'm trying to bring you home, and then we'll play such wonderful games together."

Gwendolyn gritted her teeth. "So, you can use the Figment to get into my head, is that it? You think you know a thing or two about me?" she shouted over the roar of the storms.

"Oh, Gwendolyn," he said in the singsong way he always said her name. "I know everything about you. The lonely little girl, the oddling who never fits anywhere. Always the wrong puzzle piece. I know about the darkness inside you. But I can fix you. You'll have a place where you belong. You won't be alone."

"You don't know everything. I'm not alone!" she shouted.

"Oh, you mean the two bird children? The girl sees you as a distraction, another whiny child to babysit. And the boy? You'll fascinate him for a moment, but he'll drop you and move on as soon as he sees something shiny. You know it, in your secret heart. They're not *really* your friends. They're not *real* at all."

But as deep in the darkness as she was, our Gwendolyn was not foolish enough to listen. Whatever grains of truth might lie in them, her time with the faeries had taught her that truth makes the best tricks.

"You know, I'm not sure this is entirely polite," Gwendolyn said to the empty dreamscape. "You seem to know a lot about me and my friends. What if we turned the tables? What if we saw something about you?"

"What? No. What are you doing, Gwendolyn?"

She focused on the sound of the voice, and tried to picture the little boy behind it, floating in his crystal cage. But she wanted more. She imagined herself zooming inward, right into his mind.

There was a bright flash of blue. Suddenly, Gwendolyn wasn't standing in the Wastelands anymore. She was standing in the courtyard at the School. A crowd of students formed a circle around a small boy cowering in the dust.

"Give it back," he pleaded. "Don't hurt it."

An older boy towered over him, clutching something in his fist. "Shut up, bug boy. Stay in the dirt where you belong."

The older boy threw something to the ground and stepped on it with a crunch.

"No!" the younger one cried.

"Bug boy! Bug boy!" the students all chanted.

"Leave me alone! Go away!" he shouted.

There was another flash of blue. Gwendolyn was in a small bedroom, dirty and disheveled. A bedroom she recognized. A filthy mattress sat in the corner. Shelves covered the walls, stocked with jars and boxes of all kinds. Inside, Gwendolyn could see bugs, rocks, spiders, leaves, and all sorts of odds and ends. She saw the dirty little boy with long pale hair, reading a book on the floor.

The door flew open, and the shadow of a giant filled the doorway. He stormed into the room in a soiled factory uniform, carrying an insect. "I told you not to bring this trash into my house no more. You need your ears cleaned again, boy?"

"No! I'm sorry!" he scurried against the wall. "I just found one today, and it had wings, and I thought you might want to see it—"

"I'm not raisin' some freak. Readin' books all the time. Whatcha need books for? You think you're better than me? I bring you up by hand, and you disrespect me like that, bring these pests into my house?"

"But I like to study them—"

"Don't you talk back to me! Come here!" the man roared.

There was another flash of blue. Gwendolyn saw the boy being led down a long, white hallway. There were men on either side of him, dressed in dark grey suits and bowler hats, each holding one of his arms.

"I-I'm scared. I don't want to go," the boy said.

"You were selected," said one of the men.

"You are the ideal candidate," said the other.

"But . . ." the boy blubbered, on the verge of tears. "How long will I have to be in there?"

"Do not despair," said the first man. "It will only be for a short time."

Another flash. She saw the boy floating in the crystal spire. His blue eyes burned into hers, and she watched as they slowly filled with black.

The black eyes flashed white. "What are you doing? Get out! GET OUT!" he roared, his voice low and strong and terrible.

Thick black ropes grabbed her and hurled her backward. She fell through the darkness, falling, falling.

CHAPTER FIFTEEN-AND-THEN

. . . Into the Dawn

She hit the floor of her room and woke up. Light streamed through the window, crisp and golden. It seemed the faeries had found their fill of nighttime fun and decided to play in the dawn.

And what a dawn it was. Outside, the world was golden and green, and the very air seemed glad to be alive. It was the sort of morning one never finds at home, but only on trips to far-off lands, where everything is fresh and new and noticed. A mist lingered where the sun had yet to reach, and deep shadows lurked behind trees, from which colored lights twinkled in wanton temptation, beckoning her to come out and play. All was quiet.

Now, "silence" and "quiet" can be two very different things. Silence is the absence of sound, and it can be terrifying, especially to children. Some are so scared of silence that they will make all kinds of pointless noise, just so they're not alone with their thoughts. But quiet is a gentle thing, soft and serene, more of a feeling than a sound. There were noises, yes. Birds sang in the treetops. Gwendolyn could hear her heartbeat pulsing in her ears, but it was slow and steady. Even her insides seemed quiet, and she was grateful to be free from noisy thoughts. Her mind was clear, and all was right with the world. For the moment.

Gwendolyn stood and placed her hand against the window frame. A third time. It had happened a third time. Each breakdown worse than the last. How many more were to come? Would they ever stop? Was this how she would spend the rest of her life? She was awfully tired of breaking down in the middle of adventures. There was too much to do, too much depending on her . . .

"No, stop it, that sort of thinking will only make it worse," she said aloud.

"Talking to yourself? A sure sign of madness, quickling," Tree said.

"Or genius." She smiled a fragile little smile. "Tree, would you mind opening for me? I'd like to sit outside for a moment."

"As you wish," he rumbled. The window expanded into a wide archway and a balcony grew itself at her feet.

Gwendolyn sat in the center of it and crossed her legs. Her little faerie friend joined her, crossing its own petite metal legs in a perfect imitation of Gwendolyn's pose. Gwendolyn smiled, and breathed. In and out, trying to think of nothing but each breath, each one unique, existing for a second, never to come again. Each a new lifetime in and of itself.

The air was just cool enough that she almost shivered. She felt energy flow into her, the rush of excitement and power that Faeoria offered. Exhaling, she tried to let that go as well. It was just as dangerous as the depression. She pictured herself strengthening her mental walls, holding back the looming darkness and the trembling energy that both pulled at her, neither happy nor sad, but just . . . existing. Gwendolyn sat, and breathed, and watched the sun rise. And she felt quite a bit better.

"Hi," came a nervous voice from behind her. Sparrow's voice. "Um . . . I just . . . I wanted to see if you were . . . awake. And you are. So."

Gwendolyn cringed. Her heart was too raw, and even the slightest touch was like probing an open wound. Sparrow's voice was gentle, and concerned, and it sounded as if he'd let go of their argument from yesterday. But she was not ready for kindness or company. He had seen her break down, curled up and shaking, out of control. What did he think of her now that he knew the truth? That she was broken?

She took a breath to steady herself. What was it Cyria had told her? *You can't just move on from your pain, but you can choose how you go on with it.* And the inventress was alive. No matter how heavy her burden, just knowing that Cyria was alive made her feel like she truly could go on carrying it.

She turned to face Sparrow. "Yes. I'm up. Get the others together. I'll be down soon." She couldn't meet his eyes, and she turned away again.

"Oh . . . okay." Sparrow stood frozen for a moment. Then he placed something on the little table next to her bed. "Here. I got this for you in Tohk a few weeks ago. Kept forgetting I had it. I know how you like to draw, and stuff." Then he walked away, leaving the door open.

When he had gone, Gwendolyn walked over to the table and picked up the object.

It was a sketchbook. It had a bright blue cover with white flowers on it. Next to it was a bundle of pencils. Actual *colored* pencils, not the grey things she'd always had to work with. She remembered the sketchbook Father had given her for her birthday, the one Mister Zero had taken, and she nearly broke all over again. She swore to make it up to Sparrow later.

She put the new sketchbook in her new bag, then took a moment to compose herself. The tunic with the long draping sleeves and the skirt of overlapping green and brown strips had all held up magically well, with no rips or tears or dirt. Even her boots were clean.

There was a bowl of fresh water on the vanity, and she washed the grime and tears from her face. That felt marvelous, and improved her mood as much as anything. When she looked back in the mirror, the faerie makeup had returned, green swirls around her eyes, sparkling red cheeks and pink lips. The clockwork faerie fluttered over and attacked Gwendolyn's hair, fighting the tangled mess until it hung down in an elaborate braid. The faerie even wove in some flowers from a nearby vase. Gwendolyn stroked her hair, admiring its fiery vermilion color, swelling with a momentary pride. It was strikingly lovely, and it was all hers, no faerie magic required.

There is nothing quite like getting properly ready to face the day. When one looks beautiful and confident, it helps one to feel the same. Gwendolyn kissed the little faerie on the head, and it rode on her shoulder as she went down to face the others.

Cyria, Sparrow, and Starling were in the sitting room, surrounded by a breakfast of such delectable delicacies that I will once more spare you the jealousy of further description.

The inventress was sipping tea in her usual armchair, dressed smartly in a blue tweed skirt and white blouse. Her high-heeled boots were propped on the coffee table. Her eyes flicked toward Gwendolyn as she entered, and one raised eyebrow said that Gwendolyn had some explaining to do.

Starling paced by the fire. Sparrow slumped dejectedly in the other chair, though he sat up quick enough when Gwendolyn came in. Starling noticed, and stopped pacing. "We talked to Cyria, and managed to fill her in on things," Starling said.

"Yes, we're all fine friends now," said Cyria. "Stingle and Spangle have been quite helpful. I see why you were so determined to find them."

"Stingle and Spangle?" Gwendolyn said.

"Dingle and dangle . . ." Sparrow muttered under his breath.

Starling shrugged. "She said no names."

Cyria wagged a finger at Gwendolyn. "They have been much better at rule following than you were, Rose. Stingle's a girl who really knows her onions. Got a good head on her. Now that they've had a tick to get over the shock and awe of it all," she said, gesturing to their surroundings, then rather boldly to herself as well.

"But what about you?" Gwendolyn asked. "After the Blackstar, I thought—"

"Thought I was dead?" Cyria took a sip of tea. "Yes, rather thought my number was up as well. Not often that characters like me make it through to the end, but it seems your story's a bit more forward thinking than most. Postmodern subversion of conventions. I've written a whole treatise on it if you'd like to see. Suffice to say, I had a nasty bump on the head and a completely ruined laboratory. All rebuilt now, thank the magic."

"Inventress . . ." Tree rumbled.

"Yes, all right, you helped a tad."

Sparrow and Starling looked a bit unnerved to be standing in a talking room, but Cyria pressed on. "So, you've given my beloved Pistola Luminant to some bumbling inventor to make God-knows-what abominable alterations. You've recruited two airship crews, one commanded by a pirate captain magically under your control, to help you storm the castle, steal your gem, connect it to the pistol, and blast all the magic back into your world through those Lambent things. Do I have it sorted?"

"Yes," Gwendolyn said. It sounded a bit ridiculous summed up like that. "Will it work?"

"Hmm. No."

"What?" the three of them said in unison.

"Look, the Pistola Luminant was not made for such antics. You want it to overcome a power built up over centuries. You might as well try to turn back a river with a garden hose. Of course, if you had brought it *with* you, that'd be another story. Some strong Fae magic would give it quite a kick, and faerie technology is more than a little alive and would adapt itself to suit your purpose. But who knows what state my poor pistol will be in now."

"It's not like we *planned* to come here. Cut her some slack," Sparrow said.

"Is there something in your workshop we could take with us?" Starling asked, a hungry gleam in her eye.

"*Stingle* got a tour while you were asleep, and she's all obsessed now," Sparrow told Gwendolyn.

"Quiet, *Spangle*," Starling hissed.

Cyria frowned. "It's a moot point. The power in my gems is nothing compared to dark forces draining an entire world dry for five centuries."

Gwendolyn sat on a cushy footstool and poked at the food. She wasn't hungry. Instead she took some tea, the jasmine-scented brew giving off yellow sparks. She sipped and felt it fizzing all the way down to her toes and clearing some of the cobwebs from her mind.

"Cyria," Gwendolyn said quietly. "What happened to me? When I came through the portal, I mean. I fainted, and . . . and the rest. Why?"

Cyria took her feet off the table. "Rose, you ripped a hole in the fabric of the multiverse. That took tremendous energy. It could have *killed* you. You were lucky to come out of it as well as you did. At any rate, you can't risk going through any more portals. The darkness has been trying to snatch you from the In-Between as you travel."

Gwendolyn knew it all too well. "Is it Mister Zero?"

"Yes, and then again, no. There are players in this game you have not met."

"But I've heard them, in the In-Between. Who are they? The woman and the dark man?"

"If you come through this all right, I suspect she'll reveal herself. Needless to say, the Lady of Light has helped you every way she can, but each time she has to pull you out of the In-Between, it puts her into direct confrontation with the Abscess. After such an encounter, she no doubt needs time to regain her strength. Just look at the effect of the darkness on *you* when you arrived."

Gwendolyn thought about that. "The woman fought back the Abscess when I jumped from Tohk the first time. It hurt her, didn't it? That's why there was only darkness when we jumped just now. She couldn't help me." Gwendolyn took all of that in. Unseen forces, lurking in the space between worlds. "This has something to do with the Blackstar, doesn't it? The Mister Men don't like him, and he doesn't seem to be working for Mister Zero. He's working for that larger . . . something that you mentioned. The dark man."

Cyria nodded. "Clever girl. No getting the wool over you. Nevertheless, the only safe way for you to travel is through the Egressai Infinitus in the Library. It forges a secure connection between worlds and should protect you."

Sparrow piped up. "So let's go back into that Library place, dial up some worlds, and go finish this."

"Ah, well, I'm afraid you can't dash off just yet," Cyria said.

"What?" Sparrow said.

"Why not?" Starling said.

But it was Gwendolyn who answered. "I've got to see the

queen, haven't I?" She clutched her teacup tighter, for it had very rudely started to tremble.

"Yes," Cyria said grimly. "They've felt you enter. I'm afraid they won't let you leave. After your defeat, they were quite beside themselves. And I imagine your rather rude return has made them even less pleased. Double double, toil and trouble."

"Isn't there something you can do?" Starling said. "You make the king and queen sound as dangerous as the Mister Men."

"And crueler, in their way," Cyria said. "Well, Rose, I could *try* to sneak you back into the Library. You're not bound, as I am, and we might be able to break through whatever barriers they put up, though I haven't managed it yet myself—"

"No," Gwendolyn said. "I'll face them."

Cyria reached for her hand. "Are you sure?"

"No, she's not sure, no way," said Sparrow.

"Yes, I am," said Gwendolyn gravely. "I have to do this. I can't have enemies *everywhere* I go. And as you said, our plan needs work, and we'll need a little extra help."

Cyria nodded. "Do you have any idea how you're going to get such help? Or to survive the asking?"

Gwendolyn gave her a sad smile and squeezed her hand. "I suppose I'll have to bargain, won't I?"

There was more arguing from Sparrow and Starling, but in the end, it was decided. Cyria donned her goggles and wings, then led them outside and through the winding treetop paths, from one dazzling faerie neighborhood to the next.

Gwendolyn let Cyria and Starling get ahead of them a bit. Then she turned and gave Sparrow a fierce hug. It was still a bit much for her in her fragile state, but she forced herself to do it. And she was surprised at how much better it made her feel, breathing in the scent of his leather jacket.

He seemed surprised as well, but that didn't stop him from hugging her back. Even though she was a little taller than him now, both of them seemed too small for the tasks ahead.

"What was that for?" he said.

"To say thank you, and I'm sorry. I didn't mean what I said on the ship. It's just, I don't have a lot of experience with b—well, I don't suppose anyone has any experience with our . . . unique . . . relationship."

"Oh, we have a relationship now, do we?" He gave her his old mischievous grin, and her stomach fluttered. So she hugged him again. She wondered if she would ever get used to that feeling of someone being so solid and real right next to her. She never wanted to.

"And, uh . . . what was *that* one for?" he said when she pulled away.

"Because I wanted to." Then she hurried back to the others, hoping her blush would fade before Sparrow could catch up.

CHAPTER FIFTEEN-THE-LAST

Sacrifices

They soon reached the royal district of Faeoria. "Stingle" and "Spangle" were dumbstruck by the elaborate manor houses that grew around them, the enticing gardens, the dazzling display of lights. But Gwendolyn noticed something else.

"We're not headed for the palace?" she asked.

"Afraid not," said Cyria. "The king and queen are attending a masquerade at the Lady Fen's."

Gwendolyn did not like that. She didn't trust the green-clad noblewoman.

They passed through the park. None of the faeries were there, but wood nymphs and fauns moved furtively, heads down, glancing at Gwendolyn. A unicorn whinnied and shook its mane in agitation as it passed. They knew something was coming.

The door to Lady Fen's mansion opened as they approached. "Good evening. You are expected," said Krift, the doorman Gwendolyn met on her first visit.

"Thank you, I suppose," Gwendolyn said, and the four of them stepped into the anteroom.

"Whoa," said Sparrow. He and Starling spun to take in the finery. "Where are we?"

"You are in my home," said a voice. A lithe shape wrapped in a green glow glided down the staircase. The Lady Fen wore a sinister horned mask and jet-black ball gown, both trimmed in green piping and lace. "Rosecap. So, the little flower has returned," she purred. "And she brings other blossoms with her. Or should we call them weeds when they are unwelcome?"

"Lady Fen." Cyria nodded in acknowledgment. "Please show us to the king and queen."

"As you wish," she said. "But first you must be properly attired. Drizelda?"

"Hello, honeybee!" squealed Drizzy, popping up behind them. She was also dressed in black, but with bright pink accents. "Ooooo, and friends! How adorable! Now, you must have masks. They are so terribly comfortable, and *everyone* is wearing them. Let me see . . ." Drizzy put a finger to her pink lips in thought. "I know! Poof!" And she clapped her hands.

There was a swirl of fabric, and Sparrow was suddenly wearing a black tuxedo with long tails, a black shirt, and a black top hat. The only spot of color was the bright red bow tie at his throat. His face was hidden by a black mask with a beak and feathers.

"Heeey," he crooned. "Snazzy."

"Poof!" Drizzy clapped again, bouncing with glee.

Starling was caught up in a whirl of ribbons and silk. Starling wore a feathered mask like Sparrow's and a black skirt with a high front hem that revealed high-heeled boots and ruffled black lace petticoats. She was trapped inside a black corset with a puffy turquoise blouse, her matching black-and-blue hair now done up in an elaborate bun. She looked mortified.

"And poof!"

Cyria was immediately wrapped in the poofiest, frilliest thing Gwendolyn had ever seen, with enormous hoops and bustles and bows. It was as ridiculous as it was horrifying.

The young tinkerer and the inventress traded disgusted glances.

Cyria gave Drizzy a caustic look. "Nice try. I brought my own." She clapped her hands, and the inventress wore her own high-heeled boots, black slacks, and a smoking jacket of midnight blue. With her platinum hair, she looked quite handsome. For a mask, she merely lowered her goggles.

"Yeah, nope," Starling said, and tore off the corset, opting for the turquoise blouse alone.

Drizzy pouted. "Well, at least I know what to do for *you*, my *very* best friend, Rosecap!"

"No thank you, Drizzy," Gwendolyn said. "These clothes were a gift from the queen, and I would hate to offend her by not wearing them."

"Fine!" Drizzy shrieked, throwing up her hands. She sidled up to Sparrow and looped her arm in his. "At least the *boy* has some taste. This way, cutie. You dance with *me* first. Oh, I hope you don't die before the first song!" And she led him to the ballroom.

The grand ballroom was no longer full of mirrors and colors

and flashing neon lights. Instead it was a shadowy place of flickering candles, cobweb curtains, and an ebony dance floor. The faeries' glow did nothing to penetrate the gloom. Music filled the air, but it was equally dark, somber, and haunting.

Gwendolyn saw Robin wandering about, wearing a jester's mask topped with tinkling bells, and it was impossible to tell which Robin they were today. The other masks were all monstrous, some shaped like skulls, or bats, or other unnamable horrors.

"Is this a party, or some sort of funeral?" Sparrow grumbled.

"Perhaps it shall be both," said Lady Fen with a smirk.

At the other end was a raised dais. The jewel fruit willow grew out of it, magically transported from the throne room, and below it sat the two thrones of twisted bodies. On the right sprawled Oberon, as furry and wild as ever, stubbornly maskless, his dark skin seeming even darker in the murky light. On the left sat Titania, the only spot of color in the room, clad solely in three enormous rose petals wrapped cunningly around her slim form, revealing milk-white legs. To match, she had red lips, and even red eyes, though her hair was as white as snow. She held a stick with a crimson demon's mask that covered the left half of her face, though the uncovered right side was not much friendlier.

Not good, Gwendolyn thought. The toy faerie darted into Gwendolyn's bag.

"So. Again you trespass in our lands," Oberon rumbled.

"With company, no less. And you insult our host by scorning the proper attire," Titania added.

Drizzy and Lady Fen quickly made themselves scarce.

"My lord and lady, if I might intercede—" Cyria said.

"You may *not*," said Oberon. "She lost us a precious prize, tore a hole back into our realm, brought even *more* mortals here, and nearly unleashed a great evil. We are *not* pleased."

Gwendolyn stepped forward. "Then tell me how I can please you. I wish to bargain."

"Bargain?" roared Oberon. "You shall suffer in agony for all eternity."

But Titania arched an eyebrow. "For what do you bargain?"

"For your hospitality. To make amends for losing the duel. For forgiveness in my trespass here, and . . ." Gwendolyn took a deep breath. She had an idea, but a very dangerous one. "And for your assistance."

The faeries of the court murmured. The queen seemed intrigued. "What sort of assistance?"

"You are powerful, Lady Titania. I face a powerful enemy, and I need all the help I can get. If he is defeated, then the evil I led to your doorstep will be no more."

Titania smiled like a leopard. "You are quite bold to ask so much."

"I thought you rather *liked* boldness," Gwendolyn said, trying to sound confident.

"In appropriate measures. This would command quite a price. Our forgiveness is costly, our power dearer still, but I must say things have been rather *dull*. What would you offer?"

"What's going on?" Sparrow whispered to Cyria.

"She's getting the final piece for the pistol," Cyria grumbled.

"And if we don't get it?" Starling asked.

"Then the pistol won't have enough power to overcome that Collector bloke," Cyria said. "So this isn't the *worst* idea in the worlds—"

"Quiet, you three, I'm trying to think," Gwendolyn whispered back.

This was the hard part. She had no idea what she could give the queen in exchange. "What would you have, my lady? What would be valuable to you?"

Oberon scowled. "You have nothing of value to us."

Gwendolyn's shoulders drooped. "Oh."

He held up a hand. "The question is, what is valuable to *you*?"

"What do you mean?" Sparrow blurted.

"What we mean, pretty boy," said Titania, "is that dear Rosecap must offer up a sacrifice. The greater the sacrifice, the greater its value. So we ask again. What is valuable to you?"

Gwendolyn chewed her lip. She had the little faerie, but that didn't really belong to her. She needed the bracelet to control Drekk. And her clothes were from Titania herself. Instead, she took out her new sketchbook and pencils. These were important to her, and the only thing she had other than her satchel. She held it out to the king and queen. "I offer you this. It comes from someone very special, and it means quite a lot to me—"

Oberon roared a lion's laugh. "Mere possessions? No *object* is precious enough for what you ask."

"What about . . . my talents? I could make you some art, or perform a dance?"

"No," said Titania.

Gwendolyn thought harder. What was important to her?

Of course, the answer was obvious. "You can't have them." She gestured to Sparrow and Starling.

"Tempting..." mused Titania, eying Sparrow up and down. "The boy could stay with us and never age a day, joining the dance eternal. After all, Lady Fen's parties never end."

A titter of anticipation rippled through the faerie nobles. Lady Fen's smirk widened, and Drizzy giggled.

"They're their own people. I can't give away people," Gwendolyn said firmly.

"Very well, Rosecap," Titania said. "I do have something else in mind. Can you not think of anything? Surely the answer is right on the top of your head."

"I'm sorry, your ladyship, I can't think of anything else—"

"I wasn't being figurative, girl," Titania said with a flash of annoyance.

"My... my hair?" Gwendolyn said.

"You want some of her hair? That's it?" Starling said.

"Not some. *All*. I must say, I've had my eye on it since you first arrived all those years ago."

"Days, milady," Cyria said.

"Days, years, minutes, who can keep track?" she replied. "Do we have a bargain?"

Gwendolyn didn't know what to say. Her *hair*? It seemed almost silly. Sillier still was how tough the decision was, how close she was to saying no and risking a desperate escape. But... it was just hair, and what did that matter when people's lives were at stake?

Starling put a hand on her shoulder. "It's all right, uh, Rose. It'll grow back eventually."

The crowd of faeries exchanged more sinister chuckles.

"*Fala-tien,*" Titania cursed. "You mortals never understand anything. If I take her hair, I shall *keep* her hair."

Sparrow made a slightly disgusted face. "So she'll be bal—it'll be gone, forever?" He caught a fierce look from Gwendolyn, and fixed his expression right quick, adjusting his top hat nervously. "I mean, it doesn't matter to *me,* of course . . . not that I don't like your hair, I do, it's just—"

"Shut up, Spangle, you're not helping," Cyria snapped. "It's Rose's decision."

Gwendolyn was silent for a long moment. Finally, she asked, "Why?"

Titania smiled her wicked smile, tempting and beautiful and dangerous all at once. She lifted the demon's mask to her face. "I have seen into you, remember? I have gazed into your eyes, seen through those precious emeralds to your deepest heart. Those crimson locks are most precious to you. It has been your pride, what sets you apart from the rest of *them*. It makes you different. Special. And that's what I want. Your beauty. Your pride. I want your *special.*"

Gwendolyn opened her mouth to protest, but she couldn't. She did love her hair, liking it long and wild, refusing to tame it when her mother asked. Even when it made her the target of the other children's cruelty, even when people sneered at her on the street, she had liked being different.

This was ridiculous. This was no decision at all. There were people who needed help, and who knew how long Gwendolyn had to help them. But if the decision was so simple, why was it so hard to say yes?

"Do we have a bargain?" Titania crooned.

There was a long, long pause. The silence lingered in the ballroom, save for the haunting music that wrapped around them.

"F-fine," Gwendolyn said. "Take it." The words tasted sour.

Titania rose from her throne. She stepped off the dais, her bare feet hardly touching the ground as she glided toward Gwendolyn.

Gwendolyn cringed. "W—will it hurt?" She sounded like a little girl. She felt like one, too.

Titania's face actually showed a bit of pity. "Yes."

The queen reached out a pale hand, her skin glowing white. She ran her fingers through Gwendolyn's hair, her touch as tender as any mother's.

A tangle of fiery curls fell to the ballroom floor.

The queen reached out with another gentle caress, and another. Wherever she touched, the hair simply fell away. Gwendolyn had a flash of memory, of another lock of falling red hair, when Cecilia and her friends had held her down and tried to do this very thing. That had been bad. But this was much, much worse.

The court looked on in hungry silence as the queen went about her work, drinking in the scene with perverse pleasure. Gwendolyn shut her eyes until it was over. Tears slid out anyway, and she scolded herself. *It's only hair*, she thought. *It's only hair.*

An eternity later, Titania spoke. "It is done."

Gwendolyn opened her eyes. The floor was littered with hair, as red as the rubies on the willow tree. There was so much of it. Gwendolyn had never thought she could have so much hair to lose.

She ran a hand over her head. It felt smooth, cold, and foreign.

Titania waved a hand and the shorn hair floated up from the floor. The strands began to glow. Brighter and brighter, until it all burst into flame. In a flash, it was gone.

The queen's hair was no longer straight and white, but was now a tangle of wild curls. A terrific wind blew through the ballroom, and suddenly the hangings and dresses and masks were all the very color that Gwendolyn no longer possessed.

"There. See? It was not so awful," the queen said. "Though I suppose I shall take the rest of my gifts back as well." She snapped her fingers, and Gwendolyn's clothes all burst into green sparks, vanishing.

She scrambled to cover herself but found that she was once more wearing the tattered remains of her puffed-sleeve dress. Her feet were again bare. She still had her bag, at least.

"If I recall, I also gave you back your voice . . . but that I shall let you keep. No one can say I am not a kind queen." Titania held out her hands, which welled up with water. "Would you like to see?"

Gwendolyn turned away. "No," she whispered. She most certainly would not. The queen was right. It did hurt. Just not on the outside. She cast a glance at Sparrow, but he would not meet her eyes.

"Very well." Titania held out a hand, and a willow frond dropped a glowing ruby into her waiting palm, the same shade as Gwendolyn's vanished hair. "Here. Use this in your hour of greatest need, and wherever you are, I think help of some kind will come to you." She handed Gwendolyn the sphere, the size of a cherry. Then the queen planted a soft kiss on the top of Gwendolyn's bare head. It tingled.

"Now begone from here, lest you test our patience further," Oberon commanded.

There was nothing more to be said. The four of them hurried out of the gloomy ballroom. From the shadows came the sound of hundreds of voices joined in cruel laughter.

~~~

It was a cold walk back to Cyria's tree. A harsh wind cut through her rags, chilled the newly exposed skin on her head, and stung her bare feet until they ached. It was dark now, and it was even starting to rain. *Of course*, Gwendolyn thought bitterly.

Sparrow's and Starling's party clothes dissolved in the rain, rinsing off them like paint, and they were in their usual attire again. Back in the lab, Cyria tried to find some clothes and shoes for Gwendolyn, but they were all laughably large.

"Hmm. Let's try these," the inventress said. "You left them here, remember?" Cyria gave her the School shoes she had forgotten in her climb out the window to follow the imposter Sparrow.

Gwendolyn tried them on, but her feet were too big for them now. She had grown, even though she seemed so much smaller now without her mane of red hair.

"This shoe's too big, this shoe's too small." Cyria frowned. "No luck for Cinderella or Goldilocks, then."

"What?" Gwendolyn asked.

"Never you mind. Hurry along." Cyria led them to the library door.

"I don't suppose we'll be seeing you again any time soon," Gwendolyn said.

"No," said Cyria. "Best not try the faeries' patience further. Not to worry, though, I'm sure I'll find a way out eventually." She pushed a hand against the invisible barrier that trapped her in Faeoria. "Until then, consider the Library yours. Take better care of it in the future, won't you?"

"I'll make sure she keeps it clean," Starling said.

"It should be fine now that you've started the automatic repair process. The Library seems to be a little bit alive, and grows by itself. Ingenious use of my restoration spell, by the way."

"How did you know about that?" Gwendolyn said.

"Oh, pish-tosh. I should hope I know all the goings-on in my own library, thank you."

"Oh, I almost forgot!" Gwendolyn said. "How will we get through to the City? I destroyed the doorway."

"No, you've merely blocked it. A little elbow grease, and you'll be able to get through. Speaking of . . ." Cyria reached up and pulled her glowing red necklace out from under her smoking jacket. "Without the Figment, you'll need this to power the dialing console. You'll have to leave it in the Library to keep the door open."

Gwendolyn put the jewel around her neck. "Thank you."

"And don't forget. The Pistola Luminant alone won't be enough to get your little job done."

Gwendolyn held up the queen's gift. "I won't forget. This wasn't exactly easy to come by."

"Hrm. Right," Cyria said awkwardly. "The pistol, the Figment, and that potent little trinket should pack a powerful enough punch to reverse the Collector's power."

"Yes." Gwendolyn shuffled her feet, then leaned in closer to Cyria, where Sparrow and Starling couldn't hear. "But will I . . . will *it* happen again? Another episode? We're headed into some rather stressful situations, and I can't afford to fall to pieces in the middle of it."

Cyria matched her hushed tone. "I wish I could tell you it wouldn't, sprout. But all I can say is that you're stronger than you think, and more special than you know. You're a right little bearcat, you are." She lowered her voice even further, her lips brushing the girl's ear. "I've grown rather fond of you, Gwendolyn Alice Gray."

Gwendolyn's eyes widened at her true name. But the inventress only winked, a twinkle in her eye that might have been a tear.

Finally, hugs were exchanged with wishes of good luck, and the three children walked through the Egressai Infinitus and back into the Library of All Wonder.

CHAPTER SIXTEEN

Postal Insurance

Somewhere deep in the bowels of the City, a door opened. A sign on the outside read *Pressurized Postal Service: Outer Hub.*

"This is it," said Gwendolyn, entering the room.

"Are you sure?" asked Starling.

"Yes." Gwendolyn looked around. "This is where we need to be."

Sparrow burst in behind them. "I'll take your word for it. It took long enough to move all that rubble in the Hall of Records, and you've had us traipsing through these sewers for hours. Why couldn't we just take the bathysphere again?"

The room was low ceilinged but very long, filled with twisting postal tubes of all sizes. This tangle of plastic snakes was one of the many stations where the City's mail was processed and sent to the mailing slot of each recipient's home. The three children were assaulted by the *whoosh* of packages and letters zooming to their destinations.

"Wow," Starling said. "A massively implemented hydraulic delivery system. Ingenious."

"Which means it's been here since the City was built," Gwendolyn said. "No one's done anything ingenious in hundreds of years." She looked up. Above them was a City full of mindless drones who spent their lives in a passionless grey haze. Never really living. Only surviving. All their hopes and dreams forgotten.

Forgotten. Somewhere up there were her parents. Did they notice she was gone? Or were they happier without their embarrassment of a daughter? *Your parents would probably rather have a bald daughter than an embarrassment like you,* her classmate Vivian had once said. She ran a hand over her smooth head. Bald and broken. What must Sparrow think of her now?

No, she told herself. She needed focus, not self-pity. "Let's go," she said. "We've got a City to save."

Sparrow walked behind a tube and made a face at them, his features distorted through the glass. "What did we come down here for again?"

Gwendolyn forced a grin. "A little insurance. We'll need it if we're going to get the Figment back from Mister Zero and reverse the polarity on the Lambents."

"Gotta love a good polarity reversal," Starling said.

"Right. Time to bring in the backup." Gwendolyn turned, faced the door, and closed her eyes.

"Wait, Gwendolyn," Sparrow put a hand on her arm. "Are you sure you should? Last time you did this, you fainted and . . . stuff."

"Don't worry. I'm not ripping any holes in space. I'm just

moving the Egressai Infinitus down here. Like plugging a wire into a different outlet." And here in the City, there was so much imagination going unused, she had power to spare.

She muttered her magic words. "*What if . . .*"

A surge of power jolted through her, and the door sprang open. The sewers that should have been on the other side were gone. Instead, there was a long hall strung with buzzing yellow lights. Crowded into it were Kolonius Thrash, Burly Brunswick, Professor Zangetsky, and the diverse crew of the *Lucrative Endeavour.*

"Besides," Gwendolyn smiled, one that was a little more real, "we need backup."

"Gears and garters . . ." Kolonius said as they all stepped through the door and looked around. He had cleaned up nicely. He wore a clean tunic, his dreadlocks were neatly pulled back, and there was a fresh eye patch over his long scar.

Starling ran at him and they went in for a hug, but stopped and looked around at all the others. They settled on an awkward handshake instead, both of them flushing several shades darker.

"Those two have certainly gotten close, haven't they?" Gwendolyn whispered to Sparrow.

"You have no idea. It's *so* annoying."

Kolonius put his hands on Starling's shoulders. "Are you all right?"

"Yes," she said, fidgeting. "I'm fine. We just saw each other a few hours ago when we let you into the Library," she smiled.

Sparrow popped up between them. "Hello? Hi? I'm fine too. Nice to see you. Doing well? That's my sister, by the way, so if you wouldn't mind—ow!" he shouted, receiving a sharp blow to the ear from said sister.

"Oh, could this familial patty-cake *be* more sickeningly sweet?" drawled a voice. Tylerium Drekk stood in the doorway, flanked by two of his men. The collar still glowed around his neck. "Oh my!" he said, spotting Gwendolyn and her rather severe makeover. "How awful. I haven't seen anything that hideous since the last time Bucket was bathed. Little girls shouldn't play with scissors. Now it's hard to tell you're even a girl at all."

Kolonius's hand went to the hilt of his sword. "I'll say it again, Red, we can't trust him, and we don't need him. Unless we need a corpse for this plan, and then I'd be happy to provide one."

"If corpses are needed, then please, allow me. I'd like nothing better than to murder the lot of you," Drekk argued.

"But as long as you're stuck with that collar, you're stuck with us," Gwendolyn said. "If you try to pull anything, you'll be tickling yourself with your own sword. Now apologize, and say something nice to Kolonius."

The collar glowed, and Drekk's mouth opened. "I'm sorry. You look very handsome today." He choked on the words. "I'm sure you worked very hard at it. It must have taken you *hours*," he added. Then he shot Gwendolyn the look of a caged jungle cat looking for an escape and someone to maul for his troubles. It was a very specific sort of look.

Then, just like that, it was gone, replaced by a dazzling smile. "Well, for now just consider me another of Thrash's bumbling crew. Should I call him Captain? Or perhaps whatever she calls him?" He gestured to Starling. "Sweetie? Marmalade-bear? My little spice cake?"

Gwendolyn stepped forward before Kolonius could lunge at the pirate. "Let's all just get to work."

"Oh, can we? Please? Thank you ever so," Drekk sneered. "We'll see if we can cram my men in here amongst all these *feelings* swirling around."

The others began to spread out. "*Marmalade bear. My little spice cake,*" Starling muttered in a perfect imitation of Drekk. "And that crack about Gwendolyn's hair? I'll kill him myself."

Kolonius leaned in to whisper. "I didn't want to say anything, but what *did* happen to her—"

"Shh!" Starling hissed. "I'll tell you later."

Gwendolyn blushed and turned away. Instructions were given, from Gwendolyn to the captains and from the captains to the crew. The pirates and Kolonius's crew exchanged harsh looks, but the fragile truce held.

A frantic bustle ensued as they carried out the plan that Gwendolyn had devised, a plan that I have yet to reveal to you. It will be much more fun to show you as it unfolds rather than burden you now with unnecessary exposition, and I would hate to deny you the pleasure of deducing it for yourself. The clockwork faerie ducked out of Gwendolyn's pack and zipped around, watching the commotion.

"Cap'n, are you sure about this? Splitting up? It don't smell right," Brunswick complained.

"It will be fine. Stay here with the crews and follow orders.

I'll keep my eye on Drekk and the children. It'll be just like old times."

"Why do I not find that a comfortin' proposition?" he grumbled, but he clunked obediently back to the others and continued barking orders, his peg leg excusing him from any lifting.

"Are you sure your people can make this work?" Gwendolyn asked.

"They've kept my ship flying. This should be child's play," Kolonius said.

Drekk scoffed. "Your ship. You've got a puzzling sense of the possessive, you ungrateful little—"

"Shut up," Starling said.

"I surely won't," he replied.

"Shut up," said Gwendolyn.

The pirate's mouth snapped closed.

"Professor, come on," Sparrow said. "You're coming with us, remember?"

"What? Oh, yes!" he said, looking up from his tinkerings with the golden pistol. He gathered the pistol and followed, bobbing along like a squirrel, looking intently at all the whooshing tubes, frequently tripping over and bumping into them.

Sparrow shook his head.

Gwendolyn took them through the maze: Sparrow, Starling, Kolonius, the magically cooperative Drekk, the professor, and herself. She led them to a ladder set into the wall, and the six of them clambered through a hatch in the ceiling.

They were on the Edge, standing among the factories and

smoke stacks. Behind them stood the Wall, and beyond it, she presumed, the blackened wastelands of What Has Come Before.

"Well, isn't this cheery," murmured Drekk.

"Where are we going?" Sparrow asked.

"There's a stop I want to make. Something I need to see. Maybe it will give me . . . inspiration."

Sparrow gave her a puzzled look but said nothing more.

Gwendolyn led them away from the Wall, toward a place she remembered from her first visit here. She had to step carefully, as she was still barefoot. It was surprisingly difficult to find a spare pair of shoes when you needed them. Still, if the faeries could go barefoot all the time, so could she.

It didn't take her long to find what she wanted, and soon she stood alone in a tiny, filthy bedroom while the others waited outside. She touched the rows of books and jars and boxes, remnants of a young boy's collections. The boy now called Mister Zero. Where she had originally found the Figment and the book of Kolonius's adventures. She tried to imagine what it must have been like, living here with a father who didn't want you and where a mother was nowhere to be found. She shivered.

"What are you thinking?" Sparrow asked, popping up behind her.

"Only sad thoughts, I'm afraid," Gwendolyn said. "Mister Zero was only a child when they dragged him away. Who knows what that machine has done to his mind? I know I should be angry at him, Sparrow, and I probably will be later. But just now, I pity him."

"Come on, Gwen. Better get outside. No telling what Drekk will do without you nearby."

"All right." She turned and gave his hand a squeeze. "Thank you."

"For what?"

"Oh, I don't know. For everything, you silly boy." And with that, she led him outside.

Drekk crossed his arms. "Well? Are we finished with the sightseeing? So far, I only see a clueless little girl. A rather ugly one, at that."

Gwendolyn gave him a patient look. "There. That's where we're headed." She pointed toward the Central Tower, its mirrored dome gleaming, though no light could have pierced the clouds to make it shine so.

"Given your description of his photonic imagination collection system, that configuration would provide for optimum reception," the professor said.

"It's the best place to put all those mirrors and gather the energy from the Lambents," Starling translated.

"There's more to it than that. It's the center of everything." Gwendolyn glanced back at the door to the filthy hovel where the Collector had once lived. "It's where I would go if I'd spent my whole life in there . . ."

"So, what, are we walking all that way?" Kolonius said with a frown.

~~~

And that was how Gwendolyn found herself riding the monorail with a surly pirate captain, a heroic mercenary, two children from her imagination, and a bumbling inventor. The whole thing seemed ludicrous. She had ridden the mono so many times, but never in such fantastic company. She and Sparrow sat across from Starling and Kolonius, while Professor Zangetsky sat on the floor and tinkered with the Pistola Luminant. Drekk lurked nearby.

"Almost done, Professor?" Starling asked.

"Not quite, I'm afraid. But don't worry! I'll have her ready in time. You just worry about getting that power source, that Figmenty thing you mentioned."

The train slid to a stop, and she could see a crowd of older boys jostling around on the platform. It must be time for School. The notion seemed so quaint and ordinary.

Drekk's rapier sprang out of his cane and he waved it at the first boy onboard, who was so busy chatting with his friends that he nearly pierced his nose on it. The children stopped, turned, and gaped in catatonic shock.

"Tickets, please," Drekk growled.

The boys fled from the monorail, clambering over each other and screaming for their mothers. Drekk sneered. "Was it something I said?"

Gwendolyn barked a laugh, in spite of herself. If she wasn't mistaken, some of them had been the very boys she'd fought at the start of this tale. *Who's the oddling now?* she thought.

The party rode in silence after that, taking a rare opportunity to rest on the long trip toward the Central City. Even Drekk sprawled himself across the seats.

Gwendolyn lay her head on Sparrow's shoulder. The familiar scent of leather was reassuring. She focused on her breath, readying herself for what lay ahead.

"Hey," he said quietly. "How are you feeling?"

She realized she'd been running her hand over her scalp again, and stopped herself. "All right, I think. Steady. Balanced."

"No sign of another . . . episode?"

"Not so far."

"Good," he said. "I—*we* can't afford to lose you."

She snuggled in a little closer and closed her eyes, feeling the gentle swaying and clacking of the mono. She was so tired. She'd been running for days. But this was merely the calm before the storm.

Well, she thought, *at least it's calm*. And after a while, the sound of the train lulled her to sleep.

But a childish laugh rang through her mind, and she shot upright like she'd been burned.

"What's wrong? What is it?" Sparrow asked. The others glanced over.

"N-nothing," she replied. "We're here. He's expecting us."

CHAPTER SEVENTEEN

The Menagerie of Mirrors

They walked up to the front doors of the City's Central Tower. As if on cue, two Mister Men stepped out to greet them, identical and unreadable as always. Even still, these *felt* like Mister Five and Mister Six. She knew them, somehow.

The raggedy girl stepped forward to address the immaculate gentlemen. "All right then. Here I am," she said. Her voice trembled a little.

"Yes, indeed," came the high, eerie voice. "And it would appear that she brought some . . . companions, Mister Six. Should we be concerned?"

"A most amusing joke, Mister Five. They pose no threat."

Drekk snorted. "You're clearly misinformed."

The men cocked their heads and spoke in a chilling unison. "You are Tylerium Drekk, of the village of Aarvanger in the Norslo province. An unwanted child. Wandering frozen streets in search of food. Driven to wicked excess to compensate for the helplessness and abuse suffered in childhood. You pose no threat."

Drekk's mouth moved up and down, too stunned for words. The men turned toward Kolonius.

"Kolonius Thrash. Of the Ursai collective of the Sandvale region. Captured by Drekk, escaped with the help of his guardian, Brunswick. A boy pretending to be a man, desperate to hide feelings of inadequacy, overcompensates with false bravado. Driven by revenge, yet fears he is as heartless as his captor. You pose no threat."

"How do you know that? You're lying!" Kolonius shouted.

"Professor Rufus Zangetsky. Of the Sprocket neighborhood of Copernium. A coward, a fraud, and a failure. A mediocre tinkerer from a city of geniuses. You pose no threat."

The three travelers from Tohk stood, speechless, as the faceless men turned to Sparrow and Starling. "There is . . . an unknown quantity. Two medium-sized constructs with low energy output. Our previous encounter was unimpressive. You pose no threat." Their heads snapped back upright. "You may all accompany Miss Gray. Bid her farewell now or later, it makes no difference."

Gwendolyn forced herself to smile at the others in reassurance. Sparrow caught her gaze, and he gave her a quick wink.

She took a deep breath, steeled herself, and stepped through the doors. There was a blast of light, and the world as she knew it was gone.

~~~

She woke up in bed. Her head swam. She was completely disoriented, but she could tell it was not her own bed—rather, a bulky metal thing with starched white sheets. Neither bed nor sheets were particularly soft.

Harsh fluorescents buzzed overhead. They hurt her eyes, which felt heavy and crusty. She sat up and suddenly discovered the terrific headache she had, which knocked her back down. But she managed to prop up on one elbow and look around.

The floor was a checkerboard of black and white tiles. She could dimly make out more beds all around her.

City Hospital. Her thoughts were mushy, but she could piece together that much.

She took stock of herself. She wore a rough cotton gown. A needle was taped into her right arm, with a tube running up to a glass jar of some clear liquid.

A pretty young woman in a white dress, white apron, and white cap appeared. "Doctor! Come quick! I think she's lucid."

An older man materialized next to the nurse and peered at Gwendolyn over his spectacles. "Well. Hello, dear." He checked a clipboard attached to the foot of her bed. "Gwendolyn, yes? Glad to see you back in the world. This may come as a shock, but you've been in a state of delirium for nearly a month."

It was hard to think straight with all the pounding in her skull. She reached up and felt a mass of gauzy bandages. "My head . . ." she muttered, and her voice was hoarse with disuse.

"Careful there. It's likely still a bit tender," said the pretty nurse.

Gwendolyn felt like she'd been asleep for a week. "But . . . what . . ."

"Now, now, just rest." The nurse fluffed the pillows and eased Gwendolyn back down.

"Take it slow," the doctor said. "There was an accident at the School, do you remember? A—well, it's a bit absurd—a large rat fell onto one of your classmate's heads."

"What?" Gwendolyn said. "No, it was—"

"It seems that in the commotion, you were tripped by . . . Forthright, I think her name was. You hit your head on the edge of a desk. Rather hard too, I'm afraid. My apologies about your hair—there was nothing to be done. It took several operations to stabilize you, and I'm afraid shaving must come before surgery."

"My hair?" That cut through the fog in her brain. She touched the bandages that swathed her scalp.

"It will all grow back, dear, don't worry," the nurse said. "Then you could dye it, perhaps a beautiful raven black."

"No," Gwendolyn moaned. "Sparrow . . . Starling . . ."

The doctor and nurse exchanged kindly smiles.

"Yes, your 'friends.' You've been quite delirious," the doctor said. "Going on about the strangest things. Pirates, airships, fairies, and the like."

"You've quite the imagination," the nurse said. "I particularly like this Kolonius Thrash person."

"We had to tie you to the bed at times," the doctor said. "You would dance about the ward, challenging the other patients to sword fights. Though your parents said that wasn't entirely unusual for you."

Gwendolyn shook her head. "No, that's not . . . This isn't real . . ."

The doctor put a hand on her shoulder. "My dear, it can be hard to come back to the world after an experience like yours. Patients often prefer their dreamlands. But I can assure you, *this* is reality. It's good to see you in your right mind again."

"But . . . but . . ." *It couldn't be*, Gwendolyn thought. *I can't have just imagined it all.*

"They're right outside, Doctor. Should I let them in?" the nurse said.

"I think that would be best. Perhaps they'll be able to ground her. I'd hate to lose her to the delusions again."

"Very well." The nurse walked away.

Gwendolyn sat up again. "You're wrong, they're not delusions, I—"

"Now, now, don't talk. You could trigger a relapse. Stay focused on me. You're here, in City Hospital. Everything is going to be fine."

Gwendolyn wanted to protest further, but her already muddled thoughts were completely scattered by the arrival of two more people.

Mother and Father.

Their eyes were glistening. Their smiles said they obviously remembered her, and loved her very much. Any doubt she may have had was smothered by Mother's crushing embrace.

"Oh, Gwendolyn, we've been so worried! Are you all right?" Mother said. The sound of her voice nearly broke Gwendolyn's heart. She melted into Mother's arms, allowing herself just one blissful moment to enjoy it all.

Father placed a hand on her shoulder, his mustache quivering over his stiff upper lip. "We knew you'd come back to us eventually, Bless. Welcome home."

Mother held her at arm's length and looked her right in the eye. "Never leave us again."

Gwendolyn had to close her eyes and look away. Even still, she felt hot droplets slide down her cheeks.

"Ah. Look at that," the nurse said. "Happy tears."

But when Gwendolyn opened her eyes, her expression was anything but happy.

"How dare you," she said, and her voice was sharp enough to cut glass. Anger burned the fog from her mind. "Did you think this would work? That I'd suddenly believe it was all some awful dream? This needle doesn't even hurt." And she yanked it out of her arm.

The nurse gasped.

"Gwendolyn, settle down," said Father.

"You'll hurt yourself!" said Mother.

"Shut up!" Gwendolyn yelled, and put her hands over her ears. She couldn't bear to hear her parents' voices. "I had my doubts. When the Lambents were destroyed, I wondered if any of it had been real. But it was all too big. Tohk, Faeoria . . . I could never have thought of all that by myself. They're real." She got up on her knees until she was face to face with the doctor. "*This* is the illusion."

The doctor's face twisted into an evil smile. "Well, it was

worth a try. You're clearly too obsessed with your imaginary friends to listen to reason."

She glared at him. "I could have forgiven this little trick. But showing me a dream of my parents? That's going to cost you."

The doctor's smile widened to show his pointed teeth. "Who said your parents were a dream?"

Gwendolyn whipped back to Mother and Father, but their faces were blank and uncomprehending, puppets whose strings had been cut.

"No, wait!" Gwendolyn lunged for her parents, but the doctor snapped his fingers, and everything vanished.

~~~

Gwendolyn fell to the floor. A floor that was a polished mirror. The hospital, and her parents, were gone. Her insides felt like they'd been given a sharp twist, and she tried to shake it off and get her bearings.

She was surrounded by mirrors.

"So. We're doing this again," Gwendolyn said, getting to her feet, forcing herself to ignore what had just happened and focus on what was in front of her.

What was in front of her was thousands of freckled, green-eyed girls, all with expressions of anger and determination, a look that Gwendolyn supposed she must be wearing now. A look that quickly turned to shock and disgust when she saw what a fright she was.

She was bald. She'd known that, of course, but knowing and seeing are very different things. Seeing it . . . well, it was not a fetching look for her. She had never noticed how far her ears stuck out. And the skin was so pasty and smooth. If what Titania said was true, it would remain that way for the rest of her life. On top of that, she was filthy, barefoot, and dressed in rags.

Gwendolyn didn't need to see that. She turned around, looking for her friends, but the Gwendolyn behind her was not bald or ragged at all. This Gwendolyn was dressed in Drizzy's ball gown, with its tight bodice, low neckline, and glittering jewelry. Her bare shoulders sprouted an impressive set of lacy silver butterfly wings. The reflection twirled and spun in a beautiful ballet. Her hair was red and lush, long enough it nearly touched the ground, topped with a silver bow. She was divinely beautiful.

Gwendolyn didn't need to see that either. Seeing her hair hurt worse than seeing herself bald. She clenched her fists and took a deep breath. "Go on, Mister Zero. Keep teasing me. We'll see who's laughing when I find you." She glanced around. "Sparrow? Can you hear me?" Her voice echoed strangely. There was no answer. She cupped her hands to her mouth and shouted. "Starling, are you there? Kolonius? Professor Zangetsky?" But again, no answer.

"Drekk?" she said, but not terribly loudly.

"Gwendolyn!" There was a flash of movement on her left. She whirled. "Hello?"

"Gwendolyn, over here!" came the familiar voice, from the other side this time. She caught a glimpse of yellow.

"Gwendolyn, come this way!" She turned again, and spotted Sparrow.

Her heart leapt. "Sparrow! Are you all right?" She started to run toward him, but another Sparrow came up beside her.

"Gwendolyn, stop! Don't go with him! It's a trap!" he yelled.

Gwendolyn froze, seeing double. Another trick.

"They're both lying! Hurry, come this way!" cried a third Sparrow.

"No, this way!" cried a fourth.

"Gwendolyn. Listen to me. You're in danger. Run, now!" came another.

Gwendolyn was surrounded by five identical Sparrows, clad in yellow scarves, flat checked caps, and red leather jackets. Soon they were all arguing about which of them was the real Sparrow.

"This is ridiculous. It's obviously me. Just come this way," said the first.

Gwendolyn shook her head.

"He's stupid. You're stupid. This whole thing is stupid. We don't have time for this," said the next, stepping forward. He didn't *seem* to be a reflection, but that hardly meant anything.

"Nope, sorry," Gwendolyn said.

The third Sparrow looked around, perplexed. "Well, what am I supposed to do, justify my entire existence in two seconds? That's not fair!"

"No. Is that all you've got?"

The fourth Sparrow gazed at her intently with those big brown eyes. "Gwendolyn," he said. "My sweet Gwendolyn. You know who to choose. Come with me." He stepped forward and put a hand on her shoulder.

She cocked a wary eyebrow. This one had potential. Maybe

she should keep him, real or not. His hand certainly *felt* real enough. "Let me ask you a question. Would you ever, oh, I don't know, push me off the top of a building?"

He looked aghast. "No! I could never do such a thing to you! You mean everything to me."

The fifth Sparrow scoffed. "Forget him. We're here to kill Mister Zero! He has to pay!"

"Oh, please." She rolled her eyes. "Obviously, none of you are real."

Instantly, the Sparrows all shattered into glittering dust, and a sixth one stepped forward from nowhere. "What gave it away, Gwen?" Sparrow asked.

She walked up and patted him on the head. "They all have hats. You lost yours. And I don't let anybody but you call me Gwen." She looked around at the mirrors. "It seems none of Mister Zero's traps are terribly original. I've seen that one before. Robin was better at it. But I don't fall for the same trick twice. How was *your* trip?"

"Fine. A few nasty pictures here and there, no big deal," he said casually, but his eyes said otherwise. "Come on, let's find the others. Who knows where that sister of mine is." But he grabbed her hand a little more tightly than was necessary, and Gwendolyn wondered what he had been through to find her.

Hand in hand, they continued through the maze. "Sparrow," she said.

"Yeah?" He was feeling around, running his hands along the glass to find any gap they could slip through.

"Are we . . . all right?" Gwendolyn asked. "I just . . . I would understand if . . . if you moved on without me when this is all over."

He turned to her, surprised. "Why would you say that?"

Gwendolyn fidgeted. "There were those things I said about your parents. Not to mention that now I'm—"

"Bald?" Sparrow filled in.

Gwendolyn cringed.

"I'm sorry, I didn't mean to be—"

"No, it's fine. I have to get used to it sometime." Though, seeing it reflected all around her hurt like a thousand mocking pinpricks. It was a very specific sort of hurt. "But it's not just that. You saw me in Faeoria. The *real* me. Inside, I'm . . . I'm broken."

She didn't know how she expected him to react, but she had certainly not expected him to laugh and roll his eyes. "You're not broken. A little different, maybe. From what Cyria said, it's part of who you are, and I *like* who you are. I mean, I'm reckless and impulsive and blabbering, so I can accept your different if you can accept mine. No reason we can't be friends."

"Friends?" Gwendolyn said with a raised eyebrow.

"You know . . ." And now it was his turn to fidget. "Among other things. I don't know. Words are hard. Hey! Look up there!" he said, pointing to a small gap where two mirrors came to-gether. "Think you can squeeze through?"

"What a rude question to put to a lady," Gwendolyn teased. "Are *you* strong enough to help me up?"

Sparrow flexed his muscles and made an exaggerated gri-mace. He cupped his hands, and she put her foot in them. Then he boosted her up and she scrambled through. Then she turned and helped him climb through as well.

They were in another cul-de-sac, and a figure lay on the floor in a shivering heap. At his side was a pile of tools and equipment.

"Professor Zangetsky!" Gwendolyn cried. "Are you all right?"

He did not answer, his eyes wide with panic. Small squeaks escaped his lips, and tears ran down his cheeks.

"Gwendolyn. Look." Sparrow pointed.

She did. All around them, the mirrors played horrible and gruesome scenes. A kaleidoscope of terror, a bubbling stream of evil not usually seen outside of candy factory boat tours.

"Professor!" Gwendolyn said. She shook his shoulder, but to no effect. "They're only pictures, like your show! They're not real!" But he didn't respond.

"Any ideas?" Sparrow asked.

Gwendolyn nodded. "I happen to keep a few for any occasion."

She stretched out a hand and imagined. The images changed. Soon they were surrounded by a peaceful underwater landscape. A glowing creature like an enormous manta ray, with two large fins and colorful markings, swam past them, keening its mournful song.

"The Neyora," Sparrow murmured.

Others appeared, and the song grew louder and louder, until the notes shook the very walls around them. Finally, the music faded, and all the images vanished.

"Professor Zangetsky?" she asked. "Can you hear me?"

The professor slowly looked up at her. "That was . . . that was . . . beautiful. That song. Positively wonderful. Thank you, young lady."

The two of them helped the professor to his feet and no more was said about the horrible images. They gathered up the professor's equipment, and he handed Gwendolyn the Pistola Luminant.

"I managed to finish the alterations just before—ah, well, I finished them." There were now two rings of copper and wires on top, just the right size for the Figment and the faerie globe.

"Thank you," Gwendolyn said, putting the pistol in her bag for safe keeping. "Now we need to find the Figment and the others."

Suddenly, Starling and Kolonius leapt out from a hidden corridor. They collapsed against the walls, sinking to the floor and gasping for breath. Each was bleeding from several scratches.

"What happened to you?" Sparrow asked.

"Whirling mirror knives of death," Kolonius said.

"Obstacle course of razor blades," Starling added.

"Are you hurt?" Gwendolyn asked.

"Nothing serious," Kolonius said.

"Speak for yourself," replied Starling. "This was my favorite vest." She poked a finger through a hole in the orange fabric. A sweaty lock of hair fell into her face. She pulled off her goggles, took a scrap of ribbon from one of her many pockets, and tied her hair back up into a ponytail with a weary sigh.

Suddenly, there was a loud *bang* behind them.

Starling and Kolonius leapt to their feet, and the five

travelers hastily formed a circle. There was a second *bang*, closer this time, and they looked around to see where it was coming from. They heard a third, much closer *BANG*, and a mirror exploded in a spray of silver confetti. Tylerium Drekk stepped through the hole, a smoking pistol in his hand. They gaped at him in astonishment.

"What?" he shrugged. He twirled the pistol into its holster and put his hands on his hips. "Good lord, what happened to all of you?" he asked, noting their cuts and tears, while he himself appeared completely unscathed.

Starling and Kolonius glared at him as they nursed their wounds. Sparrow shook his head in amazement. Drekk just admired himself in a mirror, picking something from his teeth and adjusting his hair.

They did not have long to catch their breath. Into the mirrors around them stepped hundreds of Mister Men. A high-pitched voice rang through the mirrored hall.

"Is it time, Mister Five?"

"So it seems, Mister Six."

"The Menagerie of Mirrors has planted its seeds."

"He is waiting for you."

The men vanished, leaving them in awkward silence. Then there was a rumbling from below. It grew louder and louder, and the mirrors began to move.

CHAPTER EIGHTEEN

Shall We Play a Game?

The mirrors separated, pulled apart by mechanical arms. Then they clicked back together, re-forming into the immense mirrored dome of the Origination Regulation Bureau. The ORB.

Into the middle rose the jagged spire, a hundred feet high. Mister Zero was as pale and thin as before. The energy in the dome rippled across Gwendolyn's skin.

Professor Zangetsky gaped. "My, my, my. A crystalline-photonic resonance absorption chamber and a potential-energy collection spire. That would explain all the mirrors, of course— the refraction serves as a focusing amplifier for the absorption matrix. Do you see how the glowing spheres at the bottom feed into the crystal?"

"Not now, Professor!" Starling hissed.

But Gwendolyn's eyes went to the ring of Lambents circling the bottom of the spire. She spotted a glint of blue: the Figment.

"Hello, Gwendolyn. Thank you for coming back. I knew

you would," said the little boy in a voice that you would find deeply unsettlingly if you could hear it yourself. Though just like Gwendolyn, you would notice that his lips never actually formed the words.

"Mister Zero. It is time for the City to be free." Which sounded wonderfully heroic to her.

A sigh rattled the mirrors. "I know that's what you *think*, Gwendolyn. But there's lots of things you don't *know*. Before we're done, you'll see it my way. You'll be my friend."

"She's won't be your anything, you twisted little creep," Sparrow growled. "Starling?"

"Right!" She drew her collapsible sword and tossed one to her brother.

He caught it and flicked it open. "I still don't see why you don't let me keep this."

"I still don't trust you with pointy objects," his sister replied.

"Children, focus," Gwendolyn said. The energy of the dome pulsed around her, and she allowed her hands to glow as she stepped into a ready pose Robin had shown her. She wished she still had that knife—people kept giving them to her and she kept losing them.

The spire vibrated. "Why do you keep playing with your imaginary friends like this? You are too old for things like them. Are they like your favorite blanket?"

"These are my friends. They're not imaginary. At least, not anymore, I think. Anyway, you and your faceless men could never understand." She didn't understand it either, but now was hardly the time for that. "Give me the Figment."

"Hmm. No. It's mine, and it is a very valuable collector's item. All the knowledge of the Old Ones. Thank you for bringing it to me."

"You took it from me."

"You stole it from me first. How rude to break into someone's bedroom and take their things," he said.

"And you took Tommy and Missy," Gwendolyn continued, ignoring him. "And everyone's memories of me, including my parents' memories," she said, almost choking on the last word. "I'll be taking all of that back as well, and putting everything back the way it was. Only better."

He laughed. "Gwendolyn, you really are so funny. You still think that this is some story, where the fearless girl and her champions defeat the evil king in his palace of glass and shadow."

The Figment flickered, and around them images of knights and monsters appeared, gruesome battles with clashing swords and gnashing teeth. The images vanished again, as quickly as they had come.

"We're all in a story, Mister Zero," Gwendolyn said, quoting Cyria.

"Fine. I will play your game, for I am so terribly bored. And when we are done and the game is over, you will see the damage that your imagination causes. How much you hurt everyone. How your plan would destroy the City."

Kolonius drew his spiral sword, activating the spinning drill-like blade. "How much longer are we going to listen to this brat?"

"Indeed." Drekk twirled a pistol absentmindedly. "I hope I

don't drone on like this in front of *my* captives. Can we murder something, so I can leave?"

"Then let's play!" giggled the voice. "Starting with a wizard's duel, of course!" His glowing eyes flashed, and the dome grew dimmer.

Gwendolyn groaned. She'd had enough of duels recently. She felt ripples in the energy around her. "Be careful!" she shouted. "Something is coming."

A shriek pierced the air above them.

"You have a knack for stating the obvious," Drekk said.

Black shapes swarmed above them, barely visible in the gloomy darkness, calling to each other with cold, unearthly wails. Their calls sounded eerily human, like a woman screaming.

She was gazing upward so intently that she did not see the thing that scuttled over her foot. She squealed, in spite of herself.

"What is it?" said Sparrow.

"I don't know!" she replied. "There's something on the floor as well!"

Kolonius looked down, but something large, black, and leathery swooped from above and slammed him to the ground. He cried out, and the black shape swooped away, then swung around for another pass.

The whole thing resembled a headless bat with the tail of a scorpion and a cluster of spider eyes. It was covered in glistening black skin, each wing tipped with a curved claw. Its powerful stinger was longer than Gwendolyn's arm.

A second one swooped toward Gwendolyn. She focused her

imagination and fired a blast of light at it, but she missed and barely dodged a strike from its tail.

Kolonius got to his feet, a line of dark red puncture wounds along his back. One flying monstrosity came around again, and Gwendolyn saw a fanged mouth stretched vertically across its entire underbelly. It dove toward the boy captain again, but he sliced it neatly in two. He was hit with a spray of steaming ooze as the pieces flopped to the floor.

"What the heck is that?" said Sparrow.

"You don't have to know it to kill it, boy, so long as it bleeds like everything else," Drekk said. He cast a look at the slime dripping from Kolonius's face. "No matter how . . . disgusting."

"Don't let your guard down," Starling warned them. "Gwendolyn, go get the Figment."

"I've got your back, Gwen," Sparrow said.

She nodded, but was distracted as something small and black scrabbled toward them. She willed a long thorn into existence and flung it at the creature, impaling it neatly through the middle.

She took a closer look, and instantly regretted it. The creature's body was a single giant eye ringed by a crust of black skin. Its ten spindly legs twitched, and it flipped over. It had four fanged pincers clicking together over a set of flat, human teeth.

Gwendolyn shuddered, but there was no time to be squeamish. Gwendolyn stretched out her hands and pictured a familiar idea. Thorny vines spread across the ORB, tangling the crawling creatures but sparing Gwendolyn's party. The vines tightened and crushed them all with a series of sickening pops.

"Thanks! But how are we supposed to move now?" Sparrow said, pointing to the vine-covered floor.

"Umm . . . hang on!" Gwendolyn closed her eyes, took a deep breath, then exhaled slowly, trying to empty her mind as Tree had taught her. It was difficult, because the ORB was not the most peaceful place for meditation at the moment. But she forced herself to focus, or rather, she *un*-forced herself, and let everything go. The vines dissolved into green sparks.

"It seems that I have learned nothing," she said, smiling to herself.

One of the flying horrors soared toward Professor Zangetsky, who covered his head with his hands and started to run. Tylerium Drekk grabbed his arm and yanked him to the ground.

"Stay down, you bumbling fool. The girl says we need you, so stay put, or we might have to find out which *parts* of you she needs, individually." He fired his pistol, and the creature screamed and flapped away, dripping slime.

Sparrow and Starling stood back to back, swinging wildly as waves of the crawling creatures swarmed at their feet. Sparrow cried out, and Gwendolyn saw him clutching a bleeding arm. A flying monster hovered above, its stinger wet.

Quick as a flash, Starling reached into one of her pockets. She palmed a small metal ball, wound it with three quick turns, and hurled it at the shrieking creature. There was a loud bang, and the monster exploded in a burst of purple smoke.

Gwendolyn dashed to Sparrow. "Let me see," she said, tearing his sleeve open. His crimson tunic made it hard to tell how much blood he had lost, but he had a long line carved into his arm. She remembered something Cyria had done once, and waved her hands over his arm, picturing the wound closing. "*If only* . . ." she whispered.

The skin on his arm repaired itself, only a faint red line marking the spot.

"Thanks," Sparrow said. "But shouldn't you be getting the Figment?"

Gwendolyn looked toward the spire and the blue gem glittering at its base. Hundreds of flying shapes darkened the air around it. "I would, but there are rather a lot of those things."

"Do you have any bright ideas?"

"I think so. Professor!" she shouted. "What was it you were saying earlier? About these mirrors?"

"W-w-w-what? The mirrors? Oh, yes! It's quite simple. They act as energy amplifiers—aaah!" he squealed as another flyer swooped in, but Drekk's sword sprang from his cane, and in one smooth motion, he caught the sword, twirled it, and sliced the creature in twain.

"So it makes my imagination bigger?" she asked.

More crawlers spawned from the mirrors and scuttled toward them. Drekk slammed his cane down on one and popped it.

"I—yes, something like that," the professor stammered.

"Perfect. Because 'bigger' is exactly what we need." She thought, and she wondered, and she imagined. "*What if* . . ." she murmured. The light in the ORB dimmed further, as Gwendolyn pictured ideas larger than she could ever have brought to life on her own.

Two massive shapes burst out of the mirrors on either side

of the dome. Shapes Gwendolyn had seen last at the Crystal Coves, guarding Cyria's secrets. Two full-grown crystal-eaters, like some mixture of rhinoceros, elephant, and mole. Their horned heads thrashed back and forth while they stamped six clawed feet. Their violet eyes glowed. Then they went berserk, stomping the crawlers like bags of wet garbage.

"That's my girl," whispered Sparrow.

Above them, a fanged flyer dove at them, but a serpentine shape emerged from the mirrors and ate the flyer whole. Three more appeared—translucent, slimy things with long needle teeth.

Deepworms. The creatures that had nearly killed them in the bathysphere were now flying rather than swimming, tearing their way through the flyers.

Gwendolyn smiled. Mister Zero wasn't the only one with monsters in his head. But she wasn't done yet, and an enormous roar shook the dome.

"MEEEEEEP!"

A thirty-foot tall orange Falderal charged into the battle, crushing the scuttling eyeballs under its enormous flippers, and chomping flyers whole. Criminy was a force of pure destruction.

It was all a bit too much. One of his giant purple feet nearly flattened Starling. The Deepworms were flying chaotically, slamming into the walls. A crystal-eater plowed into Kolonius by mistake, knocking him across the dome.

"Gwendolyn, be careful!" Sparrow said.

"Right! I got carried away." She looked down at her glowing skin. Ignoring the battle, she sat right down on the floor and crossed her legs. "Cover me for a second."

"What are you doing?" Sparrow asked.

"Sitting," Gwendolyn said. "When I can't think of anything, I try to think of nothing."

"Do what you need to do, as long as your nothing does something," Starling said. She and Sparrow took up positions beside her.

Gwendolyn closed her eyes and tried to slow her breathing and her heartbeat. It was difficult, as I'm sure you can imagine if you've ever tried to block out a horde of rampaging monsters, perhaps in the hallways at school. But eventually, Gwendolyn regained control of her creations. Between the giant orange furball, the Deepworms, and the crystal-eaters, the ORB was cleared of Mister Zero's monstrosities.

Sparrow walked over to one of the crystal-eaters and rubbed its horn affectionately. "Good job."

Gwendolyn shouted up at Criminy. "Thank you!"

"MEEEEEEEEEEEP!" he roared in pride.

Mister Zero's giggle reverberated through the dome, setting Gwendolyn's teeth on edge. "See how much fun we can have! Are you ready for the next game?"

"This isn't a game!" Gwendolyn shouted. "You've been stealing from everyone! You've stolen my entire life!"

"How quickly you forget. I haven't stolen anything. They gave it to me. I only do what I have to. But that doesn't mean we can't have fun along the way."

"I'm not fond of his idea of fun," Starling muttered, tending to Kolonius's wounds with supplies from her belt.

"Oh, cheer up. You've passed the physical trial. Now is the

part of the story where I should test your insides as well. A true hero must be tested, right Gwendolyn? So first, let's clean up our toys—" There was a flash of light from the Lambents at the base of the pillar. Criminy, the Deepworms, and the crystal-eaters vanished instantly. "Nice and tidy. No distractions."

The Lambents glowed again. Beams of color erupted from them, red, orange, yellow, green, indigo, and violet. The beams bounced like lasers from one end of the dome to the other.

"Be ready," said Kolonius.

"For what, exactly?" said Drekk.

As if on cue, the answer presented itself. The beams ricocheted off the peak of the dome and struck the floor. Six floor panels glowed, one in front of each member of the group, and six shapes rose out of them. As the glowing shapes solidified, Gwendolyn was startled to find that she was facing . . . herself.

CHAPTER NINETEEN

Reflections and Revelations

Not quite herself. Not exactly. This Gwendolyn had hair. Not red, though, but rather a deep green. Her green dress was whole and intact, with shiny green shoes, and even her freckles had a hint of emerald. But for all about her that was green, her eyes were a plain, pale grey.

"Hello, Gwendolyn," said the green girl.

"Hello yourself. Or should that be myself?" Gwendolyn replied.

The Green Gwendolyn gave a shy titter, a hint of a smile on her dark lips. The dome had grown dark, so dark that all Gwendolyn could see were the glowing doppelgängers of various hues: a Red Kolonius, an Orange Drekk, a Yellow Sparrow, an Indigo Professor, and a Violet Starling. And none of them were doing anything but . . . talking.

"Why are you doing this?" asked the Green Gwendolyn.

"What?" she replied, snapping back to attention.

"Fighting Mister Zero. Your life has not been so bad. Your parents loved you. Why fight? Aren't things better the way they are?"

"No, they are not!" Gwendolyn blurted. She was so angry at the suggestion that she leapt to defend herself, when she probably should have stopped to consider why she would bother talking to this imitation at all. But luring a thirteen-year-old into an argument has never been especially difficult. "People should not be controlled this way! It's just . . . it's wrong!"

The Green Gwendolyn played with her seaweed hair, teasing her bald counterpart. "What gives you the right to decide what's best for the entire world? They voted for this." She gave her a pitying, pouting look.

"I've told you, I—"

"I'll tell you why you're doing this," interrupted the Green Gwendolyn. "You never cared about the City. You're just lonely. Growing up with no friends, no one to talk to but trees and chairs. Everyone thought you were simply horrid. Is it any wonder you can't make friends? Unless, of course, you *make* them yourself."

The real Gwendolyn smirked. "This is the best you can do? Bring up my Schoolyard teasings? It's not going to work. I'm not that girl anymore."

But the Green Gwendolyn wasn't done. "You're right. You've grown into a selfish and bitter child who lives her life inside her own head, more interested in stories than in actual, real people. You cling to your little imaginary friends, but they aren't enough. You want something real. You want to make the whole world love you and thank you and understand you. If you can't fit into the world, you'll make the world fit you."

Gwendolyn opened her mouth to reply, but the words stung as only truth can, even if it was a twisted sort of truth.

"Why should everyone *else* have to change so that *you* can feel normal? Why should everyone have to be like you? That's not fair. That's the sort of sameness you've always hated."

Gwendolyn knew this was a trick, and she covered her ears so she wouldn't hear any more of it, but the Green Gwendolyn's voice was inside her head now, feeding her doubts and depression. Her breathing came a little faster.

"Of course I'm not real," the Green Gwendolyn continued. "I come from your mind, just as your friends do. But that doesn't make me wrong. You know it, which is why I'm saying it, because I'm you. You can't change the world just because you don't like the way it works. It's time to change the only thing you can: yourself. Isn't change what you're fighting for?"

Gwendolyn looked to her friends, and heard snippets of conversation as they all stood mesmerized by their doubles.

"You're not clever enough, no, no, no. Pretending will only hurt them in the end."

"What are you even doing here? Ordered around by a tiny child."

"Is it really worth it? You don't owe them anything."

"He'll never love you."

"You'll just have to leave her eventually."

Sparrow looked over at her. The expression on his face was

the saddest she had ever seen, and there were tears in his eyes. Gwendolyn's chest ached to see it.

The dark thoughts rose with a sudden vengeance, the attack taking full control in seconds. Her breath came in rapid gasps. There was a tightness in her chest, her stomach felt like it was clawing to get out, and a heavy weight landed on her shoulders. It pushed her down to her knees. She knew these feelings, and knew they were not Mister Zero's doing. She trembled uncontrollably.

"You see, Gwendolyn? You are not well," said the green voice in her head.

And there it was—her real weakness. She *was* broken inside. What right did she have to decide that everyone else should be like her, when *she* didn't even want to be like her?

"You only end up hurting everyone you try to help. Do you want to hurt the whole City? Everything is working just fine. The only broken piece is you."

She was right. There was no getting around it. She couldn't handle her training with Titania. She couldn't defeat the Blackstar. Why did she think she could do this? Everything in the City was just fine without—

But then something sparked inside her. Something Cyria had said, when they'd looked at the tapestry of the City. The bottom edge had been ragged, blackened, and torn. *"Something is wrong with your world,"* she had said. *"Something has been ripped from it."*

As she remembered the kind inventress's words, Cyria's image appeared on the mirror she knelt on, looking up at

Gwendolyn like a reflection on a pond. "Everyone *is born different. None of us are born to fit in.*"

The mirror showed the two of them together, Cyria's arm around her shoulders. *"They* do *like you, my molly—they go mad for a bricky girl like you.*"

And suddenly, a gleaming golden Cyria rose up from the mirror, standing next to the doppel-Gwendolyn, outshining the green girl. Cyria Kytain, in all her glory, clockwork wings outstretched and shimmering like an angel, all her kind words tumbling out of Gwendolyn's memory together.

"You're not broken, Rose. You're changed. Trees don't grow in straight lines, and neither do people. You can never tell what direction they'll go, but they're always growing upward, never backward. You can't just move on from your pain, but you can choose how you go on with it."

The golden Cyria knelt down and put a hand under Gwendolyn's chin, bringing them face to face.

"I've only known you a short time, but I can tell you true: You are not a freak. You are wonderful, and beautiful, and kind, and clever. And anyone who tells you different? You give them a sock on the jaw from me."

Gwendolyn reached out a hand, and laid it on Cyria's cheek. It was warm.

"You're stronger than you think, and more special than you know. I never could have predicted you."

And that was it. Cyria disappeared. Gwendolyn didn't feel any better, and her burden didn't feel any lighter, but she managed to get up on one knee. *I'm not broken. I am wonderful,* she told herself.

And she believed it. She got another foot under her. "I am kind," she said aloud. "And clever. And beautiful." She stood, despite her shaking legs. She may have felt like a worn-out scrap of cloth, ready to drift away on the wind, but she wouldn't let that stop her. The yawning emptiness inside might always come back to haunt her, but there was too much to do to lie around and wallow. She would choose how to go on with it. And in that choosing, she found an idea.

"You still don't understand, Mister Zero. This has not all been in my imagination or in some book. These other worlds are just as real as ours. After all, there's a book or two about us as well. There are things I know that you don't, and that is what makes you so furious at me."

The Green Gwendolyn gave her a look of disappointment. "Oh, dear, you don't understand. Mister Zero isn't mad at you, not one bit."

But Gwendolyn's thoughts were moving like a snowball down a hill. "Oh, he's terribly angry with me. He does everything he can to break me." Gwendolyn stepped right through her emerald counterpart like she was nothing more than a bit of green fog. She addressed the boy hidden in the dark. The others and their doubles all turned to look at her.

Gwendolyn opened her bag and drew out the Pistola Luminant, making sure to leave the flap undone. "And you know what else? I'm going to stop you. Because you may be a lot of things, Mister Zero, or the Collector, or the Abscess, or whatever else you call yourself to feel important—but I don't think *creative* is one of them. I may be lonely. But you're just selfish."

The Green Gwendolyn came up from behind and put a hand on her shoulder. "Gwendolyn, please. Think about what you're saying. You—"

"That's quite enough out of you, if you please and thank you very much," Gwendolyn said. She spun on her heel and fired the Pistola Luminant in the Green Gwendolyn's face, which for a moment took on a beautiful shade of chartreuse. There was a flash of yellow light and the sound of a thunderclap, and the green girl disappeared.

Gwendolyn turned the pistol's beam on the rest of the doppelgängers, vanishing them all in one sweep of her arm. The light in the dome returned, and she faced the crystal spire.

"Now, where were we?"

"You were saying lots of mean things about me," Mister Zero rumbled.

Gwendolyn smirked, still feeling horrible inside, but more than happy to heap that misery on someone who deserved it. "I have a theory. If I were going to select someone to keep watch over all the world's imagination, I would want someone who had none of his own. Someone who could keep all that power, but couldn't really use it."

The rumble came again, shaking the mirrors and distorting their reflections. Gwendolyn's companions crept closer to her.

"You never wanted me to join you. You wanted my power. But you can't just suck it out—like you said, people break if you try. You needed me to give it up *willingly*. Everything you said was a lie, a trick. You wanted me to want you because no one ever did. I know the feeling."

She looked down at the Figment again, stuck in the bottom of the spire, her initials suddenly flashing at her in the dim light. "You say that Figment is yours, and it might have been, once. But ideas are wild; they like to spread. I don't think it wants to be with you anymore. That's why it came to *me* in the first place. That's why it came back to me after I lost it in the In-Between. That's why it has my initials on it. Imagination wants to be *used*."

Sparrow leaned close. "Lovely speech. I hope you know what you're doing," he whispered.

"You know what? For once, I think I do. Because he doesn't have any imagination. Which is why he won't expect *this*," she said.

"Expect what?" the little boy asked.

Gwendolyn pointed. "That," she said. Zipping through the gloom, barely visible, was the clockwork faerie. It held the Figment in its tiny hands, and its tiny wings whirred like mad to carry it. "We are alike in one way, Mister Zero. We're both easily distracted. But at least *I* don't fall for the same trick twice."

"No! That's mine, you can't have it!" The voice was practically a scream.

Two mirrors rose up from the floor and smashed together, crushing the tiny contraption. The Figment slid across the glass and bumped into Gwendolyn's bare foot.

All her bravado vanished instantly. She snatched up the Figment and ran to the little toy.

"Gwendolyn, wait! Stop!" Starling shouted, but Gwendolyn

didn't listen. She cradled the pieces of the loyal little invention. *Stupid girl*, she thought in spite of herself. She had been cocky. It may have been just a toy; it hadn't even had a name, but she didn't care. It had been there for her when she needed it.

"Come on, girl!" barked Kolonius. "You've got the thing! Let's get this over with!"

"If you do this," Mister Zero said, "the City will be powerless. Everyone will starve and die."

An adult might pause to consider this, to weigh out the options. But Gwendolyn had the benefit of teenage recklessness and the unquestioned certainty that she was right. She stared down at the broken bits of her faerie friend. "That's just one more lie. It won't stop me."

"You saw what happened after you blew up my Lambents. Things got worse."

"Only because we had nothing to replace it with. No ideas on how to make things better."

The spire vibrated. "You're gambling with an entire City."

Gwendolyn glared. "Then let's roll the dice."

"Fine," said Mister Zero. "It's my turn anyway." Out of the mirrored floor rose several identical bowler hats, followed by identically faceless men. "When I first discovered you, I wanted you erased. You and your changes were just a problem to be dealt with, like all the others before you. But then you destroyed the Lambents, and I saw your *power*. And I *wanted* it."

A dozen Faceless Gentlemen stepped forward.

"You're right, little Gwendolyn. I can't take your power without completely shattering your tiny mind. But you have become *so* much more trouble than you're worth. There will be others like you. You aren't special. Goodbye."

They were surrounded by Mister Men. Sparrow pressed his back against Gwendolyn's, sword drawn. Kolonius and Starling squared off on her right, and Drekk whirled his rapier and cane. The professor clutched his bag of tools, looking nervously from one man to the next.

"Now, Mister Five, it appears we may have to sully ourselves in a childish physical confrontation."

"Most distasteful, Mister Six. But the Status Quo must be preserved. It is time this girl faced her . . . consequences."

The army of men removed their bowler hats. Slowly, ever so slowly, as if it were some sort of magic trick, each of them drew a long black cane out of their hats. They put the hats back on and stood at attention, hands resting on their canes.

Kolonius looked at Gwendolyn. "We've got this, Red." Then he glanced at her bald head. "I mean . . . well, you know. Just go stop all this." With a yell, he lunged at the two men closest to him, who whipped up their canes in response. Starling and Drekk joined in as well, and the sound of battle rang through the ORB.

Gwendolyn raised the Pistola Luminant, determined to blast the awful men out of existence, but one of them moved with blinding speed and knocked the pistol out of her hand. The Pistola Luminant flew through the air and came down on the other side of the dome with a loud clang. The man seized her wrist in an iron grip.

"Don't you touch her!" Sparrow yelled, and charged. The faceless man did not so much as turn his head. He just planted his cane on Sparrow's chest and pushed. Sparrow flew through the air, landed hard, and slid a dozen feet more.

"Now, Miss Gray," said the man, reaching for his hat. "Might I have your undivided attention?"

"No!" With her free hand she shoved the Figment into his unreadable face, hoping its light would drive him back. But Gwendolyn caught a glimpse of something in the blue gem. Something that made her stop struggling and bring the jewel to her eye. The Figment showed her a horrifying sight.

Standing in front of her was not a Faceless Gentleman at all, but her own mother.

Marie Gray, wearing one of her plain white dresses, hair pulled back in a bun, her face expressionless. She clutched Gwendolyn's wrist, the same way she would when Gwendolyn would daydream on the streets and need to be pulled along. Gwendolyn felt as though she were falling from the *Lucrative Endeavour* again, watching everything she loved destroyed, her stomach lurching, wind rushing through her ears.

Time slowed to a crawl as she looked at the others. Tylerium Drekk was fighting a balding man in a soiled factory uniform that looked vaguely familiar. Kolonius was attacking a little boy that Gwendolyn did not know, but I can tell you that it was the same boy who had watched her and Sparrow and Starling plummet from a building on their first meeting. They were both fighting furiously, but they might as well have been asleep, their expressions blank, their eyes glassy.

Gwendolyn turned again, and found Starling fighting Missy Cartblatt and Tommy Ungeroot. The two children wielded their canes like expert sword fighters. And Gwendolyn realized why the men had always appeared faceless, why their appearances shimmered like heat haze, why the sight of them seemed to get lost somewhere between eyes and mind.

But the Figment revealed them all. Most of the "men" scattered around the dome were people she didn't recognize, old and young, men and women. These must be the dreamers who had come before her. All the people like her, who wouldn't look into the Lambent. The ones who resisted and were erased.

But something was extra queer about the two men menacing Professor Zangetsky. They did not look like the rest. Somehow she knew it was Mister Five and Mister Six, but they were not men at all. The gem made them look like they were made of shadow, two man-shaped holes of inky blackness that sucked in all the light around them.

Last of all, Gwendolyn saw Sparrow lying on the floor, and her own father had his cane raised, poised to strike the boy where he lay.

"No!" Gwendolyn shouted.

"You wanted the truth, Gwendolyn," said Mister Zero. "Is it everything you hoped for?"

She turned back to the Faceless Gentleman gripping her wrist. "Mother, it's me! Gwendolyn!" she gasped. "You have to remember! Please, let me go!" She tried to pry the fingers off her wrist, but they might as well have been made of steel. The instant she took the Figment from her eye, her mother reverted back to one of the grey-suited men, the face under that bowler hat swimming away from her mind. Her mother's face was surely there, but unseeable once more.

"Please," Gwendolyn pleaded, nearly crying. "I can help you, I can save you, I'm your daughter!"

"Your struggle is over," said Mother, but the voice was the eerie drone of a Mister Man. She clutched her daughter's wrist with the hand that had caressed Gwendolyn's cheek, tucked her in at night, and struggled to tame her hair each morning. Then she tightened her grip and broke Gwendolyn's wrist with a sickening crunch.

CHAPTER TWENTY

Thought Piracy

She collapsed with a howl of pain, cradling her hand. The Figment clunked to the floor and rolled away. Fire raced up her arm. It was even worse than when she'd broken her arm during Titania's training. Gwendolyn moaned, and faced the crystal spire. "My mother. My father. Tommy, Missy . . . why? Wasn't—" she gasped at a jolt of pain. "Wasn't I enough? You had to . . . take them too?"

"Oh, I am sorry," came the voice of the little boy. "But I'm afraid that was your fault."

"M-my fault?" she wailed, oblivious to the battles that raged around her. "You did this! You horrible little monster, you turned them into these . . . things!"

"It couldn't be helped. Your parents were too far gone. They kept *thinking*, and *questioning*. They wouldn't give you up. And Tommy Ungeroot, well, he spent a little too much time with you and your stories. And poor Missy Cartblatt was never quite right after those ears."

Gwendolyn had no more words. All that was left was pain.

"This is where your story ends. But don't worry. You'll be one of the faceless ones. I'd like to say that you'll be happy that way, but you won't really be *anything*."

Drekk snarled as he fought off two men, sword and cane whirling, but he was clearly tiring. Kolonius took a strike to the knee and collapsed. Starling threw herself toward him, barely managing to block a blow that would have caved his head in, but the force of it drove her to her knees. Sparrow dueled her father, barely hanging on. The light of a bowler hat was already hypnotizing Professor Zangetsky.

"I'm so sorry," Gwendolyn muttered to all of them.

"No!" Sparrow bellowed. "Don't let him get inside your head. Follow the plan!"

The plan? She'd almost forgotten. The shock of seeing her parents had nearly made her give up hope completely. But Sparrow was right. They weren't beaten yet. She forced a grimacing grin.

"Oh dear," said the little boy. "You're smiling. Am I missing something? I thought I was winning our little game."

"Of course you did, Mister Zero," Gwendolyn said, as smug as she could be while biting back the pain. "But you don't know what's going to happen next. It's your biggest weakness. You just have *no* imagination."

She placed her uninjured hand on the cool glass floor, drawing on the energy that filled the dome. There was so much *power* here. Her Mister Mother reeled back to strike, but Gwendolyn blasted her back with a burst of light from her injured hand, and wrapped her in imaginary vines.

Sorry, Mother. She ordered herself to block out thoughts of her parents so she could form a clear picture in her mind, feeding on the energy of millions of people all across the City. Hundreds of thoughts and images and ideas coursed through her mind, a million distractions from all the Cityzens who'd ever looked into a Lambent. She fought to control the flow, to bend it to her will, to tell *her* story.

"*Once upon a time . . .*" she said.

A tremendous explosion rocked the ORB. Mirrors shattered.

"What? What was that?" cried Mister Zero.

Another explosion sounded, then another. Gwendolyn smiled as the entire side of the dome was blasted open in a tremendous shower of glass and metal and concrete.

The *Lucrative Endeavour* and the *Swift Retribution* hovered just outside the ORB, shining like the sun the City had never seen. Cannons spat fire. Wasps zoomed through the hole and circled the crystal spire. Kolonius let out a loud whoop. Wind rushed through the hole, pulling at Gwendolyn's tattered rags.

"NO!" roared the boy in childish rage. "What are you doing? Stop! Everyone will see!"

"That's sort of the point," said Starling.

The Wasps fired at the Mister Men, driving them back, and the men retreated to the other side of the dome.

"Okay, when I said to follow the plan, I wasn't entirely sure that would work," Sparrow said.

"Mister Zero's not the only one who can use all this energy.

I couldn't have brought them into the City if it weren't for the power in the ORB," she replied.

Burly Brunswick zipped down a pneumo line and unsheathed his great two-handed broadsword. "All right, ye snot-nosed babes, what the devil's taken ye so long?"

"Only waiting for you, old man. That peg leg been slowing you down?" called Kolonius, his face beaming with boyish glee.

Carsair landed with a heavy thump, hammer at the ready. "Too much waiting. I am not deliverywoman."

More Mister Men appeared, an army of them. As they engaged Kolonius and his crew, Gwendolyn wondered how many had been like her, once. Imaginative rebels, erased from existence.

Pirates zipped down from the *Retribution* to join in the action.

"Look, Muffins, a real fight! We's get to smash heads!" shouted a large and filthy pirate.

"Yes, Bucket, jus' make sure it's the *right* ones this time," said his scrawny companion.

Five masked pirates dressed all in black flipped from their pneumos and drew twin swords from their backs. Silently, they attacked the lines of Mister Men, jumping and twirling and generally performing astounding feats of acrobatics.

"Gwendolyn, now!" shouted Kolonius. "End this!"

Gwendolyn found the Figment a few feet away, snatched it up, and put it in her pocket, then looked desperately for the Pistola Luminant. It was all the way on the other side of the dome.

She bolted, running as fast as she could while cradling her

broken wrist. She tried to imagine it becoming whole again, and the pain lessened, though she had no time to focus and heal it properly.

"Don't hurt them!" she shouted to Kolonius.

"What?" Kolonius roared, partly in disbelief, partly because things had gotten very loud.

"They're my parents! Or my friends. Or . . . *someone*. But they're prisoners!"

Kolonius groaned, clashing sword against cane. "I'll . . . try my best, but they don't seem to be giving us a lot of options."

"I, however, will be making no such promises," snapped Drekk. He danced around three of the Mister Men with no apparent effort, having found fresh energy. "The faster you finish this, the less likely it is that I'll skewer some member of your family. No matter how much I'd like to."

"No, I forbid you to hurt them!" she ordered, bracelet gleaming. Gwendolyn managed to cross to the other side of the dome and scoop up the Pistola Luminant. She jammed the Figment into the copper coil that Professor Zangetsky had rigged up. She reached into her bag for the faeries' gift and fitted it into the other coil. The pistol vibrated in her hand, humming with terrific power. One of the bulbs on top glowed blue, another glowed red, and the third glowed gold.

"Everybody down!" Gwendolyn shouted. She pointed it at the spire, focused everything she had left, closed her eyes, and pulled the trigger.

The pistol jerked in her hand. There was an explosion of

light, and the bulbs on top all shattered. Then it fell silent in her hand.

"Shoot, girl!" Brunswick bellowed.

"I can't! It isn't working!"

Sparrow groaned. "I'm shocked. That thing never works when you need it to! I'm going to have words with that Cyria lady," he shouted. He deflected a blow from a Mister Man's cane.

Gwendolyn rattled the pistol and examined the new connections. She saw the problem: some of the wiring on the makeshift attachments had broken when it had been knocked across the dome. "It's damaged! It won't fire!"

"Professor, go help her!" Kolonius ordered. "Blast it, Zangetsky, where are you?"

"H-here! I-I-I'm coming!" The gangly professor emerged from wherever he'd been hiding and toddled toward Gwendolyn, weaving and ducking unnecessarily.

"None of that," Mister Zero said. "This isn't how I want to play. In fact, I think playtime is over. Say goodbye, Gwendolyn." Something black ran through his tubes, pumping into him. The boy's body shuddered, and his glowing white eyes turned black as well. The dome rumbled.

Then vaporous black tentacles shot out of the spire, grabbed two Wasps, and smashed them against the dome wall. The other Wasps opened fire, but more tentacles shielded the boy, and the Wasps had to break off as shadow hands grasped at them.

More shadows sprouted from the spire, forming claws and fingers and hooks, and another Wasp went down in flames. The airships opened fire again, sending streams of hot lead at the darkness, but it had little effect.

The tentacles split into hundreds of smaller strands. They wrapped up Kolonius's crew in cocoons of darkness. Brunswick hollered in rage and swung his enormous sword, but there were too many of the tiny threads, and he was engulfed.

Shadows wrapped around Kolonius, and Sparrow, and Starling. Huge pillars of darkness leapt from the spire and spread across the *Lucrative Endeavour* and *Swift Retribution* like ebony coral. Every one of her companions, every ounce of help she had, was held tight in the grip of Mister Zero's shadow. In moments, they would all be erased. Again.

Frantically, Gwendolyn tried to think of something. She could create more vines, or bring Criminy back, but the childish voice rang out again.

"Did you think I would just let you keep using my power? None for you, I'm afraid."

The mirrors around her glowed white, and the energy in the air disappeared. She felt it go, and it felt like when she'd destroyed the Lambents. Empty, and powerless. There was not enough magic for her to create anything.

They had not planned for this. The pistol wasn't supposed to be damaged, the battle should have been over already, she didn't know what to do—

Yes, she did. She had one idea left. And it was a bad one. But a bad idea was better than nothing. She pulled the glowing ruby out of the Pistola Luminant, and held it high in the air. The faerie gem that she had sacrificed so much to get.

"Help!" she cried, then smashed it to the ground.

Suddenly there was a battalion of faeries in the dome. Three neat rows of a dozen each, all clad in woodland armor, barefoot, winged, and glowing.

Puck Robin sprang from nowhere, dressed in her usual black suit, knickers, and orange shirt. "Forward, men! To battle we go! Though what we fight, I do not know . . ."

With a thunder of hooves, the entire wild hunt sprang into the dome as well, fiery-tailed Night Mares leaping over the soldiers' lines. King Oberon rode at the head of the parade of haunts, terrors, and ghouls. "Forward! I would have my hunt!"

The soldiers fanned out and lifted their bows. Arrows of golden light filled the air, piercing the shadows that trapped Gwendolyn's friends. Wherever they hit, the shadows burst and dissolved, leaving the occupants free and unharmed. The shadows fought back, lunging at the soldiers, but the mounted hunters drew glowing golden swords and fought back the darkness.

The shadows began changing shape. Suddenly there were liquid shadows, and claws, and talons, and clouds of black insects. Spears and arrows flew through the ORB, but ones made of darkness rather than light. Monstrous black creatures burst from the spire. But no matter the shape, they were no match for the faeries' glowing weapons.

"Go to your friends, my darling dear. We've come to help, so have no fear," Puck Robin said to Gwendolyn.

Gwendolyn nodded. She thought back to Puck's lessons, and she began to dance. She moved through a thicket of shadow thorns, twirling, leaping, keeping just out of their reach. But she was brought up short by an enormous shadow bear. It reared back to maul her. Suddenly, an even more enormous foot came out of nowhere and stomped the shadow bear flat. The impact shook the entire dome. The foot in question was attached to a giant wooden automaton, far bigger than any she'd seen before. Its clockwork gears ticked loudly and its limbs pumped with glowing fluid.

"Oh, yes, and Cyria sent you a present," Robin said.

Gwendolyn didn't stop to think, but just kept dancing through the chaos. Puck Robin was moving faster than Gwendolyn had ever seen, a glowing golden knife in her hand. The faerie severed shadows left and right.

Kolonius and the others were being herded together by the army of Faceless Gentlemen. The tide was turning in the heroes' favor, but the humans were all clearly tiring. She had to end this battle quickly.

"Professor!" Gwendolyn said as she reached him. "We have to repair the pistol!"

"R-right . . ." He produced some tools, and began to work on the damaged wiring. "Hold this for a m-moment, would you?" He disconnected the Figment and handed it to her.

The Tohkians fought the Mister Men while the Faeorians battled the shadows, archers firing and hunters slashing. Cyria's wooden automaton towered a dozen feet over everything else. It sent men in bowler hats flying through the air with each swing of its giant arms.

"King Oberon!" she called. "I need more help! I need to power the pistol!"

The king rode his flame-tailed mount through a pack of shadow wolves, cleaving them in two with a wickedly curved golden sword. "You have had your favor. You called for aid and here we are."

She was afraid of that. Cyria had warned her. Without the faerie globe, the pistol wouldn't be strong enough. She had sacrificed her hair for nothing. Though she supposed it wouldn't matter how bald she was if she was also dead.

She needed something else to help reverse the massive power in the spire . . .

Power. She noticed the glowing gems in the bracelet on her wrist.

It seemed she had nothing but bad ideas left.

She slipped the bracelet off, trying not to be noticed. "Professor!" she whispered. "Use these instead. They can help power the pistol so it can still broadcast the information stored in the Figment, back through the spire and into the Lambents." She handed them to him.

"I-I'll see if I can, but how am I supposed to work under these condi—"

Professor Zangetsky froze. A sword blade sprouted from his chest. His mouth opened and closed like a stunned fish, and he slumped to the ground.

Holding the more cooperative end of the blade was Tylerium Drekk.

"About time he shut up. His blubbering was quite unbearable." The professor lay on the ground, crumpled and motionless. Drekk pulled the sword from his back, and the professor did not so much as flinch. Then Drekk stomped on the bracelet with a sickening *crunch.*

"Ah," he said as his choker disintegrated into twigs, golden threads, and glowing gems. He rubbed his neck. "That is *much* better."

"Drekk! What are you doing?" Gwendolyn shrieked, but he casually waved his sword at her.

"Betrayal, of course. I don't need you. I'd much rather help *him*"—Drekk nodded toward Mister Zero—"and then I can be on my merry way."

Gwendolyn stood in shocked silence. Her hopes were dying along with the professor.

"And does the floating gentleman agree?" Drekk asked, addressing Mister Zero. "I will dispose of the girl, and for this favor, I will sail the skies of some other world. Though I must admit, I'd probably kill her for free."

Mister Zero giggled. "I'm afraid not. I do hate to lose anything from my collection permanently, particularly something from my favorite story, but it's safest to be rid of you altogether. After all, you clearly can't be trusted. Just delete them."

"Wait, what?" Drekk stammered.

One of the Mister Men grabbed his shoulder from behind. Drekk tried to turn, but the faceless man forced the pirate to his knees. Another Mister Man stepped in front and removed his bowler hat. There was a bright flash of light, and Tylerium Drekk simply vanished, his final scream lingering long after his body had gone.

"Kolonius!" Starling whirled, but she was too late. Faceless

Gentlemen forced him to the ground. With a man on either side holding him down, a third removed his hat and pointed it at Captain Kolonius Thrash.

"Do it, then," he spat.

There was a flash of light, and then nothing.

Starling was yelling, screaming something at the boy in the spire, but Gwendolyn's ears no longer seemed to be working. The world had gone silent. Everything happened in slow motion. Mister Men pinned Starling's arms behind her back. Sparrow struggled to reach his sister, but he was easily overpowered. Beams of light lanced from the central spire, and both airships vanished completely.

"A shame, but necessary," Mister Zero said. "And this time, they'll be completely erased, not even a trace left in my own collection. That way no little girls can bring them back."

"Lords of the Fae! To me! This hunt is over. Our work here is finished," Oberon roared, and the Night Mares whirled toward his call.

"King Oberon! Puck!" she shouted. "Where are you going? It's not over yet!"

The pixie bowed and gestured to the dome, which was now free of shadows. "Our bargain filled, the shadows gone. This battle is no longer fun. And don't forget—you owe me one." There was a flash of light, and all the Faeorians vanished.

"No!" Gwendolyn shouted. Blasted faeries. Cyria was right; they turned on you as soon as they got bored. They'd taken the inventress's giant clockwork man, too. With the Faeorians vanished and the Tohkians erased, Gwendolyn found herself alone in the dome, save for Sparrow and Starling. And the Mister Men—hundreds of them, circling the three friends.

"Now. Where were we?" Mister Zero crooned.

"Gwendolyn!" Sparrow called. He tried to reach for her, but his arms were held tight. Starling struggled angrily, but it was no use.

The floor shuddered. A spiderweb of cracks spread across the floor as the mirrored segments pulled away from each other. The floor disassembled, and the dome was a sphere again. An orb. Gwendolyn, Sparrow, and Starling were each on their own separate platforms, the three of them twirling in midair around the spire.

Gwendolyn stood alone, struggling to keep her balance. Two Mister Men flanked Sparrow, with two more on Starling's platform as well. The other Faceless Gentlemen whirled around them. Mechanical arms from the sides of the sphere moved the glassy platforms around the sphere in clockwork motion. All the others that had been like her, all the oddlings, all erased.

"You just watch, little Gwendolyn. You won't be alive much longer, so try and enjoy it at least a little. I saved them for last, since I know they're your favorites."

The Mister Men removed their hats and pointed them at Sparrow and Starling. Sparrow looked at her, his brown eyes sad and resigned. He opened his mouth, but before he could speak, there were two blinding flashes of light.

CHAPTER TWENTY-ONE

The Woman in White

But Sparrow and Starling did not vanish. There they were, kneeling on their floating platforms, grey-suited men still holding them down. The hats flashed again, and the two children seemed to flicker, but it was as if her friends stubbornly insisted on existing. Gwendolyn's heart gave a little flutter.

"So that's what you did," Mister Zero said. "I understand now. Oh, well. They'll vanish once I take care of you."

Black tentacles whipped out from the central spire and wrapped around Gwendolyn. "I *am* sorry, Gwendolyn. I only wanted someone to play with. Well, I wanted your power to play with, anyway. You were never really important."

Wherever the tentacles touched, her body went numb. The shadows lifted her off the platform and her feet kicked at empty air. She tried to cry out, to scream, to throw one last stinging retort at this stupid boy, but the shadows wrapped themselves around her throat.

The tentacles brought her eye-to-eye with Mister Zero. "And

that was the end of Gwendolyn Gray and all her marvelous adventures," came the voice of the boy whose mouth never moved.

She could no longer even feel the tentacles that held her. Her thoughts sped up as time slowed down. The plan hadn't worked. Even their backup plan from the postal hub seemed to have failed. All that effort, and it hadn't worked. *He still wins. I'm just another part of his insane collection. Will he turn me into one of those men? I'm sorry, Mother. I'm sorry, Father. I'm sorry we argued, and that I was rude and cross and difficult.* She would give anything to take it all back. It pained her to know that in the end, it hadn't just been her life she'd thrown away, but so many others with her.

The darkness crept over her chin, filling her mouth, spilling down inside of her. There was a rush of cold.

Help me, she thought, though she did not know to whom. *I'm scared. And I'm alone.* But there was only cold and darkness. Her thoughts slowed and ground to a halt.

Nothing.

Emptiness.

Black.

~~~

Then, something. A blur. A flicker of light. Gwendolyn opened her eyes and found herself somewhere quite unexpected.

She was in a forest.

Not her own favorite forest, and not Faeoria, but somewhere far older. Slender white trees reached high into a glittering night sky. A staggering number of stars flickered overhead as galaxies and nebulae displayed their colorful finery. Moonlight filtered gently through the branches, creating strange shadows in the fog that rolled across the mossy ground. And in the moonlight, she noticed that the trees were full of tiny emerald leaves.

Gwendolyn caught a glimpse of movement. A flicker of white cloth. She spotted a woman gliding through the mist. Tall and graceful, passing in and out of view between the thin white trunks. Long red hair flowed around her. It was not curly like Gwendolyn's had been, but straight and silken. She wore a sheer white dress that fluttered in the evening breeze, billowing out behind her, pulled taut against her lithe silhouette.

This was certainly *not* Titania. The woman in white seemed to float through the fog. A warm glow spread wherever she walked. Gwendolyn couldn't see her face, but she felt a stirring in her chest, a deep and inexplicable longing.

The woman passed her by and began to move away. Gwendolyn tried to cry out but could make no sound.

But the woman heard her anyway, one delicate hand coming to rest on the smooth white bark of a tree. The woman turned, and suddenly all Gwendolyn could see was her eyes, blue and piercing.

"Don't be afraid," the woman said, though the voice was in Gwendolyn's head and not her ears. A voice she'd heard before, just like when she'd plummeted through the skies of Tohk.

"You are never alone."

~ ~ ~

The scene dissolved in a rush, and Gwendolyn was back in the mirrored dome of the ORB. She felt as though she were waking from some impossibly long dream. There was the crystal spire in front of her, and the black eyes of Mister Zero.

Except. There was something else. Something that floated between her and the crystal. Something so small it would have gone unnoticed save for its bright color.

As I'm sure you have guessed, it was a tiny, emerald leaf. Just the same as the ones in the Lady's forest. *Lady of Light, Woman in White*, Gwendolyn sang silently, the tune springing unbidden to her mind, though being engulfed in blackness was hardly the time for singing.

But the blackness that coated Gwendolyn's skin wasn't so black anymore. It dried to a pale grey and flaked off like old dirt. The tentacles that held her quivered, buckled, then snapped like dry branches. She crashed back onto her platform.

"What? What's happening? What are you doing?" rumbled Mister Zero's voice from the surface of the crystal.

Gwendolyn tried to catch her breath. She shook herself and rid her body of more of the flaking shadows. Sparrow and Starling were staring at her in open-mouthed amazement. The Faceless Gentlemen stood frozen, waiting for instructions.

The boy in the crystal spire was as frozen as ever, but his voice quavered. "I don't like this. How did you do that?"

A black tentacle burst from the crystal in front of her. But then it trembled and broke. It fell to the floor and burst into dust.

Gwendolyn looked up at Mister Zero, and a smile crept across her face. Her wrist throbbed, her body ached, but she stood up straight and tall, a fire rising inside her. "Just a little postal insurance. Better late than never. Why? Is something wrong, Mister Zero?"

The black drained from Mister Zero's eyes and they blazed white again, flickering uncertainly. "What did you do?"

"Don't you have an idea? No, I suppose you never have any. And soon, you won't have anyone else's either. Take a look. Look at the City."

There was a flash of light from the crystal tower, and the walls of the sphere showed images of the City, tall grey skyscrapers under an equally grey sky. Crowds filled the streets, casting shocked glances upward, pointing at where the airships had been.

The mirrors shifted, and now they showed people in their homes. Gwendolyn wondered how often this terrible boy had used the Lambents to spy on the Cityzens. But now in all of these images, the people were holding *books*.

Books of all sizes and colors, books that poured out of their mail tubes. Books that Gwendolyn and her friends had taken out of the Library of All Wonder and shipped all over the City. The Cityzens read from them and passed them around excitedly, all of the City waking up to a sea of ideas and possibility. And not a single person anywhere was watching the Lambent.

"I did the one thing you wouldn't expect, Mister Zero, because it's the one thing you would never do. I decided to share. Ideas want to spread, and I've just spread them across the City like thousands of tiny sparks. Can you feel it?"

He shrieked like an animal in pain. The central spire

shuddered. The entire ORB shook as well. "NO! You can't! It's MINE!"

"It wasn't yours to begin with. For all your talk about comfort and safety, these people are choosing freedom. And the more the power spreads out there, the less of it that's left for us in here."

As she said it, the light in the crystal dimmed. The little boy in the spire moved for the first time, his body sagging against the wall of crystal around him, no longer floating, held up only by the tubes plugged into him. The light was fading from his eyes.

"You can't win," the disembodied voice said. "I'll turn them all into my Mister Men. I'll wipe everything out and start over. Nothing will change. Nothing will ever change. I won't let it!"

Gwendolyn almost felt bad for him. "It already has. You can't stop an idea once it's shared with so many people. You can't collect it or erase it. When will you learn? No matter where you take Kolonius and the others, they'll never be gone as long as someone remembers them." And she tapped her head. "I'll bring him back. Just like before. And everything else you've taken."

She pointed at Sparrow and Starling, trapped on their platforms, held by the Mister Men. Starling nodded solemnly. Sparrow gave her his trademark wink and wolfish grin.

"They're all still here," Gwendolyn said. "Because they're as real as you or me. Every one of us has a story. But I think yours is over. Everything changes eventually. Every little boy has to grow up sometime."

Gwendolyn bent down to the scattered objects at her feet. The Pistola Luminant. The Figment. And the remains of the faerie collar, the gems and twigs and golden thread.

"Do you really think those toys are going to save you?"

She smiled. "Yes. Yes, I do. And that's what makes it real."

"Get him, Gwen!" Sparrow shouted from across the dome.

"Don't stop now," echoed Starling.

Gwendolyn moved her hand over the mess, and racked her brains for the right words, the best words. She couldn't remember the ones Cyria had used when the inventress had waved her hand and created the necklace for the Figment. But she did remember Titania's advice, that magic was different for everyone. Gwendolyn had to use her own words.

"Happily ever after," she whispered. Though she had never heard the phrase before in her life, it sounded heavenly.

The pistol, the Figment, and the pieces of the broken collar rose into the air. The faerie magic sensed her will and twisted itself to her purpose, just as Cyria had promised. The wooden collar assembled itself around the Figment in a ring of smaller glowing jewels, and the golden threads connected the Figment to the pistol as the three bulbs on top repaired themselves. A seamless combination of three worlds: the Pistola Luminant of Tohk, the collar from Faeoria, and the Figment from her own City.

If only she'd thought of this earlier. But as she'd said, ideas are wild and don't always come when called.

The Figment glowed a bright sapphire blue, her initials twinkling encouragement at her. She hoped it could work without the immense energy of the faerie globe to power it. But Mister Zero's power was weakening, so maybe her own strength would be enough. Maybe it wouldn't take everything she had, and she'd survive the experience.

"You don't understand," Mister Zero pleaded. "You're just making things worse. Everything will spin out of control. Remember the Wastelands, Gwendolyn. That's what the City will become. You *need* me."

"No, Mister Zero," she said coolly. "We don't need you. You don't scare me. You're just a shadow. And only children are afraid of the dark." She looked at her friends again for strength. "I may be small, and I may be different, but I'm *not* helpless. You may have all the power in the world, but I don't have to out-fight you if I can out-*think* you. At the end of the day, you're just. Not. Clever. Enough."

She focused her will into the pistol once more, giving all her energy to one last spell.

"*What if . . .*"

Every gem and bulb and tube on the pistol glowed with the Figment's blue light. She pulled the trigger.

Lightning flew across the sphere. Not golden, as before, but a shocking blue. The sapphire bolt slammed into the pillar with a crash of thunder.

The blue lightning did not fade, but instead forged a crackling strand of energy between the pistol and the spire. It pulsated, and the light in the crystal slowly turned from white to blue. She could feel the pistol faltering, the connection fading. The gems from the collar burst under the strain, and the bulbs on the pistol popped again. But Gwendolyn poured whatever magic she had inside herself to push back against the energy in the spire, to reverse it.

Blue light spilled from the Lambents at the spire's base,

sending out all the ideas and information the Figment had stored, along with everything Mister Zero had taken over the centuries. The walls of the sphere showed that everywhere in the City, the Lambents had flared to life, beaming blue light at anyone who was nearby. The entire ORB glowed blue, until Gwendolyn could hardly see through the haze.

With a final chilling scream, the pistol, the Figment, and the central spire shattered into a thousand pieces, and she was blinded by a burst of white. She threw her arms up to shield herself from the blast of heat and wind and noise.

Her platform plummeted to the bottom of the sphere. It hit the ground with a crash, throwing her forward, and she cried out as she landed on her broken wrist. The pain was so intense that she nearly blacked out, sprawled on the curved mirrored floor of the sphere.

There was a long moment of silence.

Gwendolyn's vision was a cloud of black spots, and her head was so fuzzy that everything seemed like a dream. She tried to look around, but she seemed to be moving in slow motion, and even the tiny movement of her head took a monumental effort. She suspected she had a concussion. The idea of getting to her feet appeared somewhere in her dazed mind, but her body would not obey the slightest command, all her muscles jelly.

Every mirror in the ORB was cracked, and the bottom of the sphere was littered with shards of crystal. All the platforms had crashed. Part of the roof had caved in.

Sparrow and Starling were struggling to their feet. Gwendolyn saw the unconscious bodies of Tommy Ungeroot and Missy Cartblatt, her mother and father, and dozens of other former Mister Men, now returned to normal.

There was a crunch of broken glass. Gwendolyn barely managed to look around, and felt a dull twinge of horror as she saw a masked man in a black coat, hat, and single black glove stroll through the wreckage. He looked down at a pile of blue shards, the remains of the Figment. He crushed the shards into powder with his heel.

"Well. You've all made a mess," he said.

Slowly, ever so slowly, two men in crisp charcoal suits and bowler hats stepped toward the Blackstar, polished shoes clicking as they walked. The two faceless men who were not like the rest.

"This is a most unfortunate turn of events, Mister Five," said Mister Six.

"Most unfortunate indeed, Mister Six," said Mister Five.

"Wouldn't be a problem if you had any brains," said the Blackstar. "I served that girl up on a silver platter. Twice."

The Mister Men ignored him. "This world has fallen."

"It is no longer sustainable."

"Indeed. We will start again."

The Blackstar scoffed. "From scratch? Good luck."

"And what of the girl?" said Mister Five.

"We can't touch her. For now, at least," said the Blackstar.

"Then we shall bide our time, and deal with her later," said Mister Six.

"All the easier with the proper leverage, Mister Five. Shall we take these?"

"A wise suggestion, Mister Six."

The two men crouched and picked up the unconscious bodies of her parents. Gwendolyn screamed in her mind, tried to stand, but she was too weak. She tried again, and managed to hobble to her feet and take one shaky step forward, but the broken glass cut her bare feet and she fell, earning more cuts in the process.

The Blackstar loomed over her. "Well, I'm impressed. You've got power. But look around. It's like I said. Take care of yourself first, kid, because no one else will. And now, things are only going to get worse." He stepped back toward Mister Five and Mister Six, held up his hand, and made a cutting motion. A rip appeared in the air in front of him. Through it, Gwendolyn saw the rippling not-colors of the In-Between.

"No . . ." she moaned.

But she was not alone. Sparrow and Starling had gotten to their feet and were charging at the three villains.

They were too late. The men carried her parents through the portal, and the tear began to close.

"Don't worry, Gwendolyn, we'll find them!" Starling yelled as she leapt through the hole.

"We'll be back, I promise!" Sparrow said, and then he was through as well. Vanished. The hole sealed itself, and they were gone.

"Wait . . . come back . . ." Gwendolyn moaned weakly, her hand outstretched. She let her arm fall, and she rolled onto her back. "Not again."

But she was weak. Drained. The energy in the ORB was gone, and she'd used all of her own energy to fuel the pistol, compensating for the loss of Titania's gift. The shattered pistol lay beside her. The Figment was crushed to powder. Her insides were likewise broken. She tried to stay conscious, but her eyes began to close.

"Hello?" said a weak voice.

Her eyes opened. She forced herself to sit up, which might have been the hardest thing she'd ever done.

Mister Zero was in the center of a metal ring where the base of the spire had once been. He sat up, wobbling slightly. Then he spotted Gwendolyn and crawled toward her, but the tubes in his arms and legs held him back. He winced with pain.

Gwendolyn cringed and tried to shuffle backward. "Stop . . . get away . . ."

"W-where are we?" he asked.

"It's over, Mister Zero. You've lost."

"What do you mean?" he asked, voice trembling. "Are they done with me? Do I have to go home? My father will be furious, I promise I'll go into that machine thing, I'm sorry I threw a tantrum." This outburst seemed too much for him, and he collapsed flat on his stomach.

Gwendolyn noticed that his mouth had moved for the first time. His voice was different as well, not the childish teasing from the spire. It was slightly lower, and had an old-fashioned accent that the Collector had not.

"What's your name?" she asked.

"B-Bill." He tried to push himself up again, long white hair falling into his face. "Please don't hurt me."

"Bill. What's the last thing you remember?"

The boy sniffed. "There was a machine, and . . . these men. They came to my house, they did things to me, and—" He broke off in a fit of coughing. His limbs were so thin Gwendolyn could practically see through them.

Gwendolyn tried to respond, but the ORB suddenly spun around her, and she vomited. Her wrist hurt. And she was tired. So tired. Her vision was clouding, and she hardly knew where she was anymore.

"Sparrow?" she said deliriously, talking to the empty air. "What's happening?"

She fell to the floor with a thump she never felt, her head turning to the side. With her last moment of clarity, she saw something lying on the floor next to her. It was a tiny, impossible, emerald leaf.

Isn't that odd . . . she thought, but it was her last before she slipped fully into the black.

CHAPTER TWENTY-TWO

... Ever Truly Ends

*T*ick. *Tick. Tick.*

The sound roused Gwendolyn. She opened her eyes hesitantly, feeling a sudden rush of déjà vu. A cozy silence embraced her, disturbed only by the familiar ticking.

Her other senses returned, and she found herself once more alone in her old bedroom. The same grey walls, the same dull and practical furniture. Why did she always end up back in her bed? The Woman in White at work again, no doubt.

Sure enough, there was a small green leaf on her bedside table.

Maybe with the darkness weakened, the Lady of the Light was free to act more directly. Either way, Gwendolyn sat up slowly, expecting numerous aches and pains all over, but she did not seem much the worse for wear. She prodded her wrist, but even that was only a little sore, instead of pulverized. *Thank you, Lady,* Gwendolyn thought.

The mirror on her desk had quite a sight for her. She was

filthy, covered in scratches, and bald. Proof that none of it had been a dream.

Something seemed different about her room, though. Warmer. Had the light through the window ever quite been so bright? Had she ever seen the dust dance in it quite so cheerfully? Gwendolyn hopped out of bed and peered through her curtains. The sight that met her eyes nearly took her breath away.

The sun, she thought. *I can see the sun.*

Yellow and shy, it peeked cheerfully from between scattered breaks in the clouds. *I've never seen our sun before.*

She turned back to her bedroom. *Hers.* Her furniture, her clothes, even her drawings that wallpapered everything. A sense of comfort and relief flooded over her to see it all again.

There was nearly nothing left of her green dress. Her feet were still bare. And her red dress was still torn and much too small for her now. She opened the drawer and pulled on some black tights and a simple grey shift that had always been too big on her, but fit just fine now. None of her shoes fit, but she was getting used to going faerie-footed, as she thought of it.

She reverently laid the remains of her beloved puffed-sleeve dress on the bed and looked around the room again. It did not seem to fit her anymore either. She felt strangely calm. And more than a little disoriented, if she was honest. The final moments in the ORB were still a hazy mess.

Lacking any coherent course of action, or any coherent thoughts at all, she drifted out of her bedroom. But she stopped just outside the door. Her parents. Would they remember her?

Or would they be shocked to find a strange girl traipsing about their house?

"Mother? Father?" she called, creeping into the living room. "Hello! I'm home! Mother, Father!"

There was no answer, nor would there be.

Her parents were gone.

~~~

Some time later, Gwendolyn found herself sitting at her father's typewriter, staring at the heavy black thing. He had spent so much time here, tapping out memos for work.

She had searched the whole house, but there was no sign of them. Perhaps they'd just gone out to the store for some bread. Together. In the early hours of the morning. In the middle of a Citywide breakdown. Gwendolyn concocted a hundred theories for why they might be back any moment, walking through the door to give her a hug and tell her to brush her hair. Not that she had any left to brush. But she knew it would not happen.

Her memories had cleared. Visions from the ORB played on an endless loop. The Blackstar and the Mister Men carrying her parents into the void. Sparrow and Starling leaping in after them. Gone again.

"Don't worry, Gwendolyn, we'll find them!"

"We'll be back, I promise!"

She believed them. They would be back, no matter what got in their way. She would be waiting, no matter how long it took. And she was absolutely right—we have not seen the last of her two little friends.

But Gwendolyn had other friends to worry about too. Would Ian and Jessica remember her again? Were Tommy and Missy all right?

Was *she* all right?

Gwendolyn didn't know what to do. There was no Figment anymore—it was shattered and ground into dust. Gone for good this time.

And her powers too. She could feel that much. With all the imagination spread throughout the City, she was . . . normal again. Or normal for the first time. Or not quite normal at all, but at least her imaginings would stay safely in her head from now on. Whether she liked it or not.

Gwendolyn felt numb, as though she'd reached her limit of sadness today, thank you very much, and her insides had simply turned themselves off for a while. She found her satchel, the new one that Starling had bought for her in Archicon. Inside was Sparrow's gift, the blue sketchbook and the colored pencils. She suddenly remembered the smashed faerie toy, and a fresh pang of grief cut through the haze.

The empty apartment suddenly seemed too small for her, and she headed for the door. But as her hand touched the knob, something colorful caught her eye.

There was a mail tube by the front door, just like everywhere else in the City. And three books had spilled out of it. One was black, with no title, but she knew her old sketchbook immediately. The one Father had given her for her ill-fated birthday. The second book was red and gold. *Kolonius Thrash and the Perilous Pirates.* Mister Zero had taken these two, but here they were—another gift from the Lady, she supposed. A small nudge to reality.

Gwendolyn looked through *Kolonius Thrash*. All here, all restored. Mister Zero couldn't erase an idea that was safely in her own head. Though she supposed the professor would not be around much anymore. He had died an honest death, by the sword, and she doubted there was any coming back from that.

She put those two books in her bag and picked up the third. It was heavy, wrapped in dark green leather with veins like a leaf.

The Annals of the Fae.

She gave it a scan and was greeted with colorful pictures. Titania, Robin, and Oberon were there, along with fantastic animals and winged people and beautiful forests. The writing was dense, thousands of tiny words scrawled in an elaborate flowing script she could barely understand. The words all wrapped around the classical illustrations.

Which reminded her. She still owed Robin a favor. The thought of the androgynous faerie randomly popping up in her apartment someday was an odd one, to say the least.

She put the book in her satchel for later, nestled alongside the others. She was building quite the collection. Somewhere in the Library of All Wonder was a book about a little girl who felt like no one wanted her. A little girl with fiery red hair who'd had a family to love her and take care of her. A girl with a life.

How long had it been since she'd brought her first tiny leaf to life? There was not much left from those early days. She didn't even look the same. Her body was taller, among other changes. Her head now permanently smooth and bare.

At that thought, something snapped deep inside her. The battle was over. She had no more reason to keep pushing against the depression, and she let the black take her for a while.

She was not sure how long she spent balled up on the floor, sobbing, but she must have stopped at some point, because eventually she found herself on the street outside her house. Her feet must have brought her here. Old habits. Dull and predictable.

Not the City, though. For the first time in her life, the Middling was buzzing with energy. These were not the serious and subdued crowds she was used to. Instead, people huddled in groups, sharing brightly colored books that shone like jewels in the grey landscape. They shoved them under each other's noses, eager to share some story or picture.

Everything seemed a bit cheerier with the sun peeking through the thinning clouds. People gazed at it, basking in its light, smiling. She'd never seen people smiling on the street before.

She passed the window of a clothing store and noticed two people holding a very animated conversation behind the front window. She could not hear what was said, but a woman was holding a violet book in her hand and was pointing from the book to the grey outfit on display. The man nodded thoughtfully. She supposed the woman wanted to make clothes of the same color.

It was a pleasant reminder of Iona, the dressmaker in Tohk. No more portals for Gwendolyn, though. No Figment, no Library, nothing.

She noticed some people using their Lambents. Only there

was no ghostly glow now, but a kaleidoscope of colors that danced in the air before their eyes. One boy, years younger than Gwendolyn, rushed up to her and shoved one in her face. "Have you seen this?" he shouted. "Lookit! It's amazing!"

Before she could protest, she was blasted with a torrent of images. After a moment, her eyes focused, and she saw that the boy had been watching a mechanical puppet cavorting about a stage. She recognized it with a shock. "That's a Cyrio Kytain puppet! I mean, Cyria," she said. "Where is this coming from?"

"No one knows! That's what's brilliant, see? Do you know what it is?"

"Yes, I do." Gwendolyn leaned down to whisper in his ear. "It's Professor Zangetsky's Projectraphonic Clockwork Phantasmagoria."

His eyes grew wide, and he tore off down the street to show his mates, leaving Gwendolyn with several questions dangling off the end of her tongue.

She supposed that all the stories from Kolonius Thrash had flowed from her, through the pistol, and out into the world. Then she tried not to think of the marvelous places she had visited. There was plenty on the street to distract her. She caught snippets of conversation as she wandered.

"Bloody great airship, floating in the sky."

"Central Tower exploded, look! The top's blown to pieces."

"Do you think we're under attack?"

"By who?"

"It's not like any book *I've* seen before. All just showed up in the post, piles of the things. If we'd had these when I was a lad . . ."

So Mister Zero had been wrong. The City seemed fine. Better than fine—it was *changing*. Gwendolyn looked downtown. The Central Tower still stood, but the mirrored dome had collapsed, leaving a jagged ring around the top. Gwendolyn looked away.

She blinked and found herself at the door to her classroom at the School. Her feet working on their own again. She'd have to have a talk with them about the places they took her.

There was no way on earth she was going in *there*. Her hand went to her bare head, suddenly self-conscious as she had not been out on the street. But she peeked through the door, doing her best to keep out of sight and listen.

All of the students were there, clustered in excited groups, sharing books or Lambents or wild stories about airships.

Gwendolyn read the covers she saw. *101 Magic Tricks to Fool Your Friends*. *Carl Carlsby and the Big Puddle*. *The Mystery of the Enormous Turnip*. *A History of Mythical Horses*. Gwendolyn smiled at that. She'd read that one, recognizing it with the familiar feeling of warmth that any good reader has when seeing an old friend. It is a very specific sort of feeling.

She was even more pleased to see that Tommy and Missy were in their usual places, and she allowed herself a small fist-pump of triumph. But her thoughts were interrupted by Mr. Percival.

"All right, students, a little less noise there, a little less noise. Let's call the roll."

And Gwendolyn listened as he called out the names of her peers. Children she knew well, but now felt separated from, as though a thousand miles and a thousand years lay between them.

"Anders?"

"Present," said a boy named Michael.

"Barbington?"

"Present," said Armand.

"Cartblatt?"

"Present," whispered Missy.

"Coleridge?"

"Present," said Vivian.

"Finkmeyer?"

"Present," said another boy, Bernard.

"Forthright?"

"Present," muttered Cecilia.

"Haldrake?"

"Present," piped Ian.

"Gray? Gray? Gray?"

Her heart leapt. So they *did* remember her.

"No? Can't say I'm surprised, what with the . . . *ahem.* Situation. It's all very unusual, but rest assured, I will not desert you. Even in this time of turmoil, you will receive a proper education."

Jessica Tawny raised her hand. "Sir? We've all brought our own books to read today. Might we share them with the class?"

"That's right!" shouted Ian. "I've got one on mermaids! I don't know what they are, but it looks cool."

Gwendolyn smiled. It seemed their days of playing and reading in the Schoolyard had taken a hold on those two.

Jessica stood. "And this one is called *The Emily Sisters of Inglesbury.* Listen: 'Chapter One. My name is Sarah Beth Emily.

I was only a little girl, all alone in the big house on the hill, save for my sister, Emily Emily—'"

"No, none of that. We will not be changing the running of our class one bit." Mr. Percival puffed out his chest. "You can take pride that no matter what may occur outside these walls, here you will have the comfort of *consistency*. Always *consistency*. Hmm . . . except for those Lambents, I'm afraid, as they seem to be behaving quite oddly . . . Wildly inappropriate for Schoolwork. But not to fear; put them away and bring out your Lists."

The students groaned, and Gwendolyn took that as her cue to leave.

She had done it. *Really* done it, finished what she had started the day she had destroyed the Lambents. But saving the world wasn't about destruction; it was about creation. And now the Lambents were full of all the knowledge and stories the City had ever known. How long before people began to discover its history? Before they knew what she knew?

Perhaps it was that thought that carried her out to the Edge. She sat on the roof of her favorite building, legs dangling over the side. Her pile of throwing bricks and bottles lay undisturbed next to her.

For that moment, she was at peace. The feelings of despair hovered at a distance, the blackness always waiting to suck her up again. But she had found some temporary space, as if she could watch the sadness from afar.

She wasn't broken. She knew that now. Her depression and her mania were different, but they were *her* different. Like her drawing, or her dancing. Like her hair had been. Not better or worse. Just part of what made her, her.

She looked beyond the Wall, where the grey sky turned black. Perhaps she could keep the depression at bay the way the Wall kept the Wastelands out. She could not see it, of course, but she knew it was there. The cratered, ruined landscape their ancestors had left them. And no one but Gwendolyn left to witness.

Right at the very end, she thought. And just like the first time, she was back, and her friends were gone, and her parents as well, and she sat out here alone on the Edge of everything—

"Watcha lookin' at, Freckles?"

The voice made her jump, and she nearly fell over the edge. She spun around, hand going for a loose brick, but she stopped when she saw Tommy, Missy, Ian, and Jessica standing on the roof behind her.

"What is this place?" Jessica said, staring in slack-jawed wonder.

"What . . . what are you all doing here?" Gwendolyn asked.

Ian gazed up at the Wall. "Tommy saw you peeping through the window. He followed you, and we followed him. Gosh knows there's not much point hanging around the School anymore. Just walked right out on Percival. Saw you get on the monorail and never saw you get off. I didn't even know it came out this far. Of course, we almost didn't recognize you."

"Yeah, you look different now," Tommy said.

Gwendolyn flinched away. "Yes, I know, I'm—"

"Taller," he said. And she knew that was all he'd meant.

"And . . . you know." Ian patted his head.

"Ian!" Jessica chided. "Be polite. But . . . where *have* you been?"

"She did it," Missy whispered, looking away and hiding behind her hair.

"Did what?" Ian said.

"All of this . . . stuff," Tommy said, waving to indicate the sky and the tower. "She did somethin'. Just like when she came back last time and blew up the Lambents."

"Do you remember it?" Gwendolyn asked. "Being . . . you know . . ."

"Some." Tommy shrugged. "Flashes. Pictures. Nothin' that makes sense."

"You saved us," Missy said in her quietest voice. "Saved me. *Again.* I never did say thank you."

"And I never did say sorry," Gwendolyn replied. "For the ears, and for getting you into this."

Ian looked frustrated. "*What* are you all talking about? This stuff with the Lambents, and those flying ships and everything . . . that was *you?*"

Gwendolyn hesitated. "Well, yes. I suppose I have quite the story to tell you."

"And we've got ones to share with you too! Look!" Jessica pulled several colorful books out of her bag. "Now you're not the only one. There's tons of them now! Everyone's got them!"

"You first, Gwendolyn," Ian said.

"No, *you* first," Gwendolyn replied. "If you don't mind, I'm not . . . I don't feel like talking about it. Not just yet. Could you read some of that mermaid book, Ian? I'm quite fond of mermaids. Or Jessica could read that *Emily* book. It sounded nice."

"Oh," said Jessica, a little surprised. She looked at Ian, who shrugged. The four of them sat down next to Gwendolyn, five pairs of feet dangling over the edge of the roof.

Jessica began to read. Missy leaned her head on Gwendolyn's shoulder, and Gwendolyn smiled a quiet smile. This was *not* like last time at all.

Sparrow and Starling would be back. She would find her parents, powers or no powers. She would bear up, and carry on. She would stumble. She would fall. But she knew she would get back up again. How many more books would she fill in the Library of All Wonder? This particular volume was coming to an end. But it would not be the last.

They all listened to Jessica as she read from *The Emily Sisters of Inglesbury*. There is nothing like spending time in the company of good friends. Shy, pale Missy, the opposite of bold, dark Jessica. The two boys—Ian, a brash young thing, and Tommy, a little more cautious after his own misadventure. His hand inched closer to hers. But she pulled her hand away and stood.

She turned away from the Wall and walked to the other end of the roof, facing the Central City and its ruined tower. There was a clear patch of sky directly above it, through which she glimpsed the fresh yellow sun.

Jessica stopped reading. Gwendolyn felt them rise and gather behind her. All of them, standing together, facing a new day, a new world, a thousand new possibilities.

"What happens next?" Gwendolyn murmured.

"What?" said Tommy.

"Nothing."

But Gwendolyn heard a now-familiar voice whisper in her ear.

"You are never alone."

Or perhaps she just imagined it.

And So Ends

The Fantastical Explotis
of
GWENDOLYN GRAY

ACKNOWLEDGMENTS

First, thanks have to go to my amazing wife. Without her support, there would be no book. Thanks to my son Teddy, for always wanting to read this. And thanks to my dad for his constant support and encouragement.

Thanks to my editor, the freckled witch Caroline, for walking beside me, always having my girl's back, and fighting to keep my completely unnecessary jokes.

Thanks to all the people at Jolly Fish Press and North Star Editions, particularly Mari. You've all understood my vision from day one and have been one hundred percent supportive of this quirky project. Just look at the title on the cover—it's ever so slightly cracked and rough, just like Gwendolyn herself this time around. I didn't tell them to do that! That's how hard they've worked on this. So of course, an extra huge thanks to the cover designer Jake Nordby and the illustrator Sanjay Charlton, who never complain about my long lists of notes and always bring Gwendolyn to life in a way I hardly thought possible.

Kim and Amanda, I couldn't do this without you. You're my best friends, and thanks for going down this rabbit hole with me. And thanks for pulling me out of it when I needed it.

A huge thanks to all my kids, students, thespians, apprentices, mentees, padawans, and deshi for loving this story. Especially those of you who came up to me every day to talk about Gwendolyn, ask what would happen next, yell at me for what

I put her through, and share with me how much Gwendolyn's struggles helped you with your own. It meant more to me than you can ever know, and I'm sorry for making you late to class. You know who you are.

Another big thanks to Andy Hoffman at Blissful Kiss Photography for his encouragement and all his hard work on our amazing photos (seriously, go check them out at gwendolyngray.com). Thanks to Haylie and her family for getting up super early to dress in gorgeous costumes and traipse around the woods, standing in weird poses for extended periods of time.

Thanks to all the other books, movies, and stories that I have ruthlessly pillaged for quotes and references. This is a story about stories, after all, and I thought it only fitting to pay my respects to some of my favorites, such as Shakespeare, or *Anne of Green Gables*. Imaginative redheads must stick together, after all. Good luck finding all my Easter eggs, dear readers.

ABOUT THE AUTHOR

B. A. Williamson is the author of *The Marvelous Adventures of Gwendolyn Gray* and *The Fantastical Exploits of Gwendolyn Gray*. When not mining the unfathomable depths of consciousness for new words to sling, he can be found wandering Indianapolis, directing plays, child taming, and probably singing entirely too loud. Please direct all complaints and your darkest secrets to @bawrites or gwendolyngray.com.